Not just about love

By

Gina Thompson

Text copyright © 2018 Gina Thompson

All rights reserved

I dedicate this book to my family and friends for their continued love and support.

Table of contents

Chapter One	5
Chapter Two	15
Chapter Three	23
Chapter Four	33
Chapter Five	42
Chapter Six	52
Chapter Seven	63
Chapter Eight	71
Chapter Nine	80
Chapter Ten	88
Chapter Eleven	98
Chapter Twelve	110
Chapter Thirteen	125
Chapter Fourteen	142
Chapter Fifteen	156
Chapter Sixteen	167
Chapter Seventeen	180
Chapter Eighteen	194
Chapter Nineteen	210
Chapter Twenty	222
Chapter Twenty-One	237
Chapter Twenty-Two	258
Chapter Twenty-Three	279
Chapter Twenty-Four	297
Chapter Twenty-Five	319

Not just about love

Chapter one

Jo-Anne placed the notepad inside the book closing it with a sigh and laid back in the chair. Her eyes were burning and she sighed deeply as she rubbed them with her forefinger and thumb, then leaned forward to pick up her glass. She got up slowly from the chair and stretched before heading into the kitchen to put the kettle on. She glanced out of the window to see a figure coming up the garden path and head towards the back door and with a feeling of relief she opened the door.

"Couldn't have timed it better," she said with a smile, "I've just this minute put the kettle on, you must have smelled it!"

Darcy grinned widely, "Yep! I did. And the chocolate chip cookies that go with it!" She sauntered over to the biscuit tin and pulled the lid off, saying, "You want one?"

Jo-Anne shook her head as she filled the teapot, and placing the mugs and the milk jug on a tray with the teapot, she said, "Let's go back into the conservatory – make the most of the sunshine. Where are the boys?

"They're at a school friend's birthday party – I've to pick them up at half past four. That's the pleasure of school – they make lots of friends and go to lots of birthday parties, so mummy often gets a couple of hours to herself on a Sunday!"

They both laughed as they walked through the side door into the conservatory and Jo-Anne placed the tray on the small table, while Darcy picked up the book that Jo-Anne had been working on, then put it back down with a grimace, "Ugh! That looks boring!"

"If I want to pass my BTEC in Hospitality Management, I need to do some serious studying. I've been at it all afternoon."

"What a waste of a beautiful Sunday," said Darcy, sipping her tea and leaning back in the chair. "Anyway, I came to ask you if you want to go out for a drink tonight? Just you and me?"

"Well, I'll have to ask Trevor when he gets back, he may have made plans. But if not, then yes, I'll go with you. Any particular reason……….you want to talk or something?"

"No, not really, I just need to get out of the house for a couple of hours. Mark said he'll come round and babysit for me," Darcy replied.

They sat in comfortable silence for a few minutes before the sound of the garden gate alerted them to someone coming up the side of the house towards the conservatory where they were sitting. A few moments later a figure dressed in cycling gear walked in peeling off his safety helmet and wiping his brow with the back of his hand.

"Hi, Darcy," said Trevor, smiling at her as he bent to kiss Jo-Anne on the top of her head.

"Been out for a ride?" she asked him, "Anywhere nice?"

"Just across the moors – blows the cobwebs away," he replied as he undid the zip and peeled off his cycling jacket.

"Have you planned anything for tonight?" Jo-Anne asked him, "If not, Darcy's asked me to go out for a drink with her. I quite fancy it because I've been hard at it all afternoon with my studying."

Trevor shook his head, "Nah, nothing planned. You go, I'll find something to occupy myself with."

At that moment, his phone buzzed denoting a text message. He took it out of his pocket and looked at it. "Well, how about that for co-incidence………..Sam's asking if I fancy a game of pool down at the club! We're all sorted then, what time is dinner?"

"I'm going to start it now. You go and have a shower and you can help me when you come back down." Jo-Anne placed her cup back on the tray and Darcy stood up.

"Right then, I'll get off," said Darcy, "I'll come round about seven, if that's OK. I'll let Mark play a few games with the boys, then they'll go to bed without grumbling. They love their uncle Mark, he's got much more patience than me – I cannot play video games to save my life!"

*****

They were settled in a window seat overlooking the river, the sun casting sparkling ripples and long shadows in the trees across the other side as they watched the many dog-walkers and couples walking hand-in-hand on the warm early summer evening. Jo-Anne sighed contentedly and smiled at Darcy.

"What a good idea this was. I didn't realise how much I needed this till now! I'm enjoying my course and I think I'll do well, but I was starting to get a bit bogged down with it all." She raised her glass towards Darcy. "Here's to a bright future for us both."

Darcy raised her glass in return and grimaced ruefully. "I'm a bit in the doldrums at the moment – I need a good shake-up! I'm stuck in a rut and I need to get out of it, but I don't know what to do."

"Have you heard from Peter lately?" asked Jo-Anne.

"Nope!" Darcy pulled her lips together in a thin line. "He's not replied to the voicemail I left him yesterday. I know he said he was going to be busy, but for goodness sake – surely he can make an effort to ring to talk to his children!"

"And everything's OK? I mean, he's not ill, or in hospital or anything like that? You don't want to be bad-mouthing him then find he's been laid up in hospital, do you?" Jo-Anne leaned towards her friend, "Have you checked?"

"I'll ring the office tomorrow. He said he was going to be busy this weekend......but surely he can make a phone call! Bloody job! I tell you Jo, I'm getting fed up with it! It's starting to take priority in our lives – and that doesn't sit well with me! You know what I'm like – I should come first!" She smiled and threw her head back rebelliously, then picked up the wine bottle and re-filled her glass, leaning over to top up Jo-Anne's glass.

"Anyway," she said softly patting Jo-Anne's hand, "How are you feeling since you had your final session with your counsellor? There's been a lot written lately about the psychological effects of a life-changing trauma like you've undergone and how long it can take to adjust. I know you've recovered physically - and thank goodness it was caught before it became life threatening, but no-one but you knows if you're healed psychologically." Darcy looked carefully at Jo-Anne, her brow furrowed with grave concern.

Jo-Anne took a deep breath in and looked out across the river at the tranquil scene set out in front of her. She'd suffered for many years with endometriosis and last year a scan had found polyps and fibroids and a biopsy showed pre-cancerous cells and after long discussions with her gynaecologist she had eventually recommended a hysterectomy as she said Jo-Anne's chances of getting pregnant were very slim, and this would remove the very real threat of cancer and resolve the monthly agony she went through. However, it would also remove completely the possibility of her ever becoming a mother. She was only twenty-eight at the time and had been married for just over a year, so it was a terrible blow to her and to Trevor, but Trevor had insisted that there was no choice – her health was most important and the risk of cancer erased any doubt about such drastic surgery. She was off work for three months and on her return had thrown herself into making a career, now that there was no chance of ever having a maternity break.

"I think I'm getting there," she replied to Darcy, "At least I can look at a pregnant woman without bursting into tears, I couldn't do that for a long time – as you know." She took a sip of her wine. "I want to do well in my job; if I get this qualification, it'll open so many doors for me. I want to have choices, I have no choice over motherhood, but I can have choices in my working life."

They both lapsed into quiet contemplation, Jo-Anne thinking about what she had gone through over the past couple of years, so soon after her marriage. It had been a terrible time for everyone. Jo-Anne had cried bitterly, railing against God and the Universe for what had been thrust upon her, and Darcy had held her friend in her arms trying to soothe her, saying that it was more important that she was healthy, but in her anguish, Jo-Anne could only cry brokenly that she wanted to have a child of her own, and now this had been denied her.

Whenever the subject was raised between Jo-Anne and Trevor, the elephant in the room was always Savannah! Savannah was Trevor's child to his first wife, and she was living in Spain with her mother, Dawn, and her grandparents. Dawn and Trevor had divorced when Savannah was six years old after they had attempted to live in Spain as a family with Dawn's parents. But Trevor was miserable in Spain – he didn't take well to hot weather and he couldn't get a job in marketing, and after a few months of misery, he decided he wanted to come back to England. Dawn refused point blank to leave her parents and so they finally decided that a divorce was the best option rather than try to maintain a long-distance marriage, as Dawn had subsequently admitted that she had fallen out of love with Trevor a long time before. Even knowing that, Trevor found it was a difficult decision for him to make, as he knew this would curtail the amount of time he would be able to spend with his daughter.

Later, when he told Savannah that he had met someone that he would like to marry, she had screamed and cried that he mustn't do it, he had to wait and not marry anyone else. He realised that Savannah held firmly to the belief that her parents would get back together again, although neither of them wanted this to happen – they had both accepted their divorce and moved on from it.

When Jo-Anne was heart-broken over her enforced barrenness, she wanted to scream at Trevor, "It's alright for you – you have a child!" But she knew that Trevor missed Savannah and it was hard for him to accept being the father of a child that he only saw a few times a year. As Savannah hated the thought of her father having a new wife and refused even to acknowledge Jo-Anne's existence, she wouldn't tolerate the idea of Jo-Anne being anywhere near the villa, so whenever they went to Spain to see her, Jo-Anne stayed at the hotel nearby while Trevor went to Savannah's home to spend time with her, or took her out somewhere, just the two of them. It wasn't a satisfactory arrangement for either of them, but they accepted that this was how it was going to be until Savannah finally recognised Jo-Anne's existence.

"How are the boys doing at school?" Jo-Anne asked, dragging herself back to the present.

"They're doing well, I'm relieved to say. They appear to have their father's intelligence, thank goodness! I don't know how I'm going to manage as they get older and ask me to help with their homework – I'm struggling now so God help me when they get into senior school!" Darcy grimaced and they both chuckled. Jo-Anne knew that Darcy always played down her own intellect and she wasn't the dumb blonde that she made out she was. She was very beautiful, her shoulder length fair hair framed perfectly proportioned features and her eyes were a startling blue that she emphasised with clever make-up, though Jo-Anne thought this was unnecessary, she was beautiful without make-up at all. She had a tanned and toned body, sculpted by regular visits to the gym because she certainly didn't deny herself any food pleasures. She was also very smart, and before she had her children she had worked her way up in a very competitive area in fashion retail. She and Jo-Anne had been friends for many years, during high school and then college, and to their joy when Jo-Anne married Trevor two years ago they had bought a house just a few streets away from Darcy and Peter, so the girls' friendship became even closer.

Now that Jo-Anne's health problems were resolved, she had started to take an interest in her appearance again. She'd had highlights put into her chestnut hair and had it shaped into a bob that framed her face which accentuated her brown velvet eyes. She was smaller than Darcy and quite petite in size, which sometimes worked to her advantage when she could buy clothes and shoes from the children's range at a much lower cost. She was working as a Function's Administrator in a large hotel in the city and had been there for almost five years. It was here that she met Trevor when he attended a conference that was being held in the hotel's Conference Centre, and she had co-ordinated the function for his company. They were instantly attracted to each other and Trevor asked her out – his first date after his divorce. He had been divorced for over a year then, and the following year he and Jo-Anne were married in a quiet ceremony in the Register Office with only immediate family and close friends attending.

The sun had gone down and the room had filled up substantially with lots of young people standing around the bar, and the tables and chairs around the perimeter and the centre of the room tending to be occupied by couples or groups of older people. In the dusk outside, the streetlamps had come on casting a magical glow across the river and the path alongside it and the ghostly figure of two swans gliding silently towards their home caused a feeling to take form deep inside of Jo-Anne. She was suddenly filled with a sense of elation –

she'd not felt anything like this for such a long time, that it overpowered her and took her breath away. Darcy noticed the wave of emotion that came over her friend's face and leaned over to touch her arm.

"Are you OK, Jo? You look as though something's upset you." She looked intently into Jo-Anne's eyes, and Jo-Anne shook her head slightly and gave a little laugh.

"On the contrary - I've suddenly become aware of how blessed I am," she said, "After all that's happened …….the way I was ………..how bitter I was………….there are so many people worse off than me! I've suddenly realised how fortunate I am, and I'm going to make the most of the life that I've got! This summer is going to be the best yet!"

"Well, good on you!" said Darcy, "I'll drink to that!" she said as she raised her glass. "I know I moan a lot, and I shouldn't. We're both blessed! Here's to us!" They both laughed and raised their glasses again.

"I'll tell you what I've been thinking about," said Darcy, leaning towards Jo-Anne and lowering her voice to a whisper, "Andy Johnson!" She leaned back in her chair with a sly smile on her face.

"Darcy!" exclaimed Jo-Anne, a shocked expression on her face. "Who is he?"

"He's a personal trainer at the gym, and we've been chatting lately."

"About what?" said Jo-Anne, a trickle of unease settling on her.

"Oh, you know……this and that! He's a lovely guy, so interesting to talk to – he used to be a teacher but gave it up when his wife died. They were only married a short time." Darcy sat up straight and looked around for a waiter or waitress. "I'll get another bottle, shall I?"

"Darcy, don't be doing anything..........you're a married woman!"

"A very BORED married woman! Honestly, Jo, If I didn't go to the gym I think I'd go insane! You know me..........low boredom threshold!"

"Then get a job!" snapped Jo-Anne.

"A job? Doing what? Checkout girl, waitress, cleaner? What would I do?"

"Well any of those would be a start! Don't be a snob! You've been out of the workplace since you had George, that's over six years now! You'd need to get back into it slowly, and you'd only work part-time anyway."

When she'd married Peter, Darcy had a position in the fashion division of a major Department Store, but had given up work when her first child, George, was born, then when Lewis was born nearly two years later she had given up all thoughts of returning to work till the boys were much older.

"What about when Peter's away?" said Darcy, smiling in acknowledgement at the waitress who brought their fresh bottle of wine as she handed her a twenty-pound note. "How would I manage when he's away?"

"What do you mean? That's got no bearing on anything! You'd only work for as many hours as you currently spend at the gym – you manage to do *that* when Peter's away!" Jo-Anne said ruthlessly.

"I'm not giving up going to the gym!" said Darcy emphatically, "You know how much I enjoy it."

"No, I'm not saying to give it up, just go on an evening, or on the days when you won't be working – Peter's not away ALL the time, and when he is, well, I can babysit one night and your Mark will sit one night, or you can get a babysitter in on a regular basis – what about that young girl from the agency that sat for you a few times when Mark and I couldn't do it?"

Darcy sipped her wine and said nothing for a while. Then she slowly put her glass down and sighed deeply, a worried frown creasing her face. "Actually, I think Peter might be having an affair!"

"What? Peter?" Jo-Anne's eyes grew wide in astonishment. "Is that because he's not been in touch this weekend? That's a bit of a quantum leap! You know that he's very busy! You know he's got a demanding job, it keeps you in a comfortable lifestyle, and that doesn't come cheap! What makes you think he's having an affair?"

"Just the way he is with me when he comes home – he's………..I don't know………..sort of ….…..distant, as if he's thinking of something………..or someone! He's edgy and impatient with the boys, and that's not like him. And …….. we don't ………..you know………..make love any more………..we're more like brother and sister! I need to feel loved and………..wanted! That's why I think a lot about Andy, he looks at me like he really WANTS me………..he makes my legs wobbly! Peter used to look at me like that, but not any more – not for a long time!"

"Oh, sweetie, I didn't know you felt so bad!" Jo-Anne moved across and took her friends hand in her own. "You need to talk to Peter, let him know how you're feeling. Please, please, don't do anything rash with this Andy………you're a very beautiful woman, Darcy, and if you're strutting around the gym in lycra with the figure you've got, then it's no wonder he's looking at you like that! He's a man, and as a personal trainer, he'll be very body-conscious."

Just then, Jo-Anne's phone rang. With a tut of annoyance she glanced at it and gave a puzzled look when she saw Trevor's name on the screen, and when she answered he said in a rush, "Please come home, sweetheart, something's happened!"

Chapter Two

As Jo-Anne got out of the taxi, Darcy quickly thrust a ten pound note into the driver's hand, then followed her up the garden path, noticing the lights were on upstairs in the bedroom as well as downstairs. Jo-Anne opened the front door and immediately saw a travel holdall at the bottom of the stairs.

"Trevor?" she called, her heart in her mouth, and he immediately appeared at the top of the stairs, hurrying down taking two stairs at a time.

"It's Dawn and her parents……….they've been in an accident…….the police have been ……….it took ages for the Spanish police to trace me …………I have to go and see to Savannah. Oh, God! I don't know how bad they are. The British police didn't know much……..there's a plane at 11.15, I should just make it. I'll get a taxi to the airport, leave the car for you." As he was talking he was gathering his stuff together, checking his passport and wallet as he grabbed his travel bag. He gave the briefest of nods in Darcy's direction.

Jo-Anne was stunned. How could life take such a sudden turn? Twenty minutes ago she was deep in conversation with her friend who was confiding marital unrest, feeling so blessed that her own life was so secure, and now this! What was going to happen? She and Darcy looked at each other in stunned silence.

There was a buzz from Trevor's phone, and he glanced at it saying, "Taxi's here. I'll let you know what's happening, I'm so sorry I'm rushing off, sweetheart, but I have to go! I'll call you!"

"I know, you have to go………keep me informed……have you got your phone charger?"

He nodded, patting his pockets once again. "I'll need to call for some cash – I'll do it on the way to the airport. Are you OK? I'm sorry, I'm not thinking clearly!"

"It's OK, you just go. Let me know when you can,………. Take care." Jo-Anne's voice was breaking, but she tried to keep a brave face. He pulled her into his arms and kissed her then with a slight wave of his hand he went out of the door. Jo-Anne stood still, an overwhelming feeling of emptiness swamped her and she buried her face in her hands, feeling sick with dread.

After a few moments, she walked into the sitting room and sank onto the sofa, where Darcy joined her.

"Oh, my Lord!" exclaimed Darcy. "I wonder what kind of accident they've been in! They must be hurt badly if the police have traced Trev. What about Savannah? I wonder where she is!"

"I don't know……I don't know anything at the moment. Neither does Trevor by the sound of it. The Spanish police apparently had to trace him and pass his details to the British police. He's gone over there not knowing what he's going to face. I've got a really bad feeling, Darcy!"

"No, honey, don't think the worst! Do you want to come to my house for the night? I don't like leaving you on your own when you're feeling like this. Chuck a few bits in a bag and come with me."

"You know what, I think I might just do that. I don't really want to be on my own with my thoughts tonight. I'll just get some things."

She went upstairs and selected some toiletries to put in a bag, then decided against it – she was only going a couple of streets away, she could come home tomorrow morning and shower and get ready for work in her own home. She grabbed some fresh pyjamas and her phone charger and went back downstairs. She shoved both items into her bag and they headed out of the door.

*****

It was after six the next evening before she heard from Trevor. She'd had a nerve-wracking day at work, constantly checking her phone in case she'd missed his call, and feeling sicker by the hour when he didn't phone. She'd just got in from work and had stood for the last five minutes with the fridge door open, gazing at what was on the shelves, trying to tempt herself with something, but not having much appetite.

When her phone rang, she slammed the fridge door closed and grabbed her phone from the bench, relief apparent in her voice as she answered.

"Hi, sweetheart, sorry It's taken so long," said Trevor, sounding exhausted. "I've not slept, I've had so much to see to. It's not good news, I'm afraid. Dawn was with her parents in a car travelling to a hospital a few miles outside Madrid for some treatment her dad was having, and they were coming down a hill when they were hit from behind by a lorry that had gone out of control and it pushed them over and down the side of the hill into a sort of a rocky ravine. I'm afraid her parents were both killed outright and Dawn's in Intensive Care – it's not looking good!"

Jo-Anne gasped in horror at what Trevor was telling her. Both parents killed, Dawn in Intensive Care! "What about Savannah?" she managed to whisper, "Where was she……"

"She wasn't with them, thank God, she was in school." Trevor was quiet for a few moments. "She was spending the night at a friend's house – apparently, Dawn had arranged this when she organised the trip to the hospital for her father, she knew they'd be away overnight. So Savannah went to school this morning, not knowing anything that had happened yesterday, and she only found out when I went to school this afternoon to pick her up." Trevor's voice broke, and Jo-Anne's heart went out to him. "The school had been informed by the Spanish police, and were expecting me, which is just as well. The Police had found out Savannah's school from neighbours – the couple in the villa next to theirs were good friends and could give them information they needed. She was overjoyed when she saw me, poor darling, I then had to break her little heart…………."

"Oh, sweetheart, how awful!" She waited while Trevor regained control of his emotions and he continued, "I've been to see Dawn, she looks terrible, her face is a mess, she's got multiple injuries and there's tubes and wires coming out of her all over the place. I don't want Savannah to see her like that, it'll terrify her!" She heard him cough to try to clear his throat as his voice had thickened again. "Oh, Jo, it's a nightmare! Savannah is heart-broken over her grandparents, I don't know how she'll take it if her mother doesn't make it!"

"No! Don't think like that! It's too awful! Poor little girl." Tears were pouring down Jo-Anne's face. She didn't know Dawn's parents, she'd never met them, but it didn't lessen the sorrow she was feeling. A little girl had lost her grandparents and her mother lay in a critical condition in a hospital bed – it was just too horrendous!

They were both crying, Jo-Anne allowing her tears to flow freely, while Trevor fought to clear his throat so he could continue to talk. "I don't know what's going to happen. Savannah is staying with her friend's parents and I'm at the hospital – they've told me the next twenty-four hours will determine whether she'll make it or not!"

"Oh, darling, I wish I could comfort you! I feel so useless!" croaked Jo-Anne, feeling the weight of hopelessness almost crushing her chest.

"There's nothing anyone can do, I'm afraid," said Trevor, "It's a question of waiting ……..and praying, I guess."

"Well, I can certainly do that," said Jo-Anne with a wry smile. "You get some sleep if you can, and just ring me when you've got time. Please take care of yourself……… I love you." Jo-Anne's voice was in danger of breaking again, and she swallowed and took a deep breath.

"There's a small bed just to the side the IC unit I can use, and they'll call me if anything changes. I'll let you know. You take care, you hear me, I love you and I need you more than ever now!" Trevor said goodbye and Jo-Anne pressed the *end call* button, feeling the massive emptiness in her heart expanding and she laid her head in her arms and wept in anguish.

*****

It was four o'clock Monday afternoon when Darcy heard from Peter – she had picked the boys up from school and they'd gone to the park before going home so they could run off some of their energies, and she was sitting on a park bench enjoying the sun and thinking about Jo-Anne and Trevor.

"Oh, thank goodness!" she cried when she answered her phone, "I've been worried about you! Why haven't you called me? The boys are missing you."

"I know, darling, I'm sorry! It's been hectic, I honestly haven't had a minute. I had to spend yesterday bailing one of the drivers out of jail…………..he'd punched a guy in the truck stop and ended up being stuffed into one of the police vans, and hauled away. I had to use all my diplomacy skills to get him out, plus a hefty fine – which he owes me! I mean, Darcy, you just don't do it when you're in a foreign country – they're not as tolerant as they are in England, he could easily have spent a couple of weeks in jail if we hadn't been with him and see it all happen. He's in big trouble when we get back home!"

"What was it all about?" Darcy asked him.

"Oh……. nothing important that I know of, but he'd probably

had more than a few hassles with immigrants trying to hide away under his truck and very little sleep so he was mouthing off……..showing he was a hard guy in front of some locals I think. I don't really know how it kicked off, but the owner of the café has a hotline to the gendarmerie and they were there in an instant! And because the poor stowaway was bleeding they carted the driver off – caused me no end of problems trying to cover his load and see to my own!"

Darcy tutted. "Silly man! I know it's difficult for the drivers, but they're all in the same boat – he should have been more tolerant – the poor guy must have been desperate to get to England to try to stowaway. Well, I hope he's learned a lesson! Are you in France then? Are you on your way home now?"

"Yeah. I've a load to drop off tomorrow and another to pick up on the way, so I should get tomorrow evening's ferry, so I'll be home Wednesday morning. I'm shattered, love, this has been a hard trip!"

"Before you go, I need to tell you about Jo and Trevor – he's had to rush off to Spain. His ex-wife and her parents have been in a terrible accident and her parents were both killed. She's in Intensive Care in a bad way. Trevor's had to go to be with Savannah. We don't know what's going to happen yet."

"Oh God! How awful! The poor man! Give Jo my love when you see her." There was silence for a few moments as they both silently acknowledged the tenuousness of life, and then Peter said, "Are the boys around? I need to talk to them."

"Yes, we're in the park, I'll call them." She clutched the phone to her chest as she shouted to the boys and waved her phone in the air so they could get the message that daddy was on the phone. They came running over to her, and she held the phone out so George could talk first, while Lewis hopped on one foot to another, muttering "Hurry up, it's my turn!" Her heart warmed as she saw the look of love and excitement on

George's face as he asked his daddy when he was coming home, saying, "I miss you, daddy!" He finally handed the phone to Lewis, who also re-iterated that he missed his daddy, adding "I love you, daddy," causing George to shout out "I love you too, daddy!" When the call was over, Lewis handed her the phone and with a catch in his voice he said, "I want daddy to come home now!"

"He'll be home after two more sleeps - when you wake up after the second sleep, he'll be here!" This caused the boys to jump up and down squealing "Two more sleeps! Two more sleeps!"

Darcy gathered all their belongings and herded them back towards the car. Her attention turned back to Jo-Anne and Trevor and the way that their lives had suddenly been turned inside out and she realised that she desperately needed her husband's arms around her. He wasn't there with her, but she had her boys and so she hugged them and kissed them as she made sure their seat belts were fastened, and they both said, "Ugh, mum, stoppit!"

Later that evening she was trying to get the boys in from the garden to have a bath before bed and not having much luck, when there was a quick knock at the back door and Jo-Anne walked in, her eyes moist and underlined with dark shadows.

"Oh, honey, you look so tired!" Darcy opened her arms and Jo-Anne fell into them. They hugged for several seconds, then Darcy asked, "Have you heard any more?" Turning to the boys he said, "Ok boys, you can go and play for one more hour – no longer than that!"

"OK mum," they called and scampered out of the room.

She made a coffee while Jo-Anne brought her up to date on what Trevor had told her, and they both sat staring into their cups, knowing that life was going to be very different, but not knowing how it was going to manifest itself. She asked Darcy if it was OK for her to stay and perhaps read the boys a bedtime story, anything to keep her mind off what was happening. Jo-Anne had known the boys from birth, long before she lost her ability to be a mother, so she never had any discomfort in their presence. They were the children of her best friend and she loved them for that reason, as well as the fact that they were very lovable boys.

"Of course you can," said Darcy, "By the way I've heard from Peter, one of the drivers had ended up in jail in France and Peter had to bail him out – he's not happy about it. He's due home Wednesday morning, so we can have a good chat once the boys are in school - he doesn't need to be in work till Friday. I hadn't realised how much I'd missed him till I heard his voice." She smiled wistfully as she looked at Jo-Anne.

"So where is Andy Johnson in all this?" asked Jo-Anne, looking at Darcy from under her eyebrows.

Darcy grimaced ruefully. "I guess that dream died before it even took shape! Pity! He had such a lovely body!" They both laughed, but Darcy's laugh was hollow.

Chapter Three

Trevor woke up as the door opened quietly and a nurse put her head around the door. "You are awake, yes?" she asked him.

"Yes!" he scrambled to get up, his clothes crumpled and creased. "How is she, what's happening?" he said as the memories flooded back to him of where he was and what was going on and he felt sick and drained.

"No change," said the nurse, "Doctor will be in soon to talk to you. I bring coffee for you." She handed him a cup of coffee that he accepted gratefully, and he was conscious of his stomach growling – he couldn't remember the last time he'd eaten anything. The nurse heard his stomach and said, "You go get some food, you have time before doctor is here."

He smiled thinly at her and recognised that he needed to eat to keep his strength up, he had Savannah to think of. He drank the coffee and quickly splashed water on his face – he would have to go back to the hotel and have a shower and change his clothes, but first he would get some food. He went to the hospital cafeteria and managed to eat a fairly substantial breakfast, which made him feel slightly better, though he reckoned the sick feeling inside him was of psychological origin. Dawn must still be hanging on, otherwise someone would have woken him through the night. That in itself was a positive sign – the doctor had said the next twenty-four hours were critical, and it had been twenty-two hours since he said that.

He left the hospital and called a cab to take him back to his hotel where he showered and changed, and felt much better for it. As he was gathering his things to go back to the hospital, his phone rang. It was Officer Perez from the *Guardia Civil* – the Spanish Police. Officer Perez asked how things were and when Trevor told him there was no change with Dawn's situation, Officer Perez then informed him he was free to collect the belongings that had been recovered from the crash, mainly the keys to the villa and other personal items that had been with Dawn and her parents. Trevor thanked him and said he would be there after checking in back at the hospital to see the doctor about Dawn's condition.

He checked out of the hotel, assuming that if he was going to get the keys to the villa, he could stay there with Savannah, and hopefully bring her some small comfort of being in her own bed. In the taxi back to the hospital, he sent a quick text message to Jo-Anne, bringing her up to date on what was happening, saying he would call her as soon as he could. Once at the hospital as he approached the ICU department, he asked the nurse if he could see Doctor Garcia, and paced the floor running his hands through his hair while he waited for the doctor to come.

"Ah, Senor Gainsbury," the doctor said walking towards him with his hand extended, "I am Doctor Garcia."

"Please tell me how my wife……I mean, ex-wife……..is. What's happening?" Trevor's face was etched with worry.

"I'm afraid it is not what we hoped for," Doctor Garcia's English was remarkably good. "She has not become conscious yet, and we have had to operate for many internal injuries, but she is very strong, so we can pray that while she is unconscious her body can repair some of the damage. I'm afraid I cannot say more – we are doing everything we can for her, but it will be a long road."

"Thank you, Doctor." Trevor shook his head slowly, not knowing what to ask, feeling completely in the dark and out of his depth. "Can I see her?"

"Of course," said Doctor Garcia, "there will be a nurse with her at all times, monitoring her condition, but you may visit whenever you wish."

Trevor thanked him and went into the room where Dawn lay, her face almost as white as the sheets, emphasising the red and black cuts and raw patches on her face and arms. The tubes and wires still led in and out of her body, the machines at the side bleeping and hissing, the cardiograph and vital sign monitors being recorded constantly by the nurse in attendance. He walked up to Dawn, glancing at the nurse whose gaze flicked at him then back to her chart, and leaned over the bed.

"Dawn," he said softly, "Dawn, can you hear me, sweetheart. It's Trevor, I'm here beside you. I've come to look after Savannah. She's at school just now, but we're here for you, waiting for you to get well. Savannah misses you, sweetheart, keep thinking of her and it will help you get strong."

There was no flicker of recognition in Dawn's face, and Trevor stroked her hand – a small part of her hand where there was no injury, and stood a while chewing his bottom lip. He looked again at the nurse, and she gave him a small smile as she leaned over and moistened Dawn's dry, cracked lips. He came out of the room, his stomach feeling empty and hollow which he knew had nothing to do with hunger.

He called a cab again to go to the Police Station to see Officer Perez, he thought he might as well get the keys and go to the villa. At the station of the *Guardia Civil* he was led into a room while someone went to find Officer Perez, and he sat at the small table with his head in his hands. After about ten minutes, Officer Perez entered the room apologising for his delay, and carrying a polythene bag that he placed on the table in front of Trevor.

"These are the personal items that we recovered from the car. I am afraid the car was completely wrecked and is unsalvageable." Trevor winced at the implications of this statement and pulled the bag toward him. Officer Perez continued, "We understand a lorry travelling behind their car had a brake failure and it lost control, pushing their car off the road and down into the gorge. Investigations are still being carried out, and the driver of the lorry is in hospital with injuries that are relatively minor to those of your family. We believe the car was being driven by Senora Watson, and she and her husband were killed at the scene. Your ex-wife was safely belted in the back and managed to survive the crash, though as you tell me, her condition is extremely life-threatening."

Trevor opened the bag and tipped out the contents on the table – a set of door keys, a wallet, two mobile phones with cracked screens, a ladies' watch and a man's watch, a man's large signet ring, a small plastic bag containing rings which he assumed were Dawn's mum's – he remembered she wore several rings on both hands - two handbags containing purses and various pieces of make-up, and in what he assumed was Dawn's handbag, another set of keys the same as the others and a mobile phone. There were a couple of letters, relating to the hospital visit they were intending to make, and a number of oddments and assorted bits and pieces that seemed unimportant. Trevor glanced at everything in front of him and took the sheet that Officer Perez held out to him to sign confirming he had taken possession.

"What will happen now?" asked Trevor.

"The investigation will continue to determine the cause of the accident, although we do not anticipate any criminal procedures at this point. However, I advise you to contact one of our English-speaking lawyers who can guide you through the legalities involving the insurance companies. Very recently a new system for the assessment of damages for death and personal injury caused by traffic accidents in Spain came into force, and although I do not know the family's financial status, there will be a lot of expense to face because of this accident." Officer Perez stood up. "May I once again extend my condolences and offer my prayers that your ex-wife becomes well again. Please take my card, and should you have any questions you may reach my office by this number."

Trevor stood up and picked up the polythene bag. He shook Officer Perez' hand and walked solemnly out of the room. This was all like a bad dream, but he wasn't waking up.

*****

Darcy had dropped the boys off at school and then driven to the gym – she needed to work off the feelings of anxiety and frustration she was feeling. Peter had arrived home that morning, tired lines etched into his face and although he had made a good attempt at being jovial with the boys, Darcy could tell it was rather forced and that he was under a lot of strain. The boys had woken up early and scampered down the stairs when they heard voices and thrown themselves on their father, so any attempt Darcy and Peter had for a discussion was abruptly terminated. She made breakfast and they all sat together, the boys vying with each other for their father's attention, telling him what they had been doing at school while he was away. As she picked up the car keys to take them to school, she called to Peter to go to bed and grab some sleep and she would wake him about 1 o'clock, then they could talk.

She spent ninety minutes circuit training, then stood for ten minutes under a hot shower, letting the powerful jets of water pummel her back and shoulders. She felt much better after that, and after she'd moisturised her face and body and dried her hair, she walked into the small cafeteria to the side of the reception area. After ordering a fruit smoothie, she took a seat by the window. A voice behind startled her and she turned to see Andy Johnson walk towards her.

"Just finished your work-out?" he asked her.

"Yes," she replied, "Just having some quiet time before I head out there……." She nodded her head towards the street outside.

"What've you got planned for today, then?" he asked her, pulling up a seat across the table from her.

"Erm……. A bit of a family business later on today, but that's about all." She felt a bit guilty talking to Andy after what she had confided to Jo-Anne, as if by putting what she felt into words had somehow made the thoughts into deeds. She knew it was ridiculous, but she didn't feel as comfortable talking to him today as she had a few days ago when they'd had a long conversation by the side of the treadmill. "What about you? What have you got on today?"

"I've got three new clients this afternoon for an introductory session, but I've nothing till then, I'm at a loose end." He raised his bottle of water to his lips, his eyes not leaving her face, causing Darcy's face to turn pink.

She took a deep breath to steady her racing heart, and tried to chastise herself mentally. *What do you think you're playing at – your husband is having a mid-life crisis and you're ogling another man's pecs and getting heart flutters when he looks at you! Get a grip!*

"So……….how many clients have you got on your books, then?" she asked him, desperately trying to sound nonchalant.

"About twenty-eight regulars," he replied.

"All women?" she asked, taking a sip of her smoothie.

"No," he smiled, "Men and women, about equal numbers." He tapped the sides of his water bottle, still looking at her. "You never fancied some………… personal training?"

Her heart thudded inside her chest. He was openly flirting with her, making innuendoes, and she felt the heat creeping up her neck.

"Why? Are you saying I look like I need some?" She couldn't help but flirt back with him, she was enjoying the attention, enjoying the rush of adrenalin this was giving her.

She knew she was playing a risky game, but the buzz it gave her made it worthwhile.

"There is absolutely nothing wrong with that body!" He gazed appreciatively at her as he looked up and down the length of her body. "All I'm saying is that ……a little moulding in my hands……..might ………….." As he was talking he was simulating a sculpting motion with his hands, and Darcy's heart was pounding so hard she could feel it in her jugular veins, and she inwardly gasped at the surge of heat on her groin and pelvic area. She wanted to stand up but knew her legs would give way if she tried just now, so she turned her attention to her smoothie, the heat radiating from her face.

Andy suddenly stood up. "Well, I'll leave you to think on it," he smiled at her, "You know where to find me should you want anything………." He left the sentence hanging unfinished.

"Yes, thank you," Darcy whispered, her voice unable to take form. She swallowed as he sauntered off, gazing at his muscular frame, noting how different his body was to that of her husband. Peter's strength was in his brains not his body, and although he wasn't skinny, he by no means had a chiselled shape like the man strolling casually away from her. Darcy took some steadying breaths, then finishing her smoothie, she chanced standing up and was relieved to find her legs took her weight and she could walk.

When she got home, she busied herself with washing up the breakfast things and after emptying Peter's suitcase she put a load into the washing machine. Looking at the clock, she saw it was coming up to one o'clock so she went to wake Peter. The curtains were closed in the bedroom, and as she gently called his name, he slowly opened them and as recognition of where he was crossed his face he smiled widely and pulled her down on the bed. His arms went round her and she could smell his muskiness and feel the warmth from his body, but he seemed content to just hold her – there was no indication of him wanting any more than that. They lay for a while with their bodies pressed close while Peter deeply inhaled her scent and softly groaned in contentment.

"You going to get up now?" she asked him after a few minutes, "Shall I make you some coffee and toast?"

"Mmmm, yes, please," he murmured, "I'll grab a quick shower, and be down soon."

She untangled herself from his arms and the bedcovers and smiling fondly at him she walked out of the room and down the stairs. She was relieved he hadn't wanted to make love, not while she still had images of Andy Johnson in her head, and although nothing had happened with Andy, inside her mind she had dared to allow a fantasy to take form. *That's all it is, a fantasy,* she told herself, *and if Peter doesn't want me after being away for eight days…….. at least I know that Andy does, so it's not that there's something wrong with me!*

She reined in her thoughts and made coffee and toast, and Peter came down the stairs, dressed casually in jeans and sweatshirt. He sat opposite her at the table and gratefully tucked in to the toast she had placed in front of him, carefully spreading it with marmalade. Darcy drank her coffee silently, waiting for him to satisfy his hunger and thirst before he would tell her of his concerns at work.

"Ah, that's better," he said wiping his mouth with the back of his hand and pushing his chair back from the table he reached for the coffee pot to refill his cup. "I tell you Darcy, it's been a bloody nightmare this past week. I usually relish being on the road – I've always enjoyed travelling to different countries and meeting all sorts of people, but things are changing. There are so many checks to go through every time you stop – it's getting that we're scared to leave the lorries for fear of stowaways – some have got no fear, they'll take enormous risks to get across the channel!"

Darcy said nothing – this was not something new, it had been going on a long time and she knew it bothered Peter, but why was it an issue this trip? He'd told her on previous trips that some women offer themselves and their daughters for sex if the drivers will hide them and bring them to England, and Peter was upset at the desperation they must have felt to make such offers. What kind of life had they suffered to drive them to that?

Peter continued, "This episode with Charlie Dawson – the one who ended up in jail, I found out it was something to do with a guy who was forcing his sister to have sex with a driver to get a place for himself in the driver's cab as a mate! Charlie just lost it and bopped him! It was the pressure he'd been putting on the girl, it's sickening really, she was his SISTER!" Peter was quiet for a while, shaking his head sadly, then he looked up at Darcy and cleared his throat. "How would you feel if I gave up international haulage?"

Darcy looked taken aback. "What? But you love it – the travelling, the different countries - what would you do instead?"

Peter rubbed his eyes with his middle finger and thumb, then blinking hard to clear his vision he said, "Darren has asked if I'm interested in managing the home base. In Leeds."

"Oh!" Darcy didn't know what to say. It would mean that he wasn't away for days and weeks on end, though it would probably be less money, but it might not be if he was managing, surely that would be a raise!

"I said I'd go in tomorrow and talk about it with him, but I wanted your initial reaction first. What do you think?"

"Well, until we know the detail………. it sounds good to me – you wouldn't be away so much, so that's got to be a plus, the boys will love you being home more………"

"I don't know about that. I'd probably still have to do some haulage, and I'd spend a lot of time at the depot, plus I'd have to recruit drivers and meet with new customers……..it'll be a totally different ball game to what I've always done." Peter looked down at the table and shuffled the marmalade pot and the coasters.

Darcy sat nursing her coffee cup. "Well, you know I'll support whatever you want to do, I don't want you to be unhappy at work – you spend more hours there than you do at home, so it's important that you're happy in what you're doing. And I was just telling Jo a couple of days ago that I was thinking of getting a job."

"Woah, you don't have to do that ………..unless you want to, of course. I'll still be able to support my family, and you know we agreed that the boys need their mother at home while they're still young."

"I would only work part-time, and I would make sure it fitted in with our home life," said Darcy, smiling at him, "But to be honest, sweetheart, I'm getting a little bit bored of being at home so much."

Darcy stood up and walked to the sink to wash up the few plates and mugs they'd used. Perhaps that was why Peter had been so distant and irritable at home, and why their relationship had lost its spark. Maybe it had only been the stress of the job but he hadn't confided in her, and with a less stressful job his libido would increase and they'd regain their sex life, then she wouldn't have to look at men like Andy Johnson to make her feel like a wanted woman!

Chapter Four

Jo-Anne shook hands with the clients and smiling broadly she showed them out of the room. This function was going to be fun to organise – it was a Masked Ball, an event with the purpose of raising a target of £5000, and the charity directors had approached her boss after being let down by another company, and her boss had handed over responsibility to her to organise the whole event. She knew she could make a success of this, and as she had an appraisal coming soon, it would work well in her favour. The date was set for mid-July and her stomach lurched when the thought came unbidden into her mind – *what would be her home situation by that time?* She pushed the thought away, resolving to take each day as it arose, and the intention of dealing with whatever happened only *when* it happened and not waste energy over-thinking things.

She had spent the last couple of days in a haze of *what-ifs* and had only managed to clear her head after a long conversation with her mum, who had the ability to make things sound very simple.

"Don't make yourself ill by thinking about all the different possibilities – wait till whatever is going to happen actually happens…………..then deal with it! Anything other than that is a complete waste of energy!" her mum had said. Jo-Anne knew deep inside that this was the sensible thing to do, but she was very much a planner and organiser and never liked to react to circumstances, she liked to be in control of the situation. However, what she was facing now was completely outside of her control.

"Even more reason to let it unfold itself to how it's going to be," said her mum, "If it's outside of your control, then all the thinking and planning in the world isn't going to make a jot of difference!"

Jo-Anne pulled herself back to the task in hand and went to her computer to start planning the timetable for the masked ball and create her "To Do" list. She scrolled through her list of entertainment companies to find the Strolling Magicians, the after-dinner speakers, the Master of Ceremonies, the table entertainers, the cabaret singers and the five- piece band to provide the music. She would draw up a suggested list of options for the client to choose the kind of entertainment they would want for the evening, and if the meal was being provided by the hotel she needed to arrange to talk to the chef for suggestions for a menu and organise the waiting-on staff. She was soon lost in the planning and co-ordination and her world felt comfortable again.

That evening at home, she made herself a meal and sat down with a small glass of wine when her phone rang. She expected it to be Trevor, but with surprise she saw it was an unknown number. She cautiously answered, prepared to hang up if it was a call asking if she'd suffered a recent accident, or wanted to change her energy supplier, but the voice quickly identified himself.

"Hello, Jo, I hope you don't mind me ringing, I got your number from your brother Simon. It's Dave Forrest.........."

"Dave! Dave Forrest! Gosh! This is a surprise! How nice to hear from you!" Jo-Anne exclaimed. "What are you doing with yourself these days? I didn't expect to hear from you again - last I heard you'd emigrated."

"Yeah, did that. Went to Germany, me and Sally, spent five years there till Sally found someone she'd rather be with, and hey presto! Divorced and back in England! She stayed out there with her new hubby – Alex, – nice guy as it happens, but I decided to come home. I ran into your Simon on my way to a job interview, and we arranged to meet up. He looks well, does Si, doing OK as well. Do you see him often?"

"Not really, mainly at family events. We both have busy lives, but I suppose we should make the effort to meet more often…………..Anyway, did you get the job? The one you went for when you met Simon?"

"Yeah, I did, I'm working for a construction company as a civil engineer." There was silence for a few moments, then Dave said, "How about you? Still married to ………..Trev, isn't it?"

"Yes, how did you know that? Oh, Simon would have told you!" said Jo-Anne, "Trevor's in Spain at the moment, his ex-wife and her parents were in a car crash, her parents died and Dawn – his ex-wife - is in a coma in hospital, so Trevor had to go out to see to his daughter, she's nearly ten years old."

"Oh no! How awful for you all. What's going to happen?"

"Well, that's the million dollar question! I don't know. Trevor's not able to make any plans or anything, we have to wait to see when or if Dawn recovers. The other problem is………. Savannah, his daughter, has never accepted me! She's always refused point blank to meet me, or let me come anywhere near her, so how this is going to pan out I just don't know."

Jo-Anne felt herself becoming tense as she related the current situation, feeling the weight of the worry once again. Dave didn't answer and there was a long pause, then he said, "Are you still in touch with Darcy?"

"Oh, yes, she only lives a few streets away from me, we've stayed best friends, we're really close. I'd have been lost without her over the past couple of years with……one thing and another!"

"She still married to………Peter, wasn't it? Didn't she have a couple of kids?"

"Yes, to both questions. My word, you've kept in touch without us knowing, haven't you! They've got two boys, George and Lewis, sweet little things they are as well." Jo-Anne was smiling as she talked about the boys, they were the nearest she would ever get to having a relationship with children, and she loved them like a doting aunt.

"Well me and Simon exchange emails every couple of months, I needed to keep one foot back in England while I was abroad............Simon kept me up to date with the team and the lads we used to hang out with. We should get together, you, me and Darcy, have a catch-up, all three of us," said Dave, "What do you think?"

"Yeah, why not? Where are you living?" asked Jo-Anne, it would be good to take her mind off what was happening.

"I'm in motel at present, I was waiting to see which job I got before I decided where to settle."

"Well, I'll tell you what," said Jo-Anne, "I'll speak to Darcy and work out when we can get together. Is this number you're ringing from the number I can reach you on?"

"Yes," said Dave, "You can call me anytime. I hope we can meet up soon, it'll be great to touch base with you both again."

"What about Will? Is he still in New Zealand?" asked Jo-Anne, "The whole family moved out there, didn't they?"

"Yeah, he's married, too, with a couple of kids. Met her in New Zealand, though she's English – she'd lived there since she was twelve when her family emigrated. I keep in touch by email and he keeps inviting me out there, but I've never got round to it."

"Ah, I'm glad it worked out for him, he was always such an easy-going soul, wasn't he? We had some good times, us four!"

"We did indeed!" said Dave with a chuckle.

"I'll talk to Darcy tomorrow and get back to you. I'd better go now, Dave, I'm expecting Trevor to ring soon. I'll ring you when I've spoken to Darcy. Take care, see you soon. Bye."

"You too. Bye."

Jo-Anne pressed the end call button and stood looking at the phone with a smile on her lips. Dave Forrest! That was a blast from the past! She quickly saved his number in her contacts list and went to clear up the remnants from her meal, then poured herself another glass of wine while she allowed her memories free rein.

She was sixteen when she and Darcy had hung out with Dave Forrest and Will Merrick – they hadn't been serious boyfriend and girlfriend, but had been a group of young people just enjoying life and each other's company, really good friends. Jo-Anne smiled wistfully as she remembered how uncomplicated life was in those days; they had all attended the same school but didn't become close until the last few months of their final term and they had all enrolled at the same college. Will was first to pass his driving test as his dad wanted him to help chauffeur his young sisters around to their various clubs and activities, so had paid for his lessons and his test and had bought him a small car – nothing fancy or high-powered to keep the insurance costs down, but it was enough to give the four of them some freedom at the weekends. They often met up on a Saturday lunchtime after Will had picked up one sister from her dance class and the other from gymnastics, then the four friends drove – usually to the Lake District but sometimes wherever the fancy took them - with two two-man tents and sleeping bags stuffed in the boot and no forward planning or schedule except they must be back by Sunday at six o'clock to take both sisters to their Church Youth Club.

Jo-Anne sighed deeply. They had two wonderful years of fun and laughter before they began to grow apart. Darcy was first to find an interest outside of their group – she fell in love with the young guy who came to fix the central heating in her family home, and started to miss their weekend jaunts. Jo-Anne didn't want to go by herself with two boys, so gradually the Saturday overnighters became a thing of the past. Then Will started to miss coming for them as he had met someone at his sister's gymnastic class and started taking her out. Jo-Anne and Dave had maintained their friendship and celebrated their twenty-first birthdays together but the dynamics had changed and they gradually became more distant. Then Dave had been offered a job in Wales and although they promised to keep in touch, gradually the relationship petered out.

With another sigh, she made herself a cup of tea and carried it to the conservatory where she had left her course books and settled herself down to get an hour or two studying done before Trevor rang. Although she had used his call as an excuse to end the phone call with Dave, it was usually after ten o'clock when he rang, but she thought it was more of an acceptable excuse than "I've got studying to do," though she didn't understand why she thought that – it's not as if Dave would ridicule her or think less of her! He'd always been supportive of anything she wanted to do, but then she reminded herself it had been over eight years since she'd seen him, he could have changed. She pushed all thoughts of Dave Forrest and her giddy teenage years from her mind and focused on the task in hand.

Sure enough, at five to ten her phone rang. Trevor sounded exhausted, and her heart ached for him.

"How are you, sweetheart?" she asked, "How's Dawn ………..and Savannah?"

"Oh, God, Jo, it's a nightmare!" Trevor sounded close to breaking point, and Jo-Anne's heart lurched.

"Why? What's happened now?" she asked.

"Dawn's not come round – she's still in a coma. They don't know when……or if…..she'll wake up. It's the head injuries.

She might even be brain damaged, they can't tell anything just yet. We just have to wait……it's the waiting that's the hard part………I don't know what to do……….there's nothing I can do……." His voice cracked and he paused while he regained control. "I just have to wait…….I have to take care of Savannah, there's nobody else."

"Oh, sweetheart! Would it help if I came out there? I could fly out this weekend." Jo-Anne was rapidly mentally calculating what tasks she could delegate at work, what assignments she needed to submit for her college work, and how long she could stay in Spain.

"No, it wouldn't help, but thank you, sweetheart, for suggesting it. You know how Savannah feels……. I have to tread carefully with her, and she's already had a melt-down when she overheard me on the phone to the solicitor saying that I needed to be thinking of coming back to England……that I was missing you!"

Jo-Anne tightened her lips – one day Savannah was going to have to accept that Jo-Anne was Trevor's wife now………..but she chased the feeling away at once – this wasn't the right time.

"Well, if you change your mind, let me know – I could stay away from Savannah and the villa, I'd book into the hotel same as I used to before. I just want to hold you and give you some comfort. I hate to think of you hurting and worrying in a strange place with no-one to support you."

"While Savannah's at school I've been trying to sort out the legalities – fortunately they had a very good family lawyer who has handled everything – the villa that belonged to Dawn's parents has now passed to Dawn, and I've been made legal guardian for Savannah – I know I'm her parent, but Dawn had the residence order and this way just makes things simpler. We've had to apply to the Court of Protection for what's called a Deputy appointment – it's kind of like …….Power of Attorney

– because Dawn is in a coma, so that I can handle her affairs. I've had to arrange the funeral for her parents – it's on Friday, I'm dreading that! And there's things like Savannah's school fees and the utility bills and such for the villa – that reminds me, are you managing all our stuff – bills and the like? I'm sorry that I've had to take some money from our account to pay for stuff here – but I'm sure I'll be able to get it back when everything is sorted."

Jo-Anne quickly interrupted him, "Don't be worrying about anything back here, it's all fine, all under control. You just do what you have to do there. Oh, I wish I could help in some way."

Trevor sighed deeply. "I know, darling. I miss you so much." He took a deep breath, "There's something else - I have to sort something out about work. They can't give me unlimited compassionate leave – and no-one knows how long Dawn is going to be like this – I don't know what to do! I could use up my annual leave as Neil suggested, but what'll happen when that's all gone and Dawn is still in a coma? There'll be nothing else for it - I may have to leave my job!"

Jo-Anne took a deep breath in and was silent for a few moments. "Well if that's how it has to be, then………..that's how it has to be! It's all unknown, isn't it? We're going to have to learn how to roll with the punches, and if your job becomes an obstacle …………"

Trevor didn't respond and they were both quiet, lost in thought, till Jo-Anne ventured to say, "Couldn't you ………..come back here, and bring Savannah to live here?"

"You're not serious, are you? What about Dawn? Do I just leave her here in hospital, in a coma? With no-one to see to her? Savannah wouldn't hear of it! She wouldn't come to England to live anyway, she'd never leave her mother!" Trevor sounded quite angry.

"I'm sorry, I wasn't thinking!" Jo-Anne quickly exclaimed, concerned that she'd been thoughtless, "I just thought……….I'm sorry!"

"No, no, it's me, I'm sorry I shouted, I'm just so bloody exhausted! I'd better go now anyway, I've to get up early to take Savannah to meet the coach – they're on a school trip and leaving early in the morning. Don't go worrying about anything, you've got enough on yourself with your studying – are you keeping up with it all? Your course is coming to an end fairly soon, isn't it?" Trevor sounded conciliatory now and Jo-Anne felt soothed. They rarely rowed as a couple, and Trevor had never raised his voice to her before. They were under a lot of strain, so it was to be expected that nerves would be frayed.

After more tender words and long, drawn-out goodbyes, they finally ended the phone call and Jo-Anne sat quietly in the conservatory, still curled up in the chair, watching the moths outside batting their wings against the windows, attracted to the lights that shone brightly inside, emphasising the dark of the night outside across the garden.

Something would have to be done about Savannah – not just now, but soon. They couldn't let a ten-year old dictate their lives, or break-up their marriage…………because that's what it seemed that she wanted!

Chapter Five

Darcy's excited squeal caused Peter to look up from his newspaper. He was at the breakfast table on Saturday morning, dawdling over toast and coffee while the boys ran around in the garden enjoying a game of penalty shoot-outs, and she had been sitting at the computer desk but was now standing in the kitchen doorway.

"What's up?" he asked her, raising his eyebrows at her expression. Her mouth hung open and her eyes were huge as she stared at him.

"I've got an interview!" she gasped. "Oh, my goodness! I never expected that!"

"Well done, darling! Where is it? I didn't know you'd applied for anything."

"It was only yesterday………..I was looking on job sites to see what kind of jobs were available and I saw this one……………it's in jeweller's shop in town……..Oh!" A slow smile spread over her face. "Fancy that! I thought I'd be sending applications off and getting nowhere – I never expected an interview from my first application!"

"When is it?" Peter asked, slowly turning the page of his newspaper.

"On Thursday, ten o'clock. I'd better check my wardrobe – Oh, my goodness, it's been many, many years since I had an interview! I feel nervous thinking about it!"

Peter smiled at her, "Your outfit is the last thing you need to worry about! You've got outfits for EVERY occasion. That won't be a problem!"

"I've got to ring Jo!" Darcy leaned across the table and reached for her phone, quickly scrolling to Jo's number and walking out of the room as she said, "Jo! You'll never guess! I've got an interview!"

Peter frowned and folded up his newspaper. He wasn't sure how he felt about Darcy returning to work. They didn't need the money. When he'd met with Darren on Thursday, he'd listened carefully while Darren explained the responsibilities that came with the job, and it was as he thought – totally different to what he'd always done. He would rarely have to go out on haulage, because the main part of his job would be to manage the logistics - the contracts, timetables and diaries, and make sure all the loads were picked up and delivered with as few empty vehicles as possible on the road. Darren had built the company up from a two-van household removal business that his father had founded – Hanson's Removals - and since his father's death fifteen years ago Darren had worked night and day to develop the company into the international success that it was now – Hanson's Haulage. Peter had worked with him for the past twelve years, marvelling at Darren's ambition and fortitude, but at the same time feeling sorry for the sacrifices he had made to reach this level of success. Since Darren had contacted him, Peter had thought long and hard about whether he was ready to give up the road and become office-bound, but of late he was feeling the strain of being away from home so much, missing his children and his lovely wife, and recognising that the exhaustion he felt when he came home after a long haul was affecting his ability to be the romantic, loving partner that Darcy deserved. Although he was nearly ten years older than her, he wasn't forty yet – too young to feel as fatigued as he did and devoid of any sex-drive. This was the deciding factor in his decision-making – he envisaged their life when he took up his new position, being at home every weekend, planning days away as a family, picnics, trips to the zoo, kickabouts in the park on a Sunday afternoon – things that normal families do, and the relationship between him and Darcy becoming much closer, more relaxed and loving, and his libido would probably return to normal.

He got up from the table and went outside where the boys were still playing penalty shoot-out, and called to them to let him join in. The boys were thrilled that their father was playing with them and it filled his heart with joy tinged with sadness when he realised that such a small gesture on his behalf had brought so much happiness to two little boys.

Darcy joined them all outside, cradling a cup of coffee and watching with a smile as they took turns goal-scoring. Jo had been excited for her when she heard about the interview and offered to do some practice interviews with her if Darcy thought it would help. Darcy chewed her bottom lip as she thought about Jo-Anne's circumstances – she couldn't imagine how she would cope in a situation like that, being pushed to one side to satisfy the turbulent moods of a ten-year old child and an ex-wife in a coma! Darcy was quite egotistic and Peter had always kept Darcy at the centre of his universe so she could only view the world from that position. She had thought at the beginning that Jo-Anne was courageous taking on a man who had a former wife and child, but as they lived in another country she supposed they didn't pose much of a threat. She thought Savannah was a bit spoiled when she heard about Jo staying in a hotel by herself while Trevor visited Savannah when they went on holiday, and thought then that this little madam was running the show and should be told exactly what was going to happen. But Trevor never wanted to upset her – his time with her was precious and he didn't want to lose any of it through Savannah's sulks or rages, so he let her have her way over everything. Darcy sighed and went back through to the kitchen to begin clearing up. She shook her head sadly – poor Jo, what an awful situation for her to be in.

*****

Trevor pushed himself away from the wall that he'd been

lounging against and smiled widely at Savannah as she came walking towards him from the school gate, surrounded by giggling and excited schoolchildren. She'd been attending a Saturday club that the school ran where children could either do their homework or simply hang out with friends. Savannah had attended this club before the accident, and Trevor wanted her to carry on with things as much as possible to try to maintain some stability.

"Hello, darling, have you had a nice morning?" he asked her as she slid her hand into his and they turned to walk towards the car.

"Yes, thank you," she replied, "Can I go to see mummy today?"

Peter took a deep breath in and exhaled slowly. "She's still not well enough, sweetheart. But as soon as the doctors say she's able to have visitors, you'll be the first one to go. She's still sleeping, so she wouldn't know you were there anyway."

Savannah kept her eyes downcast and they reached the car in silence. "Would you like to go somewhere, or shall we drive straight home?" he asked her as they climbed in the car.

"Can we just go home, please? I want to write another letter for mummy for when she wakes up, because she won't be able to remember any of these days, will she? I have to tell her about Grandma and Grandpa's funeral, and how sad it was." Savannah looked at Peter with such a desolate expression that his heart almost broke in two.

They drove slowly to the villa listening to the music playing softly on the car stereo. Trevor had spent most of the morning at the hospital again, but there was still no change with Dawn's condition. As he'd sat in the chair next to her bed, he'd thought back to when they were first married and how much he had loved her. Dawn was twenty and he was twenty five, and after a whirlwind courtship, they had a beautiful wedding, then flew out to Spain to her parent's villa for their two week honeymoon. Dawn's parents had settled in Spain when her father took early retirement from the fire service and her mother left her job as a civil servant, and they sold their house and bought the villa so they could enjoy the fruits of their labours while they were still relatively young. They had set Dawn up in a small flat not far from the hospital where she worked as an administrator, and soon after they left she had met Trevor, and before long he had moved into her flat with her. He knew she missed her parents enormously, but he imagined that the love he had for her would fill the gap that their leaving had created. When they got married she sold her flat and they jointly bought a small semi-detached house with a handkerchief sized garden at the front, but a larger garden with conservatory at the back, but not too far out of town that made travelling to work difficult.

Eleven months into their married life she discovered she was pregnant, and she began to panic right from the beginning when she thought about giving birth without her mother by her side. Trevor would soothe her and hold her close, telling her that he would be with her every minute, and he would go to all the pre-birth classes with her, but as the date of delivery drew closer, she cried every evening when talking to her mother on the phone, till her mother flew back to England to be with her for the last couple of weeks before the birth, and her father flew out once the baby was born. Her mother stayed on for the first month afterwards to help with Savannah, but her father flew back to Spain after a fortnight, knowing that Dawn needed her mother more than her father at this particular time in her life.

When Trevor thought back to their relationship, he realised that he had loved her far more than she had loved him. He reckoned what he thought was love from her was a dependency – a neediness, someone to cling to when her parents weren't there. Afterwards, when her mother went back to Spain, Dawn became very morose, and the Health Visitor was afraid she was suffering post-natal depression, but then identified Dawn's complete reliance on her mother and her mother's absence as the cause of her depression. Trevor worked tirelessly to keep Dawn's spirits up and to be a good husband and father, but Dawn constantly badgered him for them to go to Spain to live, but Trevor didn't want to – he enjoyed his job in England, but more relevantly, deep down he thought that Dawn needed to be apart from her parents so that she could gain some independence and be a person in her own right, but it never happened. Dawn's frequent visits to Spain with Savannah when she was a baby and toddler bled the family finances almost dry, and when Dawn realised that once Savannah started school she wouldn't be able to go to Spain as often, and she told Trevor she wanted to go and live in Spain with her parents and have Savannah educated there - either with or without him, Trevor agreed to give it a try, but his heart wasn't in it. He lasted six months – the heat and the humidity made his life miserable, he didn't speak any Spanish and could only get temporary work in a restaurant – which he hated. Dawn, on the other hand, was the bright and bubbly person he had fallen in love with, now that she was in the secure bosom of her family. They enrolled Savannah in a school with an excellent reputation – with the fees paid for by Dawn's parents, and everyone was happy. Except Trevor.

One evening after he had had the most miserable of days, he told Dawn he couldn't take any more and wanted to return to England. She refused point blank and said he would have to go back alone. They had sold their house before they came to Spain, so the family solicitor helped them sort out the finances of their joint account and they had agreed a mutual divorce on the grounds of irretrievable breakdown. They knew there was no point in trying to keep the marriage going, and Dawn promised that she would never stand in the way of Trevor visiting Savannah, so he came back to England alone and tried to piece together his life, his heart aching for his daughter that he was only going to see on pre-arranged visits.

He had felt a great weight of sadness as he sat by the side of Dawn's hospital bed. He had loved her so much, and now he felt guilty at not trying hard enough to be a firmer and stronger husband, a husband that could fill the loss she had felt when her parents were living away from her. Perhaps then she wouldn't have fallen out of love with him. Bill and Freda Watson, Dawn's parents, lived only for each other and when he had first met them, Trevor was struck by the obvious love they had for each other and he told Bill that he would cherish his daughter the way that Bill cherished his wife, and make her happy. He was slightly puzzled when Bill had laughingly slapped him on the back and said, "You've set yourself a task there, my lad!" He often thought afterwards that Bill was right – he always felt he was pushing a pea uphill when he was trying to make Dawn happy. When Trevor, Dawn and Savannah moved out to Spain, Freda insisted in keeping up their bridge nights and dinner party evenings with a group of ex-pats that they had been friends with for a long time, as if she wanted to maintain a bit of private life without Dawn. Dawn was oblivious to this, she was happy being in her parents' home, she didn't need for them to be with her all the time.

Trevor still felt that he hadn't tried hard enough. Dawn was such a lovable girl, she didn't have a bad bone in her body - she never spoke badly of anyone and she never gossiped. As he held her hand and gazed at her sweet face still bruised and grazed from the accident, he thought about how he would be able to tell her about her parents once she regained consciousness. His heart was so heavy it felt like a leaden weight inside his chest. How would she be able to accept it? How would she carry on without her parents? He had never known anyone so close or reliant on their parents before.

Once they got back to the villa, Savannah skipped out of the car and ran up to the veranda where she waited for Trevor.

"Have you got any homework left to do?" he asked her.

She nodded. "I'm going to do it now, then write mummy's letter." She went straight to her bedroom as they entered the villa, and Trevor smiled lovingly at her as he placed the keys on the table and walked into the kitchen. She was such a lovely child, so agreeable – except where Jo-Anne was concerned! Her intolerance of Jo-Anne was a mystery to him, she hadn't even met her, hadn't given Jo-Anne a chance to befriend her. With a guilty pang he remembered he hadn't been in touch with Jo-Anne all day, not even a quick text message to say how things were. He poured himself a glass of beer and went back outside to sit on the veranda to enjoy his beer in the shade and send a message to Jo-Anne. He could never understand how people could lie sunbathing, letting the sun beat down on their bodies! He kept out of the sun as much as he could, and kept the air-conditioning on all day and night in the villa!

Just as he picked his phone up to send the message, he heard a car pull up and looking up he recognised Savannah's friend Holly and her mum Jodie. He waved in greeting and stood up. Jodie didn't turn the engine off, so Trevor walked towards the car. He could tell they were disagreeing about something, and Jodie looked up as he got near.

"Oh, Trevor, I'm sorry we've called without phoning…….." she began.

"No, don't apologise, I've told you - you're welcome anytime. It's nice that people just drop by without having to ring for permission……...that's one of the things that I don't like about modern society!" He smiled at her, "Would you like to come in for a drink?"

She smiled in return and opened the car door, and as Holly got out of her side of the car, they all turned at the sound of Savannah's shriek as she bounded down the steps and hurled herself at Holly, grabbing her hands and dancing in joy at her friend's appearance, then both girls ran off hand in hand towards Savannah's bedroom. Trevor's eyebrows raised in amazement as he witnessed the transformation in Savannah, and turning to Jodie he said, "Well! That's the first smile I've seen on her face, never mind seeing her jump for joy! What a pleasure to see!"

As they walked up the step to the veranda, Jodie asked how Dawn was. Trevor told her that things were pretty much the same – Jodie had phoned almost every night to ask about Dawn's progress. They'd been very close friends for the past four years, ever since the girls had become best friends at school, and as Jodie and her husband had divorced when Holly was a baby, she too was bringing up a daughter without a father, except for the contact visits a couple of times a year.

She had been central to all the funeral planning that Trevor had been forced to do. The only remaining family member was Bill Watson's brother, Eddie, who lived in Australia and hadn't had any contact for over twenty years, but Trevor didn't know about him – it was Jodie who told him. The lawyer had contacted him, but he didn't come to the funeral, just sent a condolence card with a wreath of flowers.

Trevor poured them both an iced coffee and they went back to sit on the veranda, as the cool breeze on this side of the house made it more comfortable to sit in. Jodie explained that she and Holly were going out for a pizza, and Holly had asked while they were driving if they could call by and ask if Savannah wanted to come. Jodie had argued with Holly that it wasn't polite to put Trevor on the spot and she apologised if he felt under pressure to let Savannah go with them.

Trevor laughed. "Well, I've got a solution – why don't we all go? I need to eat too, so we can make it a joint decision to eat out and we all go to the same place! I don't think we'll get a refusal from Savannah, do you?"

"It must be so hard for the poor child," said Jodie soberly, "I know I was shocked to the core when the accident happened, so I can't begin to imagine what she must be going through in her poor little head. She loved her grandparents so much, they were all very close. Well, you know how close Dawn was to her parents, that's what finally broke your marriage, wasn't it?"

Trevor looked uncomfortable and fidgeted with his coffee glass. "Well," he cleared his throat, "It wasn't as simple as that."

"Oh, I know, it never is. But there's always one final straw that breaks the camel's back – it was the same with my own marriage, lots of things accumulate till it becomes impossible to carry on."

Trevor stood up. He didn't want to have a discussion about his marriage and break-up with Dawn, not while she was lying in a coma in a hospital bed. "Shall we call the girls down and give them the news about going out for pizza?" he said walking through to the kitchen and placing his glass on the side of the sink.

Jodie accepted the cue of changing the subject, and finishing her iced coffee, she followed him through to the kitchen and waited while Trevor went up to Savannah's room. She heard the excited squeal and smiled as she heard the footsteps tumbling down the stairs and two very animated young girls bounded into the kitchen. Following behind, Trevor smiled and thought to himself, *"This is what normal life should be like for a ten-year-old, this is what she needs – fun and excitement with her friend, not tears and heartache every night crying herself to sleep."*

As they walked towards the car, Trevor didn't notice his phone lying on the small table on the veranda, the text message to Jo-Anne still not sent.

Chapter Six

Jo-Anne and Darcy were supposedly doing practice interviews, but they hadn't as much as sat down and tried – Jo-Anne was sprawled on Darcy's bed and Darcy was rummaging through her wardrobe, holding up then discarding outfits one after the other. The boys were in bed and Peter had gone out for a drink with Darren so that they could finalise the change of Peter's work role.

"So when did you last hear from Trevor?" asked Darcy as she held up an outfit against her body and looked long and hard at the full-length mirror.

"Last night – just after six o'clock……… a text message! Just to tell me the funeral had gone OK – well, as OK as a funeral can go! And that he missed me….. and loved me," said Jo-Anne, "And before you say anything……….No, I haven't phoned him – he doesn't like me contacting him because we don't know whether Savannah is around or how private his phone is if I send a text message. If she got to see his phone, it would cause a rumpus if she saw a message from me. During the day most days he's at the hospital anyway so his phone is off. So I have to wait for him to get in touch with me."

"Well, I cannot understand how a ten-year old child can have so much power over two grown-up people," declared Darcy hooking the chosen outfit on the wardrobe door and starting to rehang the clothes she had discarded previously.

"Well she HAS lost her grandparents very suddenly, and her mum is in hospital in a coma and very seriously ill, so she'll be even more possessive with her daddy as he's the only person she's got at the moment," replied Jo-Anne, feeling that she ought to defend Savannah.

"Mmm," said Darcy through pursed lips, "I still think Trevor is too soft with her – I mean, this behaviour towards you went on long before the accident. That's when he should have made his stand, but he pussy-footed around her terrified in case she refused to see him again. He should have called her bluff!"

Jo-Anne didn't answer. She agreed with Darcy but didn't want to say anything against Trevor while he was so far away. She'd tried to imagine what could have happened to cause him to maintain telephone silence, and could only surmise it was something to do with Dawn. She shook the thoughts out of her head and said to Darcy, "So tell me more about Peter's job."

"Well, he'll be in charge of the logistics – sorting out cargo deliveries and pick-ups, transportation, customers, legal aspects for drivers and so forth. As far as I'm concerned it can only be good – I hated him being on the road all the time, I know he loved it, but since Dawns parent's accident I've worried myself sick. There's so much that can go wrong these days, the drivers don't just have to worry about the security of their cargo – in fact that's not such a problem of late, it's the illegal immigrants that cause the most grief. I feel sorry for them, don't get me wrong, but their attempts to cross the channel puts our drivers in total jeopardy! It's a nightmare for them!"

Darcy had finished putting the clothes back into her wardrobe and picking up her phone she said, "Let's go downstairs and open a bottle of wine – I've worked hard sorting out my interview outfit!"

Jo-Anne swung her legs off the bed and followed her out of the room. As they passed the boy's bedroom, Darcy looked in on them, opening the bedroom door slowly and quietly. They were both fast asleep, the nightlight between the two beds illuminating their sweet, innocent faces and Darcy tiptoed over and kissed each one on their forehead, stroking back the stray curls. From the doorway Jo-Anne smiled fondly as she gazed on and Darcy looked at her as they came out of the room, quietly closing the door. "You OK?"

Jo-Anne nodded and they went downstairs and into the kitchen where Darcy pulled a bottle out of the fridge and Jo-Anne got two glasses, then they headed back into the lounge, sprawling out on the floor with big cushions that they threw down from the sofa.

"What about Dave Forrest," Jo-Anne asked her, "Shall we meet up with him or what?"

"Yeah!" said Darcy emphatically, "I'm curious to know about his life. He got divorced you said, did he give any details – what went wrong?"

"No," replied Jo-Anne, "We didn't spend all that long on the phone to be honest. Shall I ring him now and arrange a date?" When Darcy nodded, Jo-Anne added "We'd better make it sooner rather than later, I don't know what's going to happen with Dawn and Savannah, I may have to go to Spain……..I just don't know. But this will give me something to think about instead of constantly worrying about Trevor."

"Oh, definitely!" smirked Darcy, "There's nothing like a date with another man to stop you worrying about your husband!"

"Darcy! You know fine well it's nothing like that! Dave and I were always good friends, nothing more!"

"OK, OK!" laughed Darcy, "You know I was just kidding you! Go on, ring the man!"

Dave answered on the third ring, and Darcy nudged Jo-Anne before she had a chance to speak, "Put him on loudspeaker, we can all chat then."

"Hi Dave," began Jo-Anne, "I've got Darcy here and before you say anything bad about her, I'm warning you I've put you on loudspeaker!"

"Hiya Dave!" trilled Darcy.

Dave's loud laugh made them both smile, "Darcy, you haven't changed, you sound the same as when you were seventeen!"

"Well that doesn't get you any brownie points, Davie boy! You need to tell me I LOOK the same as when I was seventeen!"

"Which I'm sure you do, my pet! How's things with you, anyway? You're a mother, I believe? Two boys you've got, right?"

"Yes indeed," said Darcy, "Did you have any children – Jo tells me you're divorced."

"No, no children, fortunately, it made the separation easier, I suppose. What about you, Jo? You never made the leap into motherhood?"

The sentence hung in the air like a thick cloud, and Darcy looked quickly at her friend, her heart in her mouth, wondering how Jo was going to respond. Jo-Anne licked her lips and swallowed hard.

"No," she finally managed, "I had health issues and had to have a hysterectomy, so – no womb at the inn!" She gave a shaky laugh.

"Oh, I'm so sorry, pet, I didn't know ....Are you well now, have you recovered?" Dave sounded genuinely upset and sorry.

"Yes, I'm fine, it was last year." She took a deep breath to steady her stomach that had lurched at the topic. "Anyway, we've phoned to arrange a meeting with you, let's look at some dates. We were thinking maybe soon, because of Trevor being in Spain, I can't plan too far in the future in case I have to go out there." Jo-Anne was brisk and business-like, her emotions regarding motherhood pushed way down below where they had to remain so that she could function in life.

"What about tomorrow?" asked Darcy, "I know Peter will be at home with the boys. Is that too short notice?"

"That's fine by me," said Dave, "I've got zero in my diary at present."

Jo-Anne nodded, "Yes, I'm OK with that. Where are you, Dave, which motel are you in?"

"I'm in the Travel Lodge just off the motorway. But I'll come to you, just text me your addresses and I'll pick you both up and we'll go somewhere. Do you want to eat, or just a drink?"

They looked at each other, then Darcy took the lead. "We'll eat. Tell you what, Jo can come to mine for lunch and you can pick us both up here, then I can introduce you to Peter. What do you think?"

Jo-Anne nodded, "Yeah, that suits me, I love your Sunday dinners!"

"That sounds great," said Dave, I'm really looking forward to seeing you both. I've chuckled many times over the years thinking back to some of the things we used to do – those "camping" weekends we used to have………and that time that Will found the tree swing over the stream and took a flying leap………..and missed the rope!"

They were all laughing, each memory stirring another one and the laughter getting louder, till Darcy remembered the two boys sleeping upstairs who were now in danger of being woken up at the shrieks coming from the two girls. They finally said goodbye to Dave, Jo-Anne promising to text Darcy's address so he could collect them both the next day.

*****

Trevor and Jodie were smiling indulgently as the girls giggled and whispered about their heart-throb boy band and then pretended not to have said anything when either parent asked what they'd just said, gazing with exaggerated innocence and blinking meaningfully with eyebrows arched, causing both girls to fall against each other laughing like only children can.

They had finished their pizza and the girls had ordered ice-cream, while Trevor and Jodie had been served coffee. When the ice-creams arrived, they tucked in, still going into fits of giggles as they caught each other's eye. Trevor was gratified to see Savannah in this mood - he had never witnessed this side of her before as he had never seen her in the company of any of her friends when he used to visit her – he would want to spend the whole of his visitation time just with Savannah, taking her places, but just the two of them. Jodie had noticed the emotions flitting across his face and she leaned across the table and squeezed his wrist.

"It's good to see and hear children's laughter, isn't it?" she said softly, "Even more so in this case. I can guess how you're feeling right now." She looked at him tenderly, then back at the girls who had now decided to play a game of "Hangman" on a paper napkin as Holly had a pen in her little shoulder bag, along with a lip gloss, a small hairbrush and a small wallet.

Trevor nodded silently, and said very quietly, "There have been so many tears ……….so many…………. Most times I feel completely out of my depth. I wish that Dawn would come out of the coma - if she would only wake up so Savannah could visit her I'm sure they would both benefit so much from seeing each other."

Jodie sighed deeply. "I think you're right, if Savannah could see her mum she would be able to accept things better, I think the worst thing is not seeing something because your mind makes its own pictures and sometimes they're worse than the real scene, if you know what I mean."

Trevor nodded. "I know. But Dawn is such a mess I couldn't take her into the hospital, it would scare her too much. Maybe in a few days when the swelling and bruising has subsided a bit………." He looked at his watch, and Jodie said, "Do you need to go? Have you something to do?"

"No," said Trevor, "It's just that I forgot to send a text to Jo before we came out, just to keep her up to speed on how things are going. I didn't get a chance last night – Savannah had another crying fit – she found some things of her Grandmother's – I really should start sorting things out! That's what I need Jo for, she's so good at stuff like this, she'd just ……..get it done! " He had purposefully dropped his voice very low when speaking about Jo-Anne in case Savannah heard him, but she was enthralled in the game with Holly.

"Is there a problem…………" Jodie nodded her head towards Savannah, "Does she still not approve?"

"That is the understatement of the century!" sighed Trevor, "There is point blank refusal to even meet, I can't use her name, I can't make contact with……." he nodded his head backwards to signify someone far away, "as it creates a form of hysteria like you've never seen! It's a nightmare – has been from the beginning."

"Oh, how awful for her – for them both! I hadn't realised. And you're caught in the middle." Jodie looked sadly at Savannah. She'd known her since the girls first started school together, and the four of them used to spend a lot of time together – she and Dawn were good friends, and they had so much in common with each of them being divorced and raising daughters, but Dawn had the added benefit of living with her parents, whereas Jodie lived in a small apartment with Holly and visited her own parents who lived a fair distance away in the next town. Dawn had never said very much about Trevor's life since their divorce, and Jodie had never questioned her, guessing that she didn't like talking about it.

"Dad, when we go home can Holly stay for a while, there's no school tomorrow – it's Sunday?" asked Savannah, as Holly grabbed her mum's hand saying "Please, please, can I?" Jodie said nothing, but looked at Trevor, who blinked rapidly and looked at Jodie beseechingly.

"It's OK by me if it's OK by you," he said.

"Alright then, but not for too long, OK?"

"Yes, yes, thank you." The girls had clutched each other's hands and were dancing in their seats.

"We'd better head off back home then, if our chauffeur is ready." He smiled at Jodie as he beckoned for the waiter to bring the bill, and as Jodie took out some notes to pay her share, Trevor pushed it back to her and said, "Let this be my treat tonight, I'm so much in your debt for everything you've done to help me with ………things………and it's done us both good to have such pleasant company."

"Thank you," said Jodie as she took out her car keys and they all stood up, the girls starting to giggle again as they talked about which CDs they were going to listen to in Savannah's bedroom when they got back.

As soon as the car stopped they jumped out and ran up the steps of the veranda, hopping from one foot to another while they waited for Trevor to come and unlock the door. Once inside they scooted up to Savannah's bedroom and Trevor turned to ask Jodie if she wanted a drink.

"I've got to drive home so I'll just have a coffee, but if you want a drink……..don't let me stop you," she said dropping her bag on the side table with the car keys, and sinking into one of the big armchairs. She loved this room. She and Dawn had spent many evenings here with Dawn's mum while the girls played together and Dawn's dad was at one of his 'meetings' as he liked to call the evenings he spent with his ex-RAF buddy in a *taverna* putting the world to rights.

Trevor came back into the room with two mugs of coffee which he placed on the coffee table and said apologetically to her, "I'm sorry, it's instant coffee, I hope you don't mind. The kitchen is very much depleted in stock – I'll have to do some shopping, but it's not one of my favourite pastimes!" He took a seat in the opposite armchair so they were facing each other.

"I don't mind getting shopping for you, I'm going to the supermarket tomorrow for my own stuff. Do you want me to do a recce of your kitchen and stock up for you while you're at the hospital?"

"Would you? Gosh, that would be great! But I have to admit.......I can't go to the hospital tomorrow, if she's not at school - I can't take Savannah, so I'll have to miss going to see Dawn. I really hate shopping, I never know what to get, and I can never find what I'm looking for when I do decide what to get!" Trevor sounded frustrated at the prospect, and Jodie laughed.

"You're so typical of all the men I've ever known! I'll still do your shopping, you can spend the day with Savannah," she said, "Do you know, my fantasy is to meet a man who loves to shop – regardless of what we're buying – food, clothes, shoes, furniture!"

"Well I don't know any, so I can't help you there!" said Trevor grinning back at her, "When I was with Dawn, she did all the shopping – and did that woman love to shop – as you well know! And these days it's Jo that does it all, but she's very organised, she has lists of what's going to run out soon, so nothing ever does! She's brilliant – God! I still haven't messaged her, I must remember to do it tonight before I turn in for the night!" Trevor had a surge of guilt as he silently acknowledged that the reason he hadn't messaged his wife was because he was in the company of his ex-wife's best friend - and thoroughly enjoying the company of another adult after a week of being on an emotional roller-coaster. *But it's completely innocent*, he told himself, *Jo would understand, this is all for Savannah's benefit.*

They chatted for a while about what to do about Bill and Freda's clothes, and Jodie told him about the local church group who collected items for needy people and who often were donated deceased peoples wardrobes to clear. She offered to arrange this while he was at the hospital if he would sort out personal items that he wanted to keep for Dawn and Savannah and box them up. Then Jodie suggested they go to the kitchen to take stock, and Trevor fetched a pen and paper as she began to jot down what basic foods were needed, then she asked him what kind of food he liked to eat, and what he could cook.

"Oh, I can cook," he replied, "I'm not bad at all, Jo taught me a lot. I can produce some fine meals as long as the stuff is there to do it with! I often used to do the meal on a Saturday evening for Jo and me, and sometimes we'd have guests and I'd cook for them!" he boasted.

"Have you got a signature dish," Jodie asked him, smiling at his obvious pride.

"I have indeed!" he replied, "It's slow cooked lamb shank, with creamed potatoes and honey-glazed carrots with seasonal vegetables, and a rich onion gravy!" He drew himself up tall as he recited his menu smugly.

Jodie's eyebrows arched as she said with surprise, "Wow! I thought you'd say spaghetti bolognaise, or chilli – that's what most people claim to be their speciality! I'm very impressed!"

"Well, I'll have to cook it for you one night, when things……….when I know what's happening." Trevor's eyes clouded as he remembered the reality of his current life.

"Listen to me rabbiting on," he said suddenly, "Talking as if life was normal and we were two …….friends planning a normal evening, when ……… Oh, God! I still haven't messaged Jo! I really should try to get back to England to see her! I can't stay here forever - I just rushed off and…………"

"NO! NO! NO!" the scream from the doorway startled them both as Savannah hurled herself at Trevor. "You can't, daddy! You mustn't! Don't leave me! Don't go back! Stay! You've got to stay!" Trevor bent down and encircled her in his arms, "Savannah, darling, please don't cry! I'm sorry!" He hugged her to him as she screamed and wailed, throwing her head wildly from side to side.

Holly stared at Savanah and crept past her to her mother's waiting arms, fear and pity showing in her face as she witnessed the tsunami of emotional distress sweep over her best friend. She groped blindly for her mother's hand as she pushed herself as close to her mother as she could get, and Jodie hugged her tight as they both watched the scene before them.

Trevor held Savannah and whispered soothing words in an attempt to calm her and eventually her sobbing grew quieter. "Please don't leave me, daddy! Don't leave! What will happen to me? What will happen to mummy? I've got nobody! I'm all alone without you! What will I do?" Her eyes were wild and her face was blotched from crying, and Trevor looked beseechingly at Jodie, silently asking for her help, but Jodie was crying too. She shook her head at Trevor, and stood motionless, tears pouring down her face, and when Holly saw her mother crying she burst into floods of tears also.

Trevor was distraught. He had no idea how to handle this situation. He sank down till he was sitting on the floor and pulled Savannah towards him so she was lying in his arms, still crying, but not hysterical now, just a lost and lonely grief-stricken ten-year-old child who mourned her grandparents and ached for her mother to be returned to her. Jodie followed suit, slowly sliding her back down the kitchen wall till she was also sitting on the floor with her weeping child encircled in her arms as she sobbed brokenly for her own best friend lying in a coma in hospital unaware that her beloved parents had been killed in the car crash that had put her there.

Chapter Seven

Darcy opened the door and Dave stood on the threshold, a big grin on his face and two bunches of flowers in his hands. He was broader than when they used to hang out together, and his face had filled out making him look more handsome. His dark blond hair was shorter than he used to wear it, too, but the grin on his face and the twinkle in his eyes was the same.

"Just like the old days, this!" he laughed, "Except for the flowers – I never brought you flowers, just called for you to go on one of our jaunts!" He handed her one of the bunches.

Darcy laughed with him and stood to the side motioning with her head for him to come inside. Peter came into the hallway with his hand outstretched, "So this is Dave – the man who is taking my wife out for a meal tonight!" he joked and shook hands vigorously with Dave as they both laughed. "You'd better be prepared, she's hard to handle!"

Darcy pretended to swat Peter on his head, and Peter ducked in mock terror. They walked into the lounge where Jo-Anne sat with the boys, playing a video game with them, and losing quite drastically. She looked up as Dave came in, her eyes lighting up at the sight of him and her heart giving a little somersault as she said, "Thank goodness I've been saved, these two little monkeys are slaughtering me in this game!"

Dave handed her the bunch of flowers and she smiled at him, "All the years we've known each other and this is the first time you've bought me flowers!" As she spied Darcy's similar flowers, she corrected herself. "I mean US! The first time you've bought US flowers!"

Dave coughed, pretending to be embarrassed and said, "Well they're just a small token for the years I never bought them………… and they were two-for-one at the petrol station, which seemed to be hinting at me!" They all chuckled, and Darcy swatted him with the flowers.

Peter walked forward, "Have you time for a drink before you go? What time have you booked the table for?"

"I've booked for 7.30 at *Rodrigo's* on Main Street. Is it OK?"

Peter nodded, "Good choice. They do a nice steak, just how I like it. Well you've time for a drink, what will it be?"

Dave shook his head, "Thanks but no thanks. I never touch alcohol when I'm driving."

Darcy pulled at Dave's arm. "Meet my little monkeys………this one is George – he's six and a half, and this one is Lewis and he's almost five five!" The boys smiled self-consciously at Dave and bounced on their bottoms on the sofa where they were sitting. "I'm winning at this game," said George, "Lewis is rubbish at it!"

"I'm not!" retorted Lewis, "You're not that good!" and he launched himself at his brother, and George giggled, taunting Lewis, "Yes, you ARE rubbish! I win every time!" Jo-Anne said loudly, "Well I'm more rubbish than either of you!"

"Yes, you are!" shouted both boys, their attention now turned to Jo-Anne and their brotherly spat forgotten. "OK guys!" called Darcy, "Fifteen minutes more on that game, then daddy is taking you upstairs for bath and bed. And NO arguments!"

She turned to Dave and Jo-Anne and said conspiratorially, "Shall we get out while the going's good?"

"Oh, yes! Just leave me with the water-babies! Honestly, they create so much water on the bathroom floor, with their 'accidental' splashing…………..if I'm not ready with a mop, I'm sure it'll come through the ceiling!" Peter ran a hand through his hair in mock despair, and Darcy said, "Yes, dear, you're so good! I'm sure it'll be fine! They love you letting them play pirates………….. and it keeps the bathroom floor clean!" She grabbed Jo-Anne and Dave by the hand and called, "Bye, boys, bye darling, we won't be late. See you later! Love you all!" and she rushed them out through the door.

Darcy laughed as they got outside. "Doesn't it take you back," she said to Jo-Anne, "That's how we used to get out when dad went on one of his 'lectures'.......Yes, dad, you're right, dad, yes, we'll be careful! Love you!" They both laughed and Dave said, "He seems a nice guy does your Peter."

He opened the car and they both clambered in. It was a two-door hatchback, so Darcy pulled the seat forward and climbed in the back, leaving Jo-Anne to sit in the front passenger seat. "Oh, he's a darling," she continued, "He loves the boys to bits and he doesn't mind one scrap about the bath and bed routine. He spent so many years on the road and missed things like that while they were growing up."

Dave started the engine. "Ready, girls? And off we go!"

At the restaurant they were taken to their table and the waiter took their drinks order. The girls ordered white wine – a bottle, and Dave ordered tonic water. Dave looked at Jo-Anne, "You OK, Jo? You seem a bit quiet."

"I'm fine, thanks, can't get a word in for this one, that's all!" she thumbed in Darcy's direction, and Darcy wrinkle her nose at Jo-Anne. "I get starved of adult company and conversation so I tend to go overboard when I get it!"

"Yeah, whatever!" said Jo-Anne fondly and they both laughed.

The waiter brought their drinks and they began to peruse the menu. "Dave, before we go any further, I want to insist that we each pay our own share – same as we used to – just in case you had any chivalrous thoughts about picking up the tab!" Jo-Anne looked steadily at him, and Dave looked as though he was going to argue, but then spread out his hands in meek acceptance.

"I was going to say it was my treat, but if it makes you feel uncomfortable, then I'll do whatever you think best."

Darcy placed her menu on the table, "In that case, I'm having risotto – if you were paying I'd have ordered a basic salad like I used to! What you having, Jo?"

"I think I'll have bolognaise – *Rodrigo* special. I was going to have chicken, but after that beautiful roast chicken dinner today, it would put any other chicken dish to shame!"

Dave stroked his chin in contemplation, "I think I'll go by Peter's recommendation and have steak – No! Tell you what, I'm going to ask them to do me a mixed grill – for old time's sake!"

Jo-Anne laughed. "Remember that time we were in that restaurant in Kendal – you and Will both ordered a mixed grill and me and Darcy shared a small pizza and a salad? We kept asking for bits of your meal, and you shouted "Why didn't you order one between you then instead of pizza!" Then when Darcy got upset because you'd shouted and we couldn't afford a mixed grill – it was twice the price of the pizza – you got all contrite and apologetic and we ended up eating most of your meal!"

They all laughed and that started the course of the conversation. They talked and reminisced and chuckled as they brought back memory after memory, and as the evening progressed Jo-Anne felt the weight lighten concerning her worry about the non-contact from Trevor, till her phone buzzed and she saw Trevor's name as she looked at the screen, and her heart lurched.

"Sorry, guys, got to take this," she said as she rose from her seat and made her way to the ladies' room. "Hello, Trev, sweetheart I've been so worried!" she said quietly into the phone as she crossed the room and into the silence as the door closed behind her screening out the soft background music from the restaurant.

"Angel! I'm SO, SO sorry I haven't been in touch! It's been an absolute nightmare!" Trevor's voice was hoarse, but Jo-Anne was so relieved to hear from him she hadn't noticed at first.

"Oh, darling! How was the funeral? How has Savannah been since?" Jo-Anne felt the tears prick her eyelids at the thought of a little girl grieving her beloved grandparents.

"You could never imagine………..it's been heart-breaking…….." Trevor coughed to clear his throat and give him a moment to get his emotions under control. "The funeral was ………as sad as you would expect! I don't think Savannah really understood – it was a cremation, so there wasn't the trauma of seeing the coffins lowered into the ground – I think that might have freaked her out! The funeral director – *tanatorio* they're called – didn't speak any English, so that was difficult, as you can imagine. But Jodie was with us, she was brilliant – I don't know how I would have managed without her these past few days."

Jo-Anne felt a prickle of alarm creeping from the back of her neck up across her head.

"Who is Jodie?" she asked.

"Oh, sorry, I forgot, you've never met her – she's Dawn's best friend. And the girls are best friends too – they go to the same school. Jodie and Dawn spent a lot of time together, they're both raising girls as lone parents so they have a lot in common. Jodie is really cut up about what's happened. It was her that Savannah was staying with when the accident happened."

Jo-Anne was silent for a few seconds while she swallowed the niggle of jealousy that she was feeling. "I miss you so much, Trev. Can't I come and help you out? I feel so useless here while you've got all this going on. I'm sure we could think of some way to get Savannah on side."

"I miss you too, sweetheart, more than you'll ever know. But I don't want to cause her any more upset than necessary – last night she became hysterical when she overheard me saying to Jodie that I should start thinking of coming back to see you. I didn't know what to do with her, Jodie ended up crying, Holly was crying because she was so scared, it was ………..a nightmare! I couldn't console her! She won't trust me out of her sight now – she's scared in case I leave her!"

"I suppose it's understandable, she's lost her grandparents and her mum is……….. how is Dawn? Any improvement?"

"No," Trevor said sadly, "She's just the same. Her wounds are healing, but she's still in a coma, still on life support."

"It must be costing a fortune!" said Jo-Anne, "Is the insurance going to cover the medical expenses?"

"Oh, that's another nightmare – to be honest, I don't really know what's happening with all that. I know that Bill was diligent with making sure they were covered for every eventuality, and the family lawyer is dealing with everything – he's been brilliant, Manny he's called – might be short for Emanuel or something, or Manuel, but he speaks perfect English and he's a superb lawyer. He's dealing with everything. I wouldn't know where to start. There's the insurance from the accident as well, that's for medical cover, I think. I'm leaving everything in Manny's hands – he knows what he's doing. Bill trusted him implicitly, so that's fine by me."

"Where are you now, then? Where's Savannah?" asked Jo-Anne.

"I'm at home – the villa, I mean. Savannah's in bed, she didn't sleep much last night, so she was exhausted tonight. Anyway, my darling, how about you, how are you coping?"

"Oh, I'm fine – just out with Darcy for a meal and a drink," said Jo-Anne quickly, her heart skipping a beat as she realised she was deliberately not mentioning Dave, but justifying the omission by telling herself she didn't want to give Trevor anything else to worry about – *not that there WAS anything to worry about,* she consoled herself, *Dave is and always has been a very dear friend and nothing else. But Trevor may not understand that, so best not to say anything! After all, it's only a meal and a catch-up, I might not see him again! And Darcy is here so it's not a lie!*

"Well if everything is OK, I'll get off. I must say I'm exhausted myself, I've never experienced anything like this before and I'm out of my depth most of the time! I really want to come back to see you and to sort out my job and stuff – but I don't know how I'm going to manage it………….." He left the sentence hanging but Jo-Anne didn't feel that she could offer a solution that would comfort him, so she said nothing.

"Well, darling," he said at last, "I'll say 'bye for now, I love you and miss you like crazy. I'll try to phone you as often as possible, but you know how it is with Savannah, please just bear with me for a while longer – things have to change, it can't go on like this forever. If only Dawn would wake up, that would solve so many problems!"

"I don't think Dawn has much control over the issue, does she?" said Jo-Anne, "I mean, it's not like she's just having a lie-in!"

"I know that!" said Trevor sharply, "But you know what I mean………..oh, I'm sorry, sweetheart, I sounded really grumpy then! I'd better get to bed, I'll perhaps be more patient after a good rest."

They bade each other goodbye with many words of love, then Jo-Anne pressed the *end call* button and stood with the phone against her lips, gathering herself together before going back into the restaurant to her friends.

Dave looked up as she came back to the table.

"Everything OK?" he asked.

Darcy looked at her with concern. "Was that Trevor?" she asked and as Jo-Anne nodded she continued, "Did the funeral go OK? How was Savannah?"

Jo-Anne hunched her shoulders slightly and spread her hands open. "As funerals go – it went! Obviously, Savannah was upset. Dawn's still in a coma, still unaware that her parents are dead! Let's not talk about it, I was hoping to forget about it for one night!" She picked up her spoon and fork and wound the spaghetti, concentrating on the task in hand. Dave and Darcy glanced at each other, then Dave leaned over to her.

"We were just talking about that festival we went to, do you remember? In Kendal?" he had dropped his voice to a conspiratorial whisper, and Darcy joined in.

"He means that guy in the tent............." She giggled and Jo-Anne put her hand across her mouth while she swallowed her food, and joined in the laughter.

"Oh, my word, yes I do!" she laughed, "He was absolutely stoned, wasn't he, and decided to light a fire inside his tent when it began to rain! Fortunately for us around him the tent didn't catch fire – the FIRE didn't even catch fire because the kindling was wet, but it produced copious amounts of smoke and he staggered out coughing his lungs out! Will had to dive in and chuck water on the smouldering sticks, then the guy sat in the rain trying to light another spliff!"

They laughed and chatted all during the meal, recalling many fun times they had all shared. The atmosphere was cheery and pleasant, just what Jo-Anne needed. She would have plenty of time later when she was alone to dwell on Trevor's words, or between the lines of what he was saying.

Chapter Eight

The following week when Trevor sat in the lawyer's office, he stared open-mouthed at the man across the desk. Manny had known the Watson's for many years and had handled Bill and Freda's affairs since they first came to Spain to live. He knew Bill was a shrewd businessman who had invested wisely and had made ample provision for his only daughter. The whole family had good medical insurance cover which Bill had insisted upon as he had witnessed how ex-patriots could find their entire life savings swallowed up by serious illness requiring long hospital stays when they had neglected to make this essential investment and had lived their lives assuming that their health would always be good with a wholesome Mediterranean diet and vitamin D in the form of constant sunshine. But excessive alcohol consumption and cheap cigarettes, as well as a blatant disregard for sunscreen protection and a sedentary lifestyle lazing by the pool often outweighed the benefits of the former.

He spread the documents out in front of him and with very little emotion showing in his face he summarised the details of Bill and Freda's last will and testament. He explained that there was a trust fund for Savannah of £100,000 for when she came of age at 18, and this was primarily to ensure she had the fees for University. The rest of their capital, amounting to almost £340,000 was left to Dawn, plus the villa and cars - these assets realising a further £300,000. As Trevor had been granted Lasting Power of Attorney over Dawns finances and decisions regarding her health and welfare, he was now in the position whereby had no need to use his own money as he had been doing up to now.

Trevor's eyes were wide and his heart was racing. He was silent for several minutes, letting the enormity of what Manny had told him gradually seep into his brain.

"I'm so sorry for asking, but can I use some of this money to repay to my wife the amount of money I've had to take from our bank account since I've been living here?" he asked of Manny when he could finally find his voice. He had no idea Bill and Freda were so wealthy – he knew they were quite well-off, but not to this extent.

"Of course," said Manny, "You now have the authority to do as you wish – as long as it is in Dawn's best interest. It's still her money, her inheritance while she lives, but on her demise everything will go to Savannah. But it isn't fair that your wife in England should suffer financially for this cruel strike of fate that has brought us to this current situation. So you may refund your expenses so far, then you will use the money left by the Watsons for all your living expenses and any other expense you may incur. All medical treatments are covered by the health insurance that Bill was astute enough to take out, and there is the accident insurance still to be finalised. You do not need to worry about medical care costs – there is ample provision. Any other treatments that are non-medical that you may require for your…………..ex-wife……….. that are not covered by the insurances will be met by Dawn's own finances that are in your care."

Trevor shook his head slowly from side to side. "I had no idea there was so much money involved. It feels wrong of me to spend someone else's money."

"Well I don't expect you to fritter it away, but to have Dawn and Savannah's well-being and happiness as the focus of any large expenditure. But to all intents and purposes, live comfortably! You are going to earn a decent lifestyle – it's not going to be easy this journey you have undertaken! If there are any more questions………….?"

"Can I call you if I need advice any time?" asked Trevor, still nervous about the massive change that would be his future way of life, with wealth like this at his fingertips.

"Of course," said Manny, "I have been the family lawyer for many years and will still be available for Dawn and Savannah – therefore for you also." Manny smiled and stretched out his hand to Trevor, who took it in a firm grasp and gave a warm handshake to this man that he was truly grateful to. Yes, he was a lawyer doing his job, and no doubt would charge exorbitant fees, but Trevor couldn't begin to imagine how he would have coped with the legalities involved in this situation.

He left the office and walked out into the mid-day heat of Valencia, cursing the blazing sun that attacked him whenever he set foot outside an air-conditioned building, wondering if he'd ever get to feel comfortable in temperatures above 25 centigrade! He went into the nearest café-bar where the air-con would give him some respite and sitting at the farthest side of the room he took out his phone. He needed to talk to Jo-Anne.

The waiter came and after he'd ordered an iced coffee, he called her. He knew she'd be at work, but this was important – it was 12.20 GMT so it would be her lunch time. She answered immediately, concern evident in her voice, "Trevor? Are you OK? What's happened?"

"Hi, darling, I'm sorry to ring you at work……………" She interrupted him, "Is it Dawn? Has something happened?"

"No, no," he said, "Everything's still the same, no change I'm afraid, she hasn't woken up yet. No, this is something else – not bad news, so don't be alarmed. I've just spent the last couple of hours with Manny – the lawyer I told you about. He's sorted out the Power of Attorney for Dawn's finances, and he's given me a breakdown of how much Bill and Freda left for Dawn and Savannah – and honestly, sweetheart, the capital stands at £340,000 and the house is worth around £300,000! Can you believe it?"

"Oh, goodness me! I didn't realise they were wealthy!" Jo-Anne gasped.

"I know! Me either! The thing is – I can put back into our account the money I've used since I got here. Manny agreed that we shouldn't suffer financially because of this, and it's not like the money's needed here. So I'm going to transfer some cash after I've worked out what'll be a fair repayment."

"Oh, that feels a bit stingy……….. I mean nobody asked for this to happen, so we shouldn't profit from it."

"We won't profit! I'm only taking what's rightfully ours!" Trevor spoke sharply, but then quickly added, "Manny said we should do it, he actually said we should live comfortably as long as Dawn and Savannah are well cared for. And don't forget, I have no job now – I've had to give that up so that I can stay here, although I'll have to find some work……………." He left the sentence unfinished.

"Is there any way I could come to see you?" Jo-Anne asked, "I miss you so much. I could stay in the hotel nearby like I used to, and I'll keep out of Savannah's way. There's plenty for me to do – it's the City of Arts and Sciences after all, and we could spend time together when she's at school……………?"

"Yes, I miss you so much, my darling - I think it'll work as long as we're careful. She's very fragile – the least hint of insecurity sends her into a sheer panic. I'm going to take her to see Dawn tomorrow – it's the first time, so let's see how that works out, then I'll look up some flight times and book you in somewhere. Leave it with me. What about getting the time off? Can you do it with little notice?"

"Well, obviously the more notice I can give the better it is, but they're all aware of the situation, so I can get cover. And I've kept up to date with my assignments and college work, so that shouldn't be a problem. See what you can do, sweetheart, I can't wait to have your arms around me." Jo-Anne had dropped her voice so Trevor guessed there were people around, so he re-iterated his plans for the following day, and they said their farewell with whispered words of love.

*****

Jo-Anne hugged her phone to her chest after saying goodbye to Trevor and with a big smile on her face she quickly called Darcy. The phone went immediately to voicemail, so Jo-Anne reckoned Darcy was at the gym, so she left her a brief message to call when she was free. She wanted to share her news – she might be going to Valencia to be with Trevor, even though it would be very cloak-and-dagger so as not to upset Savannah, but the secrecy made it even more exciting! When her phone rang a few moments later, she thought it would be Darcy, but glancing at the screen she saw it was Dave.

"Hi, Dave," she said lightly, "You OK?"

"Yes, I'm great," answered Dave, "I'm sorry to ring you at work, but I've just been given the opportunity of attending a big Charity Auction event, I've got two tickets, and knowing that you're arranging this Masked Ball, I thought you might fancy coming along to see if there were some tips you could pick up, for now or for future events? It's being held in the Majestic Hotel in Harrogate this Saturday."

"Oh, that sounds great! I'd love to go, it'd be really interesting looking at it from a planning point rather than a partaker's point! But......I might be going to Spain but I don't know when, but........... oh, sod it! When Trevor next rings me I'll tell him I've got something booked for this Saturday so to make it next week, which it probably will be anyway...... so, yes thank you, Dave, I'd love to go. How much are the tickets, I'll pay for mine."

"Great stuff! Forget the tickets – I told you I was given them, I'll call you tonight and we'll talk more about it, OK?"

"Lovely! I'll talk to you later, 'bye." Jo-Anne ended the call feeling happier than she'd felt since the news of the accident in Spain, when her life – and Trevor's - was thrown into turmoil. Then she felt immediately guilty for feeling that way, what about poor Dawn, still in a coma and her parents both dead?

And Savannah? Her mother in hospital, her grandparents gone, and desperately clinging to her father whom she had had limited contact with over the last four years ………..neither of them would feel happiness for a long time. She shook her head sadly and turned her attention to the task in hand. She had a booking in the function room later today - a wine tasting event whereby participants were instructed on the qualities of different wines and taught how to compare. These events were usually well attended, and Jo-Anne was always amused at some of the pompous and supercilious participants who, because they were learning how to distinguish a wine by its colour and aroma, suddenly thought that they were superior to everyone else!

The day passed and when she eventually arrived home it was after six o'clock. As she let herself into the house, she noticed the side gate was slightly open. It was a six foot wooden gate the same style as the fence that surrounded the back garden and she always kept it firmly closed, so she relocked the front door and went through the gate to the back garden, looking immediately at the conservatory door for any signs of anything unusual. Her heart was beating rapidly, but everything seemed to be in order. She checked all around the door and all the windows, but nothing was amiss. She looked around the garden, noticing that the lawn needed attention, and the flower beds were looking bedraggled, and then she noticed the shed door was open and the lock was lying broken on the ground. She hurried down the path and pulled the door open. Trevor's bike was gone!

She gasped, her hand flew to her mouth and she grabbed the doorframe to steady herself. The bike was Trevor's pride and joy, it was the most expensive thing he owned – apart from the car, but he loved his bike. He would be devastated! She pulled her phone out of her pocket and called Darcy's number.

Darcy answered immediately saying, "Oh, babe, I'm sorry I didn't get back to you – I was leaving it till the boys were in bed then we could have a proper chin-wag!"

"That's OK, don't worry! Darcy, I've just got home and our shed has been broken into! Trev's bike's gone! His precious bike!"

"Oh, no! Anything else? Or have they just gone for the bike?"

"I can't see anything else missing – and the house doesn't look as if it's been tried! It appears to be either a sneak thief that got lucky, or somebody who knew Trevor's bike was there." Jo-Anne had calmed down by now, and was peering in all corners of the shed and looking carefully again for any sign of an attempted break-in round the doors and windows of the house.

"You'll have to phone the police to get a crime number to give to the insurance when you make a claim," said Darcy.

"Yes, I will," replied Jo-Anne, "Trevor will be gutted, you know how he loved his bike!"

"Are you OK, babe? Do you want to come here for tonight?" said Darcy, "You might be a bit unnerved by it, you can spend the night with us."

"No, thanks all the same. I'm OK, there's no damage apart from the padlock being wrenched off, so I think it was probably a sneak thief who got lucky. I'll go and ask the neighbours if they saw anything. I'll talk to you later."

She went next door to Mrs Willoughby and asked if she'd seen or heard anything, but she hadn't. Jo-Anne told her there was probably a sneak thief about so they should all be vigilant from now on. Then she went across the road to Mr Tomkins, a retired schoolteacher who spent many hours pottering in his garden. Mr Tomkins said he had seen a person riding a bike away from her house, but her didn't think anything of it as he was so casual about it – he certainly didn't look like he was stealing it. He told her the man was wearing a grey track suit and a baseball cap – he said he thought he was a friend of Trevor's, so didn't pay much attention. Jo-Anne thanked him and gave him the same advice as she did to Mrs Willoughby about being vigilant.

She then rang the police and reported the crime to a wearied officer who sounded as if he'd heard tales like this a hundred times – the thought made Jo-Anne smile wryly……….. *of course he does,* she told herself ………..*that's the nature of his work. It's not a drama to him, just to me!* He asked for details of the bike, hers and Mr Tomkins address, then gave her a crime number, telling her that an officer would be round in due course to get a statement from her.

Jo-Anne went into the kitchen and busied herself making a meal, but she kept glancing nervously out of the window, and as dusk approached her nervousness increased. She pulled the blind down and double checked that the back door and the conservatory door were both locked. As soon as she'd eaten, she went into the lounge and after closing the curtains she rang her mum. She needed to hear the calm rational tones of the woman who had talked her through some of the worst months of her life, when she had lost the opportunity to ever have a child of her own.

Her mum answered after the fourth ring, and Jo-Anne immediately felt relief at hearing her voice. She brought her mum up to date with Trevor's situation in Spain and his Power of Attorney role with Dawn's inheritance, then told her about the bike being stolen. As she was telling her, a slow wave of realisation washed over her – it was only a possession! Dawn lay in a coma, her parents were dead, and a bike was replaceable so in the grand scheme of things, not at all important!

Her mum said very quietly, "Oh, dear, sweetheart. Are you feeling vulnerable? Do you want me to come and stay with you for a couple of days?"

Jo-Anne was sorely tempted. To have her mum stay with her would be such a comfort, but in practical terms it would be a waste of her mum's time as Jo-Anne would be at work all day leaving her mum alone in the house. Her mum had moved to Grassington after her husband, Jo-Anne's dad, had died and she had bought a small souvenir and gift shop with a flat above it and had lived there happily, enjoying the peace and beauty of the Yorkshire Dales and the company of her golden Labrador, Bessie.

"No, thanks mum, I'm OK. It shook me up a bit to think that someone had been prowling around, but after all, it's only a bike and the insurance will cover it. I don't think I'll bother Trevor with the news just now – he's got enough to think about. I'll replace it when the insurance comes through and tell him when he eventually comes home. There's no rush. How's things going with you, anyway? Did you and Sarah join the pottery class?"

Sarah was a friend her mum had made since moving to Grassington and they met dog-walking. They had attended many classes in the Village Hall and gone on lots of workshops for different things – Jo-Anne was quite envious of the varied interests her mum had picked up since her retirement, and her social life was the best it had ever been.

They chatted some more about various things, then Jo-Anne said she'd better go as Trevor would probably be ringing soon. "If you need me, then just call," said her mum, and Jo-Anne promised she would as they said their goodbyes.

Chapter Nine

Darcy walked into the gym, surreptitiously glancing around to see if Andy Johnson was in. Her eyes lit up when she saw him on the treadmill, his body glistening with sweat and his attention focused on what he was doing. She started her warm-up stretches and as she turned, he was suddenly behind her.

"Hi, beautiful," he said softly, "I've missed you, you haven't been in for a couple of days."

Her heart skipped a beat! He'd missed her! She wasn't just a passing flirtation then, he actually noticed whether she was there or not! She swallowed nervously and said, "I've had a few things on lately……….."

He moved closer so his head was near her ear and said very quietly, "You'd look better with a few things off!"

Her stomach flipped, and she felt the heat rise in her face. "I've got a job, so I probably won't be coming as much," she managed to say, noticing the gleam of perspiration on the hairs of his chest and feeling warmth spread through her loins. Her heart was racing and her breathing was shallow.

"Oh, where are you working?" he asked, still standing dangerously close to her and looking down at her slightly upturned face. He was taller than her – her head was level with his chest and she had to peel her eyes away from his rippling biceps.

"I'm starting at James Family Jewellers on Main Street – do you know it?" she asked him her cheeks burning, and her eyes flicking from his face to his pectoral muscles feeling the urge to touch his firm body and stroke away the beads of sweat that were trickling down his chest. He noticed her gaze and glancing down at his chest, he smiled and pulled the towel from round his neck and mopped his face and chest, his eyes not leaving her face.

"I know it," he murmured, "We'll have to meet up at your lunch time and have a ………coffee together."

"Well, I haven't started yet – I begin next Monday. But I expect the first few days will be training, and I probably won't be able to get out and ………….."

"There's no rush, I'm not going anywhere." he breathed.

Oh my God! She felt faint with yearning. It had been so long since Peter had paid her any attention, she was soaking up Andy's admiration and desire like a plant starved of water. She looked at his face and saw the longing she was feeling mirrored in his eyes. *I so want to feel his arms around me, his body next to mine, his strength and power washing over me!* She thought wildly. *What am I going to do? I can't keep fighting this ……...it's too strong!*

He raised his hand to her face and took a tendril of hair that had escaped from her golden locks piled high on top of her head and tucked it behind her ear, letting his fingers dawdle around her lobe, then gently tilted her face upwards with his finger and said softly, "Whenever you're ready, I'm here………..no rush…….. now you'd better get your workout started, I've got a session in ten minutes, I need a cold shower first!" he smiled ruefully.

Darcy stood motionless as he walked away, her whole body quivering, then mentally shaking her head, she lifted her water bottle to her lips and drank greedily, trying to drown the ache she was feeling inside. She walked unsteadily over to the treadmill and forcing herself to focus, she set the machine off, gradually increasing the pace till she was running at full speed, trying to drive all thoughts out of her mind – and failing miserably!

*****

Trevor was feeling incredibly nervous as he and Savannah walked into the hospital. She had been eagerly waiting for school to end so that she could go and visit her mummy. Trevor had told her all about mummy's injuries so she knew her face would be bruised and that she had a tube helping her breathe, and that machines would be making noises, but she didn't care about any of that – she just wanted to see her. Trevor looked down at her as they neared the room door.

"Are you OK, sweetheart? Are you ready?" he asked her gently.

"Yes, daddy," she replied, "I'm ready, and I promise I'll be brave."

Trevor opened the room door slowly and stepped inside, still holding Savannah's hand. She walked in slowly, looking steadily forward till her eyes rested on the bed where her mother lay. She dropped Trevor's hand and ran forward.

"Mummy, mummy, I've missed you so much," she cried. "Can I hold her hand, daddy. Please?"

"Of course you can, darling, and talk to her – she may be able to hear you."

Savannah, gently took her mother's hand and stroked it lovingly, "Oh, mummy, I've missed you so much, and I've got loads to tell you. I hope you can hear me, because I want you to know everything is going to be alright now. Daddy's here, he's been looking after me, and you, so it's all going to be alright now. He's back. Daddy's back."

Trevor winced at her words. She truly believed that he was back to stay, that they were going to be a family again ………………..how could he destroy her world by telling her it wasn't so?

Savannah had continued, "Jodie and Holly have been spending time with us, it's been fun. We've done lots of stuff, and I'm keeping up with my homework, and I've been on two school trips, one to a vineyard and one to a museum that you and Grandma took me to............." Her voice tapered off and her eyes clouded at the mention of her Grandma and she looked nervously at Trevor who shook his head and put his finger to his lips, telling her not to mention her grandparent's death to Dawn. Savannah swallowed and took a deep breath. She started talking again, telling her mother things that had happened in school, what some of the girls were wearing on Saturday morning club that were totally just...........wrong, and if they had asked her she would have told them that what they *should* wear with those shoes............. it went on and on. Trevor had switched off to her voice – he had to think about how he was going to get Savannah to understand that he had a life in England, he had a *wife* in England, and he wasn't back with her and Dawn. How was he going to do it?

After about forty minutes, he noticed Savannah was running out of things to say, and the lapses in conversation were getting longer. He leaned over and said softly to her, "I think we need to let mummy rest now, you'll have worn her out with all your news and gossip!" He smiled at her, but she looked anxiously at her mummy.

"Have I? Have I made her tired? Have I made her worse?" she fretted.

"No, no, of course you haven't, I was joking. She'll have loved hearing your voice. It might even make her wake up, we'll have to see. But sometimes things like that happen. That's why I've been coming every day to talk to her, hoping that one day something I say will prompt her to wake up. Now she's stronger, you can come and talk to her every day."

Savannah smiled widely at this and leaned across Dawn, kissing her gently on the cheek and saying softly, "I'm going home now mummy, but I'll be back tomorrow. It would be really good if you could wake up and be sitting up in bed tomorrow when we come, so do your best, please."

Trevor ruffled her hair as she stood up, and he leaned over and pecked Dawn on the cheek, saying, "Bye-bye, Dawn, we'll see you tomorrow."

They walked out of the hospital, Savannah skipping happily by his side, a big smile on her face. As they got into the car Trevor said, "Savannah, I …………err………it's not……….err ……..oh, never mind." He shook his head. He couldn't do it, he couldn't tell her he wasn't here for good. He would have to wait till the time was right.

When they got back to the villa, Trevor went inside to prepare a meal for them, leaving Savannah on the front porch swing seat. She was playing music on her CD player and singing along with the songs, sounding happier than she had for a long time, when she shouted, "Daddy, Holly and Jodie are here!"

Trevor wiped his hands on a paper towel and went to the door. Jodie smiled as they came up the steps and Holly veered to the end of the porch where Savannah was swinging idly on the swing.

"How did it go at the hospital?" asked Jodie as Trevor stepped aside to let her into the villa.

"Remarkably well, considering," answered Trevor, "She didn't flinch at Dawn's bruising, nor the tubes, and she just talked and talked to Dawn, telling her all that had happened since………..Dawn went into hospital."

"She didn't mention her grandparents, did she?" asked Jodie.

"No, she was very good." Trevor took a pan off the stove and stirred it. "Would you like to stay for something to eat? There's plenty, I'm just doing a pasta with salad."

"No, thank you, we've eaten. I was wondering, though, now that Savannah's seen her mum, can I visit Dawn? I'm desperate to see her!"

"Yes, of course you can. Tell you what, we'll alternate – I'll take Savannah one night, then you can leave Holly here the next night while you visit Dawn. How does that sound? Of course I'll have to check that Savannah's OK about it – I told her she could visit her mummy every night, but I think Holly being here while you visit would be acceptable to her."

"Ah, brilliant! I've really missed Dawn. Are you sure you don't mind?" Jodie looked anxiously at Trevor, "I don't want to be a nuisance to you."

"Rubbish!" said Trevor, "You've been an enormous help to me during all this, and I'm afraid I may need some more of your valuable expertise in the next few weeks!"

"Anything I can do to help, I will," said Jodie brightening at the prospect of being useful.

"Just let me put this out for Savannah and if you want to make a pot of coffee, you can join us at the table while we eat, if you're OK with that." Trevor had spooned the pasta meal into a serving dish and placed it next to the salad bowl. He called Savannah to the table and all four of them sat round. Holly looked longingly at the pasta, till Trevor said, "Holly, would you like some tuna pasta?"

"Can I, mum, please?" she asked Jodie, who looked at her with arched eyebrows.

"You've already eaten this evening. Are you still hungry?" she asked.

"Mmmm," said Holly, "I love tuna pasta."

Trevor laughed and fetched a plate from the kitchen, handing it to Holly to help herself to the food. They sat in companionable silence, eating their meal while Jodie served herself and Trevor with coffee. After a few minutes, Trevor put down his fork and turned to Jodie.

"What I wanted to ask you about............I need someone to help with the garden and grounds, before it becomes a wilderness. I don't have time to see to it, and Manny has suggested I hire someone. I hoped you could recommend someone to me that is trustworthy."

She pursed her lips and pondered a while, then she said, "Yes! I know! Carlos will do it, I bet. He's a friend of my neighbour, Nicolas Moreno, and he was looking for more work – he looks after properties while the owners are away. I can ring Nicolas if you like and he can ask him."

"If you don't mind, would you. I need to start getting things in order now that the Power of Attorney is completed. I was restricted in what I could do before." Trevor looked relieved that Jodie was taking another responsibility from him, and he smiled and squeezed her wrist. "Thank you."

Jodie smiled and took her phone out of her pocket and scrolled till she found the number she wanted then called it. She stood up from the table and walked towards the veranda while she spoke into the phone, her initial greeting was in Spanish, then she reverted to English, mainly for Trevor's benefit, but then ended by chatting comfortably in Spanish. Trevor heard her laugh a few times, and he smiled in admiration at her relaxed ability to converse with people, then she said goodbye and walked back into the dining area.

"He'll ask Carlos and ring me back when he has an answer from him. If Carlos wants the job, shall I arrange for him to come and meet you?"

"Yes please. Is there any chance you could be here when he comes, just in case I have problems with the language?" Trevor looked imploringly at her, and Jodie smiled at him.

"No problem," she said, "I'll make it about this time on an evening then, shall I, then we'll be back from the hospital, whoever's turn it is."

"Is there anyone who could come and do the house and laundry?" he asked. "I might as well get it all sorted now, I don't want the place falling into ruins while Dawn's in hospital, and it has to look nice for when she gets home."

"Is it going to be long, daddy, till mummy gets home?" asked Savannah.

"I don't know, darling, but we'll make sure everything is ship-shape for when she does come home."

"Let's see what Carlos says," said Jodie, "His mother or one of his relatives could very well want a job, so we could ask him."

Trevor leaned back in his chair and sighed in contentment. Jodie was worth her weight in gold. Now that there was no financial restriction, he intended to make his life a lot easier. It had been hell so far, worrying about the villa, the gardens, always finding some expenditure or another, scrimping and struggling, but now the villa and grounds would be taken care of and he could concentrate on Savannah and Dawn.

Chapter Ten

Dave drew the car to a stop outside of Jo-Anne's house and turned towards her, the engine still running quietly.

"So, you think it was worthwhile going tonight then?" he asked her.

"Oh, definitely!" she replied, "Apart from really enjoying the auction, I found it very useful. I picked up some useful tips that could save me a lot of angst and sleepless nights!"

"Well as long as your angst has been saved, then it's OK," said Dave, causing Jo-Anne to laugh. She felt relaxed and comfortable with Dave, and always had done since their college days. She fleetingly wondered what her life would have been like if they had made a go of it all those years ago – but their relationship had never been romantic, she reminded herself, it was platonic, but special.

"Can you believe some of those lots up for auction tonight? There's no way I could ever afford anything like …………the helicopter flight, or the weekend in the luxury spa hotel in Venice, or the cruise down the Norwegian fjords………..I mean, they didn't go cheaply, did they? But it was nice mingling with rich people – you couldn't really tell who was rich and who was ……….like us, could you. Ah, it was fun! Thank you, Dave, I had a great night."

"Me too," said Dave, "I met some interesting people, as well. It was well worth going."

"Do you want to come in for a coffee?" asked Jo-Anne, "Actually, you'll be doing me a favour, I'm a bit nervous going in late like this after having that sneak thief in my garden."

Dave switched off the engine. "Say no more! Helping a lady in distress is what I'm good at! Lead the way!"

They both climbed out of the car and Jo-Anne rummaged in her bag for the key while Dave checked the side gate.

"It's locked," he said, "Did you lock it from the other side?"

"Yes," she replied, "Peter put a lock on after the burglary, and I keep it locked so no-one can get through unless they're let in from the other side. It makes me feel safer."

"Good thinking," said Dave as he joined her at the front door. She unlocked it and turned on a light immediately inside the front door.

"Why don't you get a Crime Prevention Officer to visit?" suggested Dave, "He – or she – can give you some advice, or even put your mind at rest by saying you're quite secure as you are."

"That's a good idea, you know, I think I might do that! I'll ring them tomorrow." Jo-Anne set the mugs down on the kitchen table and Dave perched on one stool while Jo-Anne sat across from him.

They chatted idly for a while about the evening, then Dave asked about Trevor and how he was doing in Spain. Jo-Anne told him about Trevor taking on Power of Attorney and the extent of Dawn's inheritance, but that she was still in a coma so he was dealing with all her financial affairs. She told him about their conversation about her going to Spain, but he hadn't arranged anything yet, as Savannah had just started visiting her mummy in hospital and he needed to concentrate on her at the moment.

Dave remained silent while she spoke, and offered nothing except a sad shake of his head. Jo-Anne looked at him.

"You're not saying anything," she said tersely, "What are you thinking?"

Dave still shook his head slowly and sadly. "I'm thinking how awful it is for everyone concerned. I can see it from everyone's point and it's very complicated!"

"Darcy thinks Trevor should be firmer with Savannah – he's always been soft with her, but now she says she's ruling all our lives!"

"Mmm, that's a bit harsh, I think. She's a ten-year-old child whose grandparents have died and whose mother is seriously ill in hospital and her relationship with her father has not been consistent or easy, so she's behaving like any ten-year-old would in this situation I should think. I'm not a father myself, but I can see it from Trevor's point............. but I can also see it from *your* point, and the sacrifices you're making in regards to your marriage - I think you're being pretty magnanimous!" Dave smiled at Jo-Anne.

"Do you? Really?" she asked him, "Thank you for saying that – to be honest I do sometimes think I'm being rather over-generous in my attitude, but then I think of what poor Trevor is going through." She sighed deeply, then said, "Let's not talk about it, it'll spoil the night and I've had a really good night tonight!"

"Well, I'd better get off now, anyway," said Dave, draining the last of his coffee as he stood up. "I'll give you a ring through the week to see how you are, and don't forget, if there's anything you want, just ring me."

"I will," said Jo-Anne following him to the door, and after they had said goodnight she double locked the door and went through checking the kitchen door and the conservatory door. She made a mental note to ring the Police station the next day to ask for a Crime Prevention visit, and she slowly went up the stairs to bed, wondering what Trevor would be doing at that very moment.

*****

Trevor breathed a sigh of relief as he closed the door and walked back into the lounge where Jodie was sitting on the sofa. He sat on the chair opposite.

"His English is really good, isn't it?" he said to Jodie, "And his mother is so typically Spanish she makes me smile."

"Well I thought I might as well mention to Nicolas that you wanted a housekeeper as well as gardener, then Carlos could ask his family members. It's a stroke of luck his mother wanting work – with her in the house there's no chance of Carlos skiving, her pride will make sure he works VERY hard. Spanish mothers are like that – well, I should say ALL mothers are like that, they want their children to do their best and gain respect, no matter what age they are!"

"You've been brilliant, Jodie, thank you so much for all you've done!" said Trevor, smiling at her, "You've been such a help to me."

"It's not a problem," she smiled back, "I think you've got enough to worry about with Dawn and Savannah, and then there's your poor wife back in England! She must be missing you like crazy."

Trevor's eyes clouded. "I know. She's been so patient, it can't be easy for her. I must look at flights for her – she wants to come out for a few days, but she'll have to stay in a hotel – Savannah still won't accept I have a wife. It's so difficult, I know I should be firm and tell her I have a wife and my home is in England, but………well, you heard her that time when she overheard me saying I should go back to England and she went hysterical! She does that every time I even hint that I'm going back. The problem is that she thinks I'm back with her and Dawn – that we're a family again, and the truth is, Jodie, I'm scared to challenge her belief!" Trevor looked so distraught, Jodie's heart went out to him.

"Do you want me to talk to her?" she asked him quietly.

Trevor didn't reply for a few seconds, then he leaned towards her. "What would you say? Do you think she would listen to you? I've been thinking she may need professional help – I mean this is not just since the accident, her refusal to accept Jo-Anne has been from the beginning. Lots of people remarry and their children accept step-parents, but Savannah's mind-set seems…………unnatural!" He was wringing his hands, obviously upset. "She's getting worse…………. Believing we're back as a family…………I don't know what to do!"

"Shall I try talking to her? I've purposely never mentioned anything, but if you want me to broach it………casually, when she and Holly are together, then Holly can kind of………act as a buffer!" Jodie looked apprehensive, and she certainly felt it. She'd never tackled anything like this before, although she worked for the Ministry of Education, her job had always been with adults as a teacher of English. But she felt that she needed to do something to help, it was an intolerable situation for Trevor AND for Jo-Anne. She'd never met Jo-Anne, but Trevor was such a lovely man and he needed her help.

"I'll not rush into anything, don't worry, and I'll be ultra-sensitive! I'd better get off home now and get Holly into bed. Can you call the girls down, please Trevor," said Jodie as she was gathering her things together and taking her car keys out of her bag.

Trevor nodded and walked towards the door, calling upstairs to the girls to come down. They'd been closeted in Savannah's room while Trevor and Jodie talked to Carlos and Fabiana about coming to work for them.

"Oh, by the way, Trevor, the school is closing for the summer in two weeks, the 21st of June – I thought you should know that for any future planning." Jodie looked steadily at him and he sighed deeply and put his hand to his head.

The girls tumbled down the stairs, laughing at some silly joke they'd shared, and Trevor was taken aback again at the difference in Savannah when she was with Holly and Jodie – perhaps it would work, perhaps Jodie could get through to Savannah and make her see that her life could be enhanced by having Jo-Anne in it. They all said goodnight as Trevor and Savannah walked to Jodie's car and Savannah waved furiously, laughing and pulling faces at Holly as the car pulled away.

Trevor tidied up the kitchen as Savannah got ready for bed, telling himself he wouldn't have to worry about it soon as Fabiana would be coming three times a week to clean the house and do the laundry! What a relief!

Savannah called that she was ready, and Trevor went upstairs and walked into her bedroom, but the bed was empty. He went into his bedroom and there she was, sitting up in his bed with her book open ready for him to read.

"Darling, you'll have to stop this!" he said gently, "You have to stay in your own bed! This bed is for me, you have your own bed in a beautiful bedroom!"

"But, Daddy, I always come into your bed when I wake up in the night and I'm scared by myself," said Savannah petulantly, her mouth turned down at the corners, "I feel lonely now that Holly has gone home and I don't want to be by myself."

"It's different when you wake up through the night," explained Trevor, "I don't mind you getting in my bed then, but you must start the night in your own bed!"

"But WHY?" Savannah looked perplexed, "What difference does it make WHEN I get into your bed? Mummy let me sleep in her bed all the time – SHE never complained!"

Trevor ran his hands over his face. "Sweetheart, please don't make it difficult for me. Just go into your own bed, I'm coming with you and I'll read you a story same as we always do. If you wake through the night and you feel scared or lonely, then you can creep into my bed – same as you always do, but you must start the night in your own bed!"

Savannah sighed deeply and tutted as she scrambled out of bed and sulkily stamped her way to her own bedroom. It was indeed a beautiful room, pink tulle drapes cascaded from the ceiling over a princess bed and were pinned back at the sides but could be let down to encircle the bed to act as a mosquito net if necessary. The walls were a darker shade of pink, with white bedroom furniture and a deep pink sofa where over twenty-five teddy bears and other soft toys all stared sightlessly into the room. The room was at the back of the villa and did not have a balcony, but very large windows ensured it received plenty of daylight, and curtains lined with blackout material made certain the light was kept out at night. Subtle night-lights and carefully placed fairy-lights gave the room a magical feel that any little girl would be thrilled with.

Trevor sat on the side of the bed after Savannah had thrown herself on to it, her lower lip still protruding, and Trevor decided not to give any more explanations or any attention to the subject, and he picked up the book they were currently reading and opened the page, asking her, "Can you remember where we were in the story? What had Imogen found when she opened the door to the secret chamber?"

"It was the table with the clue on it, daddy, remember?" Savannah bounced on the bed in her excitement, recalling the adventures of The Secret Life of Imogen Brown. Trevor smiled and began to read, both of them soon lost in the wondrous world of childhood fantasy.

Later, when Savannah was asleep and Trevor was downstairs nursing a glass of wine, he mulled over the problem of Savannah climbing into his bed. When he'd been married to Dawn and Savannah was a much younger child, it was a normal part of being a family – a child climbing into a parent's bed was expected behaviour. However, he had been an absent parent for almost five years, and now it was a ten-year-old pre-teen that was climbing into his bed – and there was no mother in the bed to make it .... acceptable? Was he making an issue out of nothing? It just didn't feel comfortable............he was worried about how it looked. Why did he feel this way? Was it HIS issue? She was his daughter for God's sake – why was he making such a fuss? He shuddered a sigh and stood up, then remembered he hadn't been in touch with Jo-Anne and sat back down to ring her. He looked across to make sure the door was closed so Savannah wouldn't hear him, and his eyes lit up when her heard Jo-Anne's voice.

"Hello, darling," he murmured, "How are you? How are things?"

"Oh, Trevor, I miss you so much," said Jo-Anne, "Everything is fine here, nothing to report." She crossed her fingers as she told the little fib – no need to worry Trevor about the theft of his bike, nor the re-appearance of her friend from her college days, nor the visit with him to the Hotel in Harrogate, she didn't want to give Trevor any cause for concern while he was away, she could tell him all when he returned home………*when or IF he returns home,* a little voice deep inside her whispered!

"How is Savannah?" she asked him, "Is she coping with the hospital visits?"

"Yes, she's being very brave about it. It helps having Holly come to visit while her mum is visiting Dawn, they've become very close – it's good for her to have a friend like that." Trevor hesitated, then continued, "Jodie has offered to talk to Savannah, to try to get her to be more accepting of…………..our marriage. Savannah seems to be of the mind that I'm back to stay…………with her and Dawn! I don't know how to handle it - every time I try to broach the subject she freaks out and ends up hysterical and it feels like we're back to the beginning. I'm at my wit's end with it all!"

Jo-Anne was silent, not knowing how to respond. She was also out of her depth with the raw feelings of a ten-year-old as she had no experience with children, and Darcy was quite unforgiving of Savannah calling her a spoilt little madam, so Jo-Anne had stopped mentioning her to Darcy. Even though

Savannah was making unrelenting demands on Trevor, Jo-Anne was trying desperately not to hold bitterness towards her.

At last she spoke. "Oh, my poor darling," was all she could manage.

"Well, changing the subject a bit – guess what? I'm now an employer! I've hired a gardener and a housekeeper! What do you think of that – I've actually got staff!" Trevor laughed to try to lighten the mood a bit.

"Oh! Do you need staff then?" asked Jo-Anne, "Couldn't you manage to do it yourself? You don't go out to work."

"God, no! The villa is huge – five bedrooms, reception room, lounge, dining room, massive kitchen, utility room, veranda on three sides………and the grounds are extensive - there's the lawned area, the flower beds, the orange trees, the hedges, the driveway, not to mention the pool – way too much for me to cope with! My day is spent taking Savannah to school, I've then had to fit in meetings with the lawyer sorting out all the financial stuff, then a few hours at the hospital, then pick Savannah up from school, then taking her to whatever activity she has, then home, then cook a meal………Ha,ha, I've just realised - I sound like a stereotypical moaning housewife!"

"Sounds a lot different to our little two-bed semi, and tiny garden," said Jo-Anne quietly, her heart feeling a slow, creeping coldness steal over it. "I'd love to be able to see it."

"Oh, I'm sorry, sweetheart, I haven't had a chance to look at flights or anything yet," said Trevor, "The problem we've got now is that the schools will be finishing soon for the summer, so Savannah is going to be around all day. I've suggested to her that we go on holiday – maybe to England, but she's adamant that she won't leave her mum. She's afraid to go far in case Dawn wakes up."

"Oh!" Jo-Anne could feel the tears start to well up, and her throat was constricted with deep disappointment. She couldn't speak and coughed a few times to try to release the tightness in her throat, which caused the tears to flow unchecked down her cheeks.

"I'm so sorry, sweetheart," said Trevor, "this whole nightmare is killing me. I miss you so much, but I don't know which way to turn – if only Savannah would accept Dawn and I are divorced and that I'm married to you! I'm just praying that Jodie can get through to her. She's been such a help to me – it was her that found Carlos and Fabiana – my staff, haha, and she helped me interview them, well, not really an interview but I needed to act like an employer! So she may be able to work a miracle with Savannah, fingers crossed!"

"Yes, I'll pray for that too," said Jo-Anne through her tears. She sniffed loudly, "I'm going to go now – I want to carry on with my college work – I've only this last unit to get through then the course is completed."

"I'm so proud of you, my angel, you've done so well, holding down a job and doing a college course as well. I've not been much help to you, have I?" Trevor was anxious – he had heard Jo-Anne weeping quietly, and he had an ominous thought that he could be sacrificing his wife for his daughter, but didn't know what to do to make it right. "I'll let you go, sweetheart, but remember that I love you and I want us to be together, I can barely think straight without you!"

"Yes, I love you too, and I can hardly bear being without you. I just wish that things could somehow become OK again." Jo-Anne was still crying softly. She felt as though her heart was being ripped open. It wasn't fair! She didn't ask for any of this! She just wanted her husband back – she wanted her life back to how it was.

Chapter Eleven

Darcy had been at her job for a week and was loving it. She began at ten and finished at four, which meant she could take the boys to school and they could attend the after-school club when school was finished, then she could pick them up at five o'clock. She worked on Monday, Wednesday and Friday, which left her with Tuesday and Thursday to go to the gym. She had tried to stop going since Andy had made his desire clear to her, and had busied herself on the first week by giving the house a good clean and making extra special meals for dinner, but she couldn't get him out of her mind. She knew she was playing a dangerous game, but she was powerless to stop it.

Yesterday her manager in the shop had praised her on her customer service after she made a fabulous sale to a man who wanted to express his feelings to the wife he had been married to for twenty-five years, and Darcy spent time listening to him to get a feel for the kind of gift she thought his wife would appreciate. The man went out of the shop with a gift-wrapped box and a contented smile on his face and Darcy felt very pleased that she had a satisfied customer, and her manager was pleased at the lucrative sale.

Now she was in the changing room at the gym and she was ready to go in, but her heart was beating so fast, she needed time to compose herself. She knew Andy was in there, she could feel his presence! Then she told herself to stop being silly, he was probably flirting with somebody else at this very moment. She took some deep breaths to calm her racing heart and pushed the door open.

Her eyes scanned the room and immediately found him. He was in the weight-lifting area with a client, watching the man lift the dumbbells and making sure that he did it correctly. As

Andy observed the man's posture through the mirror, his eyes caught sight of her as she walked towards the stepper and began her stretching, and a slow smile crept over his face. Darcy's heart leapt inside her body and she smiled back, feeling the heat surge into her face. She started her workout, knowing that as soon as he could he would come to her.

She was forty minutes into her workout, the sweat pouring down her face and her breathing laboured, but she knew that some of these symptoms were because of the possibly imminent arrival of Andy. She watched him surreptitiously, pretending to concentrate on her exercise regime, and her heart began to race uncontrollably when she saw him walk towards her. She stopped the treadmill and wiped her face and neck on her towel as she stepped off and held on to the side of the machine in case her legs shook.

"I missed you last week," he murmured, "I thought I'd scared you off."

"I started my job, and I had to get stuff organised," she replied trying desperately to be casual, but her eyes told a different tale as she looked at him, her breathing laboured and her heart racing madly.

"I can't get you out of my mind," said Andy quietly, "What have you done to me?" He took her towel from her hands and slowly and sensually dabbed her face where beads of perspiration were trickling down to her chin.

She stared at him, afraid to answer, knowing that she was a heartbeat away from breaking her marriage vows. *Oh, somebody help me, please,* she begged silently, *I want him so much, I can't help myself.* She tried to conjure up images of Peter, but her mind refused to co-operate. She tried to visualise her children, but instead of taking away her fantasy, she imagined Andy on a football field with her boys, running with them, picking them up both at the same time and swinging them – what they were always asking Peter to do, but he couldn't manage, teaching them self-defence, being a fit and healthy role model for them. *Stop!* Her mind screamed, *what am I doing? If only Peter did this to me, if only I felt like this towards Peter, but this is more powerful than anything I have ever experienced!*

"Me too," she croaked at last.

He looked deeply into her eyes, then without a word, he very gently placed his fingers under her elbow and with no pressure, just pure magnetism he guided her across the floor to a door which said "Staff Only". Oblivious to the other gym members she followed as if in a trance, then turning right he led her down the corridor and stopped outside a door. He looked at her for a few seconds and she met his eyes, unable to utter a sound, her heart beating wildly, then he opened the door and she followed him inside, briefly noticing it was an office, with a desk and a couple of chairs, and a row of coat-hooks where an outdoor jacket hung. His fingers moved down from her elbow and took hold of her hand and he walked to the window and closed the blinds, then looking at her steadily he walked back to the door and hardly taking his eyes off her he slid the bolt on the door.

Her mind was screaming, *STOP! STOP! Before it's too late! There's no going back from this! Darcy, what are you doing?* But her body was in control, not her mind, her body was quivering, aching to feel his arms around her, being teased by his nearness. He stood motionless in front of her, looking down at her, saying nothing, but saying everything. She took a step nearer and her hand slowly lifted and touched his arm, creeping higher till it was touching his bicep, then her other arm followed, touching his hand, then his forearm, then both hands were raised and resting on his shoulders. He slowly slid his arms around her back and very gently coaxed her towards him, then he lowered his head and his lips found hers
………………………………….and she was completely lost.

*****

It had been a taxing day at work and Jo-Anne just wanted to get home and put her feet up. She walked out to the car park waving goodnight to the night staff on the front desk. When she got into her car she looked at her phone again, but there was no message from Darcy – again. She couldn't understand why Darcy had been so silent, it wasn't like her. She'd been full of her new job last week, phoning and texting Jo-Anne, but then Jo-Anne had told her she wanted to focus on her final assignments to get her course completed and Darcy had been silent since. In the past when Jo-Anne had said she was going to be busy, Darcy had sent one or two text messages, just to check that Jo-Anne was OK. She'd never been silent like this. *Oh, well*, thought Jo-Anne, *I'll ring her tonight and find out what's happening.*

She put the key in the ignition and turned it. Nothing! She turned it again – still nothing! Not a sound. She laid her head on the wheel and groaned. This was all she needed to add to the misery she was feeling right now. She scrabbled around in the glove compartment for the breakdown card to call for assistance, and when she found it her eyes rested on the words "expires 29th May 2004." It was now 9th June! She wanted to cry.

She sat staring ahead, breathing deeply, trying to calm the irritation she was feeling. This was something that Trevor was supposed to do, he had responsibility for the tax, insurance, MOT and breakdown cover for the car. What else had expired while he was busy being an employer of staff in Spain, she fumed? She sat staring at her phone, then with a defiant toss of her head, she rang Dave's number. He answered almost immediately, "Hi, honey, what's up?"

"I'm sorry to bother you, but I've broken down and the breakdown cover has expired, so I'm kind of ………stuck here!" Jo-Anne hated to sound like a helpless female, but she was too tired to care.

"Where are you?" asked Dave.

"I'm in the car park at work, there's absolutely nothing when I turn the key, and I know nothing about cars………..which is why we're supposed to have breakdown cover, if Trevor hadn't let it expire!" Jo-Anne's irritation had crept into her tone.

"Don't fret, my little pet, I'm on my way to save the day!" said Dave theatrically, and as Jo-Anne laughingly thanked him, he said "Go back inside and have a coffee, I'll ring you when I get there. You'll recognise me – I'll be wearing my underpants on the outside of my trousers!" She laughed loudly as she hung up her phone.

Jo-Anne went back into the hotel and after notifying the night manager of her predicament, she went up to her office. She thought she may as well finish one of the tasks she had listed for the next day, and it would take her mind off things. Thirty minutes later, her phone rang and Dave said he had arrived in the car park. She went past the night staff again, telling them that her rescuer had arrived, so hopefully she was off home now.

She motioned to Dave where her car was parked and he parked up next to her car. She opened the door and slid behind the wheel, pushing the key into the ignition and turning it. When the engine burst into life, her face registered absolute shock.

"What! I don't understand! It was dead, there was nothing!" she turned to Dave, her cheeks crimson. "Honestly, it was stone dead – not a peep from it!"

"It could be a faulty wire or something, it's working OK now. Turn it off and then try it again."

She did so, and the engine burst into life again.

"Well, seems fine now, though I would suggest that you book it in at a garage for them to check it out, just in case it happens again," said Dave smiling ruefully at her.

"Oh, Dave, I'm so sorry for dragging you out here. I feel such a fool!" Jo-Anne was appalled that she'd brought him twenty-five miles to help her out, and it was completely unnecessary.

"Don't worry about it, flower, I had nothing else to do anyway."

"You would say that, even if you were in the middle of something, wouldn't you? Have you eaten yet?"

"As it happens, I was in the middle of..........looking for somewhere to eat." Dave was still living in the motel and ate out most nights.

"Then let me treat you to a meal, for coming to my rescue," said Jo-Anne, "There's a lovely little Italian restaurant just up the road from here."

"OK, say no more! I'll follow you. Oh, incidentally, you'd better phone up and renew your breakdown cover first thing tomorrow as well." With an exaggerated smirk, Dave got back into his car and turned it round ready to follow Jo-Anne. They pulled up outside the restaurant and Dave waited while Jo-Anne checked her face and hair in her interior mirror, and satisfied that she didn't look a wreck, she clambered out and took his arm.

They were seated in a quiet corner in the restaurant, and Dave was smiling at her.

"What are you smiling at?" she asked him accusingly.

"You! You make me smile. You act all independent and in control, but then you're thrown completely off guard when your car doesn't start, and suddenly you're a helpless, feminine wimp! I like it – it makes me look good when I have to come and sort it for you!"

"Err, excuse me, but what exactly did you do? Eh? Nothing, that's what! So don't get all clever on me!" Jo-Anne huffed and hid her face behind the menu, trying not to smile – Dave always made her feel better, he could cajole her out of her worst mood.

They chatted for a while over little things that had happened lately, then Dave said, "I've seen a house I'm thinking of making an offer on."

"Oh? That's great. Where is it?"

"You know where I used to live when I was a kid?" Jo-Anne's eyes grew wide. "Well," Dave continued, "It's nowhere near that!" Jo-Anne tutted and playfully slapped his arm, as they both laughed together.

"You! Stop teasing me! Have you really seen a house you like?" she asked.

"I think so, well – it's an apartment, not a house. Houses take a lot of upkeep, but this is a bachelor's dream! It's third floor out of a four-storey building, it used to be a convalescent home or something – it's in Crosley Park. It's got all mod cons, fitted and working kitchen, two bedrooms, a lift, security entrance, a doorman…………" he looked at her keenly.

"Crosley park? A doorman? Sounds a bit classy, will you not be out of place?" she said jokingly.

"Mmm….maybe!" said Dave pursing his lips, "But I want something that I don't have to fix up or spend much time on. Apparently, the doorman – well, he's more of a building manager – he's called a 'concierge' – can also provide, and manage, a cleaner for inside the apartments as well, all I have to do is pay a monthly fee! They're advertised as 'luxury serviced apartments'! I've no pets, no kids, it's a perfect set-up for me, don't you think?"

"Wow!" Jo-Anne leaned forward, "It sounds brilliant! Can I come and look at it?"

"Sure! I'd love you to! I've booked a viewing for Friday at 3.30 – I'm finishing work at lunchtime on Friday so I thought I'd fit it in then. Can you make it?" Dave was watching her anxiously. "I really would value your opinion. Seriously."

Jo-Anne beamed. "Well, at last! You've admitted you need my common sense and organisational skills!"

"Well, dunno 'bout that, but I'll drink to it anyway!" Dave laughed and raised his glass of tonic water in salute.

*****

Trevor and Jodie were sitting on the veranda relaxing with a glass of wine while the girls practised cartwheels and handstands on the lawn. Carlos had worked his first day on the garden and grounds and had made the lawn his priority as it was in dire need of attention, and now it transformed the whole area. Trevor was smiling as he looked around.

"Isn't it strange," he remarked, "When I was living her with Dawn and her parents, I detested this place! I'm certainly not a sun-worshipper, and I couldn't manage without air-conditioning, but ……….I'm beginning to feel comfortable living here now!"

Jodie smiled at him. "That's good………I mean, for Savannah's sake."

Trevor inhaled deeply, enjoying the smells on the evening air – the blossoms from the garden, the orange trees, wafts of garlic and barbecue meats from neighbouring villas. Life had settled into a pattern lately, and now he didn't have financial worries, he could relax. Jodie gazed around her.

"I always loved coming here – Dawn and I had some good laughs. My mum used to take Holly for a weekend and I spent my time here – it felt like my second home. I miss Dawn. She looked so vulnerable in the hospital bed tonight, and I just kept thinking how unfair it is that she should be in this situation." Jodie felt her eyes brim. "She was…………I mean, she IS…. a lovely person. She was so devoted to her parents, especially her mum."

"You don't need to tell me that," said Trevor, "She never settled in England after her parents re-located in Spain, and it finally drove a wedge into our marriage that we couldn't repair. I feel particularly bad about it now, because I don't feel so resentful about Spanish life as I did then! I wonder why that is. Makes me think I should have tried harder."

"It just wasn't the right time for you. Anyway, you're here now when Savannah………and Dawn need you, that's the most important thing."

"I don't think Jo would see it like that," said Trevor sadly. "I feel as if my marriage to Jo was in a different life, somehow not real, and every day that goes by I can feel that life growing more distant. I really need to go back to see her, but Savannah is so terrified of me leaving her, and she won't go anywhere while her mum is in hospital………I'm caught between a rock and a hard place!"

They were both silent for a while. Then Jodie said, without moving, "I should really be getting off home."

"Not yet, don't go yet," said Trevor, leaning forward and resting his hand on her wrist, "It's still early, and the girls are having so much fun. I'm enjoying the company and I'm unwinding. I'll make us some supper. I'll make pancakes! Girls, I'm going to make pancakes!" he shouted, and they both stopped their cartwheeling and Savannah yelled, "Pancakes! Yummy! Can I have chocolate spread……or peanut butter?"

"You can have maple syrup or honey!" called Trevor, "I'll call you when they're ready." Jodie picked up their wine glasses and followed him inside. She perched on a high stool at the breakfast bar, and Trevor said, "There's another bottle in the wine rack if you want to open it, you might as well, you said you're getting a cab home anyway."

Jodie smiled and sighed contentedly; she was enjoying the evening so much, she felt comfortable in Trevor's company and as her gaze followed him around the kitchen she had to admit that she found him a very attractive man. It had been a long time since any man had interested her – since her divorce she had concentrated on being a good parent to Holly, and the few dates she had been on had proved to be unsuccessful. One man had kept her interest for three dates, but even though he was a very nice chap, there was no chemistry between them. Trevor certainly had the ability to make her pulse quicken, but he was the ex-husband of her best friend, so there was no question of taking it any further. *Such a pity*, she thought, *another time, another place, another life………..it would have been a very different story!*

*****

Darcy was watching Peter at the breakfast table as he perused his newspaper and his hand groped absently for another piece of toast. She held her coffee cup near her mouth, both elbows on the table, as her tongue slowly licked her lips, recalling the feel of Andy's kisses and the minty taste he left on her mouth. Her heart lurched every time she remembered what she had done – she had been unfaithful to her husband! She was having an affair – a mad, passionate, heart-stopping, all-consuming affair – but there was no guilt! Only joy! Joy and supreme happiness, and that pushed away any thought of wrong-doing. Peter was happy enough with their life together, she told herself – but he didn't crave her body the way Andy did. When they were first married he was a considerate lover, never the one to sweep her off her feet, but brought her flowers after every trip away and was gentle and thoughtful in all areas of their life. When the children came along, it did cool their passion somewhat, but she thought that was normal, surely it happened to most couples when they became a family. As time went on they slipped into a comfortable lifestyle where they were as close as any couple could be, but the passion had dulled, and of late Peter hadn't shown any interest at all. The few times that she had made the first move to him and he had rejected her saying he was tired or had indigestion and this rebuff had hurt her to the extent that she would not now initiate any sexual contact, other than a cuddle.

She could keep this secret, she thought, she could be the wife that Peter wanted, and she could be the shameless lover that Andy wanted! She wouldn't give up her husband or her children, but neither would she give up her lover! She couldn't give him up now. He had awakened something in her that could not be subdued – he was like a drug, and she needed more! She would have to be satisfied with Tuesday and Thursdays with Andy – she would have her workout first and then another workout with Andy in the office before having a shower and returning to her life as a wife and mother. She could have the best of both worlds. She inhaled deeply and contentedly, causing Peter to look up from his newspaper.

"You look hot," he remarked and she stared at him open-mouthed, blood rushing to her already flushed face. "You OK? You're not coming down with something, are you?" he asked.

She gave a small laugh, "Oh, THAT kind of hot!" she said, "Actually, I do feel a bit over-heated, but it's very warm in here."

Peter went back behind his newspaper. He realised after he'd spoken, what connotation could be placed on his words, and he felt embarrassed that he didn't feel comfortable pursuing the innuendo because he was aware of his lack of desire. He should have said something a long time ago, when he first noticed that something was……….different, but he put it down to stress, or the children, or tiredness………...it was quite some time before he realised that it was unnatural to feel sexually dead when he loved his wife so intensely. She was beautiful, clever, funny, and he couldn't imagine life without her, but when he pulled her to him in bed, his heart would be over-flowing with love and emotion, but his body was inert. Darcy didn't put him under any pressure, she was content with cuddles and she was very often tired because of the children, and she went to her gym quite often so she seemed happy enough to be held and snuggled.

It was Darren's recommendation on all his drivers having annual medical checks that brought his 'problem' into the spotlight! Although Darren could not enforce his request, his claim that as his vehicles had to have an annual MOT, then so should his drivers, even more so since they had branched out into European haulage. Peter had realised his problem was not just a temporary lull in his sexual appetite when he went with a couple of mates to a lap-dancing club and even the madly erotic squirming and caressing of the dancer did absolutely nothing for his carnal desire. He normally would never frequent clubs or bars like this one, but he needed to know if he could be aroused at all, and a stag do was an ideal opportunity. He was distressed but strangely relieved when it happened, because he now knew that this was a medical problem and nothing to do with losing sexual interest in his wife.

So, three months ago he had been to see his doctor, who had immediately referred him to a specialist, and he had said nothing to Darcy about any of this – he didn't want to say anything until the test results were back.

Chapter Twelve

It was just after eleven o'clock and Jo-Anne was in bed when her phone rang. Her heart lurched as a number of possible disasters tumbled through her mind that only a phone call late at night can create. She sat up in bed reaching for the phone on her bedside table and saw Trevor's name on the screen.

"Hello?" she croaked, "Trevor? Is everything alright?"

"Oh, sweetheart, I'm sorry! I've just noticed the time, it's just so damn difficult to make a phone call in private, and I've been a bit busy – well, a lot busy!" Trevor sounded as if he'd had a few drinks – she could always tell by the way he sounded the letter "s" – it sounded as though it was said through clenched teeth when he'd been drinking.

"Is everything alright?" asked Jo-Anne again. "Is Dawn OK, is Savannah OK?"

"Oh, no change anywhere!" said Trevor with a deep sigh, "Dawn is still in a coma, Savannah still believes I'm back with her and her mother and we're going to live happily ever after!"

"Oh! That's a bit ……..difficult…….what do you say when she says things like that?" Jo-Anne sat further up in the bed, her heart sinking at his words.

"What can I say?" said Trevor, "If I try to correct her, or say it's not like that, she goes into a crazy melt-down and it scares me to death. Jodie is trying her best, but Savannah just seems to switch off inside her head when there's something she doesn't want to hear! I tell you, sweetheart – this is a nightmare!"

"Well, it's not a bed of roses here!" snapped Jo-Anne, but immediately felt remorseful at her hasty words.

But Trevor continued as if he hadn't heard her. "I mean, Jodie spends as much time with her as she can, but the poor woman has her job to consider, and when Savannah's with them she just wants to hang out with Holly, so Jodie has to take it very slowly – softly, softly catchee monkee as they say!" he said.

Jo-Anne could feel irritation bubble inside her and had to bite her lip to prevent any caustic remarks slipping out. How awful that this miracle-worker Jodie – whoever she is – wasn't working miracles like she thought she could, and poor Trevor having to bear the terrible tantrums that this ten-year old child was having! Maybe Darcy was right – Savannah was being indulged and it wasn't solving any of the problems, it was increasing them!

Just bloody tell her! That's what Darcy would be saying – *just tell her how it is now, this is the way life was going to be from now on!* Yes, it was harsh, yes it was cruel, but isn't it a well-known saying that you had to be cruel to be kind?

Trevor noticed that Jo-Anne was silent, and asked, "You still there, babe?"

"Yes," she replied, "You're up late, it must be after midnight there – how come you're so late? Have you been drinking?"

"I must admit, I've had a glass or two of a very nice red wine with our meal tonight, Jodie left her car and got a taxi, we both needed to unwind, it's been a bit fraught."

Jo-Anne felt her heartbeat increase and catch in the back of her throat. *This Jodie is spending a lot of time there,* she thought, *and they're sitting relaxing with 'a very nice red wine'!* Normally she would see things from Trevor's point of view and share his anxiety about Savannah's mental health and her grief, but tonight she was having misgivings about the whole set-up! If she was totally honest she was sick of Trevor whinging about what he was going through!

She was fed up of hearing about how he was having to tip-toe around Savannah, and she was not happy about hearing how he and this woman – Jodie – were so stressed they had to unwind with a 'very nice red wine'! What about what she herself was going through? She'd been careful not to burden him with any of the issues at home – the bike being stolen, the fear of being burgled, the car breaking down and the breakdown cover having expired because he'd forgotten to renew it! She'd told him that everything was fine – no problems – because she didn't want him to have any more burdens than he already had in Spain, but now she was resenting his self-pity!

"What if I come out next week for a couple of days?" she asked him, her tone measured and even.

"I've already told you sweetheart, school's finishing so Savannah's going to be around all the time," said Trevor, "We don't want to make things worse, do we? Set her off again."

"OK, just thought I'd ask," said Jo-Anne, narrowing her eyes. She'd already looked up the school finishing date, and it wasn't till 21st June – she could fly out next week for a three day midweek break and be back home before the end of term and Savannah would never know! Surely, if Trevor missed her like he said he did, he would jump at the chance of spending a couple of days with his wife – he could miss going to the hospital to sit with his *ex-wife!* She got the feeling that Trevor didn't want her to go there – but why?

"Trev, I'm missing you so much and I'm worried," she said with a catch in her voice.

"What are you worried about, my darling? Is it money? I'm going to pay an amount every month into our household account just the same as when my salary went in – you don't have to worry about money!"

"It's not money I'm worried about. It's *us*. What about *us*, Trev, what about *us!*" Jo-Anne had started to cry softly.

"Oh, my angel, you've nothing to worry about. I love you and I miss you. But you have to understand that I have a very delicate situation here, and I don't know how to handle it. I'd be lost without Jodie helping me, she's been terrific! And I've nobody else to turn to about children's issues – nobody that would understand my situation!"

His voice had taken on a different tone when he spoke of Jodie, and Jo-Anne felt a cold chill spread throughout her heart and a sickness in her stomach. Not only was he dismissing the idea of turning to Jo-Anne, his wife – *his barren wife* – who wouldn't have a clue about what to say or do with a ten-year-old child suffering trauma and bereavement – but he was falling out of love with her and he was falling *in* love with this Jodie person! *She* was now his rock, his helpmate, *she* was taking Jo-Anne's place! She felt her throat constrict and she couldn't bear to continue this conversation, she knew she would break down and fall to pieces.

"Sorry, Trev, I have to go," she said, "I've to be up early tomorrow, I've a workshop to attend for my college work," she fibbed.

"Oh, sorry, darling, I forgot to ask how things were going – is everything alright, have you managed to keep things going – is your course nearly finished now?" he asked, his tone appeasing, but Jo-Anne was too angry to care.

"Fine!" she croaked, then taking control of her feelings of hurt and anger, she softened her tone, "I'm just very tired. I'll talk to you tomorrow……….perhaps," she added, recognising that Trevor didn't ring every day like he did when he first went out to Spain.

They said their goodbyes, Trevor saying how much he missed her, but Jo-Anne didn't believe him any more! She threw herself back into the pillows and let the rage and fear consume her, weeping loudly and brokenly and railing against the unfairness of it all.

*****

Darcy looked up as Jo-Anne entered through the back door. "Honey, you look terrible!" she cried, getting up and going towards with her arms outstretched. Jo-Anne fell into her arms weeping loudly and they stood a while till Jo-Anne brought herself under control.

"I'm sorry to disturb you so early on a Sunday morning," she whimpered, but Darcy tutted at her, "Nonsense, I was awake when you rang, I was just enjoying the silence of everyone being asleep!"

Darcy made coffee and they took it through to the lounge. They curled up on the sofa, one at each end with their toes touching, the way they always sat when they were having girlie nights in.

"I'm sorry I haven't been in touch much," said Darcy, "But I thought I'd give you space to finish your college work, I know how intense it was becoming for you with all the worry about Trevor and stuff."

Jo-Anne's eyes filled again. "I think I've lost him, Darcy. I think he's creating a life for himself in Spain and I don't think he's going to come back here!"

"No! I'm sure you're wrong! I bet he's just trying to juggle a lot of things and maybe neglecting you a bit while he does it, but the man is crazy about you! There's no way he'll be creating a life for himself without you – he doesn't even *like* Spain, remember!"

"That's what I used to think, but it's different now. He's got access to a lot of money – it's Dawn's by right, but he's got power of attorney and as long as it's of no detriment to Dawn and Savannah, he can basically spend as he sees fit. He's employed a gardener and a housekeeper, and he doesn't need to work as he's got a sick ex-wife to care for and a ten-year old ……………child………. who is running the show! But to top it all, he's got Dawn's best friend, Jodie, to help him with

Savannah and ……..God knows what else……….'he'd be lost without her'," she mimicked through her tears.

"Oh, honey, what a nightmare for you! But I'm sure there's nothing going on with her – he loves you to pieces! He's just not very good with Savannah, I mean being firm with her – and you know what I think about *that!* I've always thought he was handling her all wrong and now it's come to bite him on the bum! This Jodie probably feels sorry for him – you know how single dads always elicit loads of sympathy from women!"

Jo-Anne gave a small smile, but shook her head. "I don't know. But I am worried. He keeps putting off the idea of me going out there – his excuse now is that the school is finishing for the summer, but that's not for another week or so! I could easily go for a midweek break, it's cheap enough, and be back before the 21st."

"So why don't you just go?" said Darcy, "You have to stay in a hotel away from the villa anyway, so you can just go, and see for yourself what's going on! It'll put your mind at rest, even if you don't actually meet up with Trevor – you can spy on him!"

Jo-Anne was silent. She could easily juggle her workload, the Masked Ball was still two weeks away and she had everything under control. There was nothing important in her diary for next week. She was very tempted by the idea.

"Come over to the computer and we'll just look at flights?" suggested Darcy.

Jo-Anne sat up straight and put her coffee cup on the small table. "Yes! Let's go for it!"

As Darcy left the room to fetch a stool for Jo-Anne to sit on next to her at the computer, she heard Peter's voice asking who she was talking to and then he came into the lounge in his bathrobe.

"Oh, hi there, Jo, are you OK?" he looked at her with concern.

"Yes, thanks Peter, I'm thinking of flying out to Spain to spend a couple of days with Trevor – see if there's anything I can do to help him," she replied.

"Oh! Are things better with you and Savannah, then?" he asked.

"God, no! I wish they were! She still won't tolerate me. I'll have to stay in a nearby hotel, as usual!"

"By the way," Peter added, "I've been thinking……….when your insurance money comes through for the bike, there's no point in buying another one till Trevor comes home. You might as well just leave the money in the bank for now."

"Good idea, Peter, thanks, I'll do that," she said, and Peter went out heading to the kitchen, calling to the boys who were tumbling down the stairs to come into the kitchen and help him with breakfast.

Darcy came back in with the stool and placed it next to the computer chair, nodding for Jo-Anne to sit next to her. They sat side-by-side and Darcy scrolled through the possible flights to Valencia, as she shouted over her shoulder for the boys to make less noise. She tutted and said "Sorry about the racket," but Jo-Anne paid no attention as she was focused on the task in hand. After the pair had discussed and selected various flights, then matched them up, Jo-Anne rang the hotel that she usually stayed in when she went out with Trevor and booked a room for Tuesday to Thursday, then selected the best flight to get her there, leaving from Manchester airport in the early hours of Tuesday morning.

"How are you going to get to the airport?" asked Darcy, chewing her bottom lip, "It'll be difficult for me with the boys and the school run…………"

"Oh, don't worry, I'll take the car and leave it in the carpark, that's what we do when I go with Trevor, it's usually cheaper than going by taxi. I wouldn't dream of asking you to take me, you've got too much on already, but thanks anyway." Jo-Anne was focused on phoning the airport to book her flight and didn't see the expressions flitting across Darcy's face. Tuesday was her day with Andy, and her heart leapt into her throat every time she brought him to mind, or thought about the gym – which made her think about him!

She hadn't told Jo-Anne about her affair with Andy – even though she was her best friend, she knew that Jo-Anne would be aghast at her infidelity! Jo-Anne would tell her to end it immediately, which she knew she couldn't do, and it wasn't fair giving Jo-Anne this secret to keep, it was Darcy's own secret and no-one must ever know about it! It would create a wedge between her and Jo-Anne and she couldn't bear that – she daren't risk losing her friendship. Her face flushed as she reflected her situation – she was an unfaithful wife – but she had a lover that swamped her soul with longing, who filled her heart with joy and excitement like she had never experienced before, and she could not go back to the life she had before living with Peter like brother and sister – she needed this affair to make her feel like a woman, all her senses alive and on fire, and her body craving his touch!

Jo-Anne turned to her. "Right! All done! My flight is booked! I'll soon find out if this Jodie is the threat I imagine she is!" She scooped up the notes she'd jotted and the papers from the printer with all the information on and put them into her bag. They both went into the kitchen where the boys were sitting at the table watching the small TV in the corner, and Peter was at the far side of the table with his newspaper in front of him. Darcy chased the boys upstairs with instructions to get dressed and brush their teeth as she made coffee for her and Jo-Anne. Peter folded his newspaper and asked if Jo-Anne had succeeded in her booking.

"Yes," she told him, "I fly out at six o'clock on Tuesday morning and get back on Thursday about eight-thirty at night. It's long enough to see what the situation is." She glanced at Darcy with raised eyebrows, asking her without words whether she should say anything to Peter, but Darcy shrugged her shoulders giving the decision entirely to Jo-Anne.

"I need to see whether Trevor is creating a new life for himself in Spain without me," she said, having decided to take Peter into her confidence, so she told him her fears.

Peter nodded slowly. "Yes, I can understand you feeling that way. It's a massive quirk of fate that has brought you to this situation, and although personally I don't think you've got anything to worry about, I can understand your need to check it out." He smiled at her and leaned over and squeezed her hand which lay on the table, fidgeting with the corner of a coaster.

Jo-Anne smiled back at him. "Thank you, Peter," she said. His words had made her feel much better, and she would be able to relax when she got back to England, knowing that her marriage was still safe.

*****

The next day Peter sat nursing his beer, staring into the glass but seeing nothing. He had spent the last couple of hours in the consultant's room, hearing the results of the tests he had undergone over the past couple of months and the prognosis of his disease. He had said nothing to Darcy – he didn't want her to worry, but he had first sought medical advice over three months ago when he was suffering pain and tingling in his legs. He first of all thought it was because of the long-distance driving, but then when he started having episodes of blurred vision he knew he had to have tests to determine the cause. He knew that his complete loss of libido wasn't normal, but he kept making excuses to himself, and when the other symptoms appeared he knew something was wrong.

The tests and MRI scan he'd had over the last couple of weeks showed he had Multiple Sclerosis! The consultant explained to him it was an autoimmune disease, a condition that affects the brain and/or spinal cord, but was not a terminal illness. Something goes wrong with the immune system and it mistakenly attacks a healthy part of the body – in this case the brain or spinal cord. He was suffering relapsing-remitting MS which was the most common form, where he would have episodes of new or worsening symptoms, known as the relapses which would worsen for a few days then improve. The periods in between – known as the remission, may last for years at a time. After many years – in some cases decades – some sufferers go on to develop secondary or progressive MS. The life expectancy of someone suffering MS was probably 5 – 10 years lower than average, and although there is currently no cure, a number of treatments can help to control the condition.

He had left the hospital and headed straight for the first bar where he could sit and mull over what the consultant had said. He needed to get it straight in his own head before he spoke to Darcy. He didn't want her to worry, or be scared. He wasn't going to die and he would carry on as he had done – how fortunate it was that Darren had offered him the office-based job! There were many alternative therapies, the nurse had told him, and there were MS support groups where sufferers could talk to others in the same position as themselves. He wasn't worried. He mustn't worry – Darcy would pick up on that straight away.

When he felt calm and relaxed, he left the pub and headed for his car. He would head back to the office and finish the afternoon at work so he would arrive home at the same time as he normally did, so that Darcy wouldn't suspect anything.

*****

Jo-Anne had hastily packed a small flight bag and was

sitting at the table eating a ready-meal that she had picked up on the way home. She intended to go to bed for a few hours and get up at 3a.m. to get to the airport for check-in at 5a.m. The doorbell caused her to groan inwardly – *whoever it is I haven't the time tonight*, she said to herself.

On the doorstep stood a dark-haired man with the bluest eyes she had ever seen, dressed in casual chinos and pale blue short-sleeved shirt. He carried a small case in his hand and with the other hand he held out his identity card which named him as Nick Dawson, Crime Prevention Officer.

"Hi, Mrs Gainsbury? You made an appointment for a visit following your recent burglary?" he said smiling and extending his hand towards her.

"Oh………yes I did………." she faltered. She'd completely forgotten about it, but realised it would be downright rude to refuse him entry as she was the one who had requested the visit, so she shook his hand and invited him inside.

He looked at the door-lock as he entered and made a few notes in his jotter after placing his case on the floor by the front door. "Is it OK if I just wander round and see what your set-up is, then we can have a chat?" he asked her.

"Yes, that's fine," she replied, "I'll just carry on in the kitchen, I haven't quite finished my meal. Would you like a tea or a coffee?"

"No thank you," he answered looking around the windows and frames in the lounge.

After about fifteen minutes he came into the kitchen where she had finished eating, had washed up and tidied everything away, and was busy reading the paperwork for the flight that she had printed off.

"I noticed a small suitcase at the bottom of the stairs – are you heading off somewhere?" he asked her.

"Just a couple of days in Valencia, it's a last minute thing – I wasn't planning on going anywhere, but something came up and I have to go," she replied, "I'm leaving very early tomorrow morning."

"Well in that case I won't keep you any longer than necessary," he said, "Can we go outside? I'd like to see the shed where your theft took place. Was it only the bike that was stolen? Nothing else?"

"No," she replied, "Only the bike. But it was a very expensive road bike, my husband's pride and joy! I suppose whoever took it sold it for next to nothing!"

"You're probably right. Opportunist thieves – they don't know the value of the things they steal, but as long as they get a few quid, they're happy. It's those they sell to who are the real criminals – they know what they're getting, so they can make a huge profit."

She led the way to the back garden and he examined the new lock that Peter had fitted for her on the shed and the bolts on the side gate that prevented any access from the front of the house. It was very quiet, no sounds from any of the neighbours, only the twittering of birds as they nestled in the trees. "It's very peaceful here," he remarked.

"I know," she said, "That's why I was so upset at having an intruder – it takes away some of the feeling of tranquillity. I was very nervous afterwards, knowing that someone had been creeping around! My husband is away, you see so I'm on my own here just now."

"Well, you've done a very good job of making it harder for anyone to get in. You've got good door locks and window locks. I've a few things in my case I'd like to show you that would enhance your security measures, but I promise I won't take long as you've said you're leaving for an early flight so I reckon you'll want to grab a few hours sleep first."

Jo-Anne gave a small smile and led the way back inside, and after he'd picked his case up he went into the kitchen and placed it on the table. He started taking out various items and explained to her each one as he did so. Jo-Anne's attention was wandering as she was mentally checking on the things she had to sort out before she went to bed. Nick noticed her lack of interest and stopped what he was doing.

"I'll tell you what," he said, "Do you think it might be a better idea if I come back after you've returned from your holiday? Your home is pretty secure – these items would make it better, but I can see that you've too much on your mind at present."

Jo-Anne flushed at her bad manners, and started to stammer an excuse, but he smiled gently at her as he held out a card. "If it's OK with you, I'll call next Monday about the same time. This is my card if you change your mind, but I really would like to show you some items that would help you feel more secure while you're on your own."

She took the card, and grimaced slightly, "I'm so sorry for being rude, but a lot has happened lately and my mind is just too full. This trip to Valencia wasn't planned, and I don't know what I'm going to find when I get there…………"

He raised his eyebrows very slightly, as if to encourage her to say more, but she realised she'd said too much to someone she didn't know, so she shook her head almost imperceptibly and walked to the front door. He followed her and paused at the threshold.

"I hope everything works out for you," he said gently. "Have a good flight and I'll see you next week." With a cheery wave he walked down the path.

Jo-Anne closed the door and leaned against it. "*Right!*" she told herself, "*He said the house was secure enough, so forget about it, get sorted, then get to bed!*"

She went around checking everything was locked and bolted then made her way upstairs. Just then her phone rang and she saw Darcy's name on the screen.

"Hiya, honey," she said as she answered, "I've just had a very handsome Crime Prevention Officer here. Didn't I just forget all about him coming – I booked it just after Trevor's bike was stolen, but with everything happening I forgot about it."

"Oh, yeah," Darcy said distractedly, then with a rush she said, "Jo, you know how I was complaining about Peter's lack of interest in me? Well, there's a very good reason. Jo, he's got MS! Multiple Sclerosis!" Her voice broke on a sob.

Jo-Anne was stunned into silence. "What!" she exclaimed when she could speak. "MS? How long has he had it? When did he tell you? Has he never mentioned anything before now? He must have been having tests and such!" She was babbling, unable to take in the enormity of Darcy's news.

"I know! He's been seeing his doctor and a consultant for the past couple of months. He never said a word! He said he didn't want to scare me or worry me till he knew what was going on. Didn't think that the shock of it all might bloody kill me – stupid man!" Darcy was weeping, and Jo-Anne joined her, tears coursing down her face as she thought about poor Peter facing all this by himself because he wanted to spare his wife the worry of it all.

"Do you want me to come round? I'll cancel my flight and stay with you tomorrow," said Jo-Anne.

"No, it's OK. Peter wants us to carry on as normal. He says it's not a terminal illness – he won't die with it, and it's what's called relapsing-remitting MS, so he'll have periods of symptoms for a while, possibly worse each time, then he'll go into remission for a longer period – which could actually last years. It's just that he was suffering all this while he was driving abroad, and kept it to himself, I feel such a bad wife for not noticing anything! He says it was co-incidental that Darren asked him to take on the managing role, but fortunate because it may impact on his driving ability now that it's been diagnosed. He's going to tell Darren tomorrow, but just because they're good friends, it shouldn't affect his job now."

"Oh, sweetheart, you're not a bad wife at all. It's because Peter loves you that he deliberately kept it away from you. How would you even guess at something like this? Well, rest assured, the man loves you to bits! Remember when you fancied that Andy Johnson from the gym because you thought Peter didn't fancy you any more? Huh! Andy Pandy! That's him kicked into touch!"

Jo-Anne laughed as she tried to make light of what she thought was Darcy's passing crush, but she didn't hear the small gasp from Darcy, nor see the colour suffuse her face, and because she didn't know of the torrid affair she didn't understand the guilt that was coursing through Darcy's mind – not guilt because she was having an affair, but guilt that she was being unfaithful to a sick man! Nor could she know of the desperate agony she was experiencing at the thought of having to give up her lover because of that. It was different when she thought Peter was healthy and normal – it was an even playing field. But now, knowing he had MS made her feel ashamed of what she was doing to him. Her heart was breaking in two, but she knew she would have to end it with Andy before it was too late.

Chapter Thirteen

Jo-Anne arrived at the hotel at nine-thirty the following day after spending a sleepless night worrying about Peter and Darcy. She had looked up the symptoms and prognosis of Multiple Sclerosis and didn't feel so panicky after reading about it, but it was still going to have an effect on their lives, even in a small way. She hoped Darcy would be able to cope with things and not let her imagination run away with her – this would explain the lack of interest Peter had shown in their sex life, but once he started either medication or therapies, it may resolve that particular difficulty.

She arrived at the hotel feeling tired, hungry and very hot, and after Sabine and Pablo had welcomed her she went up to her room for a rest, grateful to see the kettle and array of tea-bags and coffee sachets on the dresser. Pablo had accompanied her to the room, carrying her small bag and babbling about how good it was to see her again and how he hoped her family were all well. On their very first stay in the *Casa Flora*, she and Trevor had gone out after breakfast every day, Trevor to spend the day with Savannah, while Jo-Anne did the holiday sight-seeing and taking a taxi to the beach, meeting up with Trevor at around six o'clock when they both got showered and changed for their evening meal together, and this was the pattern they adopted every time they visited Valencia. Pablo asked about Trevor, was he well, was he going to join her? She said Trevor was busy, she had some business to attend to in Valencia which was the reason for her short visit, and she left it at that. Pablo did not pursue the matter further, though she guessed he and Sabine would conjure up a story that they thought would fit the situation and that would satisfy their curiosity.

She made a cup of tea and laid back on the pillows on the bed, grateful for the air-conditioning that gradually cooled down her warm and sticky body. She sipped the tea, trying to formulate a plan of action in her head, but her brain was suffering overload after she'd spent the entire flight creating and acting out one scenario after another. She realised how tired she was and told herself she would just rest her eyes for a while before getting showered and changed, and within minutes she was in a deep sleep.

*****

Trevor had dropped Savannah at school and was on his way to the hospital when his phone rang. Glancing at the screen he saw it was the school calling him. His heart lurched as he imagined all manner of possible scenarios that would give the school reason to call him. He pulled the car in to the side as soon as it was safe to do so and with racing heart he rang the school back.

"Ah, Mister Gainsbury, thank you for returning my call," said the Head Teacher when Trevor explained he was driving and had been unable to answer. "I wonder if you could possibly come to see me as soon as possible?"

"Come to see you? Why? What's wrong?" asked Trevor, concern evident in his voice.

"It is not a matter that I can speak about on the telephone, but I would be very grateful if you could come as soon as possible," replied the Head.

"Is it Savannah? Has she been hurt?" Trevor was feeling more concerned by the minute. "Why can't you tell me?"

"Please, Mister Gainsbury, Savannah is fine, but if you could please come to the school all will be explained to you."

Trevor realised he was not going to get an answer so he said he would come at once, and he turned the car around and headed back to the school. It was a very expensive school, an international independent school that Freda and Bill Watson, Savannah's grandparents, had sought out for her education and had paid the school fees without a murmur. The school taught in English and catered for the education of children from five years of age through to University entrance, and taught the English curriculum. Trevor was aghast at the cost of the fees considering he – and Dawn – had had a very good state education in England, but assumed Bill had compared the state education in Spain and chose to have his granddaughter educated privately. Jodie's parents had done the same for Holly, so Trevor didn't question the set-up, he simply maintained the status quo.

When he arrived at the school gates – large imposing metal gates that had an intercom and CCTV to show who required entrance, he was met by a school administrator and taken immediately to meet the Head and ushered into her office.

"Ah, Mister Gainsbury," said the very tall woman striding towards him with her hand outstretched in greeting, "I am Marian Overton, the Head of the school. We met when Savannah's mother was involved in the accident and you first came to Spain, though I imagine you were in no state to remember anything about that period of time." Trevor shook her hand and was slightly awed by the woman's presence. She was slightly taller than him and was striking in appearance, with dark brown hair swept up and held in place by a scarlet clasp which matched the lipstick on her full sensual mouth and was dressed in a black pencil skirt and white blouse, with black shoes with a small heel.

Trevor swallowed nervously. "Good morning," he gulped.

"Please sit down and I will order some refreshments. Would you prefer tea or coffee?"

"Err, tea would be fine," said Trevor, looking uneasily around him. The room was light and airy and large windows overlooked a courtyard that was central to the school, with another three large buildings surrounding it. To the rear of the Head's office, visible from the corridor outside was another three buildings that Trevor had spotted as he was being shown to the Head's office. One wall in the room was filled from ceiling to floor with bookshelves, and were full to overflowing, and box files and folders were stacked to the side of the large mahogany desk that stood in the centre of the room. Behind the desk was a row of filing cabinets alphabetically marked that he assumed were the files from each child. On each wall were qualifications and diplomas belonging to the Head, and an array of awards and honours that extolled the proficiency and praiseworthiness of the school.

There was a knock on the door and a small tea trolley was pushed into the room by the same lady who had escorted Trevor to the office. Marian Overton poured the tea and handed Trevor a cup and saucer.

"If I may ask you, how is Savannah mother?" Marian perched on a chair opposite Trevor placing her cup and saucer on the desk to the side of her.

"I'm afraid she's still in a coma, there's been no change at all," said Trevor sadly.

"I'm very sorry to hear that," said Marian. "Does Savannah visit her mother very often?"

"Yes," said Trevor, "She visits with me every other evening and my ex-wife's friend – Holly Frobisher's mum, visits on alternate evenings. When Jodie is visiting Dawn, Holly stays with Savannah and me – I'm sure you know the girls are extremely close and since the accident have become even closer."

Marian smiled. "Yes. I know. They have a very strong bond."

There was silence for a minute while both sipped at their tea, then Marian raised her eyes to Trevor's and said in a halting voice, "Mr. Gainsbury, I'll get straight to the point. Some of the parents of our children have raised concerns over something their children have told them. They state that Savannah has told them that you and she sleep together."

Trevor's mouth dropped open.

"Whaaah!" he gasped, "You make it sound……….wrong…….. She's my daughter!"

"So you do not share a bed?" asked Marian.

"Well, she comes into my bed through the night if she wakes up, but that's normal for children who are bereaved – dammit – it's pretty normal for ANY child to creep into their parent's bed when they are upset! I resent the implications of what is being suggested here!" Trevor had jumped up, spilling tea on the tiled floor.

"Please sit down, Mr Gainsbury. I'm sorry to have to raise this, but if children are making statements like this to their parents, then it could be taken out of context and reach the ears of the social services. I don't have to spell it out to you what that could mean – they have a duty of care and would be forced to investigate the claim. Although it may be groundless, the procedure can be extremely distressing for you both. That is why I have asked you to come in this morning, so that I can alert you to the dangers."

Trevor had sat back down and placed his cup and saucer on the floor near his chair. "She cries so much," he said very softly, "She's broken-hearted! She loved her grandparents so much, and it rips her little heart out – well, both our hearts, to see her mother lying in a coma. Sometimes I don't even know she's crept in my bed, I find her there when I wake up on a morning. I wouldn't dream of locking my door to her! She needs a parent, and I'm the only one she's got! Whoever these people are who think there's something wrong need to get their minds out of the gutter and leave me to comfort my daughter when she needs it!"

Trevor's voice had grown louder and more assertive as he spoke and righteous indignation made him stand taller and straighter, while two spots of red on his cheeks revealed his suppressed anger. Marian turned to place her cup back on the desk and rose to meet him.

"I fully understand your anger, Mr Gainsbury, but I felt it necessary to advise you of what was being said. Perhaps you could ………..explain……. to Savannah that her choice of wording is………….. inappropriate ………for the situation, that 'creeping into daddy's bed through the night' is not the same as 'sleeping together'. But I am not trying to tell you how to speak to your daughter, I'm sure you are very capable of that. I am sorry that I have had to raise this subject."

Trevor expelled the breath he had been holding and looked as though he had deflated like a blow-up doll. His shoulders slumped and he sat back down, defeated.

"I don't know what to do for the best," he moaned softly, "I've left my wife in England, I've had to resign from my job, my daughter won't meet my wife, she won't even acknowledge her existence! Every time we're at the hospital, she tells her mum that 'daddy's back so everything will be alright now!' If I even hint at going back to England, she goes into a hysterical frenzy and it scares me! I'm at my wit's end! I don't know what to do for the best!"

Marian looked at him with pity in her eyes. "I'm so sorry, Mr Gainsbury, it must be terribly difficult for you both. Would you like me to refer Savannah for some counselling? Perhaps bereavement counselling?"

"I think that may be beneficial for us both, yes, please Ms Overton," said Trevor, emotional exhaustion dulling his wits and making him want to weep with the unfairness of it all.

She jotted something down on a pad on her desk, then turned to face him. "I hope that Savannah's mother regains consciousness soon and that she can regain her health. If there is anything I, or the school, can assist you with, please feel free to approach me. I will make the referral today and hope that it is not too long before you hear from a counsellor." She held out her hand to Trevor again and he shook it limply, just wanting to get out of the room in case he broke down.

When he was off the school premises, he walked briskly to his car, taking out his phone as he walked, scrolling down till he reached Jodie's number. Once inside the car, he rang her, and left a message for her to ring him as soon as she could. She would be teaching in class just now, but would get his message at break-time. He looked at his watch. He probably had enough time to get to the hospital before she rang him, so he set off.

*****

The phone startled Jo-Anne from a deep sleep. She looked around her in a panic, not recognising where she was, wondering what the noise was that roused her, then as realisation of her whereabouts and situation settled on her, she reached over and picked up her phone. Dave's voice in her ear sounded puzzled.

"Hello, Jo? What's up with your phone – it sounded like an international dial tone."

"I'm in Spain," she croaked, attempting to sit up and falling over on to her side. "I decided to come and check it all out."

"Crikey! What brought this on? Why did you feel it necessary? What's happened?" Dave sounded perplexed.

"It's how Trevor has been – he's very close to this Jodie woman, and always moaning about how hard it is for him, how he couldn't manage without her.......and........." Her voice petered out as she suddenly recognised how pathetic she sounded! She had jumped on a plane and travelled hundreds of miles to check on her husband who was trying to deal with an ex-wife in a coma, a broken-hearted ten-year-old and run a villa so big he needed staff to help him! What must Dave think of her? What would Trevor think if that's how she was behaving?

"Oh, sweetheart! You've let your heart rule your head! This is not like you! I bet Darcy talked you into this!" Dave's voice was soft and gentle, but she could sense the rebuke.

"Don't blame Darcy! She's only looking out for me! She thinks that this Jodie has got designs on Trev as well!" Jo-Anne bristled with defensiveness to hide the shame she was feeling. "Anyway, why are you ringing me? I would be at work normally."

"I know. I was ringing to ask if you're still coming on Friday……but if you're in Spain……"

"I'll be back on Thursday evening, and yes, I am still coming on Friday." Jo-Anne was still feeling sulky and now she felt a bit ridiculous taking the action she had, but wouldn't admit it.

"Well, the agent has asked if I could go later, at 4.30 – he's double booked or something, but I said it would be OK. Is it alright for you to go later? I'll take you out for tea afterwards." Dave's voice was back to his normal teasing, coaxing tone, and Jo-Anne relaxed slightly.

"OK. It's a deal. I was thinking of going to the hospital while I'm here to see Dawn. Do you think I should? I don't know her, I've never met her – obviously I've seen photos, but we've never met."

"It's up to you," said Dave non-committedly, "I suppose it depends on your reasons for visiting!"

"Just a mark of respect saying as I'm in the country! No ulterior motives if that's what you're thinking!"

Dave laughed. "Well, I should hope not! The poor woman has done nothing to you – or to anyone for the past few weeks! Then what? Are you going to let Trev know that you're in Spain, or just stalk him?"

Jo-Anne tutted. "Stop making fun of me! Of course I'm going to contact him!"

"I thought you weren't allowed to contact him in case Savannah got the phone?"

"That's just text messages! I can ring him because she'll be in school."

"You sure? She might not be!" She couldn't tell if Dave was teasing or being helpful, but she was unsure again of her decision to rush over to Spain to find out what Trevor was doing.

"Dave, you're not helping! I'm here now, so I'm going to visit Dawn, then I'm going to ring Trev. No! I'll ring him first, when I think she'll be in school, then tonight I'll go and visit Dawn while Trev is with Savannah! Yes! That's my plan! And I'll see you on Friday, we can arrange a meeting place when I get home on Thursday night!" Jo-Anne had resumed her control of the situation and felt much better.

Dave smiled, it was evident in his voice when he said "That's my girl! Now don't do anything rash. And if you need to run anything by me, just give me a call – and Jo…….take care!"

"I will, Dave, thanks for being such a good friend!" She pressed the end call button and smiled to herself. He was such a caring person, she'd always been able to rely on him. She swung her legs off the bed and headed for the shower. She needed to freshen her mind and her body if she was going to meet up with her husband that she hadn't seen for the past six weeks.

It was only when she was dressed and making herself a coffee from the sachets on the small hospitality tray that she remembered that the time was an hour ahead in Spain and her watch was still on BST, so it was actually coming up to two o'clock. She thought she'd better ring him at once as she wasn't sure what time Savannah came out of school.

Her heart was beating furiously as she waited for the call to connect and when it started to ring she thought her insides were going to explode. A perplexed voice said, "Hello? Jo? Is that you?"

Her mouth was very dry. She took a deep breath in and said, "Hello sweetheart. I'm here – I'm in Spain, in Valencia, at the hotel, the *Casa Flora*!"

"What? Why? What brought you here? Has something happened?" Trevor sounded bewildered.

"No, nothing, just..........I missed you so much, and I thought we could have a few hours together before Savannah finishes school on Friday." Jo-Anne was gaining confidence in her decision as she spoke. It wasn't unreasonable to want to be with her husband – even a few snatched hours together was better than nothing. "It was a spur of the moment decision and I got a really cheap flight – last minute deal, and Sabine and Pablo were only too pleased to find me a room..........and here I am!"

"Oh, sweetheart! I'm longing to see you! Wait..... let me think.........Savannah finishes school at two-thirty and I take her to gymnastics till four o'clock, then..............." his voice became muffled and she heard him saying, "Can you pick them both up and take them to the villa and I'll meet you there? Tell her I had a meeting with Manny about ......stuff!" Then he came back on the phone, "I'll drop her at gymnastics and come straight to the hotel. Jodie will pick the girls up and take them to the villa and I can spend some time with you! Is that OK? Oh my word! I can't believe you're actually here – that I'm going to see you in an hour or so!"

Jo-Anne's heart was being squeezed – she gathered from the muffled conversation that she overheard that Trevor was with Jodie while she was on the phone with him. Mid-afternoon! She was right to be concerned! It appeared that they were together *a lot*! She needed to find out just how much Jodie meant to him!

*****

Andy was slumped against the wall in the small office which in his mind had become not only his paperwork centre, but his love nest on Tuesdays and Thursdays. Darcy was facing him, tears pouring down her face as she haltingly explained to Andy that she would have to end their relationship. She told him about Peter's diagnosis and that she needed to support her husband in his illness – her conscience wouldn't allow her to betray the man she had promised to love in sickness and in health. Her heart was breaking into pieces as she said, "I have to do this – he needs me and I can't turn my back on him."

She could see the pain in his eyes as he slowly raised them to look at her. He said nothing for several minutes, but held her hand gently turning it over in his own hand as if looking for answers in her palm. After a while, he swallowed and with his voice hoarse with emotion he said, "I understand. But I want you to know, Darcy, this wasn't just about sex! It's much, much more than that! But I don't want you to suffer – and he's your husband – so, although it tears my heart out to let you go, I will stand by your wishes! But, if things change………….if you ever…………..I'm here!" He slowly lifted her hand and gently kissed the palm, then slowly released it and drew himself up straight.

Still sobbing quietly, Darcy picked up her towel and slowly walked out of the door, afraid to look back because she knew she would run back into his arms and tell him she couldn't do it – she couldn't live without him in her life – it had become more than an affair – she knew that she loved him. But this was not just about love – it was about duty, and sacrifice and loyalty and responsibility - she had a husband who needed her, and she had promised to care for him 'in sickness and in health'………..*and forsaking all others?*……. a little voice inside her head taunted her.

Andy walked over and slowly closed the door when Darcy had gone. The pain inside his heart was physical and he was having difficulty breathing. She was the first woman to mean anything to him since Shelley had died six years ago. Shelley had been his soul mate, his childhood sweetheart, the only woman he had ever wanted and ever loved………till now, till Darcy came into his life. He had tried to keep it as a casual flirtation, enjoying the chat-up, enjoying talking to her, but somehow she had gotten inside his head and he couldn't stop thinking about her. Then the magical day when she had looked at him with those beautiful eyes and he saw the naked longing in them which mirrored his own, and wordlessly they had connected on a level that only lovers can understand.

He sat at the desk, his head in his hands and swore softly under his breath. He had spent all weekend trying to work out how he could approach Darcy to tell her he wanted more than stolen hours in the office after her workout and in between his clients, that he wanted to take her out, to wine and dine her, to walk with her hand-in-hand. He knew she had a husband, he knew her husband wasn't giving her the care and attention she needed, so he had to take it slowly and not scare her off, thinking she had to leave her husband and family to be with him – he wasn't asking her to choose between them – but he wanted more than just sex.

When she came into the gym, she was later than usual and he knew by her face something was wrong. She was ashen and her eyes were bleak. She smiled wanly at him and walked towards the "Staff Only" door, leaving him to finish the training with his client before he followed her through the door to the office situated at the end of the corridor. As he approached the office, she was standing with her back to the wall staring ahead, and as he unlocked the door she began to cry softly as she followed him in. Then, with tears pouring down her face, she told him what she had decided, every word piercing his heart like a knife.

He sat like that, not moving, barely breathing, till his watch beeped, signalling his next appointment, and with a deep sigh, he stood up and slowly walked to the door, resigned to the emptiness of his life before Darcy came into it. Yes, there were women, and yes, he dated some, but they were all empty, meaningless encounters, until Darcy, and he knew when he first saw her and spoke to her that she was different, that she would be able to fill the emptiness in his life. But now she had gone and he was staring once again into the abyss.

*****

Jo-Anne was sitting at a table in the garden of the hotel which overlooked the street so that she could see Trevor as he arrived. Sabine brought her an iced coffee and asked her if she was comfortable sitting under the tree in the shade, but Jo-Anne smiled and said she was fine. She told her that Trevor was on his way – he had managed to get some time away from what he was doing so they could meet up for a short time. Sabine smiled and patted Jo-Anne's arm then continued on her way. Jo-Anne watched her, marvelling at the woman's fortitude – she was never still, she was always busy.

As the clock ticked its way round to three o'clock, Jo-Anne became nervous and chided herself for being foolish – Trevor was her husband, what was she nervous about? But this was not about seeing Trevor, it was about how involved Jodie was in his life away from her. She was nervous about what she was going to find out.

Suddenly, a car screeched to a halt and Trevor got out, quickly slamming the door shut and running up the front steps to the hotel porch. Jo-Anne stood up, but Sabine had seen him approach and after greeting him fondly she led him to the garden where Jo-Anne smiled and walked towards him. He took her into his arms and groaned into her hair.

"Oh, Jo, my angel, I've missed you so much!" he murmured. They stood in this embrace for several seconds, then he gradually let her go and they both sank down into the chairs next to the small glass-topped table. He took her hands across the table and looked at her.

"Let me look at you – oh, you look so good!" he exclaimed. "Was the journey OK? Is everything alright back home? Oh, I've missed you, I've missed our life together – this is like a different world, not one I'm used to. Oh, Jo, it's just been horrendous, I feel so trapped!"

"Oh, Trev, you've lost weight, are you eating properly? Are you looking after yourself?" She was looking at him searchingly, noticing a few lines etched on his face that weren't there before, and she felt ashamed of herself for the unkind things she had inwardly accused him of. Poor Trevor had so much to deal with, she was determined to be more understanding and be more open-minded towards Jodie who was only trying to be helpful to him.

"How is Savannah?" she asked, "And Dawn? Any changes?"

"No, though they are talking about removing the tubes soon to let her breathe on her own – if she can! That'll be a step in the right direction if it's successful. Savannah's ………..difficult! I was called into the school this morning by the Head Teacher – she told me Savannah is telling her friends we sleep together!" He grimaced, but was taken aback at the look of horror that crossed Jo-Anne's face.

"What? Why is she saying that? What on earth possessed her?" She was staring at him wide-eyed and aghast.

"No, no, don't look like that! I mean, she DOES get into my bed if she wakes during the night – most kids do! But I have to tell her to use different words – as the Head said, creeping into daddy's bed through the night is not the same as sleeping together! But some kids have told their parents that Savannah and her daddy sleep together and the Head was worried that it might get to the attention of the Social Services." Trevor shook his head slowly.

"Perhaps you should stop her getting into your bed, I mean, she's not a little child now, is she?" Jo-Anne couldn't help the feelings that were coursing through her and this was reflected in her eyes.

"Darling, you seem to forget, she's lost her grandparents and her mother is lying in a hospital bed and we don't know if she's going to get better! And she is my daughter! I'm the only parent she's got at the moment, and if she needs comforting through the night when she wakes up, I'm not turning her away!" Trevor sounded angry and looked around him to see if he could see Sabine or one of the hotel staff to order a drink.

"I'm sorry, Trevor, it's just that I've no experience with children.........." she began, but Trevor cut her short saying, "No, you haven't!"

She felt a stab of pain in her heart as the hurt of his words reminded her yet again of her enforced barrenness and the agony swamped her once more and tears pricked against her eyelids. They were silent for a few moments while Trevor caught the attention of one of the hotel staff and asked for a jug of water.

He couldn't help but compare Jo-Anne's viewpoint to that of Jodie. When he'd left her a message that morning, she phoned him back just after eleven o'clock when it was her break-time. When he'd explained what had happened, she told him she'd say there was a family crisis that she needed to attend to and she'd get out of work and meet him. They'd met up in an off-road taverna not far from the college where she taught, and when he'd told her what Savannah had been saying, she didn't flinch.

"Do you want me to talk to her? I'll explain what she should say and what she shouldn't - and without going into sordid detail, the reason why." Trevor was filled with gratitude towards her – she always knew exactly what to say, she never judged or questioned – she just made things better.

"Oh, Jodie! You're a life-saver, do you know that? What would I do without you?" He had squeezed her hand and she'd let her hand linger in his, not drawing it away, till he self-consciously pulled his hand back and leaned back in his chair. He'd told her about the doctor saying they were thinking of taking Dawn off the life-support machine to see if she could breathe on her own. The doctor had told him this the evening before when he was there with Savannah, but he hadn't said anything to her in case it went wrong and Jodie agreed with him on this. They had stayed and ordered lunch, Jodie saying she wasn't going back to work that afternoon, another tutor had been called in to cover her class.

Now he was sitting with his wife whom he had been apart from for over six weeks, and feeling outraged that she hadn't understood his position with his heart-broken child. Then just as suddenly, his anger melted as he realised that of course she wouldn't understand – how could she? She'd not witnessed any of the tumult of feelings and raw grief that he had experienced on a regular basis, she'd never even seen him with his child, so it was all unfamiliar territory for her. He leaned across the table and searched for her hands.

"Darling, I'm sorry, I shouldn't take it out on you! It's something I will have to learn to deal with – I've never spent more than two weeks at a time with Savannah over the past five years, and I'm not used to being a full-time dad. It's harder than I ever realised it would be, being a lone parent!"

Jo-Anne felt mollified by his apology. "I'm sorry too," she said smiling at him, "I can't even begin to imagine how you're managing everything."

"Well, I'm not managing very well – that's why Jodie is so useful! She has the knack of sorting things out – a bit like you do! You always had to sort me out, didn't you? Jodie knows how to manage ten-year-olds – she has one herself! Savannah and Holly are so close, they're inseparable! She tells me that I should prepare myself for Savannah starting her periods, she thinks she'll be starting soon, as she has all the signs of pubescent behaviour! Now that's a nightmare I couldn't face without Jodie!"

Jo-Anne didn't know what to say – these were topics that she felt excluded from. She had no younger sisters that she could have benefitted from, there was only her and Simon, and he was only two years younger than her. So her experience with youngsters was at zero.

She changed the subject as she was unable to make a contribution to the present one, and told him about her college course and the Masked Ball she was arranging for the Charity event and how important it would be to her position. She remained silent about the theft and the car breakdown and Dave coming back into her life – she didn't want to spoil their time together more than she already had, and when Trevor asked if they could go up to her room, she gladly agreed. She needed to feel his arms around her to feel secure in his love again.

Chapter Fourteen

Peter came home from work in a good mood. He had told Darren the news about his health and Darren was really understanding. Apparently, he had a sixty-seven year old uncle that had MS and he told Peter that he led a full and active life and he would introduce Peter to him if he wanted to talk to a fellow sufferer. Peter gladly agreed to this offer and assured him it wouldn't affect his work and Darren had replied that he didn't expect it to and slapped him on the back and told him to get on with it, but Peter could tell he meant it fondly.

"Where's my boys?" he called as he came through the door.

"Daddy!" they screeched as they hurled themselves at him, climbing up his legs, causing him to stagger slightly.

"Be careful! Don't be so rough!" warned Darcy as she turned from the oven with a casserole dish in her hands. She was slightly alarmed when she saw Peter stagger, but he shook his head at her.

"They caught me a bit off guard, that's all," he assured her, "You're getting strong, aren't you, boys? Is that because you're eating all your vegetables?"

"Yes!" they shouted together.

"I'm the strongest!" said George, "Look at my muscles!" and he bent his arm upwards to display his miniature biceps.

"No! I'm just as strong," said Lewis, copying his brother's pose, "Look at my muscles!"

Peter felt both their arms, pretending to be awed by the strength in their muscles, then pushed them both gently into the lounge telling them to start putting their toys away then wash their hands to be ready for their evening meal. He walked over to Darcy and slid his arms around her, nuzzling her neck and murmuring "Lord! You smell so good!" Then he kissed her neck and she shrugged him away saying, "Careful, I've got hot dishes here."

She deliberately kept her face turned away from him, afraid that her eyes would still be swollen from the crying that she'd done, even though she'd kept a cold, wet flannel on them for ten minutes before starting the meal.

"You heard from Jo yet?" he asked her as he washed his hands at the sink.

"No, it's a bit early. Maybe later tonight," she replied, concentrating on the task in hand.

When the meal was ready she called the boys and they all sat down at the table.

"It's good having daddy home all the time," said George, spearing a piece of broccoli with his fork and waving it at Peter. Peter smiled in contentment.

"It's good being home all the time, and us all sitting together every night! Just as it should be!" He smiled at Darcy, and she gave a small smile back.

"You don't miss the road then?" she asked him. "You always said you could never imagine doing anything else."

"I know I did. And that's how I felt at the time. But things change, people change, and I guess I changed. But this is what makes me happy now, my family round the table, my wife and my children! I'm a lucky man!"

Darcy couldn't trust herself to speak. Every time she closed her eyes she saw Andy's face, his eyes worshipping her body and she heard his voice, whispering endearments in her ear. She felt her throat tighten and tears pricked her eyes once again. How could she go on? Would she ever be able to forget the feel of his body next to hers, his gentle kisses growing in intensity as their feelings smouldered then blazed with passion.

She saw Peter look quizzically at her and she mentally shook her head and stood up from the table.

"You alright, honey?" Peter asked her anxiously.

"Yes," she croaked, then coughed to clear her throat that had thickened with suppressed feelings. "I think I'm coming down with something. I'm going to have a bath and an early night."

Peter chased the boys into the lounge. "Go and play for half an hour and then it's bath and bed for you two."

They scampered off, not needing to be told twice, and Peter picked up the remaining dishes and carried them to the sink where Darcy was piling the washing up on the bench next to it.

"You go and sit down, sweetheart, and I'll do the washing up. I'll get the boys bathed and ready for bed then you can have a nice long soak in the bath." He kissed her tenderly on the back of her neck as she filled the sink with soapy water, and she felt tears well up in her eyes again. She nodded silently and opened the back door leading into the garden. It was a still and balmy evening. The sun was still in the sky although low and long fingers of sunlight spread across the lawn from between the houses and trees at the end of the garden. She walked to the far side of the lawn, pretending to examine the flower-beds and pick off the dead blooms, but her mind was numb. She fought the tears, feeling the crushing pain of heart-ache, and wondered if she would ever feel anything other than this anguish ever again.

*****

The taxi dropped her off at seven o'clock and Jo-Anne hurried to the main entrance of the hospital. Trevor had given her instructions of where to go once she was inside so that she didn't have to ask anyone the way and have language difficulties, and he had told her that Jodie would be there about half-past seven. Trevor was at home with the girls while Jodie had her turn at visiting her best friend, and he told Jo-Anne that he would tell Jodie that she would be there so that she wasn't alarmed when she found a stranger in with Dawn.

Stranger! Jo-Anne fumed to herself, *I'm not a stranger – Dawn and I both had the same husband! And I've still got him!*

She marched to the room following Trevor's instructions and when a nurse stepped forward to confront her, she confidently said, "I'm Mrs Gainsbury – from England!"

"Ah! Si, Senora," said the nurse meekly and gestured for Jo-Anne to step into the room.

Although she'd heard Trevor's description of Dawn's injuries and the situation, she had to stifle a gasp of shock when her eyes took in the scene in front of her. She had only ever seen a photo of Dawn - and of Savannah, so she knew Dawn was beautiful, but the woman lying in the bed in front of her could not fit that description. Her head had been shaved in part for the surgery that she had undergone and her hair was starting to grow back. Where her head had not been shaved, the hair had been cut short, but the overall effect resembled that of an unkempt street urchin. Her skin had a grey pallor, and traces of blue and yellow bruising was still visible on most of her face and arms. A breathing tube was taped to her mouth and a machine hissed and spat as it fed oxygen into her inert form, and wires were taped to her upper chest monitoring her heart rhythm while another tube snaked out from under the sheets into a thick plastic bag under the bed. A bag of clear liquid suspended from a stand by the side of the bed fed into a canula in the back of her hand.

Jo-Anne stared, her heart going out to the poor woman lying there, still comatose, and she felt shame swamp her body. How could she be so selfish, thinking only of herself in her own small world, when Trevor was facing this on a daily basis, and having to deal with the insecurities of a poor little girl who had to witness her mother in this state while still suffering the loss of her beloved grandparents?

Jo-Anne tentatively moved towards the bed and drew up a chair that was near the window to sit next to Dawn, her eyes never leaving Dawn's face. She leaned across and said softly,

"Dawn, I'm Jo-Anne, Trevor's wife. I'm so sorry about your accident."

She watched Dawn's eyes intently as if she expected her to open them and turn her head to see what Trevor's wife looked like, and realized she'd been holding her breath. She exhaled slowly and spent a few minutes deep breathing to calm her shaking innards as she racked her brains for something else to say. *What can you say to someone in a coma, especially if you don't know the person?* She tried again.

"Dawn, I'm not sure if you can hear me or not, but I want you to know that everything is being taken care of. Trevor is looking after Savannah, and he will stay here as long as is necessary, until you're fit and well and able to look after her yourself. So please don't worry, and just concentrate on getting stronger." She lapsed into silence. What more could she say?

Jo-Anne sat looking at Dawn, watching her immobile face, wondering how it felt – could she feel? Could she hear? Could she smell – would she be able to know Jo-Anne in the future by her perfume? She'd heard somewhere that smell was the last of the senses to go when a person dies, so did that mean it was the strongest and most potent of all the senses? She tried to picture Dawn as Trevor's wife – he'd loved her a lot when they were first married, did she love him the same? What if she regained consciousness and thought they were still married? What if she regained consciousness and was brain-damaged? She would need to be looked after – is this what Trevor worried about as he sat here watching her day after day?

Just then there was a small knock on the door and Jo-Anne turned to see a pretty, slender brunette with short, urchin-style hair and modest make-up, dressed in white cropped leggings and a pale blue sleeveless shirt which matched the blue of her eyes.

"Hello," she said softly, "You must be Jo-Anne. I'm Jodie, Dawn's best friend." She extended her hand as she approached and Jo-Anne gave a brief handshake.

Jodie walked toward the bed and leaned over and kissed Dawn's cheek. "Hi there sweetie," she said softly, "You feeling any better today? You're looking good, the bruises are nearly gone and you're getting some colour back in those pretty cheeks. I was thinking I'd bring you some of your make-up in – I just know you'll be yelling for it once you open those beautiful eyes, so I thought I'd have it ready for you. What do you think?"

Jo-Anne looked from Jodie to Dawn, then back again. She was talking as if she thought Dawn understood what she was saying – is that what you were supposed to do? Is that how you talked to a person in a coma? Suddenly Jo-Anne felt incompetent. All this was way beyond her realm of understanding, and she was embarrassed by her own uselessness. Jodie carried on stroking Dawn's face, then she walked round to the drawer by the bedside and took out a very soft hairbrush – it looked like a baby's brush, and began to gently brush the tufts of hair on Dawn's head, making sure she didn't touch the scars on her scalp.

"Your hair is growing back nicely. Do you know - I think the colour is going to be different! That'll be interesting to see - what colour you are going to end up and all without the aid of a hair-dye!" She laughed lightly and looked at Jo-Anne. "She had lovely golden-blonde hair. I think this is going to be darker – what do you think?"

"I don't know," mumbled Jo-Anne, "I can't really say in this light."

"Yeah, it could just be the light, I suppose. Never mind. She'll be beautiful whatever the colour!" said Jodie smiling fondly at Dawn.

Jo-Anne wanted to be anywhere in the world but the place she was at that moment. She felt as though she was in a dream – none of this seemed real. It was bizarre! She swallowed nervously and said, "Well, I'll go and leave you to talk to Dawn in private. It was nice meeting you."

She stood up, and swung her bag onto her shoulder, but Jodie said, "No, don't go. We'll go and have a coffee and have a chat."

Jo-Anne's heart sank. She just wanted to escape from the whole set-up, to go back to the hotel and ring her own friend Darcy and tell her how weird and whacky this whole thing had been! She needed Darcy to make her laugh, to put it all in perspective.

Jodie leaned across and kissed Dawn's cheek. "I'm going now, honey," she said to her, "I'm going to have a coffee with Jo-Anne and I'll see you the day after tomorrow. Trev will be here tomorrow with Savannah. If you're ready to wake up, Savannah would love to see you, as would Trevor, so …………..see what you can do! Ok? Bye, sweetie."

She smiled at Jo-Anne and as they came out of the room, Jodie linked her arm through Jo-Anne's and led her down the corridor through several sets of doors till they came to a small cafeteria where she led Jo-Anne to a table and said, "You sit here and I'll get the coffees, which would you prefer?"

"Err, cappuccino, please," said Jo-Anne, recognising that to struggle against Jodie was futile, she was a force to be reckoned with, and she would rather have her in full view till she worked out whether she was friend or foe.

*****

The next morning, Jo-Anne was eating breakfast when her phone rang. Glancing down she saw it was Trevor, so she looked around to see how many guests were still in the small dining room. Realising she would have no privacy, she pushed her chair back from the table and stood up as she answered the call.

"Hi Trevor, "she said softly, walking out of the room towards the small courtyard which led to the garden.

"Good morning, sweetheart," said Trevor, but she could pick out a sense of anxiety in his tone.

"Is everything alright?" she asked him.

"I don't know..........the hospital have just phoned me. They're ready to take Dawn off the ventilator this morning to see if she can breathe on her own. I have to be there."

"Do you want me to come with you?" asked Jo-Anne, looking at her watch as she spoke and working out what time she could be at the hospital.

"I don't know...........Jodie's coming, she said she wanted to be there when it happened." Trevor sounded distracted, as if he was doing something else and not really thinking about the conversation.

"Oh!" Jo-Anne felt a prickle of resentment. He'd obviously phoned Jodie before he phoned her. "I just thought you might want me to be with you – for support – but if you think.........." She left the sentence unfinished, hoping he would calm her fears and say he needed her by his side.

"Maybe it would be better if there was just me and Jodie there........you know.......if she wakes up..........I mean, she has never met you, has she?"

"Through no fault of mine!" snapped Jo-Anne.

"Oh, I know, sweetheart, I'm not criticising, I'm trying to think what would be best." She could picture Trevor running his hand through his hair, sweeping it back from his forehead, then rubbing his finger-tips on his scalp on the top of his head – he used to say it helped him think!

Jo-Anne has a rush of shame. How could she be petty at a time like this - this was a monumental change in what had been happening, perhaps Dawn would wake up and get well and everything could go back to how it was!

"Well, why don't you – and Jodie – go to the hospital and I'll just wait and see what happens. You can phone me if you want me to come. I'll just wait to hear from you." Jo-Anne tried to not let the disappointment show in her voice. She'd travelled all this way to spend some time with her husband, thinking that they would have the day together while Savannah was in school, but it wasn't going to happen. She would spend the day alone while Jodie would be his pillar of strength!

She's a really nice person, Jo-Anne told herself, *she really cares about Dawn and Savannah.*

And Trevor? The mischievous little voice inside her head asked, *does she really care about Trevor as well?* She'd been kindness itself last night as they sipped coffee in the little hospital cafeteria, asking about Jo-Anne's job, telling her about her own job and how she lived as an English woman on her own with a child in a foreign country, even though she had the support – emotionally and financially – of her parents living on the outskirts of Madrid. They could have been two friends just enjoying time together, and Jo-Anne had to admit she did enjoy her company – there was something refreshing and open about her, but was that a ploy? Did she secretly harbour a fondness for Trevor that went beyond the bounds of friendship?

"Well, if you don't mind, sweetheart," Trevor said at last, "I'm so sorry you've come all this way and I won't be able to spend much time with you – but that's what it's been like all the time I've been here. I'm not here through choice, remember!"

"I know, I'm sorry. I'll wait to hear from you then. I hope it all goes well – fingers crossed for you!" She said goodbye to him and blinked back tears of frustration. Taking a deep breath in and exhaling loudly, she turned and walked back into the hotel and up to her room to collect her bag and purse. She might as well do some sight-seeing, then the holiday break wasn't wasted.

*****

Darcy had spent a miserable morning in work, though she tried to keep a brave face and forced herself to be the smiling, cheerful assistant that she had been previously, but inside her heart was being twisted and shredded every time she thought about never seeing Andy again. She battled with the idea of still going to the gym, but knew she couldn't handle the pain of seeing him – there was no other option but to leave and find another gym. Perhaps she should look for a women-only gym! She wouldn't be reminded of Andy if there were no other men around – but she mentally shook her head! It wasn't the sight of men at the gym that interested her – she barely noticed them. There was something special about Andy, something on a deeper level than physical attraction, something that touched her soul.

That evening while she was in the kitchen preparing the meal, Peter came in a bit later than usual and had the predictable tussle with the boys before he walked into the kitchen. After kissing Darcy on the top of her head as she was bent down in front of the oven, he said, "I've been thinking – I should start exercising regularly if I'm going to take up a new lifestyle, start looking after my body the way that you do. So………..I've joined your gym! I called in on the way home and signed up, but then I thought maybe I'd get myself a personal trainer to set me off on the right path. What do you think?"

Darcy's heart lurched madly. She slowly stood up and had to hold onto the bench for support as her head swam dizzily. Did he know something? Was he testing her? She looked at him warily, trying to work out if he was trying to analyse her reactions, but all she saw was Peter's open and guileless face.

He saw her expression and laughed. "I know it's a shock – I've never been to a gym in my life and I could never understand your passion for it, but if I want to keep on top of this MS then I have to get fit."

Darcy wanted to laugh mirthlessly at the irony of it all. Peter wanted a personal trainer! Perhaps he would choose Andy! Oh, how life was mocking her now! Her mouth was dry and she turned towards the sink and filled herself a tumbler of water.

"You OK, honey?" asked Peter with concern in his voice.

Darcy nodded, still unable to speak. Peter continued, "I thought we could go together, get a babysitter in, and we could go for a meal afterwards - make a date night of it. Something different. What do you think?"

Darcy took a deep breath in. "I don't know. I was thinking of changing my gym, going to that women-only gym in town. They do more classes, like salsa and yoga."

"Now yoga would be good for me, don't they do a class at the gym you go to now?" asked Peter.

"I'm not sure, it's just that one of the girls was telling me that she goes to this one in town and the monthly subs are less and the classes are better." Darcy was thinking on her feet. The last thing she wanted was for Peter to go to her gym, and possibly end up with Andy as his personal trainer. Even worse was the idea of them going as a couple, it would be like flaunting her marriage in front of Andy, that would hurt him too much. She couldn't bear to see the pain on his face if she did that. Nor could she bear the idea of Peter being coached by

Andy, having casual chats and Peter talking to Andy about his wife – that too would hurt hIm too much. No! It was too risky! She couldn't allow this to happen. She would have to find another gym. She'd have to talk to Andy, make him aware so that he didn't take Peter on as a client, one of the other personal trainers could take him.

    She continued setting out the meal, her heart thudding as she pictured going to the gym tomorrow, seeing Andy and explaining to him, but nonetheless seeing him once again, like a beautiful forbidden fruit being placed in front of her, for her eyes to feast upon, but prevented from touching – or being touched, and her pulse quickened as her memories flooded back.

*****

    Jo-Anne had finished her evening meal and had gone into the garden at the hotel. She couldn't understand what was preventing Trevor from phoning her, it must be something at the hospital – there was no other reason. She'd kept herself busy all day, visiting places of interest without actually seeing them, glancing every minute at her phone, checking the volume was on, checking she had a signal, checking the battery hadn't suddenly depleted. She'd finally given up and made her way back to the hotel, to have a shower and get changed, then pace up and down the garden paths, and then go for an early evening meal.

    When her phone eventually rang, her heart almost jumped out of her mouth. She answered immediately.

    "Trevor? What's happened? I've been demented!" she babbled, her words falling over each other as they tumbled from her mouth.

    "Oh, sweetheart, I'm sorry!" said Trevor, sounding exhausted.

    "What happened with Dawn?" she asked.

"It was pretty scary! Jodie and I were on edge when they removed the tube. There were several doctors and nurses there, and they'd told us that the first sixty minutes after removal were the most critical, so you can imagine how tense we were! We sat there telling her to breathe, willing her to breathe, almost doing it for her, and she kept going! It was laboured at first, but it gradually got more stable, and she's still breathing on her own! This is a major step forward, such a relief!" Jo-Anne could hear the emotion in his voice.

"Is she still in a coma?" she asked.

"Yes, but the doctors think she may come out of it – it's something they can't predict, some patients do, and some don't! But the fact that she's breathing on her own is a massive change, it shows her internal injuries have healed, we just have to pray that her brain is healing the same!"

"Oh, that's really good news!" said Jo-Anne, "Has Savannah seen her mother yet?"

"Yes. I left Jodie with Dawn and went to collect the girls from school and took them to the hospital. Holly didn't want to go in, so Jodie came out to stay with her while I took Savannah in. She was so excited, bless her, Dawn looks more like her old self with the tubes removed. Savannah was coaxing her to wake up, getting quite cross and frustrated at one point as if Dawn was deliberately staying asleep, so I took her home. Jodie stayed home with both girls while I went back to the hospital. I was scared in case she'd stopped breathing while I was away, but she's still battling on. I've just come away now, the doctor told me to go home and come back tomorrow, not that I'll be able to sleep! I'll be on edge all night!"

"I'm so relieved for you! I can't begin to imagine what it's been like for you, and I'm very proud of how you've coped with it all!" Jo-Anne was very close to tears, her emotions were in turmoil – relief that Dawn was improving, disappointment that she wasn't going to see Trevor tomorrow if he was going back to the hospital – she didn't think it was fair to expect him to come to see her when he had Dawn's fragile health on his mind, he'd probably even forgotten she was in Spain - that was the double-edged sword of mobile phones! She felt sorry for herself, but immediately swallowed her self-pity – didn't Trevor tell her it was pointless coming to Spain? *She* took it upon herself to make this surprise visit, the intention being to see if there was anything going on with Jodie and her husband! And what had she learned? That Trevor *was* having the tough time he'd said he was having, and Jodie *was* the invaluable help he'd said she was – so this trip had done nothing to ease her mind.

"Are you still there?" asked Trevor.

"Yes," she answered, "I'm just trying to digest it all." She felt perilously close to tears.

"What time is your flight tomorrow?" he asked, and her heart lifted when she realised he hadn't forgotten.

"Eight o'clock tomorrow night – I'll be leaving here about five-thirty."

"I'm going to the hospital first thing as soon as I've dropped Savannah at school, but I'll come away as soon as I'm happy that she's still stable and I'll come to the *Casa Flora*. We can have a couple of hours together and lunch and …………..will you be OK getting a taxi to the airport? I'll have to pick Savannah up and take her to the hospital."

"Yes, that's fine. I'm so glad I'll be able to say goodbye properly! I'm going to miss you even more now. But I'll throw myself into work when I get back, and who knows, Dawn might make a full recovery and you can come back to England, and we'll all live happily ever after!" Jo-Anne was so thankful that she was seeing Trevor before she left Spain that she didn't really notice the silence that followed her giddy projections for the future.

Chapter Fifteen

When Darcy was changing into her gym kit, she suddenly had a heart-stopping thought! What if Andy wasn't here? She'd spent a crazy morning getting the boys off to school and she knew it was her own tension that made them seem like defiant, lazy slowcoaches, because she just wanted them in the car and then into school so she could get to the gym. Every task they had to do – like getting dressed, eating their breakfast, putting their shoes on, seemed to be done in slow motion, and her rational brain told her they were like this every morning, but *today was different* her mind screeched!

Now she was here! What would she do if he wasn't here? *Shut up, chatterbox!* she told her butterfly brain! *Just go and do it!* She opened the door and went into the gym, the heat from the active bodies, the drone from the air-conditioning, the sounds from the many machines and equipment and the heavy music blaring from the sound system assaulted her senses and she felt light-headed. She took a deep breath in and walked unsteadily towards the treadmill where she always started her workout.

Her eyes were drawn to the weights section, and there he was, standing with his back to her, correctly positioning a client with a dumb-bell, facing the mirrored wall. As he stepped away from the client his eyes met hers through the mirror, and it felt like electricity zig-zagging and flashing between them, and she gasped with the intensity of it. Her cheeks flamed and the heat raged through her body, and she knew in that instant that she would never stop loving him.

She pounded the treadmill, her heartbeat already high before the exercise had an effect and her breathing laboured from the beginning. She had to stop after a few minutes and try to bring herself under control. She drank some water from her bottle giving herself the opportunity to cast her eyes surreptitiously in Andy's direction, but he was concentrating on his client. When she had slowed her heart rate and regained some self-control she continued with her workout but her mind was racing. *What if he was going to ignore her? She'd told him that she didn't want to continue their relationship. What if he deliberately kept away from her – she would have to seek him out to talk to him about Peter's membership. He was scheduled to come for his assessment the following evening and sign up for a personal trainer so it was imperative that she spoke to him today!*

As she stole furtive glances in his direction, she saw him shake hands with his client and the client walked away. Andy walked over to the water station to refill his water bottle, and Darcy took the opportunity to do the same. As he turned away from the machine. Darcy was behind him.

"Oops, sorry," he said as he stepped back almost colliding with her, then she heard his sharp intake of breath as he saw it was her.

"Andy, I have to talk to you!" she said quietly.

He looked unsure. "Talk? You mean here, or privately?"

"I'm not sure – it's about Peter, he's signed up to join this gym and he wants a personal trainer," she said in a rush. "He's coming in tomorrow evening."

"I see," he said slowly, "And you want………..?"

"I want you to make sure you don't take him on, give him to someone else! It would be too………..much," she ended lamely.

"No problem," he said, "I've already said I don't want to take on any more clients. I'm going to reduce my hours here. I've got a position in another gym, so I'll work the two places till I know what I'm going to do."

"What do you mean?" her hand went to her throat as she felt panic rising. "Do you mean you might be leaving?"

"I don't know, my head's a mess at the moment!" he looked over the top of her head, then looked intently at his water bottle.

"Oh, Andy!" She felt her eyes well up with tears, and furiously blinked to clear them before they spilled down her cheeks. "My head's a mess, too."

"What are we going to do?" he said softly.

"I can't give you up!" she whispered.

He took a deep breath in and exhaled slowly. "The thing is, Darcy, I don't want …….this," he said, gesturing around him. "I don't want to creep into my office for sneaky sex! Just before you told me about Peter's condition, I had decided to tell you I want to have a real relationship with you, I want to take you out, I want to walk hand-in-hand in the rain, or sun, I don't just want stolen hours of passion. I love you too much for that!"

He looked down at his feet. "There! Now I've said it! You can run if you want to, but that's where I'm at! I love you and I want more than just sex!"

Darcy's eyes had grown wide and her heart was racing. *Oh, my God! He loves me!*

"I think I love you too," she whispered, "But I can't lose my family!"

His hand gently stroked her arm then he turned back towards the water machine. After a moment, he turned back to her.

"I will respect any decision you make," he said gently. "I have no ties, it's only you that has ………………complications, but I guess we've reached the point of 'all or nothing'. I can't continue the way we were, it will cheapen what we have and I love you too much for that."

Darcy nodded dumbly. What was she going to do? She couldn't go on without him, but she couldn't forsake Peter – not since his diagnosis, it felt.......wrong, and she could NEVER give up her children.

"Give me your phone," he said suddenly, and she took her phone out of her arm band and handed it to him.

"I've put my phone number in – you can change the name or file it somewhere else, but I want you to be able to contact me outside of the gym." As he handed her phone back to her, his finger softly stroked the back of her hand. "I'm going to go now. I'm sorry if this feels like an ultimatum, which....... I suppose it is, but..............it's breaking my heart," he ended in a whisper.

He gave her a wistful smile which tore at her heart, and she turned away so he wouldn't see the pain in her eyes, or hear the broken whimper that escaped from her mouth.

*****

Savannah had crept into Trevor's bed as she normally did, but she couldn't get back to sleep. She tossed and turned and in the end Trevor sat up.

"Savannah! You're like a spinning top! Can't you sleep?" he asked her softly.

"No, I keep thinking about mummy. Do you think she's woken up?" she asked bouncing up from the bed.

"I don't know, darling." He looked at the clock on the bedside cabinet - it was ten to five. "Shall we get up – we can have a nice breakfast and you can play for a while before you go to school."

"Can I go and see mummy before I go to school? Please? Please? She might have woken up!"

"Well, they probably won't let us in before six o'clock, but we can try!"

Savannah bounced out of bed and ran to the bathroom. "I won't be long," she called as she slammed the door.

Trevor went downstairs and started the breakfast and when Savannah finally came downstairs Trevor had already eaten his and her breakfast was waiting on the table. Trevor went upstairs to get showered and dressed, all the while thinking about Dawn and whether she'd had a comfortable night. He reckoned if something had gone wrong the hospital would have contacted him through the night, so the fact that they hadn't was a positive sign.

They arrived at the hospital at ten past six, and there were no objections to them going into Dawn's room – all the staff were carrying out their chores and the hospital was quietly humming with activity. Trevor felt nervous as he pushed the door open, but was relieved when he saw that Dawn was still breathing quietly. The nurse attending to her smiled when she saw them both and said softly to Savannah, "She is doing well, your mama."

Savannah took hold of Dawn's hand and said, "Mummy, can you hear me? I want you to wake up! Please wake up, mummy, it's been such a long time."

Trevor stroked Savannah's hair and said quietly, "I'm sure she's trying very hard, darling, but it's a very, very, deep sleep that is so hard to come out of. But she'll do it, we just have to be patient."

They sat either side of her for more than an hour, talking softly to Dawn and to each other, then Trevor said Savannah needed to be thinking of going to school – there were only two more days till the summer break and she'd be able to spend much more time with her mummy then. Savannah kissed her, and stroked her face and said she would be back later, and for mummy to keep on fighting to get out of this deep sleep.

Trevor felt a sense of anti-climax. He'd nurtured the idea that Dawn would slowly regain consciousness after she was taken off the ventilator, but nothing had changed. He held Savannah's hand as they walked out of the hospital, both of them rather subdued, and as soon as they got into the car Savannah burst into tears.

"What's the matter?" asked Trevor in alarm.

"I just want mummy to wake up!" wailed Savannah. "I thought when they took the tube out she would wake up, but she hasn't!" She banged her head against the side window of the car repeatedly, till Trevor got out and came round to the passenger side of the car and wrenched the door open.

"Don't do that sweetheart, you'll hurt yourself!" He tried to take her into his arms to comfort her, but she pushed him away.

"I don't care! I want mummy! Why don't you do something? Why does nobody care! I want my mummy!" Her voice was rising and Trevor was afraid she was going to go into one of the frenzies again and he looked around anxiously to see if anyone was around that maybe could offer help, but people just carried on with their business and paid no heed to a man trying to calm his hysterical daughter. He thought angrily about the Headteacher's offer of referring Savannah for counselling, but he'd heard nothing yet. He'd mention it again to her when he went in today – they needed to know that Dawn's situation had changed in case Savannah had one of these rages while she was in school.

When Savannah had exhausted herself and lay limply in Trevor's arms, he gently coaxed her back into the car and fastened her seat belt. When he got behind the wheel, a wave of fatigue washed over him. *How much more of this can I take?* He'd asked himself the same question a hundred times since this nightmare first began.

When he arrived at the school, Savannah was calm although quiet. As the car pulled up, she looked around anxiously for Holly, then relief washed over her when she saw her and waved madly as Holly and Jodie walked towards them. Jodie was smiling and when she saw Trevor's face she asked if he was alright.

"We've been to the hospital to check on Dawn – she's fine," he added quickly as he saw Jodie's face crease in concern. Then dropping his voice to a conspiratorial whisper he added, "She had a melt-down in the hospital car park!"

"Oh, poor you," said Jodie as she rubbed his arm in comfort, "She looks OK now."

"Yeah, she is. I'm going to speak to the Head to see what's happening about the counselling she was making the referral for."

"Do you want me to come with you?" asked Jodie, "I've time, I've no class till ten this morning."

"If you don't mind, I'd appreciate the support," said Trevor, and all four of them walked towards the main door.

They bade goodbye to the girls and waited till they'd gone inside, then after a minute or two, they went up the front steps to the reception office to ask to see the Head. They were shown into a waiting room and within a few moments, Marian Overton appeared.

"Ah, Mr Gainsbury, good morning, and Ms Bradshaw, I trust all is well?" she said.

"Yes, thank you. I came to tell you - Savannah's mother has been taken of the ventilator, but it's had a massively disappointing effect on Savannah – she believed her mother would wake up when that happened, but she hasn't! Not yet, anyway."

"I see. Yes, I can imagine that Savannah would feel disheartened by this. Thank you for telling me, we will be watchful for any impact this has on her behaviour."

"The other thing is………..you said you would make a

referral for counselling, but I haven't heard anything , and with the summer break coming I wondered if you could perhaps chase this up?"

"Of course. I'm sorry you haven't heard anything yet, though it is early days, but I will certainly contact the department again."

"Thank you," said Trevor, and when there was a small silence, Marian Overton turned to the door and pulling it open, she said," Thank you for coming to see me, I do hope that Savannah's mother regains consciousness soon for the poor child's sake."

They walked out and Jodie turned to him, "You OK?"

"Yes," he replied, "Thanks for coming in – she's a bit imposing, isn't she?"

"All Headteachers are!" laughed Jodie, "She's probably a very gentle soul in her outside life, and that's the professional persona she wears like a mask!"

They went out of the main gates towards their cars, and Trevor's phone started to ring.

"It's the hospital!" he gasped, his face blanching. "Hello?" he said

Jodie tried to read his expression, and when she saw his eyes widen and a small tentative smile play round his mouth, she knew it wasn't bad news.

"Thank you, I'll be there as soon as possible<" he said disconnecting the call.

"They think she's coming round – she's showing signs, her eyes are fluttering!" he said excitedly as he searched his pockets for his car keys. "I've got to go!"

"I'm coming!" shouted Jodie as she ran towards her own car. "I'll see you there!"

*****

Darcy had tossed and turned the entire night and when the alarm went off she got out of bed immediately as if it was a relief to be up. Peter turned over to look at her.

"You were a bit restless last night – are you OK?" he asked her with concern in his voice.

She sighed heavily. "It's nothing," she mumbled, "Just…….everything!" She rubbed her eyes with the heel of her hand. "I mean………just thinking about the future and stuff!"

Peter sat up in bed. "You mean about me……about MS? I've told you, sweetie, there's no need for you to worry. It's not a terminal illness, the worst it'll get will be bouts of symptoms – which I've been having - and neither of us knew anything and we weren't affected, so don't fret over it! I promise you – nothing will be any different!"

Darcy nodded dumbly and went into the bathroom. She turned on the shower and under the cover of the noise, she broke down in tears. It was hurting so much, the pain was tearing her apart. *Oh, Andy,* she cried inside her head, *why did you show me what passion was, how could someone enter my soul, consume me completely, make me feel so…..so…loved, and then leave me bereft? I can't live like this – it hurts too much!* She looked at her face in the mirror, her eyes were bleak, tears poured down her cheeks and she stared at the face in front of her, imagining the future – her life with Peter……..safe, comfortable, monotonous, unexciting, sexless! Could she settle for a life like that? There had been no sex in their marriage for many months before she met Andy and she didn't make a big issue out of it, she thought it was just a normal part of a marriage, a blip, nothing to create a scene over. Until she met Andy - and she was transported to a realm she never imagined possible! She had never experienced such all-consuming love for a man!

Suddenly she heard the voices of her children – arguing over who had the worst nightmare! This had the same effect as a bucket of iced water being poured over her head!

Her boys! Peter's children! He was their father and they loved him intensely! If she divorced Peter it would break their hearts – they may even choose to live with him, not her! She shook her head wildly – she couldn't bear to think of life without them! She wouldn't even consider the possibility of leaving them to run off with Andy. As these thoughts chased round and round her head she pressed her fist into her mouth and bit down on her clenched hand to stifle the scream that was threatening to burst out of her.

A frantic knocking on the bathroom door forced her back into the present moment and reality.

"Mummy, hurry up, I need a wee!" shouted Lewis, "Let me in, quick!"

Darcy grabbed a flannel and rubbed it quickly over her face to wipe the tears, and as she opened the door with one hand she shoved her toothbrush in her mouth with the other hand and bent over the washbasin so her face was hidden. The room was full of steam from the still-running shower, so she quickly slipped out of her pyjamas and climbed into the shower while Lewis regaled her with details of the monsters in the dream he'd had. He didn't expect an answer from her, he simply wanted to get his nightmare into her awareness before his brother beat him to it.

"Wasn't that the most scary dream EVER?" he shouted above the sound of the shower.

"Yes," she answered automatically.

"See!" shouted Lewis, "George, mummy said my dream was the most scaryiest! So there!"

Then Peter's voice intercepted what would have been a sibling competition that would have continued over breakfast and all the way to school – but he cleverly diverted attention to something happening in the garden with a squirrel, so Lewis ran out of the bathroom leaving Darcy to finish showering in peace.

She needed to talk to Jo! She hadn't heard from her all the time she was in Spain. She felt bad at not getting in touch with her, but she wasn't sure whether Jo would want to be bothered, but the honest truth was that all Darcy's attention had been focused on Andy. She hadn't told Jo anything about her affair with Andy – she knew Jo would tell her to end it. But it was different now – it wasn't an affair, it had the potential to completely change her life! *Stop!* she shouted inside her head, *stop this train at once! Wrong track!*

Jo would be back later this evening, she would see how the land was lying when she saw her and decide then whether she was going to confide in her or not. If she told her, if she put all this into words and they came out of her mouth, they were there – in the air – what was said could never be unsaid, and she would have to accept the consequences.

Chapter Sixteen

Jo-Anne looked back one last time as she went through the boarding gate, but there was no sign of Trevor. She'd heard nothing from him all day – she'd waited to have lunch, but when he hadn't arrived at two o'clock she knew he wasn't going to appear, so she'd ordered food but pecked at it and shuffled it around on her plate. Her appetite was as absent as her husband!

There was no place for her here, she wasn't valued, in fact she was an encumbrance! Tears welled in her eyes as she sat down heavily on the seat in the plane and turned her face to the window. She just wanted to get back to England, to her life, her friends, where she had a place, where she *was* appreciated. She glanced sideways as someone – a woman - sat next to her and turned her face back to the window – she didn't want to start up a conversation with anyone, she just wanted to close her eyes and forget the past couple of days. She felt humiliated – she'd travelled all this way to spend time with her husband, and he couldn't make time for her! Tears started to trickle down her face and she allowed herself to tumble into a chasm of desolation and self-pity. He mustn't love her as she loved him! Yes, he had a daughter and an ex-wife in a coma in a hospital bed, but that wasn't his life! He didn't belong there! He belonged in England, with her, in their little semi, going to work every day and coming home to her every evening, and the pair of them going to the cinema, or the pub, or going out for a meal, him going out on his beloved bike while she buried her head in her studies or went out with Darcy, but doing whatever they wanted to do on a weekend!

But not any more – he had given up his job to look after his ex-wife and daughter – in Spain! *He's not going to come back to England*, the little voice inside her said, *he's happy in Spain with his daughter and his……..…ex-wife's friend, they're like a little family already.* Her shoulders shook with suppressed sobs, and she sat curled up near the window for the entire flight, ignoring any requests from the flight attendants for drinks or in-flight purchases, and by the time they had landed she had constructed a steel shell around her heart to prevent any more breakage.

She switched her phone back on as she trundled to the exit doors – she had only taken a weekend case so she didn't have luggage to wait for – and found a message waiting for her from Dave.

"Am waiting by W H Smiths" it read.

Her face creased into a frown. *What did he mean? Was he here? In the airport? Why?*

She looked around as she came through the doors, and sure enough, sauntering towards her from the front of the shop was Dave, a huge smile creasing his face.

"What are you doing here?" she managed to say as he grabbed her in a bear hug.

"I got a lift from Ben – a guy from work – he's off to Malaga for a week, and I thought you might be tired so I've come to drive you home." As he was talking he had pulled her arm through the crook of his arm, then picked up her bag and led her towards the external doors. "Tough, was it?" he asked.

She didn't reply but hugged her face into his arm and he gently kissed the top of her head. She could feel tears well up, but she was determined not to cry any more, so she cleared her throat and said, "Yep!"

When they neared the car, she gratefully handed him the keys and realised that she had been dreading the drive home. It would be about half-past eleven when she got home, and Dave would have to then travel to his own place, but she couldn't be bothered to feel any guilt or remorse for that, she just wanted to get back to her own little nest.

When they'd exited the airport car-park and were on the road home, Dave asked her if she wanted to talk about her trip. She was silent while she thought about what she wanted to say, and when he glanced across at her, she took a deep breath in and said, "I think my marriage is over."

Dave didn't respond, so she continued, "I can't see any way back from this. He's created a new life for himself, and I don't figure in it."

"I see," said Dave softly.

"I only saw him once, for a couple of hours on Tuesday, then the hospital withdrew the breathing tubes from Dawn so he stayed with her all day Wednesday, and he was supposed to come to the *Casa Flora* to spend some time with me this morning and have lunch together, but he didn't come and didn't phone or text me, so I've no idea what's happened today, but I'm obviously not important enough to keep informed!"

"So it was a bit of a wasted journey then?" said Dave.

"Yep! But at least I met Jodie!" Jo-Anne turned her face away from Dave and looked out at the darkness outside. "She's actually very nice!"

Dave was silent, and they travelled the next few miles without speaking. He finally spoke.

"Are you still coming to the viewing tomorrow, for the apartment? Or do you want me to go by myself?"

"Yes, I'm coming. It'll take my mind off everything. I'm actually looking forward to it." He glanced across at her and gave her a smile.

"I need your common-sense approach. I'll be won over by the fact it's got a cleaner, then all I have to do is find a cook and I'm set for life!"

Jo-Anne gave a short laugh. "Trevor's got a housekeeper and a groundsman, and a companion who advises him on his daughter's welfare! I can't compete with that, can I?"

Dave didn't answer and they lapsed into silence again until they were almost at her house, then she said, "Oh, Dave, I'm so sorry. You've been good enough to come to the airport for me and all I've done is whinge all the way home. Are you going to come in for a coffee before you set off home?"

"Yes," he replied pulling up in the drive, "I want to check the house is OK for you. Did the Crime Prevention Office ever contact you?"

"Oh, yes, a really nice young man came on Monday evening, but I was a bit distracted having this trip on my mind as I'd only booked it the evening before, and so we've arranged for him to come back next Monday – I'd better not forget."

Dave got her travel case out of the boot and walking ahead of her he unlocked the front door and switched on the hall lights. Jo-Anne followed him in as he went into each room, checking doors and windows and once he was satisfied that all was well he went into the kitchen where Jo-Anne was boiling the kettle. He rubbed his eyes and yawned, and Jo-Anne smiled fondly at him.

"You've always been so good to me, God knows why you put up with me – I get on my own nerves sometimes!"

"Mmm," he agreed, "you are a bit of a pain............but I like you!" He used a silly voice as he said the last part of the sentence, making Jo-Anne laugh.

"If you don't want the trek home, you can sleep in the spare room if you like, it'll only take a minute to put bedding on it, and you can leave early in the morning," said Jo-Anne with her back towards him as she made the coffee.

"That's worth a thought……………actually, I might do that if it's OK with you."

"Not a problem, I'll be glad of the company to be honest. In that case, do you fancy a glass of wine? Or a beer?" Jo-Anne perked up at the thought of having someone in the house with her, and who better than Dave, her trusted friend and ally.

*****

When Trevor and Jodie arrived at the hospital and rushed to Dawn's room, they both skidded to a halt just outside the door, and Trevor groped for Jodie's hand. She took his hand in both of her own hands and they both gripped tightly in nervous anticipation. They each took a deep breath and Trevor pushed the door open.

Doctor Garcia looked up as they walked in and smiled, but Trevor's eyes flicked at him and went straight to Dawn. The nurse at the side of the bed stood back as Trevor and Jodie approached and they both leaned over to look at Dawn. Her eyes were closed, but the lids were flickering, and Doctor Garcia said very softly, "She has opened her eyes briefly, and we think she is hovering between the conscious and unconscious. We must not cause her any panic, but coax her gently into this world."

"How is she?" asked Trevor anxiously, "Is she…………okay, I mean………is there any brain damage?"

"We don't know her exact condition at present," said Doctor Garcia slowly, "If she rouses and starts to speak………we will be able to tell more, but we must be patient a while longer."

Jodie had leaned over and took hold of Dawn's hand. "Dawn, honey, can you hear me? It's Jodie. Can you open your eyes? We've missed you, wake up and talk to me, please. Savannah's eager to see you, she misses her mummy."

Dawn's eyelids moved rapidly. Trevor took a sharp breath in. "Dawn, sweetheart, it's Trevor. I've come to look after you and Savannah. Can you wake up? Open your eyes, sweetheart, open your eyes and talk to us."

They watched eagerly for any sign, and then Dawn's eyes flickered and opened very slightly. Jodie began to sob quietly.

"Dawn, honey, it's me, it's Jodie. Can you see me?"

Dawn's head moved a fraction towards the sound of Jodie's voice, and she emitted a deep exhalation of breath.

"She's trying to talk!" exclaimed Jodie. "Dawn, look at me, honey, look who's here to see you!"

"Dawn, sweetheart, it's Trevor. I've come to look after Savannah. Can you hear me? Can you wake up?"

Dawn's eyes opened a fraction more, and her hands, which had lain lifeless on the bed, started to twitch and flutter. Doctor Garcia moved forward and took her wrist, watching the machine that was monitoring her pulse rate.

"Her muscles have not been used for a long time, so she will have limited movement until the physiotherapist can do work with her," he told them.

Trevor nodded impatiently. "Yes, I know," he said, "That's not a problem if her nervous system is intact. Can you tell if she has any paralysis?"

"We will conduct many tests once she is awake, to check her physical movement as well as her brain activity. We do not want to overtire her just now, so if she becomes drowsy again, we will let her rest." Doctor Garcia moved to the other side of the room where he gave instructions to the nurse for Dawn's treatment for the rest of that day.

"I must go now," the doctor told Trevor, "You may stay with her, but please, as I said, if she needs to, let her rest. My nurse will tell you if you need to leave. Tomorrow we will start the testing."

Trevor nodded. "Thank you, Doctor."

Jodie smiled her thanks to the doctor and walked round to the other side of the bed which the doctor had vacated and gently took Dawn's hand.

"Would you like me to brush your hair and make you look presentable, now that you've decided to join us?" Jodie was smiling as she leaned across and spoke softly to Dawn. The merest ghost of a smile flitted across Dawn's face, and Jodie looked up at Trevor, her eyes wide.

"She heard me!" she whispered to him, "She heard me and understood me!"

Trevor gave a small smile. He wasn't so sure. He didn't think there was any sign of recognition, but he didn't want to dampen Jodie's enthusiasm. Jodie took the soft hairbrush and gently stroked it across Dawn's head and slowly-growing tufts of hair, humming softly as if to a child. Then she took some moisturised face wipes and carefully cleansed Dawn's face, then applied a nourishing cream. She then took her hand and gently massaged it, carefully avoiding the canula and applied a hand cream, softly stroking until the cream was absorbed. Then she walked round the bed to the other side, nudging Trevor out of the way, and did the same treatment to the other hand.

Trevor stood staring, his mind in a turmoil. What would happen now? If she was out of the coma, presumably she wouldn't want the intense medical treatment she'd been having, so the hospital would want to transfer her, either to a nursing home if she needed nursing for whatever reason, or if she was fully recovered, she would go home. And then what? Could he go back to England and just leave her with only Savannah to care for her? Even if she was fully recovered, she would need a nurse – or some kind of help, for several months at least, until he was sure that Savannah was able to live freely without being her mother's carer.

He ran his fingers through his hair absently, and Jodie looked up at him. "You OK?" she asked, concern evident in her voice.

"Yeah, yeah," he replied, "Just thinking............you know, about everything."

There had been no further signs from Dawn, her eyes were still slightly open and the pupils were visible, moving slightly every few seconds, but nothing else. Jodie kept on talking to her, trying to coax her to talk, trying to stimulate her memories by chatting about the girls and school-gate gossip and weekend trips they had been on together with the girls. Trevor felt excluded from all this, and had a niggling feeling of envy. Savannah was his daughter, and he had done none of this with her.

After a while, Dawn's eyelids began to droop and flicker, and Jodie said, "Do you want a little nap, honey? We'll go grab a coffee and let you rest, then we'll come back in a while." She leaned across and kissed her gently on the cheek, and looked up at Trevor expectantly, so he leaned across and said, "Have a little rest, sweetheart, we'll be back in a little while."

They walked out of the room and headed towards the cafeteria. Jodie linked her arm through Trevor's and said, "Isn't it great? She's coming out of the coma, she may fully recover from this! Won't that be fabulous? Savannah is going to be so excited, I can't wait to see her little face!"

"Well, we have to make sure she IS out of the coma, I'd hate to bring Savannah here and for Dawn to remain sleeping – she'll kick off big time!" Jodie looked up at him, feeling slightly disturbed about his lack of keenness in Dawn's progress, but then remembered he was divorced from her so he must be feeling a bit awkward about what he could say to her.

When they reached the cafeteria, she told him to grab a seat and she would bring the coffees over. He found a couple of seats next to the window and sat down heavily, rubbing his hand over his eyes. He stared out of the window, noticing as if for the first time the cloudless blue sky, completely unbroken, and the hum of the air-conditioning above his head, the whiteness of the pavements and the green of the shrubbery and plants, some with vivid coloured flowers and the sprinkler hosepipes snaking through, which enabled the foliage to retain its verdant colour in such hot weather.

Jodie approached the table carrying a tray with two coffees and a small plate of savoury and sweet pastries. "I thought we might need a bit of sustenance," she remarked as she sat down opposite him and emptied the tray, standing it next to the table.

"What are you thinking?" she asked him, looking at him enquiringly.

"I dunno! Everything, I suppose. Like, what's going to happen in the future – if Dawn makes a full recovery, I still can't just leave and go back as if I had just been babysitting. If she needs nursing, she'll have to go into a nursing home, and that's going to cost. I'll have to talk to Manny – I don't know what the medical insurance will cover, whether it's just for medical treatment, or if it covers nursing as well. Dawn's money won't last forever if there's nothing going into the pot!"

Jodie was silent and they both nibbled the pastries and sipped the coffee. After a while Jodie said, "It's too soon to make plans yet. Perhaps she may recover enough to come home, and I could help out with nursing her. We could manage between us till she was on her feet."

Trevor smiled and took her hand. "You're such a good friend! I honestly don't know how I would have coped without you. I guess we'll just have to take it day by day. When I try to fast forward to the future I get into a panic, so I need to try to calmly accept what each day brings. Anyway, we should get back to Dawn now."

They walked back to the room without speaking and took a seat either side of the bed, Jodie picking up Dawn's hand and cradling it in her own. Trevor suddenly leaned forward and took his phone out of his pocket and Jodie heard it buzz as he had switched it to muted ringer. He looked across to her. "It's Savannah's school!" he said.

He stood up and walked towards the door as he said, "Hello?" Jodie watched as his face creased into a frown, and after a few moments of listening he said, "I see. *Quiron?* No, but I have a sat nav – I'll find it. I'll be there as soon as I can." He pressed the end call button and turned to Jodie. "Savannah's fallen from some gym apparatus and has an arm injury – it may be broken! That's all I need! Can you stay with Dawn? She's in *Quiron* hospital, apparently it's the nearest hospital to the school and the one they use for any emergencies. I'll come back here when she's been sorted!"

"Yeah, sure. I hope it's not broken – not at the beginning of the summer holidays! Poor child!"

Trevor left the hospital and had to force himself not to catastrophise events again – he kept mentally reigning in his thoughts. The sat nav informed him it was a fifty minute journey from the hospital that Dawn was in to the hospital that Savannah was in, and it was coming up to midday so he was thankful for the air-conditioning in the car as the temperature outside was rising to thirty five degrees Celsius. When he arrived at the *Quiron* hospital he asked at the reception desk and was directed to the area of the hospital where Savannah was being treated.

As he approached, he saw Savannah sitting with a school staff member, a sling supporting her right arm, and when she turned her head and saw him coming she began to cry. "I'm sorry, daddy," she whimpered.

"Oh, darling, don't apologise! What happened? Are you in pain?" He gently placed his arm around her shoulders and gave her a gently hug.

The escorting teacher held out her hand saying, "Mr Gainsbury? I'm Julia Westbrook from the British School of Valencia. I'm sorry, I don't know what happened, I didn't witness it, but at the moment the main thing is to get Savannah treated. She's been X-rayed and the arm is broken – a greenstick fracture. She's waiting now for a plaster cast to be fitted and the doctor will explain to you the after-care schedule – I think the cast will be on for about four weeks, I hope this doesn't interfere with any holiday arrangements you've made."

She smiled ruefully, and Trevor shook his head, "No," he replied, "Savannah's mummy is in *La Fe* hospital, and we visit her every day. We don't go far from there."

Julia flushed and said, "I'm sorry, that was tactless of me – I forgot for the moment the home situation, please forgive me."

"That's ok," said Trevor, then he turned away as the door opened and a technician came out and called Savannah's name. Trevor tenderly led Savannah into the room and sat her in the chair indicated by the technician. A short while later, Savannah's arm was in the plaster cast and cradled in the sling once again. The doctor introduced himself to Trevor in strongly accented language and explained she would need an X-ray in four weeks' time to ensure the bone fracture had healed, and then the cast would be removed. In the meantime she should not get it wet – so no swimming pool activities, and she should have it wrapped in a plastic cover when taking a shower. Trevor nodded and took the card that the doctor held out to him with brief points in English about after-care of a broken bone, and the date of the next hospital visit.

When they came out of the room, Julia Westbrook was still waiting. She stood up as they approached and smiled at

Savannah. "Are you feeling better now, Savannah? Is it more comfortable with the cast on?"

Savannah nodded glumly. "I can't get it wet so I can't go in the pool!"

"Oh, dear, that's a shame," said Julia, "But four weeks isn't too long – you'll still have plenty of holiday time left."

She turned to Trevor. "I'll take you to the administration desk for the formalities, then I must get back to school. Ms Overton will ring you when she has conducted her enquiries into how the accident occurred, and obviously Savannah need not come into school tomorrow as it's the last day before the summer closure."

She leaned across to Savannah, and stroked the arm that was not in a sling saying, "Goodbye, Savannah, I hope you manage to have some fun times during the holidays – I'm sure you will – and I'll see you when we return to school in September."

Savannah smiled sheepishly, "Thank you, Ms Westbrook."

Once they got to the administration desk Trevor said goodbye to Julia and led Savannah to a chair telling her to wait there till he attended to the payment and insurance details. Once he had given the necessary details and had made a call to Manny to give him the news and check that the facts and figures were correct, he took Savannah's hand and they set out to find the hospital exit.

"I was at the hospital with mummy when I got the call," he told her. "Pity they couldn't bring you to that hospital – it would have been a lot easier!"

"I asked in the Ambulance car if they would take me to mummy's hospital," said Savannah, "But Ms Westbrook told me the school always used *Quiron* hospital – she said it's in the school information policies that all parents are given."

"Well I wasn't here when you started at this school so Grandpa would have had all that information. But it's not a problem," he added hastily as he saw Savannah's eyes fill with tears at the mention of her Grandpa.

"Can we go to the hospital to see mummy?" she asked quietly, "I want to tell her about my arm."

"Of course," replied Trevor glancing at his watch, then he took out his phone from his pocket as it vibrated to inform him he had a text message. It was from Jodie telling him she had set off from the hospital to collect Holly from school, but she would return to stay with Dawn till he arrived with Savannah.

On the way back to the *La Fe*, they travelled in silence, Savannah unusually quiet and Trevor trying to think of what to say to her - about her mother's awakening or what had happened to her at school and the cause of the accident, but he was emotionally drained and couldn't face the possibility of another of Savannah's hysterical onslaughts. So he remained quiet, casting glances at her as she stared sightlessly out of the window, trying to work out what was going on in her mind. His heart filled with pity and love and he had the urge to weep. He remembered his own heartache when his father died – he was fifteen at the time and had to put on a brave face for his mother's sake, but he cried every morning in the shower as he felt the weight of grief – not only for his father's death but also for his mother's apathy for a life without her husband.

He felt his eyes moisten and he blinked rapidly and turned on the car radio. The sound of a current pop tune filled the car, but neither of them really heard it.

Chapter Seventeen

When Jo-Anne came downstairs next morning it was to be greeted with a pot of tea waiting on the table and Dave piling hot buttered toast on a plate.

"Morning," he grinned as she came into the kitchen with her eyes wide and a huge smile on her face.

"Wow! This is a treat!" she said pulling out a chair and sitting down, helping herself to toast and pouring tea from the pot. "How on earth did you find everything?"

"Well it's not exactly a difficult task! Tea and toast was always your favourite, and I reckon you haven't changed that much." He looked at her quizzically. "Have you?"

"Not for breakfast – I have in other ways though," then she added, "For the better!"

"Of course!" Dave smiled at her. "How are you feeling this morning? Did you sleep ok?"

"Yes, I did. I was exhausted and just happy to be in my own bed!"

They ate in comfortable silence for a while, then Dave said he was heading off so he could finish his morning schedule, and he would pick her up from home at three thirty to set off to view the property. With a cheery wave he left, and Jo-Anne cleared the kitchen and washed up before finishing her preparations for her morning in work. She'd deliberately pushed all thoughts about Trevor and Spain to the back of her mind and told herself she was lucky to have Dave back in her life, he was all she needed at present to keep her from sinking into despondency.

Once in her office, she checked her mail and made the necessary responses, then checked once again that everything was in place for the Masked Ball. She had a meeting scheduled with another client later that morning who wanted to book for a wedding reception and two more email queries about wine-tasting events. The morning passed without her thinking about Trevor at all – and if he did sneak into the periphery of her brain, she instantly bulldozed him out of it. She had made this resolution on the plane on the journey back from Spain – she would disregard her marriage the same way as he seemed to have done!

She left the office at lunch time and called in at the supermarket on the way home as she needed to replenish the contents of her fridge – she'd been aware of the lack of food available when Dave had prepared the breakfast that morning! There was very little else in the fridge apart from butter and milk so he hadn't had a great choice in what to make for breakfast.

When she got back home she was surprised to see the answer-machine light flashing, alerting her to the fact that there was a message waiting for her. She pressed the play button and a male voice said, "Hello, Jo-Anne, it's Nick Dawson, Crime Prevention Officer. I'm ringing to remind you about our meeting on Monday evening. I trust you got safely back from Valencia and that everything is ok. Well, that's all – I'll see you at seven on Monday evening. Bye."

She smiled as she listened. She hadn't forgotten, but it wasn't burned into her memory as an important meeting, but it wouldn't hurt and it would keep Dave happy, bless him - he was such a comfort to have around, she thought. She made a coffee and sat at the kitchen table while she texted a long text message to Darcy – she felt guilty at not being in touch with her while she was away, but she comforted herself with the thought that neither had Darcy tried to get in touch with her! Then she mentally chastised herself for being petty – *don't be losing your best friend, Jo-Anne, you may have already lost your husband!*

She apologised for not being in touch and gave Darcy a very brief synopsis of her journey to Valencia, then she told her she was going out with Dave that afternoon and possibly evening (*he said he would take her for a meal*) and so she would visit Darcy on Saturday afternoon if that was ok and give her the full story. If Darcy had something booked already they could re-arrange. She pressed the send button and put her phone back down on the table. She didn't really expect a reply till after six o'clock when Darcy was free, but she needed to touch base now that her dramatic rush to uncover Trevor's Spanish lifestyle was over and done with.

She had a quick shower and dressed in a pair of white trousers and pale pink top with white strappy sandals. She wanted to feel smart but comfortable and thought she'd achieved the right balance, so she felt good. *Considering my marriage is a failure*, she told herself, *it's important to keep my confidence levels up, otherwise I could sink into a depressed state! Then she's won!* She stood in front of the full-length mirror in the bedroom and walking slowly towards it, she stared at her reflection and said out loud, "Pull yourself together, Jo! You don't know what was happening in Valencia – you don't know what Trevor was having to deal with – obviously something more important than me – no, that's not fair! He expects me to be here for him – to support him as his wife – he doesn't enjoy being in Spain with what he has to deal with – whatever it is! Just push everything to the back of your mind and it'll all be explained when he gets the chance!"

She heard the doorbell and picking up her shoulder-bag from the bed she cast a last look at her reflection, and making a mental note to ring her mum over the weekend to bring her up to date and get some wise words of advice she ran down the stairs to open the door for Dave.

*****

When Darcy went to make a coffee just after three o'clock in the small kitchenette at the back of the shop, she checked her phone and was surprised and pleased to see Jo had left her a text message. She had felt the chasm of Jo-Anne's absence, but had made the decision to not contact her because it was important that Jo-Anne made her own decisions about whatever faced her in Valencia, plus Darcy had nothing but Andy on her mind and she knew she would be influenced by the heartbreak she was feeling in whatever words she wrote or spoke to Jo-Anne.

She found every day a challenge. Peter had been full of hope and enthusiasm – he was taking medication that the doctor had said may help with his loss of libido, but Darcy wasn't interested. The boys had told her about their school sports day, and she promised she would go, but she was feigning interest in that as well. Her heart was aching and heavy, almost a physical weight that was pulling her down. Peter had asked that morning if she was feeling alright, concern evident in his face as he went to kiss her goodbye, but she brushed him away feeling nothing but irritation towards him.

Was it only yesterday that she had seen Andy? Pain seared through her chest like a sword when she thought of never seeing him again. *I can't bear it*, she thought for the millionth time that day. How was she going to react when – or if – Peter regained his sex-drive and wanted to make love to her again. An involuntary shudder went through her and she shook her head. *Stop this!* She cried inwardly, *he's your husband! You love him, you have two children with him! He has an illness where he may need you to care for him! Your children need you! Get a grip!*

When she read Jo-Anne's rather enigmatic text message again she still had no real notion of what the situation was with Trevor, but she knew she would get all the details tomorrow when Jo-Anne came to visit. Darcy fixed her mind on Dave's new house – wondering what it was like and where it was, grasping greedily at anything that would take her attention away from the pain inside her. It worked for a few minutes, but then the black clouds descended again and her world became a colourless, miserable existence. Her manager had asked her that morning if she was ok – her face was pale and drawn, and Darcy had replied that she didn't feel too good, probably coming down with something, she'd said. Her manager had told her if she didn't feel well she could go home, but Darcy didn't want to be alone with her misery so she said she'd stick it out and hope that she would improve as the day went on.

She was glad when her work day was over, and as she collected the boys from after-school club she resolved once again to focus on her family – after all, her family had been the choice she made when she gave up Andy. When they got home the boys ran to their room and she could hear their arguments and laughter, and she poured herself a glass of wine and took it through to the sitting room and sat slowly down in the big armchair. She needed something to take the edge off – something to calm her and help to dull her mind, so she wouldn't think about Andy. She remembered that Peter was going to the gym for his assessment and sign up with his personal trainer straight from work – how could she hope to forget Andy when Peter was going to be talking about his own training and wanting to share with her everything he would be doing at the gym? She didn't want to know – she didn't care! She wasn't interested in Peter's workouts! Nothing mattered any more!

*****

The apartment was beautiful – Dave's smile was from ear to ear as they walked around and Jo-Anne's eyes were huge as she gazed about her, taking in the walk-in wardrobe and en-suite shower room, the Juliet balcony on the lounge and the main bedroom. The kitchen was large and airy, with breakfast bar at one side and enough space for a dining table and chairs at the other side. All the utility appliances were integrated –

washer, dryer, oven, hob, dish-washer – Jo-Anne sighed with envy as she stroked the kitchen surfaces.

"Oh, Dave, this is just fabulous," she breathed, "I'm so envious! I'd LOVE a kitchen like this!"

"It is a bit........superb, isn't it," smiled Dave, "I can see me living here. I might even have dinner-parties!"

"Ooooh, lovely! Can I come?" giggled Jo-Anne.

"Course you can! You're top of the list! What do you think about the décor? What kind of furniture shall I get? Shall I get curtains or are the blinds sufficient – do people have blinds as well as curtains? Oh, there's a lot to think about!" Dave looked around anxiously.

"Calm down!" said Jo-Anne soothingly, "That's what I'm here for! Have you decided, then? Are you taking it?"

"Yes, I think so. I'm not going to get anything better, and this suits me – hardly any maintenance, and someone on site to resolve any issues before they become problems!"

They went back downstairs to the entrance hall where the agent was talking to the building supervisor and when Dave told him he wanted to close the sale, the agent shook his hand then introduced him to the concierge - Henry Rawden, who, he said, would give him details of Henry's role and responsibilities as well as details of the in-house cleaners. The agent took his leave after arranging for Dave to go to the office the following day to sign the documents and seal the deal.

Jo-Anne watched as she stood by the window as the scene unfolded in front of her, smiling fondly at Dave each time he looked in her direction. At one point he held out his hand towards her, inviting her to join them, but Jo-Anne stayed where she was feeling that she shouldn't intrude. When Dave had finished talking to Henry, he said goodbye and tucked Jo-Anne's arm through his as they exited the building. He took a deep, satisfying breath as they walked round to the car park, patting Jo-Anne's hand that lay on his arm as he looked around at the garden, immaculately groomed.

"I like it, I like it a lot," he purred in the silly voice he used purposely to amuse Jo-Anne, and it did the trick as it always did and she giggled, looking up at him.

"I like it, too," she mimicked in the same silly tone.

"Will you help me with the furnishings and stuff?" he asked her.

"I thought you'd never ask!" she replied, hugging his arm.

"Well, let's go eat and we can talk about the next steps," he said. "Will a carvery do you? There's a nice one a couple of miles down the road – I noticed it as we drove up here."

"That's fine. You know when you buy the stuff like kettle and toaster and bedding and such like? You can store them all in my spare room, if you want. The furniture you can order and have delivered straight to the apartment once you've got a date." Jo-Anne was already calculating in her head the requirements of the complete furnishing of a home, but then realised she didn't know Dave's financial status.

"How are you fixed financially?" she asked him candidly. "Are you buying cash or credit?"

"Plastic, my darling, plastic!," he said, "Everything on credit cards, so if you want to have a spending spree I'll give you a card and my blessing and you can fit out my kitchen!"

"You're kidding!" she gasped in amazement. "You'd give me your credit card?"

"Yeah, why not?" he looked at her with a puzzled frown. "Do you think I don't trust you?"

She smiled warmly at him, and as they had reached the car, she shook her head in wonderment as she climbed in and fastened her seatbelt. "I should hope you DO trust me, you're my best friend!"

"Oh? Have I usurped Darcy then? She'll kill me!" Dave smiled cheekily at her as he swung the car out of the gated driveway and headed in the direction of the carvery.

Jo-Anne pursed her lips. "Noooo," she said slowly, "Darcy's still my bestie, but she's like a sister. You're like a proper friend!"

"Well………that'll do for me!" said Dave, but his tone sounded strange which made Jo-Anne look quizzically at him, but he glanced at her and smiled then put his attention back on to the road.

Her phone buzzed to signify a text message, and she took it out of her bag expecting to see a message from Darcy and gave a small gasp as she saw Trevor's name. She quickly opened the message to read, *"Darling, am SO sorry bout yesterday - Sav broke arm and had to go hosp. Spent most of day there. Have sent email with details. I love you."*

Dave looked at her when he heard her gasp, and said "You ok, hon? What is it?"

"It's from Trevor – he's sent me a text to say he's sent an email explaining why he let me down yesterday! Well, it'll have to wait till I get home." Jo-Anne's lips were drawn in a thin line and she was breathing heavily.

"I've got my work laptop in the boot if you want to check your emails when we stop," said Dave as he pulled in to the pub carpark.

"No, thank you," said Jo-Anne, "I'm not in a hurry to hear his excuses – it's to do with Savannah again! It always is!"

Dave said nothing, but got out of the car and came round to the passenger side to help her out. She took his arm as she climbed out, and squeezing it said, "This night is ours – I don't want to think of him and spoil it. I just want to think about your new apartment."

He gave a small, rueful smile and patted her hand as they walked in through the door. When they were seated, and he'd ordered drinks for them, Jo-Anne launched into the list of things he'd need. "Have you got nothing towards furnishing a house, then," she asked him.

"Nope! Not even a dishcloth! That's why I'm in a motel." He leaned towards her and said in a hushed tone, "Don't tell anyone, but I find this exciting! I'm going to buy a bed and a sofa, and a deep armchair, and a table and chairs! I'm not bothered about knives and forks and stuff – if you want, you can buy all that stuff."

"I'd rather we did it together – it's a big responsibility choosing stuff for someone else."

"Well, if you don't mind using your weekends, I'd love your help with all that." Dave grinned and squeezed her hand. "Now let's go get food!"

*****

When they got home that night, she invited Dave in for a coffee. When they were settled in the kitchen, she said, "Do you mind if I turn on the computer and check Trev's email?"

"Certainly not," said Dave, "But wouldn't you rather do it when I'm not here – for privacy?"

"No, I need you to be here, otherwise I know I'll end up getting angry and crying with frustration. You being here will help me."

She went into the sitting room and turned on the computer, calling for Dave to come and sit in the room with her and opened up her email account. Dave concentrated on his coffee mug, but then had to look at Jo-Anne's face to try to read her expression. She was chewing her bottom lip, then she took a deep breath and expelled it slowly.

"Listen to this," she said, "He sent this at 11.40 last night. *'Blah, blah,… so sorry….. blah, blah, this is the first opportunity*

I've had to contact you to explain why I didn't come to see you today before you left. I had just taken Savannah to school when I received a call from the La Fe hospital – Dawn was stirring from the coma, so Jodie and I went to sit with her to try to coax her awake. She seems to be hovering between worlds at the moment, but we both feel that she could wake properly any moment. Her eyes are partially open, but she isn't speaking yet. They are going to conduct lots of tests tomorrow to determine whether there's any brain damage – obviously her muscle tone is wasted because of her inactivity, but we need to know whether there's any paralysis. Anyway, while we were with her, I received a call from the school to tell me Savannah had injured her arm and had been taken to Quiron hospital, which is the far side of where the school is, so I had to leave Jodie with Dawn and travel to the Quiron, then when Savannah's arm was set and put in a plaster cast, I had to take her back to La Fe to be with Dawn again. Jodie had managed to collect Holly from school and take her back to the hospital, where they waited for me and Savannah to arrive. Savannah's finished school now for the summer, the teacher said there's no point in her going tomorrow with a broken arm – Holly can collect any stuff that she needs to bring home. Oh, sweetheart, blah blah,..............'" Jo-Anne's eyes flitted across the screen as she was missing out the personal details, *"'so I still don't know how I'm fixed, not till Dawn makes more of a recovery and we can plan her rehabilitation. Jodie, bless her, has said she'll help if Dawn is allowed home for nursing, but if Dawn's capability is such that she needs more than we can manage, we'll have to look at a nursing home. I can't let myself get depressed about this – though I could very easily give in to it – but you do understand, darling, don't you – that I am doing all this for Savannah? She's my child and she has no-one else – there's nothing else I can do but stay and look after her. It doesn't mean I love you any less..........."*

Jo-Anne stopped reading and sighed deeply. "It's the same old stuff – things change – but nothing changes!" She pushed the keyboard away from her and stood up angrily and walked over to the window, adjusted the curtains, then walked back again.

Dave said nothing, and kept his eyes on his coffee mug again. She walked over to him and snatched it out of his hands and stalked back into the kitchen and made another coffee for them both. He followed and stood with his back to the worktop, his eyes cast downwards.

"Well, say something!" she snapped, "Tell me what a heartless, unfeeling bitch I am!"

"I'm not telling you that, because you're not. I think you've both got a raw deal – and it's all outside your control – both of you. I can't see what else either of you can do – Savannah won't let you near, so............" he shrugged his shoulders.

"So what do I do, then?" she asked him, a pleading look in her eyes.

"There's nothing you CAN do, sweetie, just do what you're doing – get on with your life here in England. Let it resolve itself."

"God! You sound so much like my mother! I bet she says the same when I ring her!" Jo-Anne smiled weakly, and Dave picked his coffee mug up as if in salute and said, "Yep, she always was a wise woman, your mum!"

*****

The next morning when Jo-Anne awoke, her mind immediately jumped to Dave's apartment – visualising the placement of furniture and décor. It wasn't until she was in the shower that her mind flitted back to Trevor and the situation in Spain. She felt as though she had released something – as if she wasn't holding tight to anything any more! She felt quite relaxed about it all – as Dave said, it will resolve itself. She felt a little gurgle of happiness bubbling inside as she imagined going shopping with Dave, buying an entire kitchen-full of utensils! This was going to be such a fulfilling experience, many women would envy her! Darcy would – she loved shopping!

Dave said he would ring her later after he had signed up for the apartment, and had an idea when he would be able to move in. He already had a mortgage arranged so it shouldn't take too long before he took possession. Her mind flitted to just before Dave went out the door on his way home and he'd glanced at the pile of mail on the hall table and said "If that's Trev's mail you'd better open it to make sure nothing needs attention – you don't want to find a letter from the bank saying the mortgage hasn't been paid!" She'd laughed and told him Trevor paid the mortgage by standing order and he said he would be paying the equivalent to his salary contribution into their joint account each month.

However, after she'd showered and dressed and was sitting having breakfast, she decided to go through the mail. Under normal circumstances this was something she would never do – she respected Trevor's privacy and expected the same from him, but these were not normal circumstances and she felt sure that Trevor wouldn't object. The first two were from credit card companies offering zero% interest, and the third was Trevor's credit card statement - £360.68. He normally paid this off each month, but when she looked at the "due by" date, it was two days ago – so he would be charged interest on that! She tutted in annoyance. The next letter was from the utility company – gas and electric quarterly payment of £276.97, payment due……..June 24th – Monday! She was getting annoyed as she tore open the next envelope – the car tax was due to be renewed next month! Then, it was a reminder that the house contents insurance was due for renewal on 5th August – he was lucky this hadn't expired earlier otherwise he wouldn't have been paid out for his stolen bike! The next envelope was an invoice from the garage – second request - for payment of £225, for work carried out at the end of March! She rummaged through the remaining envelopes to find a similar one, but there wasn't one, so he must have received the original invoice before he went away to Spain! She felt the anger start to bubble inside her............he must have closed his mind to his life here in England, never given a thought to what was going on back home. Home? This wasn't his home any more! He had made his home in Spain with his daughter and his............friend Jodie!

The last of the envelopes produced a couple of pieces junk mail and ....what was this? An appointment for an interview? For the post of Systems Analyst at Bletchleys! She didn't know he'd even applied for another job! The date was for 29th May – over 4 weeks ago! Oh, well, he wouldn't be getting THAT job! She slammed the letter down on the table and took a couple of deep breaths! How could someone's life change so much in such a short period of time? How could she not know so much about someone that she was married to? She felt as though she didn't even know Trevor – this wasn't the man she'd married and lived with for over two years! That man wouldn't have blatantly disregarded his life and responsibilities this way – he would have been more respectful of his duties and obligations.

She got her cheque book and started writing cheques for these outstanding bills, telling herself that first thing Monday she'd better ring the bank and check the mortgage was being paid! Fortunately, the joint account was healthy – or had been healthy before he went away, but that was another thing she'd better check – she didn't know how much Trevor was going to pay in each month, whether it would be enough to keep things afloat. Suddenly, she felt like a deflated balloon – what was the point of even telling Trevor about these bills – he'd apologise and tell her how much stress he was under! She did some quick calculations on the back of one of the envelopes - if the worst came to the worst and he didn't pay anything into the joint account, her own salary was adequate to pay the mortgage and utilities – it would be a tight squeeze, but she wasn't an extravagant person, so she knew she wouldn't end up homeless.

She decided to go to the supermarket to keep her mind off all this, she hadn't filled the cupboards and fridge for a few weeks and after that she was going to visit Darcy – she couldn't wait to see her friend and bring her up to date on how life had suddenly changed direction for her. But before any of that, she was going to ring her mum – she desperately needed her mum's viewpoint. She was such a well-balanced non-judgemental person, Jo-Anne knew that she would calmly put things into perspective for her. She also should get in touch with Simon – he hadn't told her he'd bumped into Dave and given him her number. Not that it was an issue – she was glad he had because Dave had been her lifesaver the past couple of weeks, but she needed to let Simon know that Dave was settling nearby so he could come and visit them both. She made another coffee, then took it into the sitting room and settled into the big armchair and dialled her mum's number.

Chapter Eighteen

Darcy opened the door when she saw Jo-Anne walk down the path. She'd been looking forward to seeing her friend and hearing how her trip had worked out – she hoped it would take her mind off her own anguish. They hugged and then Jo-Anne took a step back, holding Darcy at arm's length.

"Gosh, sweetie, you don't look well! Have you been ill?" she asked her anxiously.

"No, I'm fine, just……you know……. with Peter……… I'm just worried!" Darcy bustled about, pulling out a chair and keeping her face averted in case Jo-Anne could see the absolute misery in her eyes.

"Where are the boys?" asked Jo-Anne, "It's unusually quiet," she said with a grin.

"Peter's taken them out to the park. I asked him to so that we could talk in peace."

"How is Peter?" Jo-Anne asked

"Oh, pretty much same as before – I mean, I hadn't really noticed any symptoms – apart from…… ….you know………in the bedroom, he'd kept all the other symptoms hidden. It could be like this for years apparently – or he could get worse anytime! That's what I hate – the unpredictability of it all!"

"But, sweetie, life is like that – unpredictable! We never know what's going to happen – I mean, look at my life! How it's changed in the matter of a few weeks!"

"Yes, you're right, I should stop feeling badly done to! Righto! Coffee on the way – let the story commence!"

When she had a coffee in front of her, Jo-Anne began her tale, describing the short visit she'd received from Trevor on the Tuesday, then the waiting on Wednesday afternoon, then all day Thursday, waiting, waiting for Trevor to come to see her, and his excuses for not making it. She told her she went to visit Dawn in the hospital on the evening, then the next day Dawn began to come out of the coma, she told her how Savannah had broken her arm so she wasn't even in school for the last couple of days of the term, how Jodie was actually a very nice person and not the siren she expected her to be, and finished off with the list of bills that she'd had to pay because Trevor had neglected them.

"Honestly, Darcy, I'm not sure my marriage is going to survive this," she admitted, "Trevor has put his daughter and his ex-wife in front of me, and it hurts like hell if I'm honest!" She looked pleadingly at Darcy. "Tell me I'm wrong! Tell me I've got this all out of proportion and he loves me and he's going to come back to England and we can carry on like before!"

Darcy was silent, her hands clasped round her coffee mug, looking into it as if the answer lay there. After a few moments, she said almost in a whisper, "I don't know. It's hard when there are children involved."

"I know that. And I feel sorry for her, losing her grandparents and her mum being in hospital – possibly disabled, but if she would only accept me, perhaps I might have a chance! As things are, I don't know her, I've only seen photographs, she refuses to acknowledge my existence – that's pretty hard to take, you know!"

"What's your mum said about it all?" asked Darcy.

"Oh, bless her, you know my mum! She tells me to stay calm, stay positive and think only about what I want to happen! She said I'd made a bad decision when I went flying off to Spain on a whim – she said I was trying to force the hand of fate! Her philosophy is to 'peacefully accept what is outside one's control', but you know me, Darcy, I'm a control freak, and like to have everything in a well-ordered fashion!"

Darcy took a deep breath in. "Sometimes things happen that knock us for six, and there's no control – you get swept along – or swept away!"

"You're being very………deep and enigmatic today! This is not the Darcy I know and love! Who are you? Can the real Darcy Jones step forward, please!" Jo-Anne laughed, but her eyes were troubled. This was not like Darcy – she was different somehow! Normally she would have said Savannah should be made to accept Jo-Anne, Trevor should put his foot down, bring her to England, pay someone to look after Dawn – she had the money for it that her parents left to her, and eventually Savannah would learn to love Jo-Anne, and they would all live happily ever after. That's what she had expected to happen……………or that's what she'd thought she wanted.

Then Jo-Anne noticed the tears slowly oozing from Darcy's eyes and sliding down her cheeks. She gasped and leaned forward, taking Darcy's hand and squeezing it. "What is it? Darcy, what's happened? Honey, don't cry! Is it something I've said?"

Darcy shook her head and looked up at Jo-Anne, the misery and heartache etched in her face. "Oh, Jo, I'm so unhappy! I can't bear it!"

"What? What do you mean? Is this because of Peter's MS? I've looked it up – it doesn't have to mean he'll die or be disabled – he could live a pretty normal life……………." But Darcy was shaking her head.

"It's not Peter's illness, well, that's not what's breaking me – it's……..it's……..Oh, God, Jo! I'm in love with someone, and I can't live without him!"

Jo-Anne sat back in her chair, dropping Darcy's hand and looking at her with incredulity written all over her face. Her eyes were huge as she gasped, "What? Who? When? When did all this happen?"

"Couple of weeks ago," whispered Darcy, "It's Andy Johnson, from the gym!"

"Oh, for goodness sake! Darcy, it's a crush, that's all! It's a purely physical thing! He shows off his muscles and I bet half the female gym members are ogling him and salivating! It's only because you and Peter haven't had sex for months, you've ...."

"No! It's not! It's not like that. We've gradually become closer as we've chatted over the weeks – months really, but a couple of weeks ago, it ....happened!"

"What happened? Don't tell me you've ....had sex with him!" Jo-Anne's mouth was agape, as she almost choked on the words.

"It wasn't just sex! It was the most wonderful experience I've ever had in my life. It was like our souls met and merged! Jo, I love him! But I've had to let him go! And that's what's killing me!"

Jo-Anne was stunned into silence. They both sat in the stillness of the kitchen, neither aware of the ticking of the wall clock or the muted barking of a dog outside in someone's garden.

After a few moments, Jo-Anne cleared her throat. "You said you've given him up?"

Darcy nodded. "I had to. I had to choose – he wants a relationship with me, so I had to choose – my family or him. I couldn't give my kids up! That's what I meant when I said things were different when children are involved........."

"So...........what's going to happen? What are you going to do?" asked Jo-Anne.

Darcy shook her head slowly. "Nothing. Nothing is going to happen. I just ....get on with it. I just learn to live with this pain, I learn to live with a broken heart, and I................I slowly die!" She buried her face in her hands and sobbed uncontrollably while Jo-Anne stared unseeingly at the table in front of her.

When Darcy's sobs had subsided, she raised her tear-stained face to Jo-Anne and wiping her nose and her swollen eyes she said brokenly, "Do you hate me?"

"Oh, no, sweetheart, I don't hate you! I'm …………shocked and surprised ……….mainly that you hadn't said anything to me before! And I never guessed……I mean, how could I!"

"I couldn't tell you ………..I knew what I was doing……….and I didn't think it was fair to burden you with my…………infidelity, it was my own secret and I had to bear it alone! And I could have – I was prepared to have the affair with Andy and be the wife and mother my family want. But then Peter's diagnosis altered everything – and at the same time Andy said he loved me and wanted more than just ……….sex, he wanted a relationship with me!" Darcy's face creased in pain and her bleak eyes sought Jo-Anne's understanding. "How can I leave Peter when he's been diagnosed with MS? My family and friends would never forgive me – and what about the boys? I couldn't walk out on them, but I couldn't take them away from their father – they love him to bits and would end up hating me! Oh, God! It's such a mess!"

The silence hung like a dark cloud as both of them sat, their eyes fixed unseeingly as Jo-Anne tried to grasp the enormity of Darcy's confession, and Darcy tried to figure out how she was going to get through each day and act as though there was no deep aching pain tearing into her heart.

*****

Trevor raked his hands through his hair in frustration. Savannah needed to shower and wash her hair but she couldn't get the arm cast wet, so he'd bound it up in plastic bags, but still she couldn't manage. He tried to help her, but she was self-conscious about her nakedness and squirmed in embarrassment, while Trevor was just as uncomfortable washing her pre-pubescent body after he'd had the awkward and distressing conversation with Marion Overton, raising the issue again for him about what is and is not acceptable for a single father to do for his young daughter, especially a father who had not been in her life consistently since her birth.

He'd tried to make light of things, telling her to stick her arm out of the shower door and he would hold on to it, then she could use her other hand to wash herself. He'd had to place towels on the floor to mop up the water that escaped through the open shower door, but thought that was small compensation for the ordeal he was having to go through. When she was finished, he handed her a large bath sheet and encircled her in it, leading her gently into her bedroom where she could sit in her soft-cushioned wicker chair while he brushed her hair and dried it. Between them they managed to get her dressed and ready and by the time Jodie and Holly arrived, they were sitting sedately on the porch swing in the shade, with music playing quietly from her cd player.

They had arranged to go on a picnic in a beautiful spot that Jodie knew about which was in a heavily wooded area that would protect them from the midday sun. There was a nature reserve nearby which included a treasure hunt, where clues were given for objects to find, which Jodie thought the girls would enjoy. When Jodie arrived, she had the picnic basket all prepared and packed in the boot, so Trevor and Savannah climbed into her car. She had offered to drive as she knew the location and she was much more confident driving in Spain off the main highways than Trevor was. They had a pleasant journey, the mood was light and once again Trevor marvelled at Savannah's disposition when she was with Jodie and Holly. He resolved to put everything out of his mind and simply relax and enjoy what he expected would be a very pleasurable outing. When they got back they would all go to the hospital together to see Dawn, and hopefully there would be some sign of recognition from her. Up till now, she had continued to open her eyes but there didn't appear to be any reaction to anything they said to her. There were tests still being carried out, but as of yet they didn't know if her brain had suffered much permanent damage.

The glade was magnificent – cleverly hidden in the trees with several picnic tables dotted about to give a semblance of privacy without the isolation. It was perfect, and at present they were the only visitors there. After they'd eaten, the girls were playing hide and seek nearby while Trevor watched them carefully and Jodie packed up the leftovers back into the basket. They were sitting on the blanket that was spread out on the ground, and Trevor was leaning with his back against a large tree. Jodie put the basket to one side and laid down on her front, her upper body raised up on her elbows, as she looked at Trevor.

"You look very relaxed," she observed, "Was the food ok?"

"Mmm, yes, thank you, it was lovely," Trevor sighed contentedly. "I feel so relaxed here, it's almost like being cocooned from everything that's going on. It was a brilliant idea of yours to come here, I didn't know places like this existed. You're very good to us, you know. Don't know how I would've managed without you this past few weeks. Tell you what - I'll cook a meal for us tonight when we get back from the hospital, to repay you for providing such a superb lunch."

They smiled at each other and Jodie looked away, wistfully imagining that this was a normal relationship, a courtship, where there would be a future for them. She very quickly reigned her thoughts back in, mentally chastising herself. He was married and he was also her best friend's ex-husband! There were far too many complications in it to ever make it viable, and her heart sank slowly in her chest as she felt the door slam on the potential romance.

Trevor had noticed the doleful emotion flit across her face and he leaned towards her. "What's wrong? You look really sad all of a sudden – is it the thought of my cooking? I promise it'll be a lovely meal!"

"No, no," she laughed sheepishly, "It's nothing – I was just ……… thinking………."

She licked her lips nervously as her eyes met his. The air was suddenly filled with expectation as if black clouds had dispersed and sunlight had broken through, lighting up dark corners and charging the air with anticipation and hope, and as Trevor met her gaze the electricity between them crackled, then in an instant it was gone and they both quickly turned their heads, afraid to continue for fear of where it would lead.

*****

Peter walked slowly into the sitting room, balancing the glasses and plate of nibbles on a tray, and placed them carefully on the coffee table. He glanced across at Darcy who was curled up on the sofa, her legs drawn up beneath her as she flicked the pages of a magazine.

"Here you are, sweetie," he said, handing her a glass of wine. Darcy took the glass without looking at him and continued to browse the pages.

"I think I might get into this exercising, you know," he said. "I quite enjoyed this evening's session. Matty says it'll take me a while to get into shape, but he reckons it'll help with the MS. He's got a couple of clients who've got the same as me – he says with regular exercise and a good diet it could keep the symptoms at bay. That'll do for me. I'd rather do that than take a load of medication, although I know that I'll have to take *some* meds, I just don't want to be rattling when I jump up!" He gave a small laugh, but Darcy's face didn't register anything.

"You okay, sweetie?" he asked her.

She glanced at him and gave a small shrug. "Yeah, I'm just tired."

"You've looked a bit peaky for a couple of days – are you sure you're alright?"

"Yes, for goodness sake! Stop pestering me!" She took a large gulp of the wine and turned her attention back to the magazine.

"Woah! Sorree! I'm just worried about you." He picked up the newspaper that was lying on the floor and started to read, but after a few seconds he put it down again.

"Look, Darcy, I know there's something wrong. Just tell me what's bugging you! This has been since my diagnosis, so I can't just ignore it – I feel like I'm responsible for you being like this!"

Darcy flung the magazine on to the floor and straightened her legs to get up from the sofa, but Peter leaned across and held her arm to stop her getting up.

"No! Don't walk away! Let's get to the bottom of this – what is it you're worried about? Or afraid of?" His brow was furrowed and his face was a mask of concern. "Please, just talk to me!"

"I've told you, it's nothing!" Darcy still refused to meet his eyes, but she didn't pull away, simply stayed in the position she was in when his hand restrained her, as if poised for flight.

"Don't lie to me, Darcy. You've been cold and distant all week, and when I tried to hold you close in bed last night, I could practically feel you cringe! What's wrong? Is the MS bothering you? Do you think it's like …………a disease? Or are you thinking you're going to end up being my carer? Is that it? Do you think you're going to be pushing me round in a wheelchair? Is that what's bothering you?"

"No, it's not that! And anyway, our marriage vows said "In sickness and in health" …….. so……….."

"So nothing! I don't want you to stay with me out of pity! Vows or no vows, I don't want you to stay with me unless it's out of love!" Peter stood up quickly and walked to the fireplace. He stood with his back to her, his head bowed, breathing heavily. They hardly ever rowed. He couldn't remember the last time he'd even raised his voice to her, but now he felt angry – and scared at the same time.

When he turned back to look at Darcy, she had her head lowered and one hand held her forehead, the other lay limply in her lap.

"It's not that simple, is it?" she said quietly. "We're a family, we've the boys to think about. It's not just you and me and how we feel, we have to put the boys first!"

Peter looked at her with incredulity. "So are you saying………..it IS pity you feel? Are you saying that you *don't* love me? Is that what you're saying? Is that what this is all about?"

Darcy didn't speak for a few seconds, then she whispered, "I don't know. I don't know what I feel. I'm sorry, I just don't know. I don't know anything any more."

Peter sat down heavily in the chair and stared at her, but she still didn't meet his gaze. The silence between them grew as the quiet ticking of the clock counted off the seconds that swelled into minutes. Finally, Peter said hoarsely, "Do you want……….. do you want us to separate?"

"No! For heaven's sake, Peter! Why are you doing this? Why are you pushing me? Just leave it! I'll do it! I'll get there if you leave me alone!"

"Do what? You'll get where? What do you mean? I don't understand!" Peter was holding out his hands, palms facing upwards as if waiting for something to be placed in them. He needed an explanation – this conversation had gone from idle chit-chat to crazy in a few minutes and he was completely out of his depth.

Darcy stood up. "I'm going to bed. I'm tired."

As she walked out of the room, Peter looked at her retreating back and slowly shook his head. He had a sick feeling in the pit of his stomach as if he was on the brink of a precipice and didn't know which way to step.

He suddenly jumped up. He had to get out. He needed a drink. He needed a few drinks! He grabbed his jacket from the back of the kitchen chair and hastily pulled open the back door, slamming it behind him in his hurry to get away.

*****

It was five-thirty on Sunday morning and Trevor was sitting on the porch swing cradling a mug of coffee, a sweater draped across his shoulders to keep away the early morning chill. *"What have I done?"* has asked himself, feeling sick and aghast at what had happened the night before.

His mind trawled through the events of the previous day, trying to find out if there was one single incident that determined the consequence that was now making him feel so bad. But, no – it seemed so natural, the whole day seemed to flow with pleasure and happiness.

They'd had an enjoyable day, then when they were at the hospital sitting round Dawn's bed, she had slowly turned her head to look at Savannah and uttered what sounded like "Bey bey". Savannah gasped and cried, "She said 'baby', she means me, she knows me!"

Trevor and Jodie both leaned forward towards Dawn and Jodie said, "Yes, sweetheart, it's Savannah, your baby!"

Dawns face softened and the ghost of a smile crossed her face. He eyes closed slowly and a sigh escaped her lips. Trevor looked alarmed and quickly looked up at the heart-rate monitor that was still attached to Dawn, displaying constant readings of her pulse and blood-pressure, but all the readings stayed normal – there was no drop in her pulse rate. Still,

Trevor held his breath, then Savannah's excited cry of "Mummy!" caused him to look towards the bed to see Dawn's eyed had opened again, and she was very slowly turning her head to look around her. Her eyes arrested on Jodie, who was still leaning in towards her, and Dawn's hand hesitantly moved in her direction, so Jodie picked up her hand and kissed it, saying, "Welcome back, honey, you've had a good, long sleep!"

Savannah took Dawn's other hand and said, "Mummy, mummy, I've missed you SOOOO much! I've SOOOOO much to tell you. Look! I've got a plaster cast on, I broke my arm, but don't worry, it doesn't hurt now, I'm ok! We've finished school for the summer now, so we can have lots of fun – even if I can't go in the pool! Holly's here, too, can you see her? We've had a picnic today………."

"Darling, slow down! You're bombarding her! Give her a chance." Trevor touched Savannah lightly on the shoulder, and Dawn's eyes gradually lifted to look at Trevor, and a tiny frown creased her brow.

Seeing this, Jodie squeezed Dawn's hand and said softly, "Trevor's been looking after Savannah till you get well enough to do it, so you've nothing to worry about! Everything is under control, we're all here for you."

Dawn very cautiously opened her mouth a fraction to allow her tongue to lightly lick her lips, then looking at Jodie again she murmured, "Ma…mam…ma."

Jodie and Savannah both looked up at Trevor and his eyes widened. Just at that moment, the door opened and a nurse came in.

"She's been talking! She knows me!" Savannah said excitedly to the nurse, and the nurse looked at Trevor for corroboration. He nodded, smiling at her, and she looked at her watch and jotted down some readings and notes. Trevor explained what she had said, but emphasised the fact that

Dawn understood who they were, but then added very quietly, "She's just asked for her mother. What do we do?"

The nurse led him outside the room and told him he could break the news to her, or Doctor Garcia would do it. Trevor had hesitated for only a second before he asked if the doctor would do it – he didn't think he could face it. The nurse said she would contact the doctor and he would arrange to come to see Dawn, and they would all be on standby for any adverse effects the news would present for her.

They had stayed for a while longer, but when Dawn seemed to tire, they were advised to leave her. Dawn hadn't said any more, but several times they could see an emotion flicker across her face or in her eyes. When they got back to the villa, Savannah was in a joyful mood, and Trevor and Jodie agreed that it appeared that she was going to make a recovery, and they too were in high spirits. But the sobering thought of Dawn being made aware of her parents' death had the effect of cold water being thrown on their happiness.

True to his promise, Trevor made a sumptuous meal – though not his 'signature dish', he nevertheless cooked steaks to perfection with crunchy roasted potatoes and a selection of vegetables. They opened a bottle of red wine and the girls had apple juice, and there was a light-hearted conversation that made everyone smile – even Holly, who was usually in the shadow of Savannah's exuberance, was laughing heartily at the one-line jokes that were being quipped across the table. After they'd eaten, the girls went out into the garden with Savannah's portable cd player, and they sat on the porch swing laughing and chatting while the music played.

Trevor and Jodie washed up and tidied the kitchen, then took their wine glasses into the sitting room. Jodie sat on the end of the large chesterfield sofa with her knees drawn up, and Trevor pulled a small table towards them and sat at the other end of the sofa, his legs crossed and his arm draped over the back of the sofa. They both looked relaxed and continued to chat, completely at ease in each other's company.

Savannah came rushing in through the porch door. "Daddy, daddy, can Holly have a sleepover? Pleeeease, daddy?"

"I don't know, darling, it's difficult for me to manage with you having your cast on. Maybe when your arm is fixed."

"No! Please! I want her to stay tonight! She wants to stay! She can, can't she? Please!"

"Savannah! Don't put Jodie on the spot! Go back outside and we'll discuss it and let you know!"

"Okay, daddy! Come on, Holly, let's go up to my room and play with my Barbies!" And off she skipped with Holly in tow.

"Oh, honestly! Kids! I'm sorry about that, Jodie. I've had a very awkward time trying to shower her and wash her hair with her arm in a sling! It wouldn't be so bad if she was younger – a toddler – but at her age............and after what Ms. Overton said some of the parents were insinuating............I feel really uncomfortable doing personal things for her. I know........." he said, as Jodie went to say something, "I know I'm her father and I shouldn't let things like that bother me..........but I just find it difficult."

"Well, I don't mind staying over as well..........if it'll help, I mean, I can shower her in the morning and do her hair, then scoot back to my place. Holly will love it, too. And the schools are closed now, so none of us have a timetable for the next couple of months, so ………."

Trevor looked at her over the rim of his wine-glass, and said, "Well if you don't mind, I'd love for you to stay. I'll go tell the girls and quickly make the guest bedroom up."

"I'll do it, if you like. I know where everything is – unless you've changed things. We used to stay over with Dawn quite a bit especially when her parents went away for short trips. I don't mind," she said standing up and placing her glass on the table.

"Well in that case, I'll open another bottle! Tell the girls they can start getting ready for bed, not that they'll go to sleep this side of midnight!" Trevor smiled at her and went into the kitchen.

Bringing himself back to the present, he mentally pointed his finger at that moment – he should never have opened the second bottle of wine. If he hadn't been feeling so relaxed and happy, if he hadn't sat up talking with her till two o'clock, if he hadn't enjoyed the conversation so much, if he hadn't walked to the guest bedroom with her and instinctively leaned over to kiss her cheek to wish her goodnight just as she turned her face - and his lips landed on her lips, and it felt so natural, as if they belonged there, and they clung to each other as they stumbled through the door................and now he was wracked with guilt!

He leaned over and put his coffee mug on the floor and stayed bent over, hugging his knees. *What about Jo? What am I going to do?* He'd asked himself this same question a hundred times since he woke up in the bed with Jodie curled up in his arms. He'd crept out of the bed and out of the room, his mind in a turmoil. If he was honest, he'd not given Jo a single thought last night, or at any time during the whole day! He tried to justify it by reeling off the things that had happened, but in truth, none of it should have wiped the thought of his wife completely out of his mind as it had done. The trouble was – he was finding it more and more difficult to recollect his life before the accident. Yes, he had been happy with Jo and the life they had, but it seemed so long ago and so far away that it was as if that was the dream and this current life was the real thing.

He heard the screen door creak and raising himself up to sitting position he looked over his shoulder to see Jodie in the doorway.

"Are you okay?" she asked him tentatively.

"I'm so sorry, Jodie, I shouldn't have……….." he began, but she cut him off abruptly.

"Don't! Don't apologise! I'll feel bad if you do! I wanted it as much as you, it just felt ……….a natural progression."

Trevor shook his head, looking beseechingly at her.

"But I'm a married man! I can't promise……………" She raised her hand to stop him.

"No! Don't! Don't say any more! I don't expect anything from you. I'm not a kid – I knew what I was doing. I've been attracted to you for a long time, and I regret nothing! Let's not dwell on it, let's just ……………accept it happened."

He held his hand out towards her and she walked over and took it. He gently pulled her down on the seat next to him and kept hold of her hand. They sat quietly, enjoying the tranquillity of the early morning, comfortable in each other's presence, swaying gently on the porch swing, Trevor felt a calm acceptance soak into his soul and a contented smile slowly crept across his face.

Chapter Nineteen

The phone startled Jo-Anne as she sat on the conservatory floor, surrounded by text books and her notes. She was trying to get her final assignment sent off, and just had the referencing and bibliography to sort out and it was completed. She fully expected to see Dave's name on the screen, and was surprised to see Darcy's name.

"Hi, honey," she said. After Darcy's confession yesterday, they had sat and talked and Jo-Anne held her when she wept, and told her she didn't think any less of her, and Darcy clung to her, her body shaking with dry, racking sobs. Jo-Anne admitted to herself that neither of them had ever had a relationship that tore them apart like this, even when they were young teenagers and had passionate crushes that consumed their very existence. By the time Jo-Anne left her and came home, Darcy was calm and composed enough to make tea for the boys when they came in and carry on with her life with Peter.

"Jo, Peter didn't come home last night!" Darcy said in a worried tone.

"He didn't come home? Where from? Where did he go?" asked Jo-Anne.

"We had………..words. I didn't tell him………….about………….but I told him I don't feel the same way about him……………..I went to bed and he stormed off out! I don't know where – I just assume he went to the pub."

"What if he took ill, can that happen do you think? With MS? Can they kind of …….collapse?"

"I don't know. What do you think I should do?"

"Well, I think maybe ring the hospital and see if he's been admitted." Jo-Anne rubbed her hand across her brow, concern etched in her face.

"Yeah, I'll do that! I feel so bad about it, but………he kept pushing me to tell him what was wrong with me, and………I couldn't. Oh, it's so complicated! I'll ring the hospital and see if he's there. I'll let you know!"

Jo-Anne stood where she was, her arms akimbo, staring out across the garden without seeing. What a mess! Poor Darcy! Poor Peter! Her own marriage was like a car crash, too. Only a few months ago, at Christmas, they were all so happy, they'd had a fantastic time, Jo-Anne and Trevor had spent a few days in a log cabin in Scotland, and Darcy and Peter and the boys had enjoyed a trip to Euro Disney. Both families had then spent New Year's Eve together in Peter and Darcy's home and they had each said how blessed they were as they raised their glasses to toast the coming year, 2004 was going to be their best ever! Now look where they were!

Ten minutes later, her phone rang again.

"He's not been admitted to hospital," said Darcy, "They've no-one with that name. What do you think I should do now? I can't think straight. Oh, Jo, if he's done something to himself. I'll never forgive myself!" Darcy sounded distraught.

"No, don't think like that!" said Jo-Anne, "It's probably that he bumped into a friend and got drunk and went back to his friend's house!"

"He's here!" cried Darcy suddenly, "He's coming up the path! I'll ring you later to tell you!" Darcy disconnected the call.

Jo-Anne grimaced as she slid her phone back into her pocket and knelt down on the floor again to carry on with her work. Worrying about Darcy and Peter had pushed her own marital problems to the back of her mind, and when her phone rang again she thought for a second it might be Trevor, but it was Dave.

"Good morning," she said and smiled at his burst of song as he bade her a tuneful "Good morning, good mor-ning! What are you up to today, my lovely?" he asked her.

"Finishing off my final assignment, then my course is completed! Phew! The last few weeks have been difficult, but it's almost done!"

"Fancy lunch at a country pub?" he coaxed.

"Oh! What are you like! I need to get this finished!" She was sorting through books and documents as she spoke, but felt her resolve weaken.

"How long will it take you? It's ten-fifteen now, couple of hours? If I pick you up at, say, one-thirty, do you reckon you'll be finished it all by then?"

"Well…….. okay! If I'm not done you might have to wait a bit, is that alright?" Jo-Anne was building in some time to spend talking to Darcy when she rang back to tell her what had happened to Peter last night. She was itching to tell Dave about Darcy, but remembering how she herself had reacted when Darcy first told her, she didn't want Dave to think badly of their friend, so perhaps it was best to keep Darcy's secret to herself.

When Dave had hung up, she focused on compiling the information she needed for her bibliography, and checked all her referencing, and had just carried her papers through to where the computer was when her phone rang.

"He was in the police station! He was locked up for being drunk and disorderly!" Darcy's voice was dripping with disgust. "Can you imagine – a man of his age – a father - being picked up by the police for being drunk and disorderly! I'm horrified!"

"Well at least he hadn't collapsed or topped himself!" said Jo-Anne. "He wasn't driving, was he?" she asked as the ghastly thought hit her.

"No! Though he did take the car, he had the sense to leave it at the pub. He was staggering home and fell in front of the police car, and they couldn't get his name and address out of him because he was too drunk to speak, so they locked him in a cell for his own protection! If his mother finds out about this, he'll never hear the end of it! I've a good mind to ring her!" Jo-Anne could hear the recalcitrant tone in her voice and was happy to recognise the old Darcy – the one she knew and loved.

"Where is he now?" she asked.

"In the shower – he smelt like a brewery! He's going to take the boys swimming in an hour! That won't help his hangover, but I don't care! Do you want to come over for lunch?"

"Oh, thanks, honey, but I've got to finish my assignment, then Dave's going to pick me up and take me for lunch."

"I see." There was an odd pitch to Darcy's voice. A few moments went by.

"How are you feeling this morning……….about…….you know?" asked Jo-Anne.

"The same," said Darcy bleakly, "I don't expect to ever feel any different!"

Neither of them spoke for several seconds, then Jo-Anne said, "I'd better get back to my assignment. Shall I pop in tonight after the boys are in bed?"

"Yeah, but give me a ring first, just in case something kicks off here again. Not that I expect it to," she added quickly, "but life is not how it used to be." Her voice sounded so sad that Jo-Anne felt a rush of pity.

Jo-Anne was almost ready when Dave rang the doorbell, and she hurriedly let him in and ran back upstairs to finish her hair yelling for him to make himself a coffee and she'd be down soon. He went into the kitchen and switched the kettle on, his eyes catching sight of the pile of documents and files on the kitchen table. As Jo-Anne walked in the door he nodded to the stack saying, "Is this your college work? Did you get it all done?"

"Yeah," she replied, "I'll hand it in to my tutor on Tuesday at college, then my Tuesday nights are my own again! Yay!"

"I'm very impressed, you know," said Dave, smiling fondly at her, "It's not everyone who can do further education and hold down a full-time job at the same time. You've done really well, especially with everything else going on for you."

"Aw, thank you!" Jo-Anne, "I must admit it hasn't been easy. Especially when I've had a hard day at work, and all I want to do is veg out in front of the TV with my feet up. But it's done!"

Dave put the two mugs of coffee on the table and pulled a chair out to sit down. Jo-Anne stood with her back to the worktop and picked up her mug, cradling it in her hands.

"Peter got locked up last night – drunk and disorderly!" She watched carefully for Dave's reaction.

"Really? That doesn't sound like him." Dave took the news very calmly, unwilling to pass any judgement, admitting to himself that he didn't know Peter very well.

"Well, apparently, they had an argument of some sort – pretty serious from what I can gather and he stormed out. Darcy went off to bed and didn't know he hadn't come home till she got up this morning and realised he wasn't in the house. He'd staggered in front of a police car before passing out, so, as they couldn't get any information out of him, they put him in a cell till morning. Darcy is horrified!"

Dave gave a little laugh, "I bet she is! She'd be worried in case the neighbours found out and pass judgement on them."

"Anyway, if you've finished your coffee, let's get going, I'm starving!" Jo-Anne put her mug in the sink and picked up her bag. Dave put his coffee mug in the sink and saluted her, "Yes ma'am!"

They went to a quiet country pub that served home-cooked food and had a massive open fireplace and hearth, which would be welcoming and snug in the winter, but as it was a warm afternoon in early July, a basket of sweet-smelling logs filled the hearth. They chatted about the week they'd had, Jo-Anne telling him about her hopes and ambitions once she got her qualification, and then told him about the correspondence of Trevor's that she'd opened and how she'd had to pay all these outstanding bills.

"Honestly, Dave, if he'd been here I've have killed him! I was so angry! I've just trusted him to pay the mortgage and utilities and the car tax and insurances, and I didn't realise that he was so negligent with it all. I know he often tries to get cheaper deals than what we're paying for the gas and electric and car breakdown and such, and I've just left it all in his hands assuming it would all be sorted. I'm still annoyed! I'm going to the bank tomorrow to check the joint account and see what he's paying in and whether the mortgage is coming out every month. I don't know how much he took out to cover his living costs in Spain till it got sorted."

She toyed with her food for a few moments, before looking him straight in the eye. "I don't think we'll survive this, you know. I think my marriage is over!"

"What makes you say that?" Dave asked her.

"Well………..Savannah is his daughter. She doesn't like the idea that Trevor has another wife, she has never accepted that fact and I don't think she ever will. Whenever Trevor has to make a choice between us – he always chooses her! I know she's his child, and I know that a parent's love is the strongest love of all – so that says it all, doesn't it? He's not going to come back to England, Savannah will never agree to come here to live, so I might as well give in gracefully!"

They were both silent for a while and continued with their meal.

"What was it like when you and Sally divorced?" she asked tentatively.

"Oh, you know, it hurt at first – male pride and all that, but she'd found someone that she'd rather be with so………." He shrugged his shoulders.

"But………..didn't you put up a fight for her? Did you just give in? She was your wife, you were married – how many years? Six? Seven? Didn't that count for something?"

"Well not to her apparently!" Dave put his knife and fork down and poured a glass of water from the jug on the table.

"Was she…… had she been unfaithful to you? Do you mind me asking all this?" Jo-Anne looked at him with troubled eyes.

Dave leaned back in his chair and took a deep breath in. "We were both very busy – workaholics, I suppose. She had a high-powered position in the pharmaceutical business and I was technical manager in a large building company. We lived in a fancy apartment in Munich and between us we had business meetings so often we had to actually schedule in some time for us to be together. Sometimes we went days without seeing one another. A recipe for disaster, really. One day she told me she was in love with somebody else. I thought long and hard about it and came to the conclusion that if she loved someone else, she didn't want to be with me and I didn't want to stay for us to end up hating each other – so I agreed to the divorce. I met him – he's a nice guy, Alex, a bio-chemist, and an excellent tennis player! I couldn't hate him. Sally was a strong, beautiful woman - I fell for her, and he did the same! I couldn't hold it against him."

"Oh, Dave, I'm so sorry you've been hurt! You're such a nice man! You always see the best in people, don't you?" Jo-Anne leaned across and squeezed his hand.

"Jo, sweetheart, everyone has to do what feels right for *them*! Don't think that because I behaved in that way, you should do the same with Trevor. If you want to save your marriage, you have to find a way of doing it – but where you keep your self-respect, obviously!" He kept hold of her hand, then raised it to his mouth and kissed her fingers.

She gave a small grimace. "That's the point – I've thought of nothing else since I came back from Spain. I think we're both different now – well, Trevor more so than me! When he left for Spain all those weeks ago, he left me and our life together. Too much has happened for him – he has a different role now, he's a father first. I could never fit into the life he's now leading, and I don't want to. I like my life here!"

Dave pushed his plate away and picked up the dessert menu. "Okay! So shall we confirm how much you like it with a sticky toffee pudding! Or ice-cream – or both?"

*****

When Jo-Anne opened the door the following evening, Nick Dawson greeted her with a wide grin.

"Hi, Mrs Gainsbury - Jo-Anne? Nick Dawson, Crime Prevention, did you remember about my visit?"

"Yes, come in," she smiled back at him. "Do you want a drink?"

"A cup of tea would be lovely, please," he said, following her into the kitchen. "How was your trip to Valencia? Pleasant?" He was looking at his case as he placed it on the floor by the side of the table and didn't see the inward shudder she gave in response.

"It was………a waste of time, really" she admitted, "A bit impetuous, I shouldn't have bothered."

"Oh, dear, I'm sorry." He looked so concerned that Jo-Anne was quite taken aback, but she busied herself making tea, changing the subject to the safeness of the weather and how pleasant it was on warm evenings.

They made harmless chatter for a while, and then he asked if he could show her some of the devices and safety gadgets he had in his case. She agreed and for the next half hour he explained the purpose and benefit of the many different pieces of equipment, and Jo-Anne asked him to leave her some brochures and leaflets about a couple of the closed-circuit television systems. She wanted to discuss them with Dave before deciding, and it wasn't until Nick said he fully expected her to consult with her husband before coming to any decision that she realised with a jolt that the first person she thought about was Dave, not Trevor! It was as if Trevor didn't figure in her life any more.

They chatted some more, then the topic of interests and hobbies came up and Nick told her about his love of acting and how he was a member of the local Amateur Dramatic Society. Jo-Anne was interested as she had been very involved in her high school productions but didn't pursue it when she went to college. Nick said he had joined this group six years ago after his divorce and how it had helped him move on from what was an acrimonious relationship break-up.

"I'll tell you what," he said suddenly, "There's a production running this week – I'm not in it, but I've got a couple of tickets going spare from two friends who were coming, but there's been a death in the family so they've had to drive down to Wales. It's for Friday evening. Would you fancy coming – you can take a friend," he added hastily when he saw her expression alter fleetingly, "It might re-ignite your interest in local theatre?"

"That's very kind of you," said Jo-Anne. She was thinking about Darcy – having a night out at a local theatre might be something she would like to do as a change from their usual night out at the pub. She was sure she could persuade her that it would be therapeutic! "Are you sure?" she asked him.

"Oh, yes, I'd love you to come. I'm quite proud of our group

– we're very good, you know," he added self-assuredly. He said he'd be there as the members who weren't in the cast usually helped out either backstage, or front of house. He arranged to meet her in the foyer of the theatre at seven o'clock and scribbled down his mobile phone number, "In case something happens," he said and asked timidly if he could have her number, "For the same reason," he explained.

A short while later he packed up his case and bade her goodbye, saying he would see her on Friday at the Playhouse. As she closed the door behind him, Jo-Anne smiled to herself. Well, this was something different, she thought. She pulled out her phone and rang Darcy.

"Can I come round? Is Peter home?" she asked her. When she'd phoned Darcy the previous evening to ask if she could come round, Darcy had asked if she would leave it as she and Peter were trying to talk about things. So she hadn't seen her friend since the night she'd found out about Darcy's heartbreak.

"Can I come to you instead?" said Darcy. "The boys are in bed, but Peter's home doing some paperwork for work."

"I'll get the kettle on, see you in ten minutes!" said Jo-Anne.

When Darcy arrived, Jo-Anne noticed she still looked pale and drawn. She impulsively hugged her, saying "Oh, sweetie, you still look peaky, are you sure you're not ill?"

"I'm not ill, just heart-broken!" said Darcy forlornly.

Jo-Anne picked up the two coffee mugs and they went through to the sitting room, Darcy sat in the armchair and leaned over hugging her knees. Jo-Anne put the mugs on the coffee table and sat on the sofa near to Darcy so she could reach over and take hold of Darcy's hand.

"I know it's a bit late, but I've had the Crime Prevention Officer here – Nick Dawson, do you remember I told you about him?" Darcy nodded, raising her head to look at Jo-Anne.

"Well," she continued, "It turns out he's in the Amateur Dramatic Group and they've got a production running at the moment. It's only on for a week, and he's offered me two tickets for Friday night's performance. What do you think? Do you fancy it?" She smiled encouragingly at Darcy.

"Why don't you ask Dave to go?" said Darcy.

"Because I want to go with you! Go on! It'll be fun! There's a bar, so we can have a drink, and Nick says that after the show quite a few "invited" people stay back and have a chat – we could do that, as Nick's invited friends, or we can just come home. Go on! Say you'll come!"

Darcy sighed. "Okay, I'll come, but I'm not promising to be lively and entertaining!"

"You will be! You can't help it! So! That's sorted. Now tell me all about Peter's escapade!"

Darcy told her how the dispute had started, and how Peter had stormed out when she'd told him she didn't know whether she loved him or not. Then last night when they were talking, he'd asked her straight out if there was somebody else.

"What did you say?" asked Jo-Anne, her eyes wide in alarm.

"I said there wasn't," said Darcy and her whole body slumped forward as she began to cry softly. "I was scared of the consequences. But now I feel like I've betrayed Andy – I'm a Judas!" She covered her eyes with one hand and the other hand wrapped round her body as she wept pitifully.

"Oh, Darcy," said Jo-Anne gently as she leaned across and put her hand on Darcy's knee. They sat for a while in that position, then Darcy pulled herself upright and rubbed both hands across her face.

"I can't tell him, I can't take the chance of losing my boys! I just have to try to forget Andy – but I don't know how I'm going to do that!"

"Well we'll just have to fill our lives with different things – find new hobbies or interests. I'll have more free time now that my course is finished, so we can do stuff together. You can help me choose the stuff for Dave's new apartment – it's fabulous, you'll have to come and see it once he gets the keys to move in! Shouldn't be a long wait. In the meantime we can plan it, go window shopping – though he said I could start buying kitchen stuff now if I store it in my spare bedroom. He's given me his credit card – how about that for a trusting friendship? Trevor would never give me his credit card!" Jo-Anne was aware that she was talking too much, but she wanted to try to get Darcy's mind off Andy Johnson.

Jo-Anne desperately wanted to confide in Darcy about the decision she had almost reached about her own marriage – but she guessed that Darcy wouldn't take kindly to Jo-Anne thinking of leaving her marriage seemingly effortlessly, and for no other reason than she didn't want to compete with her husband's child, while Darcy was forcing herself to stay in a marriage when she'd stopped loving her husband, and was sacrificing her happiness with a man she did love. *What a mess*, she thought sadly.

They chatted idly about the boys and Darcy's job, then Darcy looked at the clock. "I'd better get home, it's ten-thirty," she said, "I hope Peter's in bed, I don't want another discussion with him tonight."

After she'd gone, as Jo-Anne closed the door and checked the conservatory and back door as instructed by Nick Dawson, her mind drifted to Trevor and what he might be doing at this moment. Was there anything going on between him and Jodie? Then with a sudden burst of clarity, she realised it didn't matter – she didn't care! Jodie wasn't the reason she was going to end her marriage – it was Savannah. A ten-year-old child had caused her marriage to fail!

Chapter Twenty

It had been three days since Dr Garcia had broken the news to Dawn about her parents' death, and since then she had made no attempt to speak or make any kind of contact with anyone, not even Savannah. Trevor and Savannah went every day to the hospital and on most evenings Jodie went by herself to sit with Dawn and hold her hand and try to coax her to come back to them from wherever her mind had gone. Savannah talked and talked to her mummy, but got no response, and each time they came away from the hospital she cried. But it wasn't the hysterical screaming that she used to do, this was simply deep sadness.

Trevor had spoken at length to Dr Garcia about what they should expect, but Dr Garcia couldn't give him any definite answers about Dawn's psychological state. Her physical condition was slowly improving – the physiotherapy was going well and she was sitting up, and her muscle tone was recovering gradually. The doctor said that soon they would need to think about future care for Dawn – she wouldn't need hospital treatment and may even improve enough to be cared for at home, if there was adequate care available, if not a nursing home would be the next option. However, her mind seemed to have been affected by the news of the death of her parents, and Trevor blamed himself for asking the doctor to tell her, he said it had been too soon, but Jodie soothed him saying that Dawn was asking for her parents, and they couldn't keep it from her.

The first week of the school holidays was over and they had eased into a routine that centred around hospital visits. Jodie and Holly stayed at the villa each night so that Jodie could see to Savannah's shower and dressing, and then she took Holly home to their own apartment while Trevor and Savannah went to the hospital. Then they all met up back at the villa, and either Trevor or Jodie would cook the evening meal, then Trevor would stay with the girls while Jodie went to the hospital.

Trevor had sent a couple of emails to Jo-Anne, but he kept them quite factual about Dawn's progress – or lack of progress, and his difficulty with Savannah's fractured arm and how it was helped by Jodie and Holly staying *in the guest room* – he always emphasised that bit – to be there on a morning to see to her bathing, but he was aware that he wasn't telling her how much he loved and missed her like he had done in the beginning. He was very careful how he worded everything – he didn't want Jo-Anne asking questions and he certainly didn't want her suddenly arriving as she did a couple of weeks ago. He didn't send many text messages, he didn't know what to say, apart from things like, "Hope all is well, not much change here, take care, luv u.xx" He could feel the distance opening up between them but felt powerless to do anything about it whereas he was becoming more and more reliant on Jodie and couldn't imagine how he would cope without her. Savannah was much easier to deal with when Jodie was around, and he had to admit that when they were all together, like at mealtimes, it felt like they were a family, and it was a good feeling.

It was Friday evening and the girls were in the garden. Carlos had made huge improvements in the outside areas, and as Trevor looked around he had a great surge of satisfaction. His life here was very pleasant, he thought, and he was looking forward to Jodie's return from the hospital. He had selected a bottle of wine from the wine cellar that Bill Watson had been so proud of when he was alive, and it was standing ready with two wine glasses by the side.

When he heard the car draw up, he walked back from the other side of the pool to where Jodie was getting out of the car and smiled at her.

"Everything ok?" he asked, taking her arm as they went up the steps.

Jodie sighed deeply. "She still hasn't spoken. The nurse said she isn't making eye contact with anyone, not even when she's having physio. It's like she's gone back into a coma but with her eyes open. It's very sad."

Trevor nodded slowly. "I know. I don't know what we can do – I don't know if there's anything anyone can do. I suppose her mind is processing the information about her parents – we just have to pray that she comes through it."

Trevor poured them each a glass of wine, and they went back to the porch swing where they could sit in the cool evening air and watch the girls. They sat in quiet contemplation for a while, then Trevor took her hand and turned to face her.

"I think I've reached a decision," he said quietly.

"What about?" asked Jodie nervously.

"About the future – well, MY future!" he said. "I've decided I'm not going back to England."

"Oh!" said Jodie, "I hadn't realised you were planning to do so."

"I wasn't – well, I mean – I have a wife and a life in England, but there are too many complications if I think about trying to join my life here with my life there! Savannah will *never* agree to live in England and I can't leave her, so……………….I'll have to leave my wife!"

Jodie didn't speak. Her mind was racing. She felt desperately sorry for Trevor's wife – she was an innocent party in all this, she hadn't done anything wrong to deserve her marriage to fail, yet deep down inside of Jodie a small bubble of excitement and joy was gurgling to the surface. If he was staying here and leaving his wife – was there going to be a future for them together?

"I feel really bad for doing this to Jo – she's a lovely girl," Trevor said sadly.

"Yes, she is," echoed Jodie. "Have you spoken to her – have you told her that you're not going back?"

"No, not yet. I don't know how to do it. This whole business has been grossly unfair on her, and she doesn't deserve to be dumped as if she was unnecessary baggage, but………I can't see what else I can do!"

"So, you haven't ………..stopped loving her," asked Jodie with trepidation.

"Well………..no, I suppose not, but ………….I don't know, it's not just about love! There are so many considerations in this situation. I can't just think about her and me. I *have* to put Savannah first! Jo will understand that!"

Jodie was silent. Trevor was Jo's husband. She'd done nothing wrong, why should she just relinquish her marriage? *I wouldn't give up so easily*, she thought. She was glad Trevor hadn't mentioned her in all this – she didn't want to be the cause of the break-up, even though they had slept together, she didn't want it to wreck a marriage.

"I hope this isn't a result of you and I ……….." she didn't finish the sentence before Trevor interrupted her saying, "No, no, it's not that."

"Well I hope not, because I told you at the time, it was something …………wonderful, but that I had no expectations from it."

"I know," said Trevor, "But I must admit that this week I've been happier than I've ever been! All four of us together ………it's so blissful! I mean, Savannah is a different person when you're around, she really loves you. And I ………..really appreciate how you've held us together when we've been falling apart! You're something special!"

"Oh, thank you, kind sir! Now go and make me a coffee to show you mean it!" she said, trying to lighten the conversation and steer away from something that what was lying under the surface, even though she really, really would have loved to pursue it.

*****

Darcy and Jo-Anne got out of the taxi in front of the Playhouse and walked up the front steps into the foyer. Darcy was looking better than she had done, thanks to cleverly applied make-up, and she was wearing white trousers with a pale pink top whereas Jo-Anne wore navy trousers and a pale blue embroidered shirt. They had spent a half hour on the phone earlier that evening discussing what they should wear as neither of them had any experience of local theatres and didn't want to go overdressed. As they entered they looked around and were relieved to see that there was a comfortable mix of all dress codes – from the be-jewelled elderly women down to the jeans and tee-shirt-wearing younger individuals. Then Jo-Anne nudged Darcy as a very handsome man strode purposefully towards them.

"Jo-Anne!" he exclaimed, "So good to see you. You look very nice."

"Thanks," she replied, then gestured towards Darcy. "This is my friend Darcy. Darcy this is Nick."

Nick shook hands with Darcy, his eyes appreciating the beautiful woman who stood in front of him, and said, "I'm very pleased to meet you."

He turned back to Jo-Anne and said, "Can I get you both a drink?"

"Yes, thank you, I'll have a white wine spritzer," replied Jo-Anne and when he turned to Darcy, she said she would have the same. He took them to a small round table in the corner of the room and said he'd be back soon and went off to the bar.

"Gosh, he's good looking!" said Darcy, "I think he likes you."

"Nah! I think he's just a nice man. I'm not interested, anyway." Jo-Anne dismissed the idea with a flick of her wrist.

"Well, you've got Dave at your beck and call – you don't need yet another guy while your husband is away!" said Darcy and Jo-Anne looked quizzically at her, unable to judge whether she was joking or being sarcastic.

"Dave is my friend! You know that! And as for my husband – I don't think he'll be that for much longer!"

"What do you mean?" asked Darcy.

"Just that I can't fight for him – he's a father who won't abandon his child, and that same child won't have me in their lives, so I'm giving in! Savannah's won!"

Just then Nick came back with the drinks so Darcy was unable to reply, and he pulled up a chair next to Jo-Anne and raised his glass in salute. "Here's to a happy evening," he toasted, and as they raised their glasses in agreement he added, "I hope you enjoy the play, it's had very good reviews. It's a murder mystery."

They chatted casually for a few minutes, then Nick said, "If you'll excuse me, ladies, I must go and help out." He reached into the inside pocket of his jacket and pulled out two tickets. "These are your tickets," he said handing them to Jo-Anne. "If I don't get to see you in the interval, I'll meet you back here at the end of the show. Is that ok?"

"Of course. Thank you, Nick." Jo-Anne smiled in gratitude as she took the tickets from him and he walked away.

Suddenly Darcy gripped Jo-Anne's arm fiercely.

"Ow!" yelped Jo-Anne, "You're hurting!"

She looked at Darcy to find her staring, eyes wide and mouth open, her face devoid of any colour. She was looking towards the door where a man had entered and was looking around, obviously seeking someone. He was a tall, extremely handsome figure dressed in grey chinos and a white open-necked shirt.

"It's Andy!" gasped Darcy. She was still gripping Jo-Anne's arm tightly, and Jo-Anne had to forcibly extricate herself from the grasp. She could see a pulse throbbing in Darcy's neck and could hear her quick breathing as Darcy looked wildly around as if for an escape route.

"Calm down, Darcy! Are you sure it's him?" Jo-Anne was watching the man carefully and saw him smile widely and stride over to a woman who had risen from her seat and held out a hand to pull him towards her, then a strangled whimper escaped from Darcy's lips as he leaned across and with an arm around her shoulder he kissed the woman fondly on the cheek.

"I can't stay here – I have to go!" whimpered Darcy.

"You'll have to walk past him to get out of the door – you're better staying here. Please! Just try to ignore him! If you're going to stay with Peter you'll have to steel yourself against situations like this!"

Darcy picked her glass up and emptied it in one gulp. Her hands were shaking and she was fighting to regain composure. She couldn't take her eyes off him even though Jo-Anne was clutching her hand telling her to look the other way.

As if by magnetism, Andy's eyes roamed the room and came to rest on Darcy. She saw his brows arch and his eyes widen as he stared. Suddenly, he leaned across and said something to the woman and stood up. Darcy gasped, but then he walked decisively towards her, his eyes never leaving her face.

"Darcy," he said quietly, "How are you?"

Darcy was having trouble finding her voice, and many seconds passed before she could croak, "I'm………okay."

"Can I sit?" he asked pulling a chair towards him and before anyone could reply he had sat across from Darcy.

"I didn't know you were into Am Dram," he remarked.

"I'm not. I mean, it's my first time here! I came with my friend……." She gestured towards Jo-Anne whose eyes were glued to the man in front of her, the man who had caused her friend such deep heartache. "……….my friend, Jo. Jo, this is ………Andy."

He turned to Jo-Anne smiling and held out his hand to shake hers. "I'm very pleased to meet you, Jo." He turned back to Darcy. "I'm with my sister – her husband is in the cast. I don't always come to the productions, just when he's playing. Support from the family and all that."

He noticed Darcy's empty glass. "Can I get you a drink?" he asked.

Darcy looked beseechingly at Jo-Anne and lifted her empty glass.

"I'll get the drinks," said Jo-Anne understanding the silent message she'd received.

"Not for me, thank you, I've got a drink on my sister's table," said Andy.

Jo-Anne scurried away never feeling more superfluous than she did at that moment. As she waited at the bar she saw them leaning closer together, their heads almost touching and such an intense look on Darcy's face that Jo-Anne had the feeling of being in a kaleidoscope – everything tumbling and changing. She desperately tried to lip-read, or at least work out by facial expressions what they were saying, but the barman distracted her by asking her order and engaging her in trivial chit-chat.

By the time she'd got the drinks for herself and Darcy, the call had come out for everyone to take their seats. The barman had given Jo-Anne a numbered card to place under their drinks to leave them on the table as no drinks were allowed in the auditorium. Andy stood up as she approached, and she heard him say, "I'll see you here at the interval." And with a smile at Jo-Anne he walked away.

"We need to go in now," she said to Darcy placing the drinks on the table. Darcy stood up. Her eyes were bright and two spots of colour highlighted her cheeks. She walked as if in a daze and followed Jo-Anne like an obedient child. When they took their seats, she looked around until she had spotted Andy and smiled when she saw he had done the same, and their eyes met. Andy's seat was two rows in front and he was on the end seat to the right of where the girls sat, so he could easily see Darcy simply by turning slightly to his left. Darcy didn't have to move in her seat, all she had to do was turn her head a fraction and he was in her sight.

Darcy couldn't wipe the tiny smile off her face, and Jo-Anne leaned towards her and whispered, "You're not going to pay much attention to this play, are you?" and wasn't at all surprised when Darcy shook her head.

Just then the lights dimmed and the music started so they didn't have a chance to continue, so Jo-Anne tried to push all thoughts about Darcy and Andy and Peter completely out of her mind so that she could enjoy the play. She kept glancing at Darcy and each time she saw Darcy's eyes were on Andy, and when she looked across at him, his eyes were on Darcy. Jo-Anne sighed – the play was actually very good, but she knew that there'd be no point in discussing it with Darcy afterwards as she was completely unaware of anything around her except Andy Johnson!

At the interval, Darcy was first out of her seat and eagerly pushed towards the bar area, and by the time Jo-Anne got there she was sitting drinking her spritzer. Jo-Anne sat down and said, "Well, what's going on?" but as Darcy's face lit up, she glanced up to see Andy coming towards them. Just behind him was Nick Dawson, and Nick looked curiously at Andy till Jo-Anne said, "Oh, Nick, this is Andy," and left it at that with no explanation to either one who they were.

"Ah, you're Ben's brother-in-law, aren't you?" asked Nick, "I thought I recognised you."

"What do you think of the play?" asked Nick, turning towards Jo-Anne.

"It's very good, I'm really enjoying it," replied Jo-Anne and when Nick looked at Darcy and Andy, they weren't even aware that he had spoken, they were in deep, almost whispered conversation.

He turned back to Jo-Anne. "We've done some wonderful productions. There are framed posters on all the walls in the corridors and up the stairs to the balcony. I'm only in a couple of them, but I'm very proud to be part of this cast – they're excellent."

They chatted some more about amateur dramatics and various other innocuous topics and Jo-Anne felt completely at ease in Nick's company. He was so easy to get along with.

"How long have you been a Police Officer?" she asked him.

"Oh, I'm not a Police Officer, it's a civilian post," he replied, "I work for the Metropolitan Police, but it's a nonsworn position. I'm into security and preventing crimes from happening rather than catching the bad guys!"

He told her he had a degree in Criminology and she told him about her current BTEC course and her ambitions for her future, then all too soon the call came over the loudspeaker for everyone to return to the auditorium for the second part of the play. Nick jumped up, "Gosh, that went quick, I'd better shoot backstage to see if I'm needed. I'll see you at the end, back here, okay?" And off he rushed.

Jo-Anne nudged Darcy's arm – she and Andy were oblivious to anything that was happening around them, and she looked up at Jo-Anne in surprise.

"Time to go back in," she said.

"I'll see you after the play," said Andy, touching Darcy's arm and gazing deeply into her eyes.

She nodded dumbly and followed Jo-Anne back to their seats, and then watched as Andy walked round the auditorium to get to his seat. She then settled back into the chair but continued to look in his direction.

Jo-Anne was feeling a tingle of excitement herself. She had very much enjoyed her conversation with Nick and found him interesting. As the lights dimmed and the curtain went up, she resolved to push everything to the back of her mind and continue to enjoy the play.

*****

The taxi dropped them at Jo-Anne's house, and Darcy walked like a sleepwalker behind her as she unlocked the door impatiently and pulled Darcy inside.

"What the hell are you doing!" she snapped as soon as the door was closed.

"What do you mean?" said Darcy with genuine puzzlement on her face.

"All this……..with Andy! Chatting to his sister as if you were a couple! Does she know you're a married woman?"

"I don't know. I don't know what Andy has told her – if anything. She's nice though, Hannah, she's got two boys as well, older than my two." Darcy kicked her shoes off and threw herself down on the sofa. "Jo, I can't be without him! I know that now. I have to figure something out, but I can't be without him!" Darcy's voice was thick with desperation, and Jo-Anne ran her fingers through her hair and pulled at it in frustration.

"Oh, Darcy!" she cried.

"Anyway!" countered Darcy, changing the subject, "What's this about *you* giving up *your* husband? You dropped that bombshell and didn't explain, so what do *you* mean?"

Jo-Anne sighed noisily and sat down heavily. "We're both in a mess, aren't we!"

Darcy got up and walked over to Jo-Anne. "Jo, honey, I need you now more than ever before. Please don't judge me or hate me for what has happened with Andy. It's so powerful, this feeling, I've never experienced anything like it before. I *have* to be with him! But I don't want to destroy my family .... so what do I do?" She knelt in front of Jo-Anne and placed her arms around her and they sat there huddled together.

Finally, Jo-Anne gently broke free and took Darcy's hands in hers. "I've realised that the Trevor that is in Valencia today is not the man I married and lived with for nearly three years. That Trevor has gone, and the one remaining is a father of a ten-year-old and that is the most important thing to him. So I'm not fighting, I'm not resisting, I'm just..........letting go." She grimaced ruefully. "I'm not saying anything to Trevor, I don't want to push anything, I'll still reply to his emails – he rarely rings or texts - but I'm just going to get on with my life here, and take the pressure off him. I think it will naturally evolve to a divorce!"

Darcy sighed. "Oh, sweetie, it's such a shame. But it's true – children cause you to make decisions that you wouldn't make if there were no children. If it wasn't for my boys, I'd just leave Peter! And I'd gladly suffer the berating I would get from his family and some of our friends for leaving a sick man!"

Jo-Anne got up. "I'll make some coffee," she said walking into the kitchen. Darcy followed and sat at the kitchen table.

"So what were you two talking about tonight. It was very intense," said Jo-Anne.

"We were saying how meeting up tonight was perhaps a sign – fate telling us something!" Darcy was picking at her fingernails. "He said he'd never stopped thinking about me, but wouldn't contact me for fear of pressuring me into making a decision. He said he loved me."

"And you love him?" asked Jo-Anne. "Enough to end your marriage?"

"Yes! It's my boys that stop me from running to him, not Peter. When he was missing the other morning – when he got locked up – I was worried, but mainly because I felt responsible after I'd told him I didn't love him any more. And I was so annoyed and ashamed to find out he'd been locked up, he was an embarrassment! I wanted to walk out then – take the boys and just walk out! And that's when I thought Andy was out of my life!"

Jo-Anne placed the coffee on the table and took a seat opposite Darcy. Then both sat cradling their coffee mugs, then Jo-Anne asked. "How did you leave it with Andy? Have you arranged to see him again?"

"Well, I said I'd ………….. talk to Peter – see how it goes. I have to come clean with Peter. I've arranged to meet Andy on Tuesday to tell him what happened." Darcy was staring into her coffee mug.

"I think that's best. It's all you can do really, isn't it? I'm not doing anything in my situation because there's no-one else involved, so I can just let things come to an end naturally." Jo-Anne squeezed Darcy's hand.

"So what about this Nick, then?" asked Darcy, "He seemed pretty keen. Has he got designs on you, I'm wondering? Have you made any arrangement to see him again?"

"No, though I have to make a decision about some CCTV stuff we talked about in his role as Crime Prevention Officer, so I said I'd ring him when I've spoken to Dave." Jo-Anne laughed, "He thought Dave was my husband, and I didn't bother correcting him – it was too complicated!"

Jo-Anne suddenly stood up. "I'd better check my phone – I put it on silent when we went to the Playhouse." She went to her bag on the sofa and took out her mobile phone. "Will you look at that!" she exclaimed, "Seven missed calls – all from Dave, the last one only ten minutes ago! I knew he'd ring – but seven times? I'd better ring him." She called his number and he answered almost immediately.

"Jo! Are you okay? I've been worried sick!" Dave sounded frantic.

"I'm fine, I'm home. Darcy's here. I forgot to turn the ringer back on when I came out of the theatre." Jo-Anne grimaced at Darcy and pointed at the phone that was held against her ear, indicating that Dave was upset.

"Did you enjoy it then? The play?" asked Dave.

"Yeah, it was good. Nick was very kind – he invited us to stay for a drink with the cast after the play was finished. It was fun. Surrounded by all those thespians high on adrenalin, it was like another world!"

"Did Darcy enjoy it, too?" asked Dave.

There was a moment's silence as Jo-Anne struggled for an answer, then finally said, "I think so, maybe not her cup of tea, but she did have a good night!" The last words were said with her eyebrows furrowed, conscious that she was not being altogether open and honest but not telling lies.

"Good," said Dave, "Now, about tomorrow, do you want to do some shopping – choosing furniture? I should get the keys in two weeks time."

"Ooooh, yes," said Jo-Anne excitedly.

"I'll pick you up about 10.30, is that alright?" When Jo-Anne had agreed, he wished them both goodnight and hung up.

"Do you think he's a bit jealous of Nick?" asked Darcy.

"No way!" said Jo-Anne, "There's nothing to be jealous about! And anyway, there's nothing going on with either of them, so…………"

"Seven missed calls?" mused Darcy, "He wasn't bothered? Hmm?"

"Oh, for goodness sake!" laughed Jo-Anne, "Stop trying to turn the focus on my love life – or lack of – when it's *you* that's in the spotlight! Seriously though, sweetie, you're going to have to grasp the nettle, and pretty soon, before it all comes crashing down around you!"

Chapter Twenty-one

A few days had passed with no improvement from Dawn, then came the day when Trevor and Savannah walked into the room and her eyes looked up at them and her mouth quivered. Trevor heard a gasp from Savannah, then she rushed to the bed saying, "Mummy, you can see me!"

Dawn's shaking hand crept up towards Savannah's face but Savannah grabbed it and held her mummy's hand in hers, kissing her fingers and hugging her hand to her chest. Trevor stood behind his daughter, smiling at her joy as he watched Dawn try to mouth her name. He leaned across to Savannah.

"I won't be long, sweetheart, I'm just going to pop out to see the doctor." Doctor Garcia was busy, but the nurse told Trevor that the change had seemed to occur with Dawn that morning as she woke up – it was as though she had needed to withdraw to heal her mind from the new trauma that had been inflicted with the news of her parents' death, and now it seemed she was aware and responsive.

"We are hoping that she will now begin to communicate," said the nurse, "She is gaining strength physically so we are going to help her get out of her bed into an armchair later today. I think we will be seeing great improvements now."

Trevor thanked her and asked if he could see Doctor Garcia when he was free. This would probably mean that Dawn would need to be transferred soon, either to home or to a nursing home. He needed to know what kind of care she would need to know whether he could provide it at home. He would have to talk to Manny about the cost of home nursing – he would have to have help – there'd be physiotherapists and goodness knows what other therapists would be needed, so who would pay the cost of this – did the insurance cover it, or would this come out of Dawn's estate? He could feel the panic start to rise in his chest – this was too much, he couldn't cope, he needed Jodie to sort it out for him. She'd told him she would help, he couldn't do it without her.

He went back into the room where Savannah was telling her mummy about her accident at school when she hurt her arm, and Trevor could see flickering and quivering in Dawn's face as she was obviously feeling some emotion at hearing that her child had been hurt. Savannah turned to Trevor, her eyes dancing with delight and brought him into the conversation, but Trevor's mind was so full of worries that he couldn't fully engage, but this didn't stop Savannah from keeping up the one-sided conversation.

A few hours later, after Savannah had fed her mummy and helped her sip her drink through a straw, Trevor said they needed to be getting back home. Doctor Garcia had been to see Trevor and he was impatient to get home and talk to Jodie. Savannah didn't put up an argument about it, she was a model of obedience. Trevor remarked on how good she'd been not putting up a resistance, and Savannah told him that she was going to be very, very good from now on so that mummy would come home quicker and she was going to help look after her.

Just before he got into the car, he rang Jodie and asked if she could come earlier that afternoon as he needed to talk to her before she went to the hospital. Jodie was concerned and asked if there was a change with Dawn – fearing the worst, but he quickly eased her mind by telling her it was all good news, but there was stuff he needed to talk to her about. She arrived within forty minutes and it was apparent that she and Holly had had a heated argument, but when Trevor asked what was wrong she muttered, "Oh, don't ask! She's driving me insane!"

"Why? That's not like Holly, she's normally so compliant." Trevor watched as Holly flounced out of the room with Savannah in tow, normally the other way round.

Trevor and Jodie went into the kitchen as it was the coolest room, and Trevor told her about Dawn's new awakening. Jodie clapped her hands in excitement but then noticed that Trevor wasn't sharing her delight. He then told her about Doctor Garcia's prognosis and the effect it was going to have on all of them.

"He reckons it'll be about two weeks, then she'll be able to come home to be nursed here. We'll have to have a bed downstairs, and a wheelchair, a physiotherapist will continue to visit three times a week………."

"Well none of that is a problem. Is it? Why do you look so glum?" Jodie took his hand across the table. "We'll manage, I've told you. I'll be here."

"I know. I guess I'm just scared. I've never cared for anyone like this before – it's a big responsibility." Trevor grimaced, but Jodie squeezed his hands and said, "Don't worry. It'll be fine."

At that moment, Savannah came flying into the room shouting, "Daddy, please can I go to visit Holly's grandparents – she wants to see her grandma so much and she said I can go, too?"

"What? But they live miles away, darling, you can't just pop in for tea, you know."

"I know that, daddy, but I don't want Holly to go without me." Savannah pouted and as if to prove her devotion, she took Holly's hand and pressed it to her heart.

"I'd better explain," said Jodie, "My mum rang this morning and said they'd waited long enough to see us, and insists that we go to visit. I used to go every two months for a weekend because our apartment is too small to have them with us for overnight visits, but I haven't been since Dawn's accident, and I explained to them that I was needed here, but………Holly wants to see them – which is only right, I just don't want to leave you in the lurch, especially with Savannah's arm the way it is."

"That's why Savannah should come with us, mummy! Then you can still look after her, and she won't be lonely without me." Holly stood arms akimbo, glaring at Jodie, daring her to object to the obvious solution.

"Please daddy, can I?" begged Savannah.

Trevor was nonplussed and looked helplessly at Jodie.

"Well, I don't mind at all, and I know mum and dad will love to see her again, but it's up to you, Trevor."

Trevor sighed. "What chance have I got against three beautiful women? Yes, Savannah, you can go."

Savannah yelped in glee and she and Holly danced on the spot before Savannah grabbed Holly's arm and pulled her outside. "Let's see if Carlos is finished in the orchard, we can play hide and seek!"

Jodie laughed and shook her head. "What are they like – little monkeys! We don't stand a chance when they team up together, do we?"

"When were you thinking of going?" asked Trevor.

"Well, if Dawn may be coming home in the next couple of weeks, we need to go as soon as possible, so we can be back to get things ready for her. We could go early on Monday morning and come back on Saturday, if that's okay."

"Sounds good to me." He looked at his hands, then up at her face. "I'll miss you," he said simply.

She smiled tenderly at him. "It's only a couple of days. Before I go, we can spend the next couple of days working out what needs to be done for Dawn's home-coming and recuperation, and you can get it sorted while we're away."

He nodded absently, still dwelling on what he'd just said. He hadn't realised until now just how much he relied on her, and to say he would miss her was a massive understatement.

"I'm just wondering, Trevor…………..whether this might be an opportunity for you to take a trip back to England and see Jo? If Savannah's with me, she won't know you've gone, and you can use the time to sort things out with Jo………..one way or another." Jodie chewed on her bottom lip.

"I guess you're right. I should, shouldn't I? Though heaven knows what I'm going to say to her. I'm choosing my life with my daughter instead of my life with my wife? It sounds pathetic when I say it, even to myself!"

*****

Peter had tried to make it up to Darcy since he had spent the night in a police cell, knowing how embarrassed and ashamed she was about his behaviour. He put it down to a combination of the alcohol and his medication, but she wouldn't accept that as an excuse - she told him he should be more responsible. She'd been distant all week, and if he tried to start a conversation with her, she deliberately found something that she needed to do urgently at that very moment. The boys hadn't noticed anything, but Peter was at his wits end trying to find a way to get a discussion going. She had told him she didn't feel the same way about him – she didn't know whether she loved him or not! She was staying with him out of pity – that's how he saw it!

He'd noticed a difference in her straight after she'd been to the Playhouse. She was brighter, more animated, still distant with him, but the times she sat quietly she had a tiny smile on her face, not the deep, depressed aura that had surrounded her for the weeks beforehand. This was all since his diagnosis, he was sure of that. Perhaps visiting the theatre had given her an interest? He hoped so.

On the Saturday evening, the boys were bathed and in bed, and he had been working on some figures for Darren – the business was doing well since Peter had introduced new systems at the head office and Darren was looking to expand or diversify. He put everything away, and noticed Darcy was watching something on TV – a wildlife programme. He sat down next to her and asked if she was watching the programme, and she said, "Not really." Then turning to face him she said, "I think we should talk." She turned the television off.

"Yes, we need to." Peter tried to take her hand, but she pulled it away. He continued, "I'm so sorry that things have come to this – I'll do anything you ask to get us back on track again. I know last week was………" She held up her hand and shook her head.

"No, Peter, shush! Let me talk. Please don't stop me or interrupt……….this is very difficult………..I don't know how to say it, so I'm just going to say it outright ………..I'm in love with someone else!" she finished in a rush.

Peter's mouth dropped open and he stared at her. "What? But I asked you and you said no, there was no-one else! How? When? Who is it?" He was shaking his head wildly. He stood up and began to pace the floor.

"I'm so sorry, Peter, I couldn't help it. I've tried to fight it, but I can't. I love him." Large tears were slowly oozing from her eyes, and she looked at him beseechingly. "I don't want to hurt you, but I can't keep it to myself – I could see how it was destroying you, so I want to be truthful."

"How long?" Peter croaked, "How long have you ……..been seeing him?"

"For a few weeks, but I've known him for several months," she whispered.

"Who is he? Where did you meet him?" he said hoarsely.

"It doesn't matter, it doesn't help anything for you to know details. We need to work out what we're going to do! For the boys' sake, we need to be civilised about this." Darcy had already decided she wasn't going to tell Peter that she'd met Andy at the gym, that she used to see him there, not now that Peter was enrolled at the same gym! It would be too cruel. If she was forced to tell him where she met him, she would make something up – say it was a chance meeting in a supermarket or something.

"Why did you lie to me………when I asked you? Why did you say there was no-one else? Why did you let me think it was my illness that caused all this?" His voice was beginning to rise, and she held up her hands to him.

"Please don't wake the boys! I couldn't tell you – I was scared to!" She was crying and wringing her hands together.

"You were *scared*? Scared of *me*? Did you think I would beat you? I've never lifted a finger to you – I've never raised my hands to you or to the children! What were you scared of?" Peter's eyes were stretched wide in disbelief. "I don't believe I'm hearing this!"

"No! No!" she sobbed, "I was scared of the consequences!"

"So what's changed? Why aren't you scared of the consequences *now?"* he asked her.

"Because I want to be with him! Because I can't go on without him!" She covered her face with her hands and let the anguish pour out, her sobs wracking her body.

Peter stood in front of the fireplace, one hand on the mantlepiece to keep himself from falling as he looked at his wife – the woman he had loved more than life itself for the past eight years, and even in his shock and grief he still wanted to take her in his arms and comfort her, his brain not able to comprehend what she had told him.

They were both silent, the only sounds were from Darcy's sobbing and moaning, as the clock ticked away the minutes. Peter was staring vacantly as he tried to come to terms with the idea that his wife loved someone else – that his marriage was over.

"What are you going to do?" he asked hoarsely. "What about the boys?"

"I can't leave my boys!" She lifted her head and looked at him imploringly.

"No. Neither can I! Oh, God! What am I going to do?" His voice was small, he had a defeated look on his face and seeing this made fresh tears gather in her eyes. He didn't deserve this, he was such a lovely man, and she was destroying him, she was devastating her family! But the feelings she had for Andy could not be stifled, the love she had for him was far greater than anything she had ever experienced and seeing him the evening before confirmed that it was not a passing fancy, nor a lustful affaire – she loved him with every fibre of her being.

Peter had one hand over his face and the other still holding the mantlepiece. He turned away from her and placed both hands on the wall above the fireplace. His voice sounded strangled as he said, "It'll have to be me – I'll have to leave! I'll have to tell them it's for my job – that it's just for now. We don't have to break their hearts as well!" His voice broke and he wrapped his arms around himself, dry sobs wracking his body. "I'll go and pack some stuff."

"No, Peter, you don't have to go tonight," she said desperately, "You can stay in the guest room and look for somewhere over the next few days. We can talk to the boys together, let them see that we still both love them, and that they will still have both parents, just in different houses." Darcy was anxiously wringing her hands, grateful for Peter's solicitude. "I'll go and make the bed up, and we can talk some more tomorrow – work out what we say to the boys." She touched his arm softly. "Thank you, Peter, thank you for being so ………….understanding." And she went out of the room.

Peter continued to stare at the floor long after she'd left the room, and gradually his face twitched and crumpled and the tears oozed from his eyes as he fell forward on to his knees and crushing a cushion to his face to stifle the noise he roared till his throat burned as the pain enveloped him.

*****

Jo-Anne was preparing a roast dinner. She'd invited Dave for Sunday lunch and then they were going for a walk. The weather was warm but not too hot, perfect for a leisurely stroll and a couple of drinks in a countryside hostelry. She was smiling to herself as she remembered the previous day and the fun they'd had trying to choose furniture, especially for the lounge. Dave had spied a huge leather chesterfield low-back sofa with an equally large high-back winged chair which he sat on proclaiming this was made for him – it felt regal, and when Jo-Anne pointed out it was far too big for the room – he wouldn't be able to walk round it – he had reluctantly conceded and then made a huge drama out of examining small cottage suites, asking if they would be large enough. They had giggled like schoolchildren but had finally decided on two small sofas that would stand either side of the glass-fronted fire which was set inside the wall about two feet off the floor with large pebbles instead of the usual imitation coal, but which was gas powered and had real flames licking round the stones. Jo-Anne loved the fire – it was the first time she had seen one like this and was quite envious.

When Dave had arrived the previous day, the first thing he'd asked about was the evening before – did she enjoy the play, was she going again, was she seeing Nick again? She'd turned to face him and said, "Stop with the interrogation! He's a nice guy who offered me two tickets for a local amateur production which he's a member of! He didn't whisk me off to the opera and ply me with champagne and caviar!"

Dave had looked sheepish and mumbled, "Sorry, I just wondered."

This time when he arrived Jo-Anne was the one to mention Nick's name, and she noticed how Dave's head shot up at the reference.

"You know when Nick came the other night to do the Crime Prevention stuff – that *you* suggested I follow up? Well, he's given me some brochures about different CCTV systems that I'd like your opinion on, if you don't mind. I was quite impressed at some of the home safety equipment he showed me, but he said my home is pretty secure as it is. Some of these CCTV systems are quite ingenious but I need you to advise me on what's practical." She walked to the kitchen drawer and pulled out a small pile of brochures and set them down in front of him. "Have a browse while I finish preparing lunch."

Dave glanced at them and flicked through while continuing to look at her. "You didn't answer me yesterday – are you seeing him again?"

"Oh, I don't know………. perhaps! We haven't arranged anything………why?"

"No reason, just interested. So, was there anyone there at the Playhouse that you knew?" Dave had started to look through the brochures and didn't see the look of alarm that crossed her face.

"What do you mean? Why do you ask?" Jo-Anne asked sharply. Did he know anything? Was he just fishing or did he know about Darcy's…………lover? How could he know? He lived over twenty miles away, he'd lived away from the area for many years – he couldn't know the same people, he couldn't know about Darcy! It was her imagination, that was all.

"Dunno!" he said, "Sometimes you meet people that you've known for years in places that you never expected to see them, simply because you don't know all the details of their lives. Just curious."

Jo-Anne relaxed slightly. It was up to Darcy if she wanted Dave to know – they were all good friends at one time, but Jo-Anne didn't think Darcy would want him to know just yet, it would put him in a compromised position with Peter, same as she was, but Darcy was her best friend and her needs came first. She started to serve up the lunch, and Dave shuffled all the brochures together and put them on the bench.

"Wow! This looks good! I'm starving!" he said and for the next ten minutes they concentrated on enjoying the roast dinner she had prepared for them.

When her phone rang, she glanced at the screen, then glanced up at Dave. "Oh, I'd better take this," she said rising from the table.

"Is it Trevor?" he asked.

She shook her head as she walked into the sitting room out of earshot, and a few minutes later she came back in and sat back down at the table. "Sorry, it was Darcy. She's in a bit of a state."

"Why, what's up?" He was taken aback that she had felt it necessary to leave the room to talk to her friend who was also his friend, to have a conversation that she didn't want him to hear. What was going on?

"She's having a bad time at the moment – she and Peter are having some difficulties, and she wants to talk. I told her we're going out for a couple of hours, but I'll ring her when I get back – when I'm on my own."

"Oh, right!" said Dave, feeling a bit restrained, as the long relaxing day had been suddenly given a time limit, and he was being excluded from Darcy's problems.

"I've got strawberry cheese-cake for dessert – or would you rather have ice-cream?" she asked him, not wanting to take the conversation any further about Darcy.

Dave asked for cheese-cake, so while she was cutting it and pouring on some double cream, she thought about what Darcy had told her. She said she had confessed to Peter that she was in love with somebody else, and they were spending the day talking things through and trying to find a way of explaining to the boys. She told her how unselfish and noble Peter was being, how he loved her so much he would rather give her up than have her broken-hearted – how many men would do that for a woman? She'd made the quick call to Jo while she was in the privacy of the bathroom and said she would give her the details later on that night when the boys were in bed.

Jo-Anne sighed deeply. Everything was changing – her own marriage was in jeopardy, Darcy's marriage appeared to be over, Dave was already divorced. Was that why Dave had so effortlessly given up his wife – did he love her so much that he gave her up rather than make her unhappy by staying together? She felt strangely disturbed by this thought, but then dismissed it. *None of this applies to me*, she mused, *I'm giving up on my marriage because I can't compete with a child!*

The conversation stilled as they finished the dessert and Jo-Anne asked Dave to clear the table while she went upstairs to get the shoes and light jacket she would need for the afternoon's walk, then ten minutes later they got into the car to drive to the reservoir where the five mile circular walk began, the previous issues forgotten as they relaxed in each other's company once again.

*****

Savannah leaned across Dawn's bed to be able to look at her mother full in the face, and taking her hand in her one hand that wasn't in a sling, said, "Mummy, I'm going to go with Holly to visit her grandma and grandpa for a few days, so I won't be able to visit you, but daddy will be here, so you won't be lonely!" She turned to Trevor with a smile as she said this, and Trevor gave a small smile back, feeling guilty that he hadn't said anything about his impending trip back to England, but knowing the kind of hysterical outburst it may create, he had to keep it secret. He'd booked to leave on Tuesday as Jodie was leaving with the girls on Monday afternoon to go to her parents' house and he would return late on Thursday evening.

Dawn raised her hand to Savannah's face and a little smile turned the corners of her mouth upward which had the effect of lighting up her whole face. She rasped, "You go, have fun!" and Savannah's head whirled round to Trevor.

"Did you hear that, daddy? Mummy spoke to me! She said I should go – have fun! Oh, mummy! You're going to be okay now, you're going to be well!"

Trevor's face registered shock and amazement – she didn't appear to have any brain damage! Although Doctor Garcia had told him they couldn't find any obvious signs of damage, Trevor found it hard to believe that someone's head could suffer such horrific injuries and come out relatively unscathed. The doctor said there may be gaps in her memory but even this may improve in time - the brain was a complex organ and a lot depended on the person's will to live. Dawn had her daughter to live for which had seemingly over-ridden her grief for her parent's death.

He turned as the door opened and two nurses entered. "We are going to sit mama in a chair next to you," said one of the nurses to Savannah, and she stood up and moved next to Trevor as the nurses used their skill and training to ease Dawn out of the bed seemingly effortlessly and sit her gently in the high-backed armchair which stood next to the bed. Trevor noticed Dawn's legs were painfully thin and knew this was because of the months she had spent in bed causing muscle wastage, but that continued physiotherapy would help to give her the muscle tone she needed to help her walk again.

Once they were sure that Dawn was safe and comfortable in the armchair, the nurses went out of the room. Trevor placed a chair next to Dawn so Savannah could sit next to her mummy, and he perched on the bed in front of her. Savannah took her mummy's hand once more and asked her if she was comfortable.

"Yes, darling," croaked Dawn, "I'm fine. What about school?" Her speech was very stilted and her voice was thin and raspy, but she was understandable.

"It's Sunday today, but it's summer holidays, mummy. That's why I've been coming during the day. That's why I'm going with Jodie and Holly, because we want to be back for you coming home. I'm so excited! You're coming home!"

Dawn looked at Trevor with a puzzled frown. "And you?"

"I'm going to look after you – me and Jodie will do it between us! Don't worry about anything, we've got it all sorted. We'll have a bed downstairs – we'll make the dining room into bedroom for you so you've got some privacy, and there's the downstairs shower that you can use – it's all in hand, so don't fret!"

Dawn looked down slowly at her hands and body, and then her gaze rested on her daughter and she smiled again. Savannah was in the middle of one of her non-stop monologues about everything and nothing that only a ten-year-old can impart and only a peer can identify with, but it was a healing comfort to Dawn who had been in a silent and grey land for the last couple of months.

Trevor's mind was racing. He had booked to fly back to England to talk to Jo about ending his marriage because he couldn't think of leaving his daughter, but what if Dawn made a complete recovery? What if she recovered so that he wasn't needed to look after Savannah? What if she expected Trevor to stay with them – as Savannah did, as husband and father? What about Jodie? She said she would help to look after Dawn, how long for? What would happen if Dawn recovered enough that she didn't need nursing? He ran his hands through his hair frantically. He hadn't expected this turn of events. Doctor Garcia had warned him that sometimes coma patients make rapid recoveries once they are out of the coma, some don't - especially if there has been injury to the head, and he had expected Dawn to be in the latter. But she suddenly had............come alive, after weeks and weeks of him sitting by the side of her bed in her comatose state, making plans that didn't really take into account her full recovery. He realised how negatively he had viewed everything – he honestly hadn't expected Dawn to recover fully and had made all his plans around her being an invalid.

Maybe in another few months he could go back to England to his wife and his life there! He tried to envisage the house he lived in with Jo, but only succeeded in remembering how small it was. He had his bike – he could resume his long cycle rides across the moors and the dales! He'd missed that! He had no job to go back to – he was unemployed. He would have no income from Dawn's estate – she would resume control of her own finances once he lost power of attorney. And Jodie? He'd miss her enormously – he had hoped that once he resolved things with Jo, he could come back to Spain and maybe develop a relationship with Jodie. He knew he was attracted to her and she had already told him she had feelings for him, even though they had refrained from any further intimacy with the two girls in the house. But how would that work out if Dawn was fully recovered – would she accept the fact that Jodie was in love with Trevor? Thinking the words "in love with" caused his heart to flutter, and he realised he was more than a little in love with her. All these thoughts chasing around in his head made him feel overwhelmed and dejected, and he had to force a smile on his face in front of Savannah.

After Dawn had eaten her lunch, which Savannah had helped her with – Dawn could use a spoon but not manage a knife and fork, so Savannah had cut up her food into manageable pieces - the nurse came in to say that Dawn should rest for a couple of hours. Trevor noticed that Dawn's speech had become slurred and more sporadic as if she had had too much alcohol, so he told Savannah that they would leave now, and go to get some special toiletries that she had asked for to take on her holiday. To his surprise Savannah agreed, telling Dawn that Jodie would be in to see her later that afternoon while she and Holly discussed what they would take to her grandparents' house, and she would see her when they came back, which was only a few days away and she expected her mummy to be much stronger then and ready to come home.

"I'm sooooooo happy that you're properly awake and talking, mummy. I'm not scared to leave you now. Bye-bye my sweet mummy, I'll see you very soon." She clambered on the bed so she could give her mummy a big kiss and hug with her uninjured arm. Dawn's eyelids were drooping by this time, and she stroked Savannah's arm and whispered, "I love you, baby," very clearly.

"I'll be in to see you tomorrow, Dawn, rest up now and Jodie will come later on to see you," said Trevor, feeling slightly ashamed that he was calling in to tell her she would have no visitors for the next couple of days, till he was back in Spain on Friday.

*****

When Dave dropped Jo-Anne back at home it was almost seven o'clock, so Jo-Anne sent Darcy a text saying she was back home and did she want her to come to the house or did she just want a phone call. Darcy's response was that Peter was going to see Darren about work, and so could Jo come to her house about eight-thirty when the boys were bathed and in bed?

Jo-Anne tidied the kitchen and washed up the dinner plates while she pondered over some of the things she and Dave had discussed that afternoon. He was in a rather reflective mood and had asked her a lot of questions about her marriage to Trevor, about her inability to have a family of her own and her non-relationship with Savannah. Jo-Anne used this as an opportunity to analyse her own feelings about the situation, as she recognised that much of her recent decision-making was made easier by Trevor's apparent uncaring attitude and his indifference to her and her own needs, and she suddenly realised that she didn't really *like* the weak person that Trevor had become – or had he always been like this but she was too besotted with him when they were first married? After her operation she had felt very much a failure and this translated as gratefulness towards Trevor for standing by her, and it wasn't until she underwent months of counselling that she regained her confidence in herself as a worthwhile person. Their relationship had seemed steady, she thought, but if the last few weeks had been a test of the strength of their relationship, then it was floundering badly.

She in turn asked Dave about his own marriage and why he hadn't wanted to start a family with Sally. He told her he had never yearned to have a family – had never thought about it much, and he and Sally had been career driven. Sally had never raised the subject, and thinking about it since he came to England he admitted that he didn't think she liked children much – she never wanted to visit her sister who had four children and referred to her as 'the breeder'! They walked and talked, her arm linked through his, and Jo-Anne had felt more relaxed and at ease with the world than she had done for the past few weeks.

When the clock ticked round to eight-fifteen, she set off walking to Darcy's house with a bottle of wine tucked into her bag. She reckoned she was going to need a drink to deal with whatever the evening was going to bring. She quickly rapped on the back door and let herself in. Darcy was in the sitting room curled up on one side of the sofa, and she hastily stood up when Jo-Anne entered, pulling her tee-shirt down and running her fingers through her hair nervously.

"I bring fortification!" said Jo-Anne dramatically but with a wide grin, and Darcy pointed to two glasses on the coffee table and the bottle of wine, saying, "Got there before you, honey!"

They both laughed and Darcy started to pour the wine as Jo-Anne settled herself on the opposite end of the sofa, a position that they had adopted many times over the years when they were having "girlie chats."

"So, come on then! All the details – spare none!" said Jo-Anne, though she felt flutters of anxiety about what she was about to hear. Darcy had lived in a comfort zone for the past few years, whereas Jo-Anne had gone through a massive life-changing event when she had the cancer threat and the radical hysterectomy, but she recognised that whatever happened in Darcy's life would have an impact on her own in some way, and she wasn't sure she was ready for more changes – that's why she was struggling with the decision about her own failing marriage.

"Our Mark came round and took the boys to the cinema so we had a couple of hours to talk with no interruptions," began Darcy, "I told Peter I had met Andy in a coffee shop near to the gym that I used to go to and that we chatted each time we were in there, and gradually got closer till we realised that we were falling in love!" She looked sheepishly at Jo-Anne than with a rueful grimace she said, "I couldn't tell him that I met him in the gym – that he worked there! I mean, Peter signed up at the same gym and has personal training himself! Not from

Andy," she added hastily at Jo-Anne's raised eyebrows.

"And how did he take it?" asked Jo-Anne shaking her head sadly.

"Well, last night when I first told him, he was devastated! I made the bed up in the spare room and he slept there, though to be honest I don't think either of us got any real sleep! I could hear him pacing the floor, and I kept crying, thinking of how cruel I was being but then thinking of Andy and wanting him so desperately – at any price. Jo, I've never felt anything as powerful in my entire life! I didn't imagine feelings like this could exist! When I saw him on Friday at the theatre it made up my mind – I can't possibly live with Peter while loving another man as intensely as I do! It's not fair on any of us. And Peter deserves to be happy, not miserable – which is what I would make him if I couldn't have Andy! I thought when Peter was diagnosed with MS that I should stay with him and be the dutiful wife, but Peter himself said he didn't want me staying with him out of pity – which is what it would have been. And that helped me make the decision – I respect Peter too much to insult him that way, and also, I didn't want to end up hating him! Please tell me you understand! I don't want to lose you - our friendship." Darcy grabbed Jo-Anne's hand.

Jo-Anne took a deep breath in. "Well, I can't honestly say I understand, because I don't think I've ever felt anything as potent or overwhelming as you describe, but we're very different personalities - you're a much more vibrant person than I am. That's why we get on so well. But I always thought Peter was the calming, stabilising influence you needed – perhaps I was wrong!"

"Yes, I thought the same, till Andy came into my life," said Darcy, "So today, we talked about how we were going to protect the boys and make sure they didn't suffer." Darcy began to cry softly. "Peter told me he loved me too much to see me hurting and miserable as I had been, and that he would always love me even though he was standing to one side to let another man take his place in my heart! Honestly, Jo, it was heart-rending! He was crying while he was saying this and I was crying at the sacrifice he was willing to make to see me happy!" She continued to weep softly, and Jo-Anne felt her own throat constrict as she imagined how Peter must be hurting and she shook her head in wonderment at his pure altruism.

"So, are you leaving and taking the boys?" asked Jo-Anne quietly.

"No, Peter says he'll move out. We're going to tell the boys that it's to do with daddy's work till they get used to us being in separate houses." She took a deep breath and wiped her eyes. "And I'm not rushing into moving Andy in, so don't worry. When Andy and I talked on Friday, and I said I was going to tell Peter and end my marriage, we agreed that we would take it very slowly and gradually introduce Andy to the boys to let them get to know each other. Andy doesn't know yet that I've done it – we arranged to meet up on Tuesday and I would tell him then what the situation is……….he didn't want me to make a decision under pressure."

"So how are you feeling now?" asked Jo-Anne.

"A strange mixture of sadness and excitement. I desperately want to ring Andy and tell him I've done it, I've ended my marriage to be with him, but I'm trying to be calm and composed about it and act like a grown-up! I'll wait until Tuesday and I'll meet him and tell him face to face. I'm trying not to think too much about Peter – he's such a wonderful person, I wish I could have loved him more!" She shook her head sadly.

Darcy turned to Jo-Anne. "Anyway, tell me about your day with Dave, did you have a nice walk?"

"Oh, yes, and we talked a lot. He's so easy to be with – he's like my soul-mate, we get on so well," said Jo-Anne with a smile. "I don't know how I would have coped the past couple of months without him."

"Mmmm?" mused Darcy, "You're becoming very close, aren't you?"

"We always were close when we were younger, when the four of us used to hang out together. When you started going out with that Gary, then Will met that girl from the dance place or whatever, there was just me and Dave, till he got the job in Wales, then………I don't know……we were young and just setting out in life……..we just drifted apart I suppose."

They were both silent for a minute or two, Jo-Anne feeling nostalgic and Darcy – unable to keep her mind on anything other than Andy - was feeling nothing but a yearning for Tuesday to be here so she could tell him of her decision.

Chapter Twenty-two

Trevor stepped out of the taxi at the front door of the house he had shared with Jo-Anne for the past three years, and could hardly believe the smallness of it – how on earth had they survived in such a tiny space? The sky was overcast and there was a nip in the air that normally he wouldn't have bothered about, but as he had managed to acclimatise himself to a Spanish summer, he contrarily tutted at the chilliness that seeped through his thin jacket. As the taxi drove off, he looked around at the tiny, neat street with the row of little box houses on either side and gave a little wave to Mrs Willoughby next door who was busily trimming the low privet hedge that separated her garden from theirs.

He knew Jo-Anne wouldn't be home. When he phoned her on Monday morning after Jodie had suggested she keep the girls upstairs to enable him to make the call without Savannah hearing, Jo-Anne was getting ready to leave for work and she had sounded cool and unenthusiastic to hear that he was making a flying visit to England while Savannah was away with Jodie and Holly. He couldn't blame her, he had thought to himself, after how it had turned out while she was in Spain – although it was all due to matters outside his control, he still realised how discourteous it had been to say the least. She had told him she couldn't get the time off work at such short notice, though she knew she could probably have done so, she didn't think he deserved her changing plans for him after the way he had treated her a couple of weeks ago when she went to Spain. Her compromise was that she would try and finish early – although she had a meeting with a couple who were planning on having their wedding reception in the hotel's function room, but she didn't expect to get away till three or four o'clock.

He picked up his overnight bag and walked up to the front door, rummaging in his pocket for the door key. Mrs Willoughby called out to him, "Hello there, Trevor. I didn't expect to see you back here. Jo-Anne's at work." She walked over to the dividing hedge, pulling off her gardening gloves as she spoke.

"Yes, I know, Mrs Willoughby. How are you keeping?"

"Oh, you know, plodding along! Are you and Jo-Anne………back together, then?" she asked him.

"Back together? We haven't been separated – well, I've been in Spain, but that was unavoidable, but we're still married – still a couple!" Trevor gave a little laugh.

"Oh!" Mrs Willoughby looked perplexed. "But I thought……….with the other man being here………..I just assumed you had split up!" She put a hand over her mouth as if she had said something she shouldn't.

"What other man? What do you mean?" Trevor's face blanched as her comment registered in his brain.

"Oh, pay no attention to me – I've obviously got it wrong! It's probably a family member or something!" she blustered.

"Yeah, that'll be it – it'll be Simon, her brother! Yeah, she did tell me he was spending some time here – he's working nearby!" Trevor nodded his head emphatically, wanting to believe the lie he had just invented, but a sick feeling in the pit of his stomach alerted him to the possibility that it wasn't her brother at all.

He gave a little wave to Mrs Willoughby, saying he needed a cuppa after the journey and opened the front door. As he stepped into the tiny hallway he noticed how neat and tidy everything was. He went into the kitchen and absent-mindedly filled the kettle and switched it on as he looked around at the well-organised and spotlessly clean kitchen, remembering how the massive kitchen in the villa showed obvious signs of a family living there, with unrelated items dotted about on work surfaces, and shoes kicked off carelessly in a corner. While he waited for the kettle to boil, he ran up the stairs with a sick feeling to see if there were any obvious signs of a man living here. The main bedroom looked the normal, immaculately tidy and organised room that it always had been and the guest room bed was made up, but tidy with no personal items lying around and the bathroom showed there were no spare toothbrushes or razors or after-shave, and Trevor felt himself relax a little as he slowly went back downstairs. When he had made a coffee, he took the mug and carried it through the rest of the house, looking around at everything and re-aquainting himself with what used to be his home and castle.

He walked through the patio and unlocked the door, wanting to feast his eyes on his beloved bike – he had missed his long bike rides while he had been in Spain. Perhaps he'd have time for a quick trip out before Jo came home, he wondered. He noticed the new lock on the shed door and placing his coffee mug down on the ground he quickly went back through into the kitchen to the drawer where the shed key was kept. Yep! It was a different key, much larger than the previous small padlock and key that had been on the shed before he went away. *She must have lost the key and had to get a new padlock,* he contemplated as he opened the shed door.

There was no bike! He stared, unable to comprehend what his eyes were telling him. His bike was gone. It wasn't in the shed. Where could it be? The shock and disbelief was slowly turning to anger. Had it been stolen? Was that why she had put a new lock on? Why hadn't she told him? What else had happened while he'd been away? And who was this bloody man that Mrs Willoughby had thought had taken his place?

He heard a car pull up and went to the side gate to go out to the street. That's when he saw the bolt half-way up the high gate, making access impossible from the front of the house. *We must have been burgled at some point,* he thought, *why didn't she tell me?* He yanked open the bolt and stepped out to the side of the house where the drive was, where Jo-Anne was just getting out of the car.

"Where's my bike?" he shouted, unable to restrain himself.

Jo-Anne blinked and looked taken aback. She had totally forgotten about the bike – it seemed so long ago and the insurance had paid up, so the money was lying in the bank ready to buy a replacement.

"Well, hello to you, too!" she said peevishly, slamming the car door shut and hoisting her bag up on to her shoulder.

"Oh, sweetheart, I'm sorry! It was such a shock! Were we burgled or something?" he walked towards her with his arms outstretched and pulled her towards him to give her a hug but noticed how she held back, as she gave him a perfunctory kiss on the cheek.

"*We*? *You* weren't here! *I* was burgled! It was shortly after you left!" Jo-Anne brushed past him through the gate towards the back of the house and Trevor followed behind, asking, "How did they get in? What did they take? Did you call the police? Were you at home or was it when you were at work?"

She stopped and turned around, "All that went missing was your bike. It must have been an opportunist thief, the police said. Which is why the bolt is on the gate – so nobody else can get in! The insurance paid out, but Peter advised me not to get another bike – to leave it till you got home. Which is what I did!" Her words were clipped and measured and as they had reached the patio doors by this time, Jo-Anne went inside calling over her shoulder for Trevor to re-lock the gate and shed.

By the time Trevor had secured everything and walked back through the patio to the kitchen, Jo-Anne had curbed her irritation towards him and Trevor had composed himself. She placed her bag down on the kitchen worktop and forced a smile as she turned towards him.

"Shall we start again? That wasn't a very welcoming homecoming, was it? How are things in Valencia? How's Dawn? How's Savannah?" She switched the kettle on and took out a coffee mug from the cupboard. She held out her hand for his mug to refill it, and he held it out to her.

"Sweetheart, I'm so sorry I've not kept in contact much, but honestly, it's been one thing after another! When I did get the chance to ring, it was usually late at night and I didn't want to wake you, knowing you'd have to be up for work. I tried to keep you informed as much as possible with the emails, but most of the time there was very little change. Till now!"

Jo-Anne sat down slowly at the table, and Trevor pulled a chair out opposite her, leaning in towards her. "A couple of days ago, Dawn started to speak. She answered when Savannah was in the middle of one of her dramatic monologues and took us both by surprise. This was after weeks of her just staring sightlessly, and by all accounts her brain is functioning pretty well! Savannah has gone with Jodie and Holly, as I told you, and when I called in this morning at the hospital and told Dawn I was taking this opportunity to sort out stuff in England, she said, "That's fine, Trevor, do what you have to do!"

Jo-Anne was silent. She looked down into her coffee mug, then back up at Trevor. "Does this mean you'll be coming back?" she asked.

Trevor stood up and walked to the window. He turned and leaned against the sink, looking directly at Jo-Anne. "Well, it's not as simple as that," he said slowly. "There's still a way to go before Dawn will be able to look after Savannah – I mean we don't really know how ……..able…..she is going to be." He raked his fingers through his hair and turned to look at her. "Jo………when I arrived Mrs Willoughby was in her garden. She was surprised to see me……….she said she thought we'd separated..........she said something about a man being here......?"

Jo-Anne exhaled noisily in exasperation and tutted. "Well, yes, that'll be Dave. He's a friend from years ago, he's recently moved back here from Germany. We all used to hang around together, Darcy, me, Dave and Will. He got in touch with us – me and Darcy - just after you went to Spain, and he's helped me out a few times..........like the burglary, the car breakdown that you let expire.......the bills you let go unpaid, Dave helped me sort stuff out. He's a good friend, so don't have a go about him!" Her face was set and her eyes were piercing, and although Trevor knew better than to criticise at this moment, he couldn't just let it pass.

"Well, what do you expect? What are people supposed to think? I haven't been away all THAT long – not long enough for you to take up with...........an old boyfriend!" he said with a frown.

Jo-Anne's eyes grew wide in astonishment. "What? How dare you! What about Jodie, then? What is *she* to *you?* You keep telling me what a good friend she is, how you couldn't have managed without her – well, I feel the same way about Dave! There is nothing going on between Dave and me – can you say the same about Jodie? Is there anything going on between you two?"

Trevor blinked and his eyes dropped for a second. "Of course not! She's ....she's Dawn's friend and Savannah's friend's mother..........and we've become close because of the circumstances, that's all!"

"Well, same for me, so let's just drop it, shall we. We've both needed a friend over the past few months. I have to say a lot has happened here since you went to Spain. Apart from the mess you left with the bills," she said in a barbed tone, "There was a job you'd applied for without saying anything?"

"Oh, that job was nothing……..I applied out of curiosity to see how my CV stood up to a challenge……..did I get a reply?"

"You were offered an interview," said Jo-Anne shortly, and had a rush of irritation at Trevor's smile of satisfaction. She continued, "The burglary was distressing – especially as I was here alone, but then Peter was diagnosed with MS! Worse still, Darcy and Peter have split up just this past weekend and I'm still in shock over that!" Jo-Anne rubbed her forehead willing herself to remain calm and not raise her voice.

"Oh, my God! Why? Is it because of the MS? I don't understand!" Trevor looked shaken by the news, then stood up and walked towards the patio.

"Don't ask me any questions about their separation – all I know is………..Darcy has met someone else and Peter has agreed to move out of the house rather than make her unhappy by staying with him. The new guy is not moving in, she's going to take things very slowly for the sake of the boys." Jo-Anne was visibly upset by the news and leaned forward with her elbows on the table, cradling her head in her hands.

Trevor shook his head slowly, a gentle whistle escaped from his lips and he looked down at his hands. "Wow! Things have certainly changed," he said quietly. He wasn't only referring to Darcy and Peter – there was a definite change in the way that Jo-Anne was behaving towards him. She'd been aloof since she first arrived home and he didn't know how to relate to her. He could almost see the chasm between them.

Jo-Anne walked over to the fridge and opened the door. "Do you want something to eat? Shall I make a meal?"

"Why don't we eat out?" said Trevor, brightening at the thought of them sitting across a table in a restaurant, the way they used to. Perhaps that would ease the discomfort between them. He didn't want any bitterness or animosity between them, regardless of how the situation finally resolved – he never could handle conflict.

"Probably the best idea – there's not much in here." She shut the fridge door then asked him, "Do you want a shower after your travelling? You go on up, I've got a few phone calls to make for work – I've got an important function on Friday and I just need to check a few things."

"Okay, I will. I've only brought a couple of changes of clothes as I'm going back on Thursday, but I could do with freshening up. Actually, I could take some of my stuff from here back with me as well," he said thoughtfully. "I won't be long." He picked up his bag and went upstairs.

Jo-Anne picked her phone up from the worktop and quickly typed a text message to Darcy, *'Plse call me asap to let me no wt hpnd.'* She was on tenterhooks waiting to see if Darcy met up with Andy and therefore ended her marriage. Once she had left the message, she rang Dave's phone. He answered on the second ring.

"Can you talk?" she asked him.

"Yes, though it's a bit noisy – I'm outside on a building site. You okay?" He sounded concerned.

"Yeah, I'm at home, Trevor's here and he's annoying me already! We're going out for a meal to try to have a civilised chat. I'm ringing you, really, to tell you I've got the tickets for Friday – the Masked Ball, you remember?"

"As if I'd forget! I'm actually looking forward to it!" She heard him call out to someone as he took the phone away from his face, then he said, "Sorry, honey, have to go, got a bit of a crisis. I'll ring you on Thursday. 'Bye, sweetness!"

She smiled as she disconnected the call, then tidied up the kitchen before going upstairs to the bedroom. She was laying out an outfit to change into when Trevor came in wrapped in a towel, his hair wet and tousled from the shower.

"Ah, that's better!" he said and smiled at her. She felt a tiny stir of longing as she glanced at his familiar body. He saw her eyes rest on his naked chest, and he walked slowly towards her. She turned to look at him, her breath catching in her throat. He put a finger under her chin and tilted her face up to meet his eyes.

"Jo, I've missed you," he said breathing heavily.

Her heart was fluttering and her pulse had started to race. He was her husband. He was the man she had vowed to love until death. She had missed him. Yes, he'd been neglectful towards her, but he did have a lot to deal with. Perhaps she'd been hasty in her decision to end her marriage simply because his daughter was taking priority in his life – things may be different now that Dawn was recovering. And Savannah wouldn't always be a child. She took a step nearer to him and his arms encircled her, his lips slowly descending on hers, and she melted in the comfort and familiarity of his embrace. The towel around his waist dropped to the floor and he gently nudged her backwards towards the bed and when the back of her knees met the mattress, she slowly laid down, Trevor following, his arms still around her, his lips still on hers.

Afterwards, as she lay in his arms, her mind flitted over the past few months, how a car accident in Spain had wreaked havoc on so many lives and she brought to mind the theory of chaos whereby the fluttering wings of a butterfly in in a remote country can ultimately influence a hurricane at the other side of the world! She remembered how jealous she had been about Jodie's involvement in Trevor's life, and acknowledged that Dave was doing exactly the same in her life! They both had really good friends who were helping them in times of trouble, and so neither of them could criticise the other. She felt much better about everything now, and the decision of ending her marriage was, she recognised, a knee-jerk reaction to her hurt pride.

She slowly sat up in the bed, and Trevor trailed his fingers down her back. "You okay, Jo?" he asked.

"Of course I am," she smiled at him. "I suppose we'd better get dressed if we're going out."

"There's no rush," he said, as he sat up and let his fingers creep up into her hair and gently coax her back down on the bed. She smiled at him and with a contented sigh she gave herself up to the moment.

*****

Darcy walked quickly to the hotel lounge that they had arranged to meet in. Her heart was pounding and her eyes were bright with excitement and joy. As she opened the door, she saw him immediately. His smile lit up his face as he stood up to greet her. He took her hands and tenderly guided her to a table in the corner of the room that was not in direct vision of the door and pulled her down on to the seat across the table from him, still holding her hands.

"How are you?" he asked gazing into her eyes.

"I'm shaking…….. excited…….. happy……..scared……..I've done it……. I've told Peter! I've ended my marriage!" Her eyes were fixed on him, and he could see the love in them.

He raised her hands to his lips and kissed her fingers, his eyes never leaving her face. "I love you," he said simply, "I want to spend the rest of my life with you. I want to get to know your boys and for them to accept me ……….I know it will take time, but I'll wait, I'm a patient man!"

"I love you so much," she said, "I've never felt like this, ever! It's as if I suddenly fit – as if I'm where I should be, where I belong!"

He smiled tenderly at her. "When Shelley died I thought I'd never love anyone again. She was only twenty-four, we were just starting out. I was very bitter. I resigned from teaching as I told you before and started doing Gym instructing and personal training. I found it a more superficial environment –

people are very focused on the physical bodies, and very few are interested in what's going on *inside!* Till I met you! Then I knew………I, too, had the feeling of ……….coming home, I suppose, so I know exactly what you mean about fitting! We are meant to be together. I'm just sorry that Peter had to be hurt."

"I felt bad that this happened just as he got his MS diagnosis," said Darcy, "But the prognosis is good, and there are support groups. He's finally looking after his health – exercising and taking care of what goes into his body, taking supplements and some medication. I decided that I couldn't give up my chance of happiness with you – I would end up being bitter and hating him. And that would impact on the boys."

They both sat back in their chairs as the waitress arrived and Andy ordered two coffees.

"Have you time for lunch? What time do you need to be back?" he asked her.

"The boys are in after-school club, so I'm free all afternoon. I've come on the train, so if I get the 4.15 back – I'm parked at the station at the other end and it'll only take about 20 minutes to get to the school."

"Great! We can spend the afternoon together – I've made arrangements to cover my sessions till 5.30, so that fits in well with me. What would you like to do? Any preferences?"

"We could have lunch then go for a walk along the river?" Darcy wanted to hold hands with him, to walk and talk like a normal couple in love, to make plans for their future.

"Sounds good to me," he said softly, "All I want just now is to hold your hand as we walk," and she began to laugh. "I had the exact same thought!"

They lunched at a small Italian restaurant, raising a glass of red wine to toast their future together, as the music played softly in the background, an Italian aria so full of emotion that created an ambience perfectly suited to their suppressed passion. Afterwards they strolled, hands entwined, along the river walk, stopping every few minutes to look at something of interest or to simply gaze at each other in wonderment at the thought of being together forever.

All too soon the afternoon was over and it was time for her to go for her train. They were standing across from the station entrance, his arm across her shoulders.

"Don't come to the station with me," she implored him. "Let's say goodbye here. I don't want the train to pull away leaving you on the platform – it's too much like "Brief Encounter" and that was a sad ending! Ours is a happy ever after, so I want to walk cheerily away from you knowing that we're going to meet up again on Friday evening – if our Mark will babysit, that is!"

He laughed and hugged her tightly. "I don't want to say goodbye……ever!" She raised her face to his and he kissed her tenderly on the lips. "Till Friday, my beloved. I love you."

"I love you, too. I'll see you on Friday." She gently touched his cheek and stepped away from him. He stood watching her as she crossed the road and as she reached the central reservation she turned and waved to him as she stepped on to the road. She didn't see the black car as it accelerated, the driver not looking out of the window - his head was down looking at something inside the car, and Andy watched in horror as Darcy was thrown up into the air and come down in front of another car, it's brakes screeching as the driver tried to take evasive action……… and failing.

There were screams from bystanders, cars braking behind each other and people running towards the inert body lying crumpled on the ground. Mothers pulled their children away, trying to avert their eyes from the horror of the scene that had just unfolded in front of them. Andy suddenly sprang to life as he cried out her name, "Darcy! Darcy!" he roared as he jumped across the railings into the road, vaulting over car bonnets that were in his way till he reached her side.

"No! No! No!" he screamed as he knelt down by her broken body, "Darcy! My darling! No! No!" Tears were cascading down his face as he helplessly looked at her, scared to move her in case he did more damage, but needing her to know he was there. He touched her face gently, caressed her hair, murmuring her name over and over, his heart breaking into tiny pieces. Her eyes fluttered and opened slightly, and her mouth moved into a small smile. He stroked her hair, leaning over as his tears fell on to her face.

"My love," she whispered, then her eyes closed.

Andy rocked back on his heels and raised his face towards the sky as he roared out his anguish. A hand was placed gently on his shoulder and a woman's voice said softly, "An ambulance is on its way. Here's her handbag." He blindly clutched the bag to him as he turned and looked at the source of the voice. Kind and sympathetic eyes regarded him, her hand still gently resting on his shoulder. He shook his head wildly, "This can't be happening! Tell me it's not happening!" But as the sound of the siren got louder, then stopped, and paramedics appeared before him, he knew it *was* happening and the world would never be the same again.

*****

Jo-Anne's phone rang, startling them both and Trevor murmured, "Leave it!" But Jo-Anne twisted out from under him as she reached over to the bedside cabinet, saying, "No, I have to get it, I asked her to ring me," as she saw Darcy's name on the screen.

"Hiya, babe," she said as she sat up and pulled the duvet up across her body. A strange voice spoke.

"Hello, Jo?" a man's voice croaked, "It's Andy, Andy Johnson........."

"Eh? Andy? Where's Darcy? What's happening?" Fingers of fear were crawling up her spine. Why would Andy Johnson be ringing her.

"It's Darcy………she's been…………a car hit her………….she's……….. it's not good, Jo, it's bad………..she's……….." His wail of anguish pierced her heart like a knife

"No! Oh, my God! Where are you? Where is she?" She'd leaped out of bed as she was talking and was grappling for her clothes strewn across the floor.

"Leeds General," he sobbed, "I rang you because……….you were the last number to call and …………..I couldn't ring Peter…………...will you ring him? There's the boys to pick up as well………"

Jo-Anne had started to cry, shaking her head in disbelief. How could this happen? How can life suddenly change so instantly? "Yes, I'll sort it. Stay there, I'll be there as soon as I can."

She threw her phone on to the dressing table and frantically started to get dressed. Her heart was hammering in her ribcage and she was breathing heavily. "What's happening?" asked Trevor, also clambering into his clothes and trying to get Jo-Anne to speak to him. "What is it? Has something happened to Darcy?"

"She's been run over! I think she's……I think she's dead!" she gasped, as she violently dragged a comb through her hair and reached for her phone again. She quickly scrolled down to Peter's number and put her shaking hand to her mouth while she waited for him to answer. Trevor stared in shock and disbelief as he took in what she had just told him.

"Hi, Jo? What's up?" said Peter, sounding puzzled.

"Peter, it's Darcy…………there's been an accident……………she's been hit by a car………..she's in

Leeds General Infirmary.........it's ....it's very bad." Tears gushed from her eyes as she said the words, and sobs tore at her throat as she heard Peter's gasp, then the roar of his pain and suffering.

"Peter, listen to me. You need to ring Mark, get him to collect the boys from school. And ring your parents, they'll maybe want to look after the boys for a day or two. I'll ring Darcy's parents. I'll meet you at the hospital. Do you hear me?" She was shouting, her tears running freely down her face.

"Yes, yes, thank you, Jo. Erm........ ring Mark, you said, yes, yes, I'll ring Mark." The line went dead.

"What do you want me to do?" asked Trevor.

Jo-Anne ignored him as she hastily threw the duvet across the bed and pulled to straighten it. Her tidiness was such an innate part of her being, she didn't realise what she was doing, until Trevor said, "Leave that, Jo! What do you want me to do?"

She looked at him as if she didn't recognise him, then swiftly gave her head a little shake. "Oh, I don't know, maybe drive me......she stopped mid-sentence as his phone began to ring. He looked at the screen. "Sorry, I have to get this..........it's Savannah, she thinks I'm still in Spain! Sorry!" He gave a little rueful smile, walking out of the room as he answered.

"Hi, sweetheart. Are you having a good time?" he asked, then in response to what she said he replied, "Yes, yes, mummy's fine. She sends you her love."

Jo-Anne couldn't hear any more as he walked down the stairs. She drew her lips into a thin line, feeling an intense loathing wash over her body. Savannah! It would never be any different, she would always come first – no matter what! Even now!

She took in a deep breath and scrolled through her contacts in her phone till she reached Darcy's parent's number. She exhaled fiercely then took in another deep breath, and then Darcy's mum answered.

"Nancy, it's Jo."

"Hello, Jo, how are you?" said Darcy's mum. "Is everything okay?"

"No, Nancy, it's not. Is Ken with you?"

"Yes, well, he's in the garden. What's up, Jo." She could hear alarm creep into Nancy's voice, and she heard her call to her husband, "Ken! Ken! Something's wrong! Come here!"

When Jo gave her the news about Darcy, her own voice broke as the pain of what was happening hit her. She was telling her best friend's mother that her daughter – her beautiful daughter, was dead. They both wept noisily, then Ken took the phone from his wife and spoke gruffly to Jo.

"Where is she?" he demanded. "Where have they taken her?"

"Leeds General Infirmary. I'm going to go there now, Ken. I'll see you there. I've told Peter, he's getting Mark to pick the children up and calling his parents to help out with the boys." She sobbed, "I'm so sorry, Ken! She's my best friend."

"I know she is, Jo, I know she is."

They said goodbye and Jo-Anne wiped her eyes and blew her nose. As she went down the stairs she could hear Trevor still talking on the phone to Savannah, humouring her. He was in the conservatory, so she gave a glance full of distaste over her shoulder and strode out of the front door, climbed into the car and drove off, leaving Trevor to cosset and indulge his spoilt brat of a daughter while she drove to the hospital to grieve over the death of her best friend.

*****

At the hospital she looked around for Andy. There was a man hunched forward his head in his hands, and she guessed it was him – she's only seen him that one time at the Playhouse.

"Andy?" she croaked tentatively as she approached, and his head shot up. She saw the raw grief and pain in his eyes and her heart went out to him. She instinctively put her arms around him as he stood up and he sobbed silently into her shoulder. They stood for what seemed an age in this position, until he gradually brought himself under control, and her own sobs had subsided.

"Shall we go somewhere?" she asked him. "It's just that her parents and Peter will be coming soon and…………"

"Yeah, yeah, I'm sorry!" He drew his hands down his face in an attempt to get rid of the tears. He handed her a handbag that he had been holding fervently, his last link with his lost love. "This is her handbag, her phone's inside."

Jo-Anne took the bag and clasped it to her heart. "This was her favourite. She loved this bag."

She put her hand on Andy's elbow and led him down the corridor. Glancing at the signs on the walls and ceilings, she worked out where the cafeteria was and headed in that direction. She needed to talk to Andy, to find out what exactly happened, but she didn't want Peter to have to deal with confronting the man who had taken his wife's love. Not just now.

They made their way to the cafeteria, a busy place with lots of hustle and bustle and she told him to find a seat while she queued for coffees. He found a small table near the window and sat staring unseeingly outside. Jo-Anne brought the drinks over, and a couple of sachets of sugar. "I'm sorry, I didn't know if you used sugar." He shook his head and picked up the cup, taking a small sip and replacing it on the table.

"Can you tell me what happened?" she asked gently. "I knew she was meeting you. I knew she had told Peter about you."

"We were so happy," he said brokenly, "We'd had such a wonderful day. We'd talked about our future, about taking it slowly, so that we were enjoying the courtship and not scaring the boys, getting them used to me slowly. She went for the train. She didn't want me coming to the station – she said it would remind her of "Brief Encounter" and she didn't want that." He smiled thinly at the memory. "She said the film had a sad ending and ours was a happy ever after…………" he was unable to carry on and rubbed his hand over his face vehemently. "I should have never let her go! I should have insisted!"

Jo-Anne's face crumpled and she wept quietly.

He took a deep breath and continued. "She crossed the road to go to the station. At the central reservation she turned and waved to me, then stepped out into the road and a car – he wasn't looking where he was going – drove straight into her." His voice broke. "If I'd gone with her she wouldn't have turned to wave – she would still be here! Oh, God help me!"

"Have you told the police?" she asked

He nodded. "Yes, I've already done all that – there were lots of witnesses."

"Can I have your phone number, Andy – to keep in touch, to let you know what's happening. If you want me to."

"Of course! Thank you, Jo. You're the only one I can talk to." He rubbed his forehead. "I can't think – here, can you find my number?" He handed her his phone and she quickly scrolled till she found his number and stored it in her phone.

"I'm going to go back now, Andy. Peter will be there and maybe her parents. I'll ring you. Okay? Have you got someone that can come for you – your sister, maybe?"

He nodded dumbly and feebly waved a hand in her direction. "You go. See to Peter and her parents. I'm going to sit here a while."

She stood up and placed Darcy's handbag inside her own larger bag, and touching Andy gently on the shoulder, she walked away, leaving him desolate and broken.

*****

As she walked back down the corridor her phone rang. Looking at the screen she saw it was Trevor. She answered curtly, "Yes?"

"Where are you? Why did you leave me?" he asked in a puzzled tone.

"Trevor, I'm at the hospital. I left because you were busy talking to your daughter and I needed to get here!"

"Do you want me to come to the hospital? Shall I get a taxi?"

"No, just stay where you are. There's nothing you can do. I'll be back later. I have to go now." She disconnected the call and shook her head sadly. Then she called Dave's number.

"Dave," she began as soon as he answered, "It's Darcy, she's been in an accident – a car ran into her, and ………..she's dead!" Her voice broke as she said the words, the words that she would never be able to say without feeling raw pain and sorrow.

"Oh, my God! When? Where? What happened? Where are you?" He sounded distraught.

She was weeping openly again and had to lean against the wall to stop herself from falling on to the floor in a heap. "I'm at the hospital – Leeds General, I'm going to meet Peter and Darcy's parents, they should be arriving any minute."

"Do you want me to come? Is Trevor with you?" he asked.

"No, I left him at home – his bloody daughter rang just as I was leaving and he had to talk to her, pretend he was still in Spain! It sickened me! Please, can you come Dave, I need you here."

"I'm leaving now. I'll come find you." He ended the call and Jo-Anne attempted to compose herself once more as she continued to the accident department where Darcy had been brought in.

Peter had just arrived and was looking around wildly. When he saw her he ran up to her and threw his arms around her. "Jo! Jo! I can't believe it. Where's the doctor? Somebody? I want to see my wife!"

"Peter!" They both turned at the sound of the voice and saw Nancy and Ken walking quickly towards them. Peter began to weep as he held Nancy, and Ken stood to the side, his arm across his wife's back, the torment visible in his eyes. Jo-Anne put her arms around Ken, and they stood silently, grief uniting them.

A door opened and a doctor came out. "Mr Jones?"

"Yes," said Peter, disentangling himself from Nancy's arms, "These are Darcy – my wife's – parents, Nancy and Ken Edwards."

"I'm Doctor Heath. I am so sorry," the doctor began, looking at each in turn and his eyes finally resting on Peter, "When your wife was brought in, I'm afraid she was already gone. She died at the scene of the accident. There was nothing anyone could do. I understand there were many witnesses."

Peter's wail of anguish tore at Jo-Anne's heart as he clutched at his head and looked around wildly. "No, no! It can't be………are you sure it's her? It might be a mistake! Can I see her?" asked Peter on a sob, and Nancy looked up sharply, but the doctor nodded.

"Yes," he said, "Her injuries were internal and there are no visible signs of trauma. Would you like to see your daughter, too?" he asked Nancy and Ken.

They looked at Jo-Anne, but she shook her head. "I'll wait here," she whispered.

Peter took one arm of Nancy's and Ken took the other to support her shaking legs, and they walked mechanically through the door following the doctor. Jo-Anne slowly sank into a chair and stared vacantly at the floor. She wasn't aware of the passing of time, she wasn't aware of the people coming and going past her, she was only aware of the numbness creeping over her body and soul. She thought she should ring her mum, and her brother Simon, but didn't want to say those words again.

A voice spoke softly to her. "Jo? I'm here." Looking up she saw Dave, his kind, beautiful face filled with concern, his eyes mirroring the pain in her own. She stood up and melted into his arms, the tears once again falling, but these were tears of relief - relief that she could share her grief with someone where she didn't have to put their needs first. Neither of them spoke. They stood for a long time like this, Dave gently stroking her back, and Jo-Anne thankful to be in his embrace.

Chapter Twenty-three

Trevor left early on Thursday to catch his plane back to Spain. They hadn't spent much time together, Jo-Anne had hardly been at home – she was either at Peter's house or at work. Trevor had gone with her on Wednesday to Peter's house to give his condolences, but the boys were around as well as Peter's parents and Darcy's parents, so they didn't stay long, then Jo-Anne dropped him at home and went into work for a couple of hours. The gulf between her and Trevor was growing wider and each time his phone rang when she was around she walked out of the room in anger.

When she was in work she'd phoned Andy to check how he was. He didn't answer, so she left a voicemail saying she was concerned about him and was checking to see how he was coping. A few minutes later her phone rang and she saw it was him calling.

"It's Andy," he said, "Sorry I didn't answer, but I didn't recognise the number and I didn't want to talk to anyone – except you, of course. I've got your number stored now."

"I understand, don't worry. How are you?" she asked him.

"Broken-hearted," he said, a catch in his voice.

"Me too," she said, "It's going to be hard without her, isn't it?"

They spoke for a short while, but neither of them truly wanted a conversation, so she said she would keep in touch and tell him when the funeral arrangements were made.

Then she rang Dave and felt comforted just hearing his voice. He'd stayed at the hospital with her the evening before and was with her when Peter and his in-laws came out of the room after sitting with Darcy. He'd hugged Nancy and though she was surprised to see him, she was grateful for his presence. Both her and Darcy's parents had liked Dave and Will, and were disappointed when their friendship didn't mature into adult relationships for any of them.

Jo-Anne told him that she wasn't sure about going to the Masked Ball, but he said to wait and see how she felt on the Friday evening – she'd already sorted out a gown to wear, and he knew that Darcy would want her to go. They chatted for a while, then she asked him to call her on Thursday evening after Trevor had gone back to Spain, which he said he would.

Jo-Anne drove Trevor to the airport before going to work, and the conversation was stilted on the journey. Jo-Anne was numb with grief, and Trevor didn't know how to deal with the situation. He felt as though everything he said or tried to do for her was wrong, so he stopped trying. He had been nervous when Savannah rang him, which she did two or three times a day, and when she asked if he could put the phone next to mummy's ear, he had to pretend she was asleep, or to say he had just come out of the hospital for some reason, and as he wasn't a very good liar, it made him panicky when she called.

Jo-Anne breathed a sigh of relief as she turned back from the airport. Regardless of what happened with Dawn, she didn't want to get back with Trevor. Losing her best friend the way she had made her realise that life shouldn't be wasted on situations that don't make a person happy. Look what Peter was willing to do – he was making such a sacrifice for Darcy's happiness. Then the realisation that Darcy would never get that happiness hit home and the pain of her untimely death struck her again and the tears gushed from her eyes as she was driving.

When Dave rang her that evening, she'd just got home from visiting Peter's house. The boys had been told originally that mummy was in hospital because she'd been knocked down by a car, but that morning Peter and his mum had sat them down and explained gently that mummy wasn't coming home and had gone to heaven. They had no experience of death and didn't fully understand the implications of being in heaven, so kept asking how long she would be there. Peter was in a bad way when Jo-Anne arrived, and the boys kept crying asking for mummy, and all Jo-Anne could say to him was, "You just have to get through it, allow them to grieve, to cry, to yell – you too, if it helps. Just don't bottle it all in."

What lay between them – the elephant in the room – was Andy Johnson. Peter made no mention of him, but he would know that Darcy had confided in Jo-Anne. She had made the decision to never mention Andy unless Peter brought the subject up, but she kept in touch with Andy – just one phone call a day – as her heart ached at his predicament. She had no doubt about his love for Darcy, and she wasn't sure how much he had told his sister about their love affair. She hoped he had told her, then at least he had someone to share his sorrow with in the hope that he could get some comfort.

At home, she settled on the sofa, pulling her knees up under her, the phone cradled on her shoulder as Dave asked her if she'd eaten. She said she'd had something at Peter's house – his mother was spending her time baking and cooking to keep her hands occupied and to try to involve the boys in the baking chores that they used to enjoy. She had made her mind up earlier that day that she was going to take Dave into her confidence about Darcy and Andy, so she'd opened a bottle of wine and poured herself a glass.

Dave heard the noise and asked, "Is that the pouring of wine that I can hear?"

"Nothing escapes you, does it?" she replied with a half smile.

"I'm just gutted that I'm not there with you!" he teased. "But I won't judge you!"

"Well, I just want to relax a bit. I've got something I want to tell you," she said in a serious tone.

"Oh? This sounds a bit heavy, should I open a bottle at this end?" he said.

"This is serious, Dave. I want to talk seriously. It's about Darcy. She and Peter were going to separate – she'd fallen in love with someone else and wanted to be with him. Peter had agreed to move out, she said he'd told her that he loved her too much to see her unhappy with him, so he would stand aside to allow her to be with the man she loved." She paused, and when there was no sound from the other end she said, "Dave?"

"I'm here, honey. Wow! Do you know the guy she was in love with?"

"She'd only told me recently – she'd been seeing him a while before she told me. She didn't want me to be in a compromised position with Peter, but she was so unhappy she had to confide in me. I met him the night we went to the Playhouse, when Nick got us those tickets – his brother-in-law is in the cast and he was there with his sister. That was all just a co-incidence. He really loved her, Dave, I mean *really* loved her. He's devastated, as you can imagine. In fact, they'd spent the day together. She'd told him that she'd ended her marriage and that they could start planning their lives together. They were going to take it slowly for the boys' sake. She was waving goodbye to him when the car hit her............" Jo-Anne began to weep softly.

"Oh, poor guy!" said Dave with feeling, "That must have been horrendous – to see your loved one............" he stopped, the scene conjured up in his mind was too bad to put into words. "Are you okay, sweetheart?"

"Yeah, I just keep crying – like, all the time!" she said sniffing and wiping her eyes.

"You're bound to. She was a big part of your life, you'd been friends for such a long time - since you were kids in school. You grew up together. Almost a sister!" Dave's voice soothed her.

"Yeah, we were." She sniffed again. "You know - I think I will go to the Ball tomorrow night, hah! *said Cinderella!*" she said in an attempt at light-heartedness and was pleased to hear Dave's laugh. "I've put so much work into it, I want to see it through. Does it make me sound heartless?"

"Not at all!" said Dave, "I think it's wise – Darcy would be the first one to tell you to go!"

"She would, wouldn't she?" Jo-Anne nodded, almost hearing Darcy telling her to go.

"Okay, then, I'll come through and pick you up. It starts at eight o'clock, you said, so shall I get to yours about seven-fifteen?"

"That's fine. I'm finishing work early so I can spend time on my make-up, my face is a mess with all the crying!"

"Nah! You're beautiful," said Dave emphatically, "Always were, always will be!"

"Flatterer!" she said, but was secretly thrilled to hear him say something like that, especially as the photo he'd showed her of his ex-wife revealed that she was an absolutely stunning woman.

*****

Trevor got back to the villa in a state of confusion and misery. He hadn't managed to sort anything out, not even his own feelings. When he'd booked to go to England he was clear in his mind – he was going to talk to Jo about ending their marriage – Savannah had to come first. He'd imagined himself and Jodie as a couple looking after both girls, but then the sudden upturn in Dawn's recovery and the fact that she may even make a full recovery had put that in jeopardy. Then to throw another spanner in the works, when he saw Jo in their bedroom – the familiar surroundings – and the way she had looked at him, he felt himself slip easily into the life he knew and had loved before the accident had happened. And for those few short hours in bed with her, he had put all thoughts of Spain behind him.

When Jo received the phone call about Darcy, she didn't turn to him for comfort as he would have expected – in fact she treated him as if he was an irritation! Yes, it was a terrible thing that had happened, but he felt as though she blamed him somehow! And hadn't she told him that Darcy and Peter had agreed to separate only a couple of days ago? What the hell had been going on? He sighed deeply, then checked his watch – he'd better get to the hospital and make sure Dawn was okay before Savannah got back. He looked at the list of things to do that Jodie had made out before she left – jobs that she expected him to have completed before Saturday when she returned. He'd have to see Carlos and ask if he would help him with the bed and furniture that she had planned out.

Dawn's bed was empty when he got to the hospital, and his heart thudded painfully in his chest. He frantically sought out a nurse to ask where she was and the nurse smiled and pointed to a room at the end of the short corridor. When he rushed in the room he discovered it was the television lounge and Dawn was in an armchair having a stilted conversation with another patient. She turned and smiled as he came in.

"Trevor, you're back," she said slowly and stiffly, but her speech was easily recognisable.

"Dawn, you look amazing," he said. Her hair had been shampooed and styled and although still very short, it didn't look unkempt as it had done. She was wearing a pretty cotton robe and she had colour in her cheeks. "How did you get here?"

"That," she replied indicating the wheelchair that was at the far side of the room. "Nurse brought me. I escaped from the room!" she said triumphantly.

Trevor raked his hands through his hair. Obviously he was pleased that Dawn was doing so well, but he hadn't expected such a speedy improvement in such a short time. He turned at the sound of his name as Doctor Garcia walked in.

"Ah, Senor Gainsbury, I am pleased you are here. As you can see your wife – excuse me – ex-wife," he corrected himself as Trevor raised his hand, " She has made remarkable progress in the last few days, so as soon as you have made the adaptions we spoke about, she can come home. This is good news, yes?"

"Yes, indeed," said Trevor, feigning excitement, "As you may be aware, I have been in England, so I haven't had the opportunity to do much, but now I am back, I will get it all sorted."

"Good," said Doctor Garcia and held out his hand for a handshake.

When the doctor had left, the lady that Dawn had been talking to stood up. "Excuse me please," she said in broken English, "I return to room now." She pulled her robe together and walked very slowly out of the room. Trevor pulled up a chair next to Dawn and smiled at her.

"How is your wife?" she asked.

Trevor had a flutter of relief – at least she remembered that they were divorced and that he was remarried.

"Oh, she's well," he said, then shook his head. "Actually, a few hours after I got there, she got a call to say her best friend had been ………run over and……. had died!" He looked at her nervously, wondering if it would spark any bad memories for her. Her eyebrows furrowed and she shook her head very slowly.

"Oh, how awful for her," she managed to say.

There was an uncomfortable silence for a minute or two, then a nurse popped her head round the door and said brightly, "Time for medicine!" and pushed her trolley into the room. She checked her list and gave Dawn a small container containing pills and a small plastic cup of water.

"I'm going back now," she said slowly after the nurse had gone. "Can you get my chair please?" Trevor pushed the chair next to her armchair and she told him where to stand and how to support her while she heaved herself into the wheelchair. She was breathing heavily after the exertion and laid back and closed her eyes. Trevor anxiously asked if she was alright, and she nodded still with her eyes closed. When they were back in the room he then had to manoeuvre her again to get her into the bed. Once she was safely tucked in she said to Trevor, "I'm going to sleep now, you can go. Thank you." He stood there, not knowing what to do, then he raked his hands through his hair and said, "I'll get off then, and get some of these jobs done that Jodie left for me. Savannah's having a great time, by the way."

She nodded as she closed her eyes again, and Trevor stood uncertainly by her bed, then when she didn't open her eyes, he turned and walked out, feeling as though he'd been dismissed.

*****

The Masked Ball had been a huge success – the Charity had raised way above their target, and Jo-Anne had received several enquiries about future bookings and functions for her to organise. Dave told her how proud he was twice that evening – once when he came to pick her up and saw her in her pale blue full-length evening gown that gently caressed her body and emphasised her slim, shapely form and also deepened the blue of her eyes. His own eyes widened when he saw her and he let out a low whistle and said how proud he was to be her partner for the evening. Then at the end of the evening, when she was finally alone with him after the crowds had dispersed after thanking her profusely, he told her again how proud he was of her for the way she had organised such an event. She grinned at him, feeling ridiculously happy that she'd made him so, feeling a sense of fulfilment for a job well done, until the pain and grief crashed in when she remembered that she wouldn't be able to tell Darcy about this – or anything, ever again.

Dave saw the sorrow cross over her face and guessed what she was feeling, so he put his arm around her and said, "She'll be watching, and she'll be so proud, too."

She turned to him, tears glistening in her eyes, and whispered, "Thank you."

"I think it's home time now, don't you? I bet you're shattered!" said Dave picking up her evening bag from the table and handing it to her. They said goodnight to the staff who were busy clearing tables and taking down the banners, balloons and table décor, and smiled at each other when one of the agency waiters called, "Goodnight Mrs Gainsbury, goodnight, Mr Gainsbury!"

"That's the penalty for being in the shadow of a successful woman!" he said light-heartedly, and Jo-Anne laughed, secure in the knowledge that he wasn't offended at the mistake.

When they arrived home, Jo-Anne asked him to come inside, and as she opened the door, she turned to him. "Do you want to stay over, it's very late for travelling back? And I want to stick my finger up to Mrs Big Mouth next door!"

"Eh? What do you mean – who's Mrs Big Mouth and why is she?" Dave closed the door behind him and followed her into the kitchen.

"Oh, Mrs Willoughby – she told Trevor that she thought we'd split up …….because he wasn't there and I had another man…………you!"

"Oh, Lord! Was he upset?"

"A bit, but I put him straight – and I asked him if his situation with Jodie was any different – he keeps saying she's just a good friend!" Jo-Anne had made coffees and she beckoned for him to come into the lounge with her, saying, "So are you staying over? You didn't answer."

"If it's okay with you and Mrs Willoughby!" he replied and they both smiled.

After spending some time talking about the success of the evening, the conversation eventually came around to Trevor's visit. Jo-Anne exhale noisily and grimaced.

"I'm afraid it was a bit of a disaster," she said sadly. "I feel ……….very confused, sad, angry, frustrated, disappointed, any other words I can think of! I was very aloof with him when he first came, but then as we chatted and got ready to go out…………well, it kind of………I don't know………..we…………..got together." She felt rather embarrassed telling him, especially as she had been so certain in her decision about ending her marriage last time she spoke with him.

Dave looked down at the rug, not wanting her to see anything in his eyes, and when he felt his face was devoid of emotion, he looked up at her and said, "Well, he's your husband."

"I know! And I hate myself for it, because as soon as Savannah rang I felt as though he'd rejected me – even though I had just received the phone call about Darcy, he put her first again. I knew then it was a big mistake! She'll always be first with him."

Dave said nothing. He chewed on his bottom lip and continued to stare at the floor. There was silence for several minutes then she said, "Oh, God! It's a mess!" They both sat quietly, then Jo-Anne spoke again. "Did I tell you, my mum's coming on Sunday? She's staying with me for the funeral, her friend Sarah is looking after Bessie, her labrador. I haven't told her about Trevor yet, there's enough for her to contend with without that. She was very fond of Darcy – she treated us as sisters when we were younger because we were so close."

"I know," said Dave, "I remember. It'll be great to see your mum again, though I'm sorry it's losing Darcy that's enabled it."

Jo-Anne's lip quivered, and to try to stem the well of emotion that lay just beneath the surface, she jumped up and said, "Come on – let's go to bed!"

Dave looked at her, his eyes widened in astonishment, and as Jo-Anne looked at him her eyebrows furrowed then she gasped and laughed. "Oh, for goodness sake – what on earth am I saying? I mean, in our own rooms – not……….together! And ruin what we've got? No way!"

Dave stood up and picked up the jacket that he had thrown over the back of the sofa, and still not meeting her eyes he walked out of the room and went to check on the doors and patio while Jo-Anne concentrated on collecting her shoes and bag and taking the coffee mugs into the kitchen. At the top of the stairs, they said goodnight and Dave leaned forward to kiss her cheek, praying he had the self-control to do it then smile and walk into the guest room without her ever guessing what turmoil he was going through.

*****

When Jodie and the girls returned on Saturday, they clambered out of the car and rushed up to greet Trevor. Savannah threw herself into his arms as he met them on the veranda exclaiming, "Daddy, daddy, I've missed you but I've had a super time! We've been to loads of places and Holly's grandma and gramps are sooooooo cool!"

Trevor laughed at her exuberance and smiled at Jodie over the top of her head while saying, "I've missed you, too, sweetheart!" Jodie flushed at the veiled declaration, and nodded in reply, as she said, "Let's see what daddy's done while we've been away."

They all tumbled through the doorway and Jodie exclaimed, "Wow! You have been busy, haven't you?" Savannah danced around the room in delight as she took in what Trevor – and Carlos – had done in preparation for Dawn's homecoming. Trevor had bought a new bed that fitted under the window in the large dining room with matching furniture that accommodated all Dawn's personal items and clothing. It was Carlos's suggestion when he had asked him to help to bring down furniture from upstairs - Carlos had asked what would be going into the empty room upstairs? If he was truthful about it all, it was mostly Carlos's suggestions and ideas that had transformed the room into a beautiful as well as functional bed-sitting room. Trevor turned to Jodie and was pleased to see an approving smile on her face.

"I thought you could help and give me some ideas to pretty up the shower room, so it doesn't look too utilitarian?" he asked and she nodded, "Of course!"

"Daddy, it's wonderful! Can we go and see mummy straight away, please? I want to see her. Is she still better, is she even better than she was? Can we go, please? Now?" She was jumping up and down in her excitement, and Trevor laughed.

"Of course you can. Do we all want to go? What about you, Holly? Jodie?"

"Can we go home, mummy? Just so I can………see my things……?"

Jodie hugged her. "Yes, sweetie, we'll go home and get the laundry done and you can see that everything is fine, and we'll come back at tea-time. I'll take your laundry, too, Savannah, then daddy doesn't have to worry about it!"

Trevor put his arm around Jodie and pulled her to him subtly whispering, "We'll talk tonight!" and she nodded. Jodie and Holly got back into their car and drove off, as Savannah danced around Trevor urging him to hurry up. He'd forgotten what a whirlwind she could be like, but before long they were in the car and heading towards the hospital, Savannah still talking about what she'd done with Holly while she was on holiday.

At the hospital she urged him to walk faster as they walked up the corridors. "Mummy may be in the TV lounge," he told her, "She's been sitting in there with the other patients during the day."

Her eyes shone. "That's wonderful news, daddy, you never told me that! Were you keeping it a surprise for me?"

"Yes," he fibbed, "I've only told you now so that you don't get worried if she's not in her room."

Sure enough, Dawn was in a chair in the lounge reading a magazine. There were three other patients in the room all idly watching the TV up on the wall, and everyone looked up as Trevor and Savannah entered. Savannah screeched as she saw her mother and threw herself at her, her arms going around her neck in a tight embrace, crying "Mummy! Mummy! You're better!"

Dawn hugged her daughter back, kissing her hair and breathing in her daughter's smell.

"My angel, my baby! " she crooned, "I've missed you so much!"

"You can talk, mummy, you sound just like you used to!" Savannah had pulled herself back to gaze intently at her mother's face. "Your hair is cool! I love it! Did the nurses do it for you?"

"No, it was the hairdresser," laughed Dawn, "She visits the hospital."

"So are you coming home now?" demanded Savannah. "Daddy's fixed up your room downstairs, you can come home!"

Dawn looked questioningly at Trevor as he stood with his

hands in his jean's pockets, and he nodded. "When you feel ready, and when Doctor Garcia thinks you're ready to be discharged," he said.

He sat on the chair next to Dawn as Savannah regaled her mother with the exploits of her holiday and how her broken arm hadn't spoiled any of the fun they'd had, and how Jodie had looked after her and Holly……….and so on. Trevor had mentally switched off, his thoughts going to Jodie, and how he was going to explain the disastrous trip he'd had to England and how he and Jo-Anne hadn't resolved anything. After all he'd told her about ending his marriage – how he had chosen his daughter and his life in Spain over his wife and his life in England, but then to return with the status quo. He felt foolish.

*****

The funeral took place on Wednesday of the following week. Jo-Anne had helped Peter with the plans as a funeral wasn't something that he and Darcy had spent a great deal of time talking about – they were a young couple with a young family, so organising a funeral wasn't high on their priorities list. Jo-Anne made suggestions when Peter asked her, but she made sure that he remained the one in control of what he thought would have been his wife's last wishes. There would be a service at the crematorium taken by a Humanist Celebrant, and Darcy's favourite songs would be played.

Peter still had made no mention of Darcy's lover, and Jo-Anne guessed he was going to act as though it hadn't happened, but as she had been a witness to Andy's grief there was no way that she could ignore the fact that when it mattered - Darcy had chosen Andy over Peter. She had met with Andy on Monday lunchtime and told him the funeral arrangements and asked if he was going to attend. He said he would as he needed to say his goodbye, but that he wouldn't approach Peter or make any kind of scene out of respect for his beloved Darcy. He was still full of self-reproach and repeated that he should never have let her go to the station without him, and Jo-Anne reiterated that he should stop blaming himself – it could have happened even if he was with her. But his eyes told her he didn't believe that.

Jo-Anne was grateful for her mother's presence at home because she was feeling the strain of trying to be strong when around Peter and the boys and Darcy's parents, when her own heart was breaking in two. It was her mum and Dave's strength that kept her going. Her mum was overjoyed to see Dave and they spent all of Monday evening going down memory lane, then as Dave was getting in his car to go home and she was waving from the front door, she turned to Jo-Anne and said, "Such a lovely boy – I mean, man! I always liked him."

When Jo-Anne had confessed to her mum that she was planning on ending her marriage, her mum wasn't too surprised. She said she'd picked up from Jo-Anne's conversations on the phone over the last few months that this rift between them was probably not going to heal easily – at least not without some kind of relationship therapy. She told her daughter that she should do what she felt was right – life was too short, as Darcy's premature death demonstrated, so if she was unhappy she should do something about it. This prompted Jo-Anne to confide in her mother about Darcy's own marriage failure, as she desperately needed to talk to another woman about how it made her feel as Darcy's friend and confidante and how she had initially made a judgement on Darcy and was now suffering massive feelings of guilt over it. They had talked way into the night, Jo-Anne weeping at recalled memories, and her mum soothing her and showing her how Darcy had made her own choices. She reminded Jo-Anne that Darcy had tried to give up her lover when Peter was diagnosed and how she'd made her children a priority, only to confess to Peter that her unhappiness was likely to create more damage to the boys and to her own feelings towards

Peter. She said they were the actions of a brave woman, and Jo-Anne should remember her as such.

"So, in a similar vein, would you think I was being noble by releasing Trevor from our marriage to enable him to create a life with his daughter?" she asked her mum.

"Definitely, if that's what he asks of you!" she replied, "But I would say, at this point – the ball is in his court!"

When the day of the funeral arrived, Dave came to pick up Jo-Anne and her mum and drove them all to Peter's house. Both sets of parents were already there, and the boys were dressed in smart shirt and trousers. It was a beautifully sunny day, and everyone had been asked to wear bright colours and come to celebrate the joy of Darcy's life, rather than to mourn her death in sombre clothes. The boys didn't fully understand what was happening, but knew they were going to say a last goodbye to their mummy. Peter kept them close to him the entire time and in the car following the hearse they kept asking where she was. No-one wanted to point to the leading car decorated in pink and white flowers with the words 'mummy', so Peter told them she was in their hearts where she would be forever. Neither of them answered but the furrows on their brows indicated that the whole event was beyond their comprehension.

The chapel room at the crematorium quickly filled up, and Jo-Anne watched anxiously for Andy to arrive. He came in quietly accompanied by his sister; his face was grey and his eyes sunken and he took a seat at the back of the room. He stared ahead at the coffin, biting his lip as his eyes rested on the photo of Darcy on the top. Jo-Anne's heart went out to him as his anguish was clearly visible. She noted how his sister held his hand and stroked his arm and deduced from this that he had confided in her his love for Darcy and their plans for their future, which were wretchedly destroyed by one man's careless driving.

Jo-Anne sat between her mother and Dave in the row behind Peter and the family, the boys positioned carefully between Peter and Darcy's brother, Mark, and she held her mother's hand and Dave held her hand, but she had to let go of both of them to try to stem the tears that poured endlessly from her eyes throughout the beautiful ceremony. The Celebrant talked as if she knew Darcy intimately, but her information was only what she had gleaned from talking to the family members and Jo-Anne, but she had spent several hours in their company getting to know about Darcy's life.

After the service, Jo-Anne, her mother and Dave followed Peter and the family outside where Peter received condolences from their friends and colleagues, and Jo-Anne slipped away to talk to Andy and his sister who were standing a distance away. She gave a watery smile as she approached, noting his red-rimmed eyes and how he pulled himself up erect as Jo-Anne drew near in an effort to regain composure. Hannah gave Jo-Anne a hug and said how sorry she was to hear of the devastating turn of events, and as she spoke she rubbed her brother's arm gently and hugged it to her. Jo-Anne thanked her and turned to Andy.

"Thank you for coming, Andy, I know how hard this is for you – at least we can all share our grief, whereas you …………." she left the sentence unfinished.

"I have no words, Jo," he said simply, and giving her a hug, he whispered, "I have to go now, but please stay in touch. You're all I have left of her." He turned away, and Hannah gave a brief smile and quickly followed him. Jo-Anne felt the tears dart into her eyes and scanned the crowd to find Dave and her mum and once she'd spotted them she hurried to their side before either of them had a chance to miss her.

The Celebrant came out to the crowd of mourners carrying seven helium-filled balloons and handing one each to Darcy's children, her parents, her husband, her brother and her best friend, she asked them to say – either out loud or in their heads – their words of goodbye to Darcy, then to release the balloons. The boys loved this and shouted out "Catch this, mummy, it's coming up to heaven!" as they let the balloons go, which caused a few more tears from several of the onlookers.

Peter kissed the balloon and let it go, never taking his eyes off it till it disappeared completely from view. Mark did the same, as did her parents, their words to their daughter too private and precious to be spoken out loud. Jo-Anne whispered "Fly high and free, my angel" as her balloon was released. Everyone stood in silence, except for the shrill voices of the children arguing over whose balloon went the highest, till the last balloon was no more than a dot, then the crowd gradually dispersed and Dave walked over to Jo-Anne and tenderly put his arm around her shoulders. Neither of them spoke as they walked back to where her mum stood, then all three of them slowly turned towards the car park and back to a life without Darcy in it.

Chapter Twenty-four

Trevor sent an email to Jo-Anne asking how the funeral had gone. He'd only been in touch with her once since he got back as he was unsure how to be with her. He knew she was devastated about Darcy's death, but it went deeper than that. The distance between them was too vast now to easily heal – if he wanted it to be healed! So he thought he'd just be cool but friendly for now. He told her Dawn was being discharged from hospital at the end of the week and her care would continue at home. He explained how a therapist would continue to visit to keep on with the physio and her medication was now down to a minimal amount. Dawn was continually improving, and her speech was getting stronger and steadier, but at present it was still unknown how physically able she would be. He mentioned that Jodie had offered to continue staying on an evening – just till Savannah was out of a plaster cast – so that she could help also with Dawn's personal care. He said he hoped Jo-Anne was coping okay without Darcy, he knew how close they had been.

Once the email was sent, he turned off the computer and turned to face Jodie. "Sorry about that, I had to send an email to Jo, her friend's funeral was today."

"Oh, dear, I hope it all went alright. Those poor children! My heart aches for them," said Jodie sadly.

"What was it you said you needed to talk to me about once the girls were in bed? Something Dawn had told you, you said?" Trevor sat on the sofa next to her, his arm draped casually over the back.

"Yeah, it's a bit difficult……….but I think you'll be okay with what she said. We were talking about her discharge from hospital, and I said that Holly and I would continue to stay overnight to help with Savannah's showers and hair and such, just while her arm is in a plaster cast. I told her how the bedrooms were allocated to make it all quite respectable....." and she glanced up meaningfully at Trevor as she said this. "Then she asked about your wife – whether you'd left her or whether you intended to go back. Knowing what you'd told me – before Jo's friend died and put paid to you discussing your marriage, I told her that you weren't in any hurry to return to England, that you and Jo had grown apart and may possibly be looking at separating." She looked quizzically at him as she spoke, giving him the opportunity to contradict her, but he nodded in agreement.

"She then said that she hopes that you don't think you're getting back with her – she appreciates what you've done for her, but she doesn't want to get back with you!"

"Well, thank goodness!" said Trevor with obvious relief, "That was one of my concerns! I feel much better now that that's in the open!"

Jodie grimaced and gave a small cough. "I......err.........I said something to her.......I was a bit forward, but I was also testing the water!"

"What did you say?" asked Trevor, his eyebrows raised.

"I told her that I quite fancied you! I said it flippantly so that if she got upset I could say I was kidding, it was just my hormones or something. But............she was elated! She said if we could 'get it together' she'd got the best of both worlds....... her best friend with her daughter's daddy, and both of us looking after her and all of us living together! That was the only time she got anxious – she repeated "We will all live in the same house, won't we." When I asked her would she not mind if she saw us......kiss or cuddle......and she said, "Oh, God, no, it wouldn't bother me at all, and Savannah loves you, so she'd be thrilled." I said that I was relieved she felt that way...............because..."

She looked at Trevor, hardly realising that she was holding her breath, till he gave a whoop of delight and jumped up, hauling her to her feet and hugging her tightly.

"Oh, boy! This is fantastic news! I was so scared of her finding out that we had feelings for each other, I never imagined in my wildest dreams that she would actually *like* this to happen!"

He held her at arm's length and with a smile from ear to ear, he said, "You can't possibly imagine how I am feeling at this present moment. It's like everything has come together – I know the girls will be ecstatic because they'll be like real sisters! That settles it! I'll wait a decent time for Jo to come to terms with Darcy dying, but then I'll talk to her about getting a divorce."

Jodie took a deep breath and exhaled slowly. "I'm so relieved that things have turned out this way because………….I think I'm pregnant!"

*****

On Friday evening Dave picked Jo-Anne and her mum up to take them out for a meal – her mum was going back home on Saturday morning so he wanted to say farewell to her. At Jo-Anne's suggestion he had booked a table in the restaurant that he and Jo-Anne and Darcy had first gone to – the first time they met up after all the years apart. Jo-Anne reminded him of the fun and laughter they had shared that evening, and she wanted to return to honour Darcy's memory.

The evening wasn't melancholic at all. They joked and laughed, recalling the conversations they had had on that evening, and Jo-Anne's mum smiled fondly at them both as she listened and feigned horror at some of the pranks they had carried out in their youth. The food was delicious, and one of the waiters, a young Italian man with swarthy, handsome features and a superb singing voice took her hand and serenaded her, finishing by presenting her with a red rose.

Although it was probably something that they did regularly in the restaurant, nevertheless, her mum was in raptures and her eyes shone like diamonds.

Jo-Anne's phone rang and with a look of surprise on her face, she saw it was Nick Dawson ringing.

"Woah! This is uncanny! Your phone rang on that night as well!" said Dave, "Is it Trevor again?"

"No," said Jo-Anne standing up, "I'd better get this – I won't be long." She hurried towards the ladies' room, speaking into the phone as she walked.

"Oh, God, Jo! I've just seen Ben! He told me about your friend Darcy – it's just too awful!" Nick sounded aghast.

"I know," replied Jo-Anne, "I'm still have trouble believing it myself."

"Are you at home? Are you by yourself? Do you want me to come round?" he asked.

"No, thank you, Nick, I'm actually out in a restaurant with a friend and my mum – she's been staying with me………since it happened, and she's going back home tomorrow, so we're having a farewell meal. But thanks for thinking of me."

"Oh, anytime you feel lonely, just give me a call and I'll come and take you out or something. Is your husband still away?"

"Yes, I don't know when……..or even if……..he's going to come back! But, one problem at a time, eh? I need to focus on helping Peter and Darcy's boys for now."

"Yes, I see," said Nick, "Ben was saying his wife is really worried about her brother, Andy. Apparently, he's taken it really hard – he was very much in love with her, it seems, and this is the second time he's lost the woman he loved, his first wife died of leukaemia – she was only 24 or thereabouts. Poor bloke, I feel so sorry for him."

Jo-Anne felt a surge of pity. She knew how much Darcy had loved him, and she was grateful in a perverse way that he'd loved her so intensely in return – that way it didn't feel that her death was so hollow. She didn't know what to say in reply to Nick and as her throat had constricted with emotion, she simply mumbled.

Nick continued, "Anyway, I'll let you get back to your meal – I just had to call you when I heard. Ben said the funeral was on Wednesday – it's so sad. Those poor boys. Well, goodbye, Jo-Anne, and don't forget, anything I can do to help, please call on me."

"Thanks, Nick, I will. Goodbye." She disconnected the call and went back into the restaurant with a thoughtful look on her face.

"Everything alright?" asked Dave.

"Yes," she replied and as her mother looked at her intently, asking without speaking who had been on the phone, Jo-Anne shook her head slightly and said, "That was Nick Dawson, the Crime Prevention Officer. He'd just heard about Darcy and passed on his condolences."

"Oh," said Dave, and opened his mouth as though he was going to add something else but changed his mind. He turned to Jo-Anne's mum and said, "Pity I didn't get the keys for my new apartment while you were here. You'll have to come back when I move in. It's got two bedrooms so you can even stay over if you like."

"That'll be nice. I might take you up on that," she smiled back at him.

"And what's wrong with my house," said Jo-Anne, "I've got two bedrooms as well."

"Now, now, children, it's not a competition!" laughed her mum and the atmosphere was lightened once again.

Jo-Anne glanced at Dave furtively and noticed he was pensive. She couldn't guess what he was thoughtful about – they'd been having a light-hearted time till she took the call. Was he thinking back to when Trevor called her last time they were in this restaurant? Did her floundering marriage cause him to think about his ex-wife? Did he miss her? The thought of it made her heart miss a beat. She didn't like to think that he cared deeply for someone else – then scolded herself silently! He was her friend, she should want him to be happy. *Yes, I do* she thought, *but not without me.*

*****

Dawn was thrilled with what Trevor and Jodie had done with the villa in preparation for her coming home. Savannah had badgered Carlos for as many flowers from the garden as possible without leaving it bare, then she and Holly had gone to neighbouring villas to ask if they could spare some flowers from their gardens, till the house resembled a flower-shop - every room, every surface, every container was filled to overflowing.

An ambulance car brought her and Jodie and the girls were waiting on the veranda, and as the car drew up in front Savannah rushed forward screaming, "Mummy! Mummy! You're home! At last!"

The nurse escort showed them how to position the wheelchair to make Dawn's transfer from car to chair and vice-versa easier, and then they wheeled her up the ramp into the villa. Carlos had ensured that every room entrance had even flooring so that Dawn would be able to push herself around without needing help, so that she was as independent as she could be. Dawn gasped at the quantity of flowers and said, "Are there any flowers left in Valencia, or do I have them all here?" This made the girls giggle, and Savannah hopped from one foot to the other in her excitement, and said, "Look mummy, we've put pretty cushions on your bed to make it look like a sofa for the daytime! And a special armchair! And all your perfumes and creams are on this dressing table – you can get your wheelchair right under it so you can do your hair and make-up! And your shower-room is SO pretty – Jodie did all that as well!"

Dawn smiled at Jodie and took her hand. "Thank you, Jodie, you've made everything so pretty. I'm so pleased to be home."

Trevor had hovered a little in the background. He owed such a lot to Jodie – she had knuckled down and made everything pretty for Dawn – he was too practically-minded to see beyond the functionality of the adaptions. Now that Dawn was here, he could see how important it was to have the feminine touch, otherwise it would all be purposeful, but with no dignity for her.

He was overjoyed at the prospect of another child and it had dwelt inside him like a secret bubble of happiness for the past few days. He hadn't realised until this had happened how much he enjoyed being a father, and that privilege would always be denied him while he was with Jo-Anne. Jodie had told him she was only a few weeks into the pregnancy and as they had only made love one time, it was easy to put a date on the conception. They had agreed to not tell anyone until the twelve-week scan and concentrate on making Dawn comfortable at home. Since they found out that Dawn would not oppose their relationship, or so she had said in the hospital, they had still decided to play it cool and let family life evolve as naturally as possible. Jodie still went home every morning to check on her apartment, water the plants and pick up any mail, sometimes Holly went with her and sometimes both girls went.

Trevor was still emailing Jo-Anne a couple of times a week but finding it increasingly difficult to know what to say. The feelings of guilt about Jodie and the baby were enormous especially as he had denied a relationship when she had asked him, but he hadn't known at the time what that one night of passion would lead to. He could hardly believe that this had been his life – that this was the woman he had married and had loved, living in their little semi-detached house, going to work every day in a job that he did well, but didn't have enthusiasm for. He had loved going across the moors on his bike – he missed his bike – but even that was no more! It was as if his life in England was slowly being erased and would one day cease to exist. Jo-Anne's replies to his emails were just as aloof – she talked only about work. He guessed that given time, the marriage would just fizzle out – which he hoped would happen as he hated conflict or even having to confront a problem, so if it resolved itself that would be great!

They all very quickly fell into a pattern of living together in harmony and Savannah was happier than Trevor had ever seen her. So, when the letter came for the appointment for counselling, he spoke to Jodie and Dawn together. Dawn was dismayed to think that Savannah had been so upset that the school needed to make the referral for counselling, but when Jodie explained how she had been and how it was probably a natural reaction to what was going on around her, and that the school had to be seen to be helping her, Dawn was pacified. She took Trevor's hand and said, "You've had it rough while I was in hospital, haven't you? Thank you for all you've done, for me and for Savannah. I don't know what would have happened to her if you hadn't given everything up in England and flown to our rescue!"

Trevor and Jodie flashed a look at each other as Trevor said, "It's been tough at times, but it's had its compensations!" Dawn caught sight of the look and smiled at them both.

"Do I detect something going on between you two?" she said with a grin.

Jodie flushed and said coyly, "It's still early days, but............yes, we have feelings for each other."

"Well I just want you to know that I'm happy for you both," said Dawn, "And I can bet that Savannah will be overjoyed. Have you said anything to her?"

"No! We don't want to rush anything," said Trevor, "And remember, I still have a wife in England! I need to sort that side of things, but I don't want to hassle her just yet while she's grieving for her friend."

"Let's just enjoy all being together and be happy that we are alive," said Dawn and tears pooled in her eyes as she thought about her parents, who bought this villa with the intention of living out their retirement years in warmth and comfort but who were taken away from her so suddenly. But fate had seen to it that her life was slightly compensated by bringing together her best friend and the father of her child - who was also her child's best friend - into her home for them all to live as one family. Although they could never replace her parents, it was a special blended family that was full of love.

*****

On Tuesday evening Jo-Anne went to Peter's house and found that Mark was there again. He had been coming every day to see the boys and to give practical and moral support to Peter, which Jo-Anne was grateful for, then she didn't feel as though Peter was being left to fend for himself. Darren had told Peter he could take as much time off work as he needed to get his home life sorted before he needed to return. The boys had gone back to school and Peter had been to see the Head Teacher and they discussed how the staff would handle any issues that came up, especially from their peers, as children's natural curiosity could lead to thoughtless remarks unintentionally causing distress.

Jo-Anne was relieved to see that Peter seemed to be handling the domestic work – there were no piles of laundry or washing up in the sink, the kitchen was clean and he was cooking decent food – they weren't living on take-aways and fast foods, which would have distressed Darcy as she always made sure they ate healthily. Mark was playing a video game with the boys and Jo-Anne and Peter were in the kitchen talking about work – she had been telling him about the positive feedback she had received after her organisation of the Masked Ball, when Peter suddenly blurted out, "Jo, I know about it! She told me!"

Jo-Anne's heart lurched and waves of sickness washed over her. "About what?" she stammered. She felt like a rabbit trapped in headlights – what could she say that wouldn't hurt him more than he was hurting now?

"I know she was in love with someone else," he said quietly, "We had discussed it and I was going to move out, as you probably know. She promised she wouldn't move him in here straight away for the boy's sake! I don't know who he is. I've gone through her phone looking for a name I wasn't familiar with, but I can't find anything. I don't know if he knows what happened."

Jo-Anne's mind was galloping, trying to figure out how much to tell him, enough to stop him thinking about it, but not too much so that he would dwell on it. After a moment or two she took his hand across the table. "He knows," she said softly.

Peter looked sharply at her. "How?" he said.

"She had been with him that afternoon and was on her way home. He saw it happen. He rang my number as it was the last call on her phone – and he knew she was going to pick the boys up from school. He asked me to call you................ I'm sorry, Peter."

"So you knew him?" he said brokenly.

"No, no, not really. Darcy didn't tell me till just recently – she didn't want me to be in an uncomfortable position with you. She only told me a couple of weeks ago, just before she told you. Truly, Peter, she kept it to herself."

"What's his name?" he asked.

"Andy. That's all I know." Jo-Anne didn't want to divulge any more than that – she didn't think more information would help him. "Honestly, Peter, it's best not to dwell on it."

Peter sat staring at an invisible mark on the kitchen table, his eyes brimming with tears. After a while he said, "I loved her so much. I thought she loved me."

"She did! Even when.........she fell for Andy, she never stopped loving you. That's why she told you - she could have carried on having an affair and had the best of both worlds, but she told me she loved and respected you too much to deceive you! Please, Peter, don't dwell on it. Dwell on the years you were together, in love, a happy family – don't let the last couple of months spoil your memories." Jo-Anne's voice was pleading and she was filled with misery. She didn't want Darcy's memory to be tarnished. It was easier for her because she had seen how distraught Andy was at losing Darcy and that somehow beautified the relationship, but she didn't think that Peter would welcome her defence of Andy's character.

Peter pulled himself up straight. "You're right!" he said, "We had a good, strong marriage up until this year and that's all I'm going to remember. Thank you, Jo. You're a true friend, and I love you for it."

Mark came into the kitchen just then saying, "I've been sent in for refreshments - my lords have ordered milk and cookies! How are you doing, Jo?" He smiled wanly at her and she noticed the dark circles under his eyes.

"I'm just about coping, Mark, how about you? I'm busy at work so that helps to take my mind off missing her."

"Yeah, I'm back at work, too. It does help, but I have to keep an eye on mum and dad – they're not coping well at all. Everyone says the same – time will make it easier, but........" He let the sentence fade, and they both grimaced at the same time.

After chatting with the boys for a while, Jo-Anne said she was going back home as she had stuff to see to. She said her goodbyes, promising to call again in a day or two and went out of the door. She had walked to their house as it was such a mild evening so as soon as she had got to the corner of the street, she took out her phone and rang Dave. When he answered she told him she'd been to see Peter and he had confronted her about Darcy's love affair. She heard Dave's sharp intake of breath as he said, "Oh, no! That must have been hard for you. What did you tell him?"

She gave him a synopsis of the conversation and tried to explain to him how she was feeling – *a sense of treachery* was how she termed it, but Dave's straight-talking and common sense eased her feelings of guilt and after a few minutes he had her laughing. He kept the conversation going till she had reached her front door and he said for her to keep talking till she was safe inside then he would hang up.

"You're like my own arm's length private security protection," she laughed as she locked the door behind her.

"Well don't keep me at arm's length!" he retorted.

There was a moments silence, then Jo-Anne said, "Right, I'm home and the door is locked behind me. I'll let you go now - will I see you this weekend?"

"Actually, I might be getting my keys this week, so I can start moving in!" he said.

"Oh, that's great! Just what's needed to give us a focus. Ring me as soon as you get signed up and get the keys in your hand!" Jo-Anne sounded cheerful and Dave smiled as he visualised her face, her eyes dancing as her mind flitted across the furnishings he had bought already and creating a mental list of what still had to be bought. He knew she had derived a great deal of satisfaction from organising his home and furnishings, and as he said goodbye to her and closed his phone, he thought, *"If I had to buy a house every year to make her this happy, I'd find a way of doing it!"*

*****

The summer holidays had eased by in peace and happiness and "the family" (as they called themselves) had settled into a comfortable routine. Savannah's cast had been taken off and her arm was good as new, Dawn was steadily improving and despite the doctor initially thinking she would need intensive care at home, she was able to do much of her own showering and personal care after a few weeks and her medication was down to the bare minimum. Every morning, before Jodie went to her own apartment, they would all sit at the breakfast table – Dawn in her wheelchair, and they would talk about what was going to happen that day.

One morning during this discussion Jodie said quietly that perhaps she and Holly should be thinking of going back to their own home now that Savannah's arm was okay and Dawn was able to do pretty much everything for herself - apart from walking. Trevor felt his heart sink into his stomach and his breath caught in his throat. No! He couldn't let that happen! He racked his brains to think of an excuse to keep them there, when Savannah jumped up.

"No!" she cried, "Don't! Why can't you just live here like you have been doing? You want to, Holly, don't you? We both love living here, all together! Why have you got to go back there?"

Trevor wanted to kiss her! Bless the spoilt, precocious little madam – he wanted to say all that, but she could get away with it!

Dawn frowned and laid her hand on Savannah's arm.

"Sweetheart, you mustn't push Jodie into doing something she may not want to do!" Then turning to Jodie she said, "Jodie, honey, you know I love you being here, you're my best friend. I would love for you to stay, make this your home – in fact, you could sell your apartment and put the money away for a rainy day and really make this your home! But if that's not what you want………………………"

Jodie gripped her friend's hand. "Sweetie, you know I love being here – I always have done. And I do feel like it's my home. I was thinking about the long term – if Trevor and I…………" and she looked at Trevor, urging him to join the conversation.

It had been very difficult for them to find time to be together since Dawn had come home and they had started living as a family and they'd had to be satisfied with Trevor sneaking into Jodie's bedroom on a night but having to sneak back again before morning or before either of the girls discovered them. Many times Trevor had groaned when he had to tear himself from her arms and clamber out of bed saying he wanted nothing more than to wake up next to her.

Trevor now looked at Savannah, then at Holly, trying to read their expressions as they interpreted Jodie's words.

"Yes," he managed to say, "We're all happy living together, and Jodie and I are ….erm ………well, what would you say, girls, if Jodie and I got married one day?"

Savannah looked quickly at her mum. "But what about you and Daddy?" she asked with a frown.

"Daddy and I are divorced, sweetheart. I don't want to be married to him again – and he wants to marry Jodie, but we'll still all live here – won't we?" She turned quickly to Jodie.

"Of course we will!" said Jodie, "What do you think, Holly? You haven't said anything."

"Will Savannah and I be proper sisters if you and Trevor got married?" she asked quietly.

"Yes, you'll be step-sisters," said Dawn.

"Then I want to stay here and I want you to get married," said Holly hugging her mum.

"Me too," said Savannah, "Will Holly and I be bridesmaids?" She clasped her hands together and when Jodie laughed and said, "Of course!" they both jumped up and down in their excitement.

Trevor leaned across the table and took Dawn's hand. "Thank you for this, it's not every woman who will welcome her ex-husband's new wife into her home!" Dawn smiled at him as he released her hand and took Jodie's hand.

"Well, I want to make this a formal offer – Jodie, will you please marry me………when I'm free?" he added quietly.

"Of course I will!" she laughed and the girls – after pausing in their bouncing, resumed their excited leaps.

Trevor could hardly believe his good fortune. Obviously he had to end his marriage to Jo-Anne, but here he had a complete family where his ex-wife and new wife-to-be were best friends and their children were best friends and although the others didn't know it yet, they were going to welcome a new member into the family next Spring, which would cement the two families together.

"I've been thinking," said Trevor, "I need to get a job. I've been scanning the recruitment agencies online to see what's available, and though I couldn't get a job last time……….." he grimaced at Dawn, "I think I've a better chance these days. I may have to go back to England for a couple of days to sort out some stuff ……….." he looked at Savannah with his breath on hold, waiting for the eruption that usually occurred whenever he mentioned going back to England, but to his surprise – and relief, there was no outburst. She looked quickly at her mother and when Dawn nodded in agreement to Trevor, she said, "You will be coming back, won't you?"

"Of course I will!" he said laughingly, "I've got my family here!"

They had decided earlier that they were going on a picnic – there were some picturesque walks suitable for wheelchairs and prams that Jodie and Dawn used to take the girls on during the summer holidays, and as they loaded the lunch and blankets into the car, Trevor contemplated his trip back to England. He'd received an email from one of his friends back home telling him about a marketing opportunity with a Head Office in Madrid. He wanted to meet up with Sam and a couple of the others that he hadn't seen since he left in April, and also he needed to talk to Jo about a divorce. Now that his and Jodie's relationship was in the open, and more importantly, once they made it public about the baby, he wanted to be in a position to marry Jodie before she showed too much.

He whistled happily as he packed everything in the car, stroking the vehicle in admiration – he'd always yearned for a SUV, and he'd been given Dawn's permission to buy one so that her wheelchair could fit in. Trevor had lost the Power of Attorney when Dawn regained her mental capacity and she was now in control of her own finances. This meant that Trevor could no longer transfer money into his and Jo-Anne's bank account, and in his recent email to her he had explained that he would have to "sort something out".

Now that things were panning out nicely here, he wanted to get to England quickly and get things sorted with Jo-Anne. She had been cold and distant in her emails to him and though he accepted that she was still grieving her friend, he reckoned she would be this way with him even if Darcy hadn't died. He sighed, it was obvious now - their marriage hadn't been strong enough to survive what had happened in Spain.

*****

As she closed the door behind her, Jo-Anne wanted to skip down the corridor in her excitement – she'd been offered a promotion! More than that, she'd been offered a choice –

there were two positions available as event/conference organisers, one in Edinburgh and one in Harrogate. The Harrogate position was as senior manager in a similar sized sister hotel which carried a substantial salary increase, whereas the Edinburgh position was as manager of a small team in a very large and successful hotel, also with a substantial salary increase and a relocation package. And this was before the results of her course were known, but the MD had said her results weren't important – the fact that she had undertaken and funded the course on her own showed potential and she had good career prospects. The results and feedback he had received from not only the Masked Ball, but the numerous events that she had organised, showed what an asset she was to the company. The Harrogate hotel was a challenge – it had lost its' sparkle and had been allowed to stagnate, so it needed an injection of her competency and expertise to bring it to the same level of success as she had brought to her current job. The Edinburgh position was in a very successful hotel whose patrons were more prosperous and distinguished, so she would be in a very different environment to what she was used to. The conference/event facilities were twice the size of the hotel she was currently in so everything would be on a much more massive scale, which was why she would need a small team.

The excitement bubbled inside her as she went back to her office, but she couldn't sit still. She reached for her phone to ring Darcy, when the pain clutched at her heart as she remembered she wouldn't ever be able to share her news with her friend again. Before the black cloud came down, she jumped up and paced the office floor as she rang Dave's number. As always, he answered immediately.

"Hi, honey, is everything alright – oh, just hold on a tick!" she heard muffled voices, then he came back on the phone. "Sorry about that, somebody needed some info. So, what's up with my little treasure today?"

"Everything is absolutely wonderful!" she exclaimed. "I've been offered a promotion! In fact, I can choose which I prefer!"

"Well! That IS good news! Congratulations, my pet, I'm so very proud of you! What are your choices?"

She outlined the two hotels and positions she could take her pick of and noticed the long pause when she'd finished. Dave finally spoke, saying quietly, "What are your thoughts? Have you got any gut feelings about either of them?"

"Oh, I don't know! I'm too excited to think properly. The awful thing is – I went to ring Darcy to tell her………"

"That'll happen often, my sweet, it's only natural! But it kind of renews the pain, doesn't it? And it hurts all over again."

"Yeah," said Jo-Anne sadly, "Well, I'll let you get back to work. I just needed to share my news. I'll talk to you later."

"Shall I take you out tonight, to celebrate?" asked Dave.

"No! Tell you what – I'll cook a meal for us, do you fancy that? If you bring your pj's and teddy-bear we can have a sleepover, then we can stay up later talking. What do you think?" Jo-Anne chewed her lip as she waited for his answer.

"What about Mrs Nosy Knickers next door?" he asked.

"What about her, indeed? She can take a running jump!"

"Okay by me! I'll get to yours about six-thirty, is that alright? Want me to bring anything?" he asked.

"Just your lovely self!" she replied flippantly, happy that he was going to come.

She went back to her desk and turned on her computer. As she brought up her emails she noticed one from Trevor. With a sinking heart she read that he was coming to England again on Friday till Monday, but he had an interview meeting arranged on Friday, and he was meeting up with Sam and some other pals on Saturday, so he was sorry he wouldn't be able to spend much time with her but if she could keep Sunday free there was a lot he needed to discuss with her. It didn't read like a letter to his wife, it read like a formal letter to an acquaintance, and although part of her was glad, the other part of her was hurt that he was so cold and distant.

"*Get a grip!*" she told herself, "*You don't want him anyway! Be happy he doesn't seem to want you – it'll make the break easier!*"

He would probably want to sleep there – it was still his house, well, in name only as he wasn't paying anything towards the mortgage and running costs now. That was something they needed to sort out! What if he wanted to sell up – could she afford to buy him out? Was this a sign that she should take the relocation package to Edinburgh? Did she *want* to live in Scotland? She resolved to push it to the back of her mind till Friday came! She didn't want it to spoil her good news today and she had Dave coming round tonight, he would help her sort her mind out, he always did.

Later that day as she was walking to her car, her phone rang. It was Andy.

"Hi," she said, "How are you, Andy? How are you coping?"

"I'm not," he said, "That's why I'm ringing you. I can't go on, I'm re-living that day over and over again," his voice broke and he fought to regain control. "I miss her so much."

"Oh, Andy, I'm so sorry you're having such a bad time – you have to remember this is twice you've been bereaved, you need to seek help. Have you been to see your GP? Or a counsellor, a bereavement counsellor?"

"No, my sister is on at me to see someone, but I don't know………."

"Listen to your sister, Andy, she loves you very much, it's obvious, and she'll be hurting that she can't help you. Do it for her sake, a bereavement counsellor is just that – to help people that have been bereaved. It'll help, I promise you."

"I'm thinking of going back into teaching, but at primary rather than high school. The new term starts in September, it might take my mind off things to have a new challenge."

"I think that's a wonderful idea! I've been offered a new challenge, too – a promotion and relocation package to Edinburgh! I'm just weighing it all up," she said with forced brightness.

"Perhaps it's what we both need. I'd like to stay in touch, though, if either of us does move away. Would you do that?" Andy said imploringly.

"Of course I will," said Jo-Anne, "We share a big heartache – that'll always unite us!"

"Thanks for talking to me, Jo, I feel a bit better now. I can get through the next hour or two now, I think!"

"That's how to do it, bit by bit, hour by hour, day by day!" said Jo-Anne, "You can call me anytime you hit the bottom, and I'll try to haul you up again!"

"Thanks, Jo," she could sense the hint of a watery smile in his voice, and her heart ached for him. She didn't feel as though she was scheming against Peter – this was a man who had nothing to live for whereas Peter had his boys. Peter would eventually come to terms with his wife's death, but she wasn't sure if Andy would even survive never mind come to terms with his loss.

*****

The meal that evening was simple but tasty, Jo-Anne had hastily produced a spaghetti bolognaise with a strawberry cheesecake for dessert (taken from the freezer), but a decent bottle of red wine had made it more of an occasion. Dave was happy with her choice and after the meal was finished they stayed in the kitchen talking, as they looked at the pros and cons of each of the positions she'd been offered.

"Do you want to move to Scotland?" asked Dave.

"I don't know. It's not something I've ever thought about," she replied. "It might be worth considering, especially if Trevor wants to sell up – which I think he might!"

Dave was quiet as he helped Jo-Anne with the washing-up and she looked sideways at him. "What's up? You're quiet."

"I'm okay," he replied, "Just trying to not influence your decision-making. When have you got to give your answer?"

"He said he'd give me a week to think about it. Do you think I should wait to see what Trevor wants when he comes here? I'm making the spare bed up for him – I think it's fairly obvious that we will be sorting out a divorce settlement and not a marriage patch-up!"

"Is that what you want?" said Dave handing her the pans to put away in the cupboard.

"Yes, it is. That's something I'm definite about – last time……when we…….you know, it was………...I don't know ……..an expectation, I suppose. I mean, we haven't put anything into words yet, either of us. But as time goes on we're saying less and less to each other, and both our lives are growing in different directions. So I think it'll be a relief for him as well as me when we finally do say the words."

Dave nodded silently. Then Jo-Anne took the wine bottle and her glass, nodding at Dave's glass on the table for him to pick it up and they went into the sitting room. She put the bottle and glass on the small table and turned the sound system on, selecting a cd from the drawer. The music drifted out and Dave smiled at her selection. As she curled up on the sofa she told him about Andy's phone call.

"Poor guy," said Dave, "It sounds like he's in a bad way."

"I know," said Jo-Anne sombrely. Then she sighed deeply. "I want to be loved like that!" she said wistfully.

"How do you know you're not?" asked Dave.

"You're kidding? Trevor isn't like that at all!" she laughed. "He's too egocentric – he hasn't got an altruistic bone in his body!"

Dave smiled back at her. "Well, lets just see what the weekend brings – he might surprise you."

"He needn't bother! Love has to go both ways, and it's broken down at this end!" she said emphatically.

"How's Peter doing?" asked Dave, changing the subject.

"As well as can be expected, I suppose. I'm calling in again tomorrow night. He's got good support from both sets of parents and Mark has been a God-send for him – he's so good with the boys. But I worry that Mark's not getting on with his own life – though it's early days, isn't it?" she frowned.

"Oh, yes, Mark will take comfort from being with the boys. As time moves on they'll all start to pick up different pieces of their lives." They were both quiet, the soft music relaxing and soothing them. Jo-Anne laid her head back on the sofa.

"I don't think I'll go to Scotland!" she said suddenly.

"You won't? What's made your mind up?" asked Dave.

"This! You! You and me – like this! I wouldn't have this in Scotland, and I'd miss having you near me." Jo-Anne's head was resting on the back of the sofa and her eyes were partially closed so she didn't see the hope and joy spring into Dave's eyes. He didn't answer, he daren't answer. It was important that she made her decision about her marriage with no input from him to influence her in any way. It was the hardest thing he'd ever done – keeping his feelings under control and saying nothing, but it would soon be over! He hoped that when Trevor came this weekend they would finally agree to the marriage being over, then he could admit his feelings. The option of her and Trevor getting back together was not something his mind would accept.

Chapter Twenty-Five

Trevor arrived at the house at six o'clock. He'd phoned her when he got out of the meeting and asked if she wanted him to bring any food, so she'd said he could call in and get a pizza. She didn't want to spend time cooking as she had quite a bit of work to do as there'd been a problem with the computer system at work and so she'd brought her work home.

When he came in, she noticed he'd lost a bit of weight, but she put that down to his busy lifestyle and Mediterranean diet. He looked well, and he complimented her on what she was wearing and how well she looked. She smiled as she realised they were conversing like mere acquaintances, and a wave of sadness washed over her, but fleetingly. They tucked in at the pizza straight out of the box and she'd taken a bottle of wine out of the fridge to help ease the awkwardness between them.

He'd asked how she was coping with Darcy's death, how Peter and the boys were doing, how her mum was, and she in return asked about Savannah and Dawn, and then grasping the nettle she asked about Jodie.

"Yeah, okay, we're all doing okay," he said, "I….er……need to talk about that……..I know you asked me before and I said no………but it's different now and it's ……er………yes."

"What are you talking about?" she said, a sick feeling settling on the pit of her stomach, guessing what he was saying, but needing him to be clear in what he was disclosing.

"Me and Jodie……….we're………an item!" he rushed.

"I see," she said calmly. It was no surprise, but she was interested in examining how she was feeling now that her husband was revealing that he was being unfaithful to her. She felt a hollowness in her stomach but couldn't work out if it was a tinge of resentment or jealousy or………..was it relief?

She stood up and walked over to the window, aware that Trevor was watching her very carefully. She gazed out of the window, noticing Mrs Willoughby "pottering in her garden". She'd have seen the taxi drop Trevor at the door so she must be trying to detect any raised voices or arguments. She smiled ruefully.

She turned back to Trevor. "So, are we talking about divorce then?" she asked, "Are you asking me to divorce you?"

"Well, yes, I suppose I am, I mean, I've given you grounds for divorce, haven't I?" he said quietly. "I'm really sorry, Jo. I didn't intend for any of this to happen. But you know what I've been through, and I've had to put Savannah first. Then when Jodie ……….."

"I know!" she interrupted him, "I know. I don't need the detail. So what do I do then, do I need to see a solicitor?"

"Well, we have the family solicitor – in Spain - he can arrange everything. You're not going to contest it, so it should be simple – we can have it on the grounds of irretrievable breakdown if you're okay with that?" he asked hopefully.

"What about the house? The car? And the bank account?" she asked him.

"I'll get Manny to draw up an agreement – I'll let you have the car, the house won't have much equity so you can buy me out for a couple of grand - can you afford the mortgage repayments on your salary?" he asked her.

"Yes, I'd worked that out when I was worried that you weren't sending any money when you first went over there."

"Oh, God! I'm sorry! I put you through it, didn't I? That's why I want to make it as easy for you as possible, to make up for what you've had to go through. The joint bank account we can close and divide what's in it." He was looking less strained now that he saw that Jo-Anne was co-operating fully.

"You need the insurance money from your bike first......." she said rapidly calculating mentally what was in the account and how much they would each take.

"Forget that. I don't want to leave you short of money," he said, "You didn't ask for any of this, did you?"

"Neither did you, in the beginning," she countered, "But I suppose what's happened has happened, and we must move on as painlessly as possible."

"Thank you, Jo, you're being brilliant about it all. Oh, that interview meeting I had this afternoon, there's a good chance I've landed a position working from home – in Spain – working as an internet sales co-ordinator, which would be just what I need to be able to be there for Dawn for when Jodie.......goes back to work after the summer." He was aware of the stumble in his speech, he nearly said *"when Jodie has the baby"* but he didn't want Jo-Anne to know about that yet – it would point to him lying to her when she'd asked him before if there was anything going on between them. He was dreading telling her, anyway - he knew how much she had wanted a baby of her own and how the hysterectomy had devastated her. Telling her he was fathering a child with someone else was really rubbing salt in the wound. Besides, Jodie had said she didn't want to tell anyone till the first trimester was over.

Jo-Anne then told Trevor about her two job opportunities, and how she was undecided which one to take. He was genuinely pleased for her and they chatted comfortably about her work and what the promotion could lead to. When it got to ten-thirty, Jo-Anne yawned and Trevor said, "Oh, sorry, am I keeping you up – are you ready for bed?"

"I am, actually, if you don't mind – you don't have to go yet if you want to watch some TV or something – I've made up the bed in the guest room for you."

Trevor looked relieved that the sleeping arrangements were already sorted so he didn't have to feel uncomfortable and said he would stay up if she was okay with that. He turned the TV on, but he didn't want to watch it, he wanted to ring Jodie but needed the cover of the TV sounds. Jo-Anne went upstairs and into the bathroom. She wanted to ring Dave and tell him what had transpired tonight but didn't want Trevor to hear her on the phone, so she needed the cover of the sound of the shower.

The next morning, Trevor left after breakfast to meet up with Sam and a few others at nine o'clock. They were meeting down by the river where Sam and his buddies were fishing, then they were going for a game of snooker and a few drinks at lunchtime. Jo-Anne said she'd be back later that evening as she was helping a friend who was moving house – she didn't think she needed to give more detail than that. She offered to drop him off down by the river which he gratefully accepted, and they parted amicably like old friends.

When Jo-Anne arrived at Dave's new apartment, he was already there. He'd told her the night before when she rang him that the furniture was arriving between one and two o'clock, and she had filled the boot of the car yesterday with all the stuff of his that she had stored in her spare room when she got the room ready for Trevor to sleep in.

As Dave let her in by the door entry system, she walked past Henry, the concierge at his desk sorting the mail for each of the apartments. "Good morning, Henry," she called to him.

"Good morning, Jo-Anne," he said, "Dave's already there, he's waiting for the furniture to arrive. He told me to expect you."

"Thanks, Henry," she said smiling.

When she arrived at his apartment, Dave was waiting at the door. He grinned from ear to ear as she hugged him, and said, "Today's the day! This is where I shall lay my head tonight!"

"So you've got everything from the motel?" she asked,

handing him a bag with kitchen equipment in it.

"All my possessions are in these suitcases!" he said gesturing with his thumb to the cases in the corner.

"Well, come and help me with the rest of the stuff out of my car, and you'll feel more like a homeowner and less like a nomad!"

He laughed and squeezed her to him in a one-armed hug, then took the bag into the kitchen and placed it on the worktop. They went down to the car and after a couple of journeys all the purchases were scattered around his bedroom and kitchen.

"We just have to wait for the furniture to get here to make the bed and store the linens, but we can be sorting out the kitchen. Do you want me to organise it for you, or would you rather have your own system?" Jo-Anne asked him.

"I don't have a system," he said, "If you put things where you think they should be, I'll find them – I don't have any trouble finding my way round your kitchen. I'll go hang my stuff in the wardrobes."

They chatted easily as they worked, a feeling of harmony and companionship making light work of it all, and before long the intercom announced the arrival of the furniture. It didn't take too long to have everything in place, and by four-thirty it was done – the bed was made up, the cushions were on the sofa and a vase stood in the centre of the dining table waiting for flowers. Jo-Anne surveyed the finished room, a smile of satisfaction on her face as she looked at Dave.

"Are you happy?" she asked him.

"I love it!" he said, "Thank you for everything you've done. I couldn't have managed this as painlessly as you've made it. It's been fun, hasn't it?"

She nodded slowly. "I'm wondering if I should sell my house once Trevor signs it over to me – get something like this? I really like this apartment."

"Well………." Dave had to watch carefully what he said. "Well, once it's yours you can do what you want – we can have a word with Henry and see if there are any apartments up for sale. In the meantime, shall we go and get some food? I'm starving!"

"Good idea! We'll eat, then we'll go and do a supermarket shop – fill your fridge and freezer so you can start cooking for yourself instead of eating out all the time like a bachelor!" said Jo-Anne.

"But that's what I am! I've been divorced over a year now, but you're right – I need to start re-learning kitchen skills." Dave grimaced.

"Yes, you can invite me for meals, and I'll invite you for meals – we can have competitions on who made the best meal!" Jo-Anne laughed as she got her belongings together and taking a last look round, they went out of the door.

*****

When Trevor left on Monday, it was a much more cordial parting than the time before. Jo-Anne drove him to the airport before going to work and had a tinge of sadness as she waved him goodbye, thinking that this would probably be the last time they parted as husband and wife. Trevor had turned and smiled rather ruefully at her and she gave a slight nod of her head to signify that she understood how he was feeling – she felt it, too – a kind of wistfulness for what once was, or could have been, but was no longer. Then with a sigh she turned away and directed her thoughts to her own life – she needed to think about the promotion offers and what she was going to do about it.

She had a very busy day at work- she had three

appointments for potential bookings – two wedding receptions and a Promise Auction for another national charity, and all of them made firm bookings. The diary was becoming very full and the Hotel restaurant was becoming more and more popular for non-residential diners, so everyone was kept busy and more staff were being employed. Although it wasn't all down to Jo-Anne, she knew that she had made a big impact on the success of the business.

She was still thinking about work as she pulled up outside her house, and decided she was going to have a long soak in the bath and an early night after she'd been to see Peter and the boys. She made a quick meal as she didn't want to leave it too late otherwise the boys might be in bed, then decided as it was only a ten minute walk she would leave the car at home – she'd been office-based all day and needed the exercise.

The boys were excited to see her and talked about their latest video game that Uncle Mark had bought them. They said he wasn't coming to see them tonight as he was going out with a "friend" and whispered conspiratorially that it was a "girl" – said in such tones of disgust that Jo-Anne couldn't help but laugh. She looked at Peter for confirmation and he nodded.

"Yes, he met a girl at a bereavement support group he's been attending – she's lost her brother, so they've got a lot in common," said Peter.

"I'm so glad he's picking up a bit – I was rather worried about him, but this is good news," said Jo-Anne. Mark was such a lovely young man, he was six years younger than Darcy and she'd always looked out for him as they were growing up, and he in turn had always adored his big sister. She watched the boys as they showed her how adept they were at the game, and she feigned interest in it as she couldn't muster up any enthusiasm.

Peter asked whether she'd made any decision about her job, and she told him she wasn't going to take the Edinburgh position and so the Harrogate position was likely to be the one she took, but she had arranged to go and visit the Hotel first before finally making her mind up. At least she could commute there every day, it was only about a fifty-minute drive.

She'd noticed lots of photographs strewn on the little table in the corner of the room and casually walked over to them. They were snaps of Darcy and the boys, holiday photos, photos of the boys when they were born, every one of their milestones captured in a photo, in fact every year of their lives together as a family. She picked up one or two, then looked at Peter – he was smiling sadly and said, "We had nine years together, lots of happiness, lots of love, and that's what we're concentrating on, my boys and me – we're thinking about how lucky we were to have her in our lives!"

Jo-Anne felt her throat constrict and she walked over to him and hugged him. She looked into his eyes and whispered, "You're right – that's all that matters!"

When the boys went up to bed, she offered to read them their bedtime story and they jumped up and down excitedly shouting, "Yay, please can she, dad?" and Peter ruffled both their heads and said, "ONE story, no more, then straight to sleep!"

When she finally came downstairs – after a story that warranted a long discussion according to the boys, Peter had poured her a glass of wine. "I thought, as you're not driving..........?"

"Oh, lovely, just what I need!" she replied and settled down on the sofa where she always sat, but Peter sat in the armchair – the other side of the sofa was where Darcy always sat. Jo-Anne told Peter about the weekend with Trevor and the decision for them to get divorced, and although it wasn't a great surprise, nevertheless Peter said how sorry he was that it had ended up this way.

"Yes, it is sad," she said, "But our lives have changed dramatically since the beginning of this summer. Who would believe that in such a relatively short period of time so much could happen to alter so many lives? But Trevor will be much happier with his daughter without me as the fly in the ointment, and Jodie is a nice person – I think she'll be good for him, and Savannah loves her so it's all worked out well."

"But what about you?" asked Peter in a concerned voice, "It's alright saying Trevor will be happier – will YOU be happier?"

"I will, actually. Savannah was a hurdle we would never be able to get over. I loved him, before everything that happened in Spain. But, it's not just about love………..it's also about responsibilities and acceptance and all the other stuff that got in the way, and it just suffocated our love. But, to be honest, Peter, since Dave came back into my life………..oh, I don't know ………..he's just so …………we were always really good friends ……..and to be honest……..the relationship I have with him makes me more content than the one I had with Trevor!" She could feel her cheeks begin to grow hot and leaned over to pick up her glass.

"Well, many relationships begin with friendship that grows into love – perhaps that's where you're headed?"

"Mmmm, maybe, but I'm a bit scared to take it any further in case it ruins the friendship! I couldn't bear that. I'm going to concentrate on my career for the next year or two, I'm happy to have Dave in my life, I'll settle for that," said Jo-Anne firmly, then looking at her watch she said, "I'd best be making tracks, its nearly half-past nine and I was going to have a bath and an early night."

She stood up and draining the last of her wine, she handed Peter the glass. She picked up her bag and jacket and walked with him to the back door. "I'll pop round again in a couple of days – I need to find out how Mark got on with his young lady!"

She bade him goodnight and walked down the path feeling pleased that Peter was dealing with his loss and doing a great job with the boys.

As she reached the end of the street, she rang Dave, and talked to him all the way home as she usually did, telling him about Peter and the boys and then about her likelihood of taking the Harrogate job once she had made the visit to check it out.

"Want me to come with you when you go?" he asked her.

"Hmm, that's a thought, you could give me your unbiased opinion," she replied, "Well, I'm home now, so............."

"'Scuse me, love!" She turned at the sound of a gruff voice and had a brief glimpse of a fist flying towards her then stars and blackness crashed down on her, causing her knees to buckle and as she fell forward her head struck the edge of the doorframe. The assailant grabbed her phone and ran off – the whole incident taking less than five seconds.

*****

Dave looked puzzled as he heard the call being ended, and re-dialled Jo-Anne's number. He was even more puzzled to hear the phone had been switched off. He drew his brows together as he tried to analyse the last sounds he'd heard after Jo had said "I'm home now," so he assumed she was at her front door, then there was a mumble – could have been a voice – then a 'whump' sound, then what sounded like a thud as the call ended! His heart began to race! It sounded like something was seriously wrong. Now her phone was switched off – she would never switch her phone off! As he was trying to piece together what he'd heard, he was gathering his jacket and car keys, had slammed his apartment door closed and was already half way down the stairs – he was too hyped up to wait for the elevator.

It seemed an eternity before he arrived at Jo-Anne's street, and as he drew up he noticed the light was on in the kitchen, so he knew she was home. He clambered out of the car and ran up the path. He knocked on the door, calling "Jo! Jo! It's me, Dave, where are you?"

He heard sobbing and the door was wrenched open. Jo-Anne had a deep cut on her forehead which was streaming blood down her cheek and blood was pouring from her nose, and his heart almost stopped at the sight.

"My God! What's happened? Oh, my poor darling! What happened?" he asked as he entered the house and took her in his arms. She pulled back, "I'll get blood on you!" she cried.

"What happened?" he asked as he led her back into the kitchen where he saw a pile of blood-stained tissues and paper towels on the bench next to the sink. He sat her down in a chair and began to clean her face. He opened several of the kitchen drawers till he finally located the first-aid box where he pulled out a large sterile pad and some tape to secure it, saying, "I think you'll need stitches in this, it's quite a deep cut!"

Her nose had stopped bleeding, but he could tell there had been some kind of blow to her face. Her sobbing had subsided and there was just a periodic shudder and hiccup. He crouched in front of her. "What happened?" he asked gently.

"When I was talking to you, somebody – I think it was a young man, he said 'Excuse me, love,' and as I turned around he…………punched me in the face!" She ended with a wail and as she began to cry again, Dave put his arms around her, rage boiling inside him. How dare he – whoever he was – how dare he hurt his precious girl!

"I think I hit my head on the doorframe as I fell, I don't think he did that," she wept, "But he snatched my phone! Thank goodness I didn't take my handbag with me tonight – he'd have taken that as well!"

Dave's rage was burning inside him, but he recognised that to voice it would cause her more distress, so he kept it to himself and said, "I'm going to take you to the hospital to get this gash looked at, then we need to report this to the police."

Jo-Anne gratefully handed herself to Dave's keeping – she could trust him completely to sort everything out, and her head was hurting too much to put up any argument.

After a two hour wait in the Emergency Department, her head was fixed with butterfly stitches and a wound dressing and her nose had been examined and found not to be broken, but she was told she may have bruising to her cheek. She was advised to have someone stay with her overnight in case of any complications and she looked at Dave questioningly.

"Of course I will," he said, "The question is – your place or mine?" As he said this he imitated twirling a moustache and spoke in a deliberately lecherous tone, which caused her to laugh.

"Oh, don't make me laugh – it hurts my face!" she said with a whimper, then a giggle.

"I'll take you back home to your house, but if you want to grab some things and come and stay at my new apartment for a few days, you're perfectly welcome," said Dave taking a more serious tone. "I don't like to think of you there on your own now."

She sighed deeply. "Perhaps it's a sign – maybe Trevor and I should sell the house, I don't want to live there any more. It would make things much simpler – a clean break! What do you think?"

"Talk to Trevor about it – I'm sure he'll think it's a good idea too," said Dave as they walked slowly towards the car park and he took her hand and drew it through his arm, and she looked up at him, grateful for his care and consideration as well as the physical support as her legs were still shaky.

*****

When Trevor received Jo-Anne's email telling him about her doorstep attack, he was horrified. He was swamped with guilt, feeling that he had brought a lot of suffering to an innocent young woman who had done nothing to deserve it. When Jodie saw his stricken face, she gently put her arms around him while he criticised himself and she quietly rationalised his distress, telling him that all that had happened since April had been outside his control and he was as much a victim of circumstance as Jo-Anne was. After a while when he was calm, he agreed with her, realising that fate had always been the director – he was simply one of the cast in this whole production – as was Jo-Anne. This latest event had persuaded them both to decide to sell the house and each go their separate ways, which Jo-Anne had said, would be the best in the long run.

He had made an appointment to see Manny soon after arriving back in Valencia, and the following day when he saw him and told him what they wanted, Manny had assured him that he would start the ball rolling and get the divorce and the financial settlement done as quickly as possible. Trevor related the news back to Jo-Anne telling her that an agent would be in touch with her soon to arrange for the valuation and sale of the property. He had expressed his horror at the attack and said he understood perfectly her reluctance to stay in the house alone and hoped she was managing okay staying with the friend she had told him had offered to put her up and accompany her each time she went back to the house.

Jo-Anne had decided not to say who the friend was because although it was a perfectly innocent relationship, the fact that Dave was a man as well as a former boyfriend, may just be enough to muddy the waters considering that they were going through divorce proceedings at the moment. She was a little surprised that he hadn't asked more about who the friend was, but then thought that as they were each making new lives for themselves and he had begun a new relationship already, he wasn't really in a position to query any friendships she had.

Trevor had plenty to keep his mind occupied – he had secured the job which gave him flexibility to work from home and although it didn't yet give him the kind of salary he had commanded previously, he at least had an income. Dawn was happy for him to manage their household finances and Manny had seen to it that she had been well compensated for the accident - Jodie was renting out her apartment and had her own income from her job, so as a group they were monetarily sound. Carlos and Fabiana continued to work three days a week because when Jodie went back to work and the girls went back to school, at least Dawn had Fabiana to keep her company and assist her if required. Besides, Carlos was a very proficient handy-man who kept the villa in good state of repair as well as the grounds and the pool. He also had two other villas to look after that belonged to British people who had bought properties as holiday homes.

When Jodie's scan date arrived, Trevor went with her to the maternity clinic. He was so excited when the picture appeared on the screen and the whooshing little thuds that signified the baby's heartbeat and Jodie laughed happily to see so much joy in his face. When they came out of the clinic, he was practically dancing, and on the way back to the car he stopped at a flower-seller in the street and bought a huge bunch of flowers, placing them in Jodie's arms as he planted a kiss on her lips. The flower-seller smiled widely, partly because of the huge sale that had been made, but also because of the infectious happiness that emanated from the couple.

When they got home, they went straight in to see Dawn who was reading in her room, and with slight trepidation, Jodie broke the news to her and showed her the scan picture. Dawn didn't speak for a few seconds, then a wide smile lit up her face.

"Oh, that's fabulous news! I must say, I kind of guessed that this was a possibility – I could see that you had a glow about you. Have you told the girls yet?"

"No, not yet," said Trevor, "We wanted to tell you first, to check that you were okay with it."

"Okay with it? I'm over the moon!" laughed Dawn, "It'll be lovely to have a new baby in the house, and that's something I can help with – I can do all the cuddling and nursing and just hand her – or him – back to you to be fed and changed! A bit like a grandma!" Then her face crumpled and she broke down, sobbing uncontrollably.

Jodie and Trevor both rushed to her side, Jodie placing her arms around her and Trevor kneeling in front of her holding one of her hands.

"I'm sorry," Dawn wept, "I just miss my mum and dad so much, and I know that they would be overjoyed for you, Jodie. I'm happy about it, honestly. It was saying the word 'grandma' that reminded me that they aren't here any more." Her sobbing had subsided, and she wiped her eyes with the tissues that Trevor handed to her.

When they heard the girls' voices coming nearer, she quickly pulled herself together. Trevor stood up and all three of them turned to face the girls as they came into Dawn's room.

"Mummy," began Savannah as she entered, then she looked at each of them in turn, "What's wrong?" she said suspiciously, picking up on the emotion hanging in the room.

"Nothing," said Dawn, smiling, "Daddy and Jodie have something to tell you both."

Trevor took Jodie's hand and said, "We're going to have a baby! Savannah and Holly – you're both going to be a big sister!"

The girls looked at each other, a slow grin spreading over their faces, then they began to jump up and down in excitement, holding hands and squealing.

"I guess they're happy about it," laughed Jodie, "It won't happen till next Spring, so we've got plenty of time to get used to the idea."

Trevor held his arms out and Savannah rushed into them as Jodie did the same for Holly, then they all hugged together, and did a staggered walk over to Dawn to include her in the group hug, everyone laughing with joy and happiness.

When Jodie took the girls out shopping for their new school clothes later that afternoon, Trevor sat for a while with Dawn on the veranda, then he said he had to go and break the news to Jo-Anne. He explained to Dawn how he would have to be very careful how he worded the email as Jo-Anne's greatest wish had been to have a child of her own but because of her hysterectomy she had been robbed of that privilege, therefore it would be a bitter pill for her to swallow to find that Trevor was going to father another child. He very nervously started the email, frequently deleting and re-writing until he was sure that he'd been as tactful as he could be, then with a shuddering sigh he clicked on the 'send' button.

*****

When Jo-Anne received the email she was just about to finish work for the day, and seeing the new mail come in she decided to open it before she turned the computer off. When she read Trevor's news, she felt a stab of anguish in her stomach. Jodie was pregnant! Trevor was going to be a father again! He was going to have the thing that Jo-Anne had wanted more than anything in her life – a child of her own! She felt hurt and betrayed. How could he? So quickly after they had agreed to separate…………..Wait a minute………..
Jodie had just had the pregnancy confirmed with a scan so she must be at the twelve week point! Twelve weeks? She quickly

calculated back and consulted her diary and realised that they must have slept together before Trevor came to England – before Jo-Anne and Trevor had had sex – the day that Darcy died! They were still together then, even if they had grown distant. Which meant Trevor had cheated on her! He had cheated and he had lied about it when she had asked him! The hurt and the anger rose up like a volcano and a wail escaped her lips. She bit down on her hand to stop the noise from alerting security, as she whimpered in despair and resentment.

She sat at her desk with her head in her hands trying to come to terms with what had happened. She thought they were going to have an amicable divorce, perhaps even remain friends, but now she felt waves of hatred wash over her! She wanted to hurt him the way he had hurt her! The tears poured down her face.

"Darcy, Darcy! I need you to tell me – what shall I do?" she whimpered. Darcy's face came into her mind clearly, her beautiful face with the enigmatic smile and her voice inside Jo-Anne's head said, *"Let him go! He's holding you back! Let him stay in Spain with his spoiled brat and his new family – don't even give him head-room, Jo, you're worth so much more!"*

She pulled herself upright and took a deep breath in then exhaled slowly. "You're right, Darcy, just let it go!" she whispered. She dried her eyes and took out a small mirror from her desk drawer to check the state of her eye make-up. After a quick dab with concealer and powder, she reckoned she could get past the night staff without anyone asking of she was alright – her face still carried substantial bruising from the doorstep assault, so they were used to seeing her eyes swollen. She hurried out of the hotel feeling desperate to talk to Dave – she needed to tell him this new turn of events so that he could calm her and make her feel better. As she got into her car her phone rang.

"Hi, Dave," she said with forced brightness.

"Are you still at work?" he asked, "Shall I start the meal?"

"Yeah, sorry, I was held up, I'll tell you about it when I get home. I'm leaving now, so I'll see you soon."

"Okay, honey. See you soon."

As she drove to Dave's apartment, she determined to not let Trevor's new life have any kind of impact on her own life. She had a lot to look forward to – she was starting her new job at the beginning of October, so she only had two weeks to get everything finalised here before handing over to the new events administrator. Dave had been quite impressed with the splendour of the hotel she was going to and the size of the main function room. She could arrange some very large events, and there were two smaller function rooms that could be used for many different purposes as well. She focussed her mind on the ideas that had been swimming around in her head since they'd seen it, and she felt confident that she could make a huge success of this venture.

She also had Peter and the boys to think about. Financially they would be secure as the life insurance would pay off the mortgage and leave a decent sum for the boys' university fund – Darcy had been insistent that the boys should have the opportunity to go to a University of their choice. Mark had begun a relationship with the girl he dated, which she and Peter were very happy about, but Mark hadn't brought her to see them yet, they had that to look forward to. There was also Andy – she'd met him briefly one lunchtime for a coffee and he'd told her that he was applying to work abroad as a volunteer – he said he wanted to work in third-world countries where his anguish would hopefully be lessened by working to bring some relief and comfort to severely deprived children and communities. His grief was etched into his face, making him look tired and drawn. Jo-Anne felt a sense of responsibility towards him and by keeping in touch she felt as though she was maintaining a link with Darcy.

She pulled into the car-park and as she got out of the car she noticed how cool the evenings were becoming. It was amazing how quickly she had settled into Dave's apartment, it felt more like home already than her own house did and she dreaded the thought of going back there. She and Dave went there every few days to pick up a few more of Jo-Anne's things and when she had joked that she was actually moving in surreptitiously, Dave's face had registered a look that she couldn't fathom so she'd quickly said, "It's a joke – I'm kidding!" She certainly didn't want to be at the house in the dark winter evenings – she didn't feel safe at all there now, so she hoped Dave would let her stay till it was sold and then she could decide what she was going to do. She would miss coming here, she loved this apartment complex - perhaps fate would smile on her and an apartment would come up for sale once her house was sold. She was contemplating all this as she walked up the stairs – she rarely used the elevator - and opened the door on to the corridor where Dave's apartment was.

A young and attractive, petite, blonde women was standing at Dave's door, her upturned face glowing as she openly flirted with him. Dave was smiling back at her, one elbow raised and resting on the door jambe, the other arm extended towards her as he gave something to her, but she was too intent in gazing into his eyes to take it from him. Jo-Anne's breath caught in her throat, and an inexplicable pain stabbed her somewhere in the region of her chest and heart. She walked forward hesitantly, her brows furrowed and her eyes clouded. Dave looked up and said, "Oh, hi, Jo!"

The girl looked quickly round at Jo-Anne then turned back and took the bowl from Dave's hands. She smiled at Jo-Anne and Dave said, "Jo, this is Suzie, she lives in the apartment at the end of the corridor. She's just moved in. Suzie, Jo's my lodger till she gets her house sorted out."

Suzie's eyes brightened as she looked from Jo-Ann to Dave. "Oh?" she said, continuing to smile up at Dave.

"Excuse me," said Jo-Anne as she tried to squeeze past her to get through the door.

"Well, I'd better go now, the meal is almost ready. I'll probably bump into you again," said Dave taking a step back over the threshold. Suzie reluctantly moved back and turned to go, batting her eyelids and smiling coyly. "I'll look forward to that," she said with a little wave as Dave gently closed the door.

He walked into the kitchen to find Jo-Anne standing with her arms folded and her back to the wall. "She fancies you!" she said accusingly.

"Do you think so?" said Dave, "She seems nice enough." He started to serve up the meal and beckoned for Jo-Anne to sit at the table. Jo-Anne was biting her lip, watching him carefully, trying to fathom the mixture of feelings that were raging inside her. There was a feeling of panic bubbling in her chest............what if Dave and this Suzie woman got it together and became an item? What would she do? This Suzie wouldn't want her staying at Dave's apartment any more and he wouldn't be there for her like he had been for any problems that she had – he wouldn't drop everything to come to her rescue like he normally did! The panic began to rise..........then suddenly she felt as though a bubble had popped in her head and she could see clearly. He was her friend, her saviour, her rescuer, her confidante, her soul mate...........her everything! Her life would be nothing without him in it. She loved him! But it wasn't just about love! It was about a deep, soul-satisfying friendship that bound two people together, a friendship that was stronger than any other relationship she had ever had – even with Trevor. She couldn't imagine her life without him in it now – but she wasn't sure if he wanted more than friendship. She knew now that she did.

She was staring at him intently, her food lying forgotten on her plate. He looked up, feeling the intensity of her gaze.

"What's up? Don't you like the food?" he asked anxiously.

She blinked and looked at her plate. "Oh, it looks nice, yes, I mean, I like it!" She put down her knife and fork and leaned across the table. "Why did you make a point of telling that Suzie that I was your lodger?" she asked.

"Eh? What's brought this on? What did you want me to say?" Dave looked puzzled.

"Well, I'm starting to feel that I'm cramping your style - I mean, that Suzie………. it was obvious she fancied you. If I wasn't here, you could perhaps………..get it together with her?" Jo-Anne's voice rose as she spoke, and she ended with a cough.

Dave looked at her with a bewildered expression. She continued, "I was thinking – perhaps I should go back to my own house. I should be alright now, I don't think about the attack very often……….and I need to get everything sorted out for selling up……….and I should start looking for somewhere of my own………..leave you in peace to live your own life and not have to nursemaid me all the time, because that's what you must be thinking about me…………" Her voice trailed off as Dave banged his fist on the table.

"Oh, you know what? I can't do this any more! I can't be the good guy, it's killing me!" Dave put down his knife and fork and took a deep breath as he stood up. Jo-Anne's eyes widened and her heart began to race…………what was he going to say? Had he had enough of her and her troubles? She hadn't yet told him about Trevor having a baby with Jodie – she knew it would open up all kinds of wounds for her, and she needed Dave to see her through it. She felt her heart break and the tears began to pour from her eyes, so she kept her face averted so he wouldn't see her misery as she waited for him to tell her it was time for her to stand on her own feet.

Dave walked over to the window, then turned to face her. "When I came back to England it was with the intention of trying to find you. Over the years I had constantly thought about you and wondered what you were doing – who you were with and so on, and when my marriage floundered I didn't put up a fight for Sally – I realised that I'd never really been 100% committed to her, because *you* were always in the back of my thoughts! So, I decided it was time for me to come back to England to find you. Then when I bumped into your brother it was as if fate had paved the way for me. But you were apparently happily married, so I just played it cool – stayed as your buddy – that came easy, we were so close when we were young. But it was different this time. As we got closer, I knew I loved you – probably always had loved you – but we were too young first time round and both needed to flex our wings. I didn't want to force you into making a decision about your own marriage. It had to be your choice. I had to just………be here…….. waiting."

The silence in the room hung heavy and Jo-Anne's heart was pounding so loudly she was sure he could hear it. She turned her face slowly towards him, her eyes wide, her face wet with tears.

"Oh, sweetheart, you're crying!" he said coming towards her his face creased with concern.

"Do you mean it? You love me? Really?" she whispered.

"I really love you! Yes!" he said, smiling and placing his arms around her.

"What did you mean ……….you can't be the good guy any more?" she asked.

"I can't pretend to be just your friend……….. not when I'm going crazy with desire for you. I can't stop myself any more from taking you in my arms and doing this………." and he gently pulled her towards him and placed his lips on hers.

All the years she had known him and all the times he had kissed her cheek, or her forehead, or even a swift peck on the lips, he had never kissed her this way. She had never felt this rush of desire! Her heart was pounding, she could feel her legs trembling and she clutched at him, her breath coming in gasps. He moved his face away from hers and looked into her eyes.

"Please tell me you feel the same way – don't say I've got this wrong! I've waited so long for you." Her response was a groan of pleasure as her arms snaked around his neck and she sought out his lips again, wanting to experience this intense emotion once more – this man who had been her best friend and her soul-mate, and now she wanted him as a lover. She felt the joy bubble up inside her and a little chuckle escaped from her. He leaned back and looked at her.

"Are you laughing at me?" he said.

"I'm laughing because I'm so happy. I'm laughing because life is wonderful. I love you, my buddy, my best friend, I love you. I think I've always loved you, too."

She melted again into his arms and knew that this was where she belonged – where she had always belonged, and where she was going to stay.

Printed in Poland
by Amazon Fulfillment
Poland Sp. z o.o., Wrocław